THE BROTHERS GRIMM

ALSO BY JACK ZIPES

Unlikely History: The Changing German-Jewish Symbiosis, 1945–2000 (editor, with Leslie Morris)

The Great Fairy Tale Tradition: From Straparola and Basile to the Brothers Grimm

Sticks and Stones: The Troublesome Success of Children's Literature from Slovenly Peter to Harry Potter

The Oxford Companion to Fairy Tales: The Western Fairy Tale Tradition from Medieval to Modern (editor)

When Dreams Came True: Classical Fairy Tales and Their Tradition.

Yale Companion of Jewish Writing and Thought in German Culture, 1066–1966 (editor, with Sander Gilman)

Happily Ever After: Fairy Tales, Children, and the Culture Industry

THE BROTHERS GRIMM

From Enchanted Forests to the Modern World

JACK ZIPES

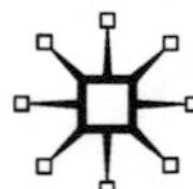

THE BROTHERS GRIMM

First published 2002 by
PALGRAVE MACMILLAN™
175 Fifth Avenue, New York, N.Y. 10010 and
Houndmills, Basingstoke, Hampshire, England RG21 6XS.
Companies and representatives throughout the world.

PALGRAVE MACMILLAN is the global academic imprint of the Palgrave Macmillandivision of St. Martin's Press, LLC and of Palgrave Macmillan Ltd. Macmillan® is a registered trademark in the United States, United Kingdom and other countries. Palgrave is a registered trademark in the European Union and other countries.

ISBN 1-4039-6065-8 hardback
ISBN 0-312-29380-1 paperback

Library of Congress Cataloging-in-Publication Data
Zipes, Jack David.
The Brothers Grimm : from enchanted forests to the modern world / by Jack Zipes.
p. cm.
Includes bibliographical references and index.
ISBN 1-4039-6065-8 — 0-312-29380-1(pbk.)
1. Grimm, Jacob, 1785–1863. 2. Grimm, Wilhelm, 1786–1859. 3. Philologists—Germany—Biography. 4. Kinder- und Hausmärchen. 5. Fairy tales—Germany—History and criticism. I. Title.

PD63.Z57 2003
430'.92'243—dc21
[B]

2002070390

A catalogue record for this book is available from the British Library.

Design by Letra Libre, Inc.

First edition: December 2002
10 9 8 7 6 5 4 3 2 1

Printed in the United States of America
Transferred to Digital Printing 2007

For Donald Haase

CONTENTS

PREFACE TO THE 2002 EDITION

Fourteen years have passed since the first edition of *The Brothers Grimm: From Enchanted Forests to the Modern World* was published. It followed numerous celebrations of the two hundredth birthdays of the famous Brothers Grimm held in 1985 and 1986 and was intended to be a "critical" tribute to their lives and works. Yet, in the meantime, their names and accomplishments appear to have been diminished and distorted, if not obfuscated—at least in English-speaking countries.

In the summer of 2001, I conducted a storytelling session with a group of ten-year-olds in College Park, Pennsylvania, and at one point I told a version of "Snow White" and asked the students whether they knew who had written the tale. None of them knew except one small boy who stated confidently, "Walt Disney."

Now, this is not exactly wrong, but I wanted to be a bit more historical. So, after agreeing with the boy, I went on to explain that there were also two brothers named Grimm who lived in Germany some 200 years ago, and they were *really* the first to have written down the tale, but the students were not particularly interested. Moreover, they had never heard of the Grimms. Did it really matter?

Does it really matter that in the film *Ever After* (1998), the Grimms are summoned to a castle by a French baroness played by a real French actress, Jeanne Moreau, who tells them a preposterously radical version of "Cinderella," indicating that they had got their story wrong? In fact, the film intends to show that the Grimms had not done their homework—and it also manipulates history to reveal how a feisty young woman inspired by Thomas More's *Utopia* becomes the Queen of France.

Films (like many historians) have a propensity to twist history to reinvent it, and we have a propensity to accept what is cinematically popular as history. Thus Hans Christian Andersen, the troubled and desperate writer, becomes a cheerful singing bungler played by Danny Kaye in *Hans Christian Andersen* (1952), and the Grimms have fared no better. For instance, there are two god-awful, kitschy films about the Brothers Grimms' lives and how they came to write fairy tales—*The Wonderful World of the Brothers Grimm* (1962), starring Lawrence Harvey and Claire Bloom, and *Once Upon a Brothers Grimm* (1977), featuring Dean Jones and Paul Sand. Both "frame" the Grimms in such a way that the background to their lives and the purpose of their collecting tales are totally distorted to create lively entertainment. In both films, the Grimms come off more as loveable fops than serious scholars, and history itself is mocked. Entertainment is always more important than truth. We live in realms of fiction. Even the news is part of popular culture.

So, perhaps the only way we can glean some truth about the Brothers Grimm will be through fiction and popular culture. For example, it is not strange to find a novel about the Grimms, *Grimm's Last Fairy Tale* (1999), written by the historian, Haydn Middleton, who has done an abundant amount of research and is obviously well-versed in German culture. Yet, he had to "resort" to fiction to write about the brothers, even though we still do not have a "definitive" biography of the Grimms in English. Indeed, Middleton comments in an author's note: "According to the German Romantic writer Novalis (1772–1801), novels arise out of the shortcomings of history. In creating this fiction based on the lives of the Brothers Grimm, I have tried to write a novel that is not in itself another shortcoming."[1]

As fiction but not as history, the novel is a provocative questioning about the personal lives of the brothers.[2] Middleton sets the story in 1863, the last year of Jacob's life, and he interweaves three plot lines: Jacob takes a trip to Steinau, Hanau, and Kassel, the places of his birth and childhood, because he knows he may die soon and wants to revisit these memorable sites; he has visions that turn into a fairy tale told throughout the novel and interwoven with the actual plot line of Jacob's journey; he is accompanied by his niece, Auguste, daughter of Wilhelm and Dorothea, who suspects that Jacob, the inveterate bachelor, may be her real father and wants to discover the "truth" before he dies. During the course of the novel, Auguste has a brief affair with a Jewish servant named Friedrich Kummel, and Middleton adds a leitmotif to his novel by revealing how much of the Grimms' patriotic dedication to building a united Germany in a liberal humanitarian sense was warped by "blood and soil" nationalists and eventually led to the exclusion of Jews and the rise of Nazism. These trends were already apparent to the Grimms during their own lifetime, and they were disappointed by them. And certainly they would have been horrified if they had lived during the rise of fascism.

Of course, Middleton's novel is all speculation. There was no Friedrich Kummel. There is absolutely no proof that Jacob had an affair with his sister-in-law. If anything, he was more in love with his brother Wilhelm (who was never called "Willy," as he is in the novel) and his research than anything else. There was no trip at the end of Jacob's life. But the knowledgeable Middleton does take the Grimms seriously, and there are revealing insights into the great tenderness and compassion among the members of the Grimms' family. Middleton also makes us think about the tragic and ironic aspect of the Brothers' achievement. Highly acclaimed as the founders of the popular fairy-tale tradition in the West, if not in the entire world, the Grimms aspired as brilliant philological scholars to glorify the greatness of the German popular tradition and believed deeply that their voluminous works on the German language and customs would have a moral impact on the German people. There was always a profound political and moral commitment to what they thought the German people and nation could be. Unfortunately, their utopian vision for Germany in the nineteenth century turned into a nightmare. It is to Middleton's credit that he uses the novel form to unveil the irony of the Grimms' accomplishment.

Fortunately, there was much more of a utopian residue in the Grimms' fairy tales than they realized, and the tales, rather than their remarkable pioneer philological studies, have continued to give hope to millions of readers and spectators in the twentieth and twenty-first centuries. Though their names may be taken in vain or forgotten, their tales will continue to be reproduced and revised in highly imaginative ways, and scholarship will seek to reorder and reevaluate their contributions to German and "global" culture as well—in part to counter the myths of popular culture, in part to assess the appropriation of the Grimms' tales in light of historical and cultural shifts.

Indeed, since 1988 the research into the work of the Brothers Grimm has continued to grow, and there have been some significant new publications and tendencies in scholarship that need to be discussed to situate my new and revised edition of *The Brothers Grimm: From Enchanted Forests to the Modern World.* Perhaps the most important development, despite the virtues of the international conferences and exchanges organized from 1985 to 1987 to celebrate the Grimms, is that there are clear divisions in the manner in which German scholars and other Western scholars, particularly the Americans and British, have approached the Grimms' tales, and it is apparent that there is now very little critical exchange among the German and other Western critics. This lack of mutual and collaborative work is unfortunate, because I believe that a greater awareness of the differences in methods and approaches can shed greater light on the relevance of the Grimms' tales throughout the world. Certainly, journals like *Fabula* and *Marvels & Tales* have been open to different analytical approaches, just as the *Grimm Jahrbuch* and the *Brüder-Grimm Gedenken*, published by the Brüder Grimm-Gesellschaft, have endeavored to document the wide variety of scholarship in all the fields in which the Grimms worked, including lexicography, philology, linguistics, ethnology, and folklore. However, certain limits have been set, especially in Germany, with regard to interpreting the tales, and the limits reveal limitations, especially on the Continent.

In Germany the historical-philological approach dominates, and there has been a plethora of superb scholarly editions and studies since 1988 that are worth citing. The most important work has clearly been done by Heinz Rölleke, who made a name for himself early by publishing the Ölenberg manuscript under the title *Die älteste Märchensammlung der Brüder Grimm* with commentary in 1975. This superb edition was the first post-1945 edition of the 1810 manuscript of the Grimms' tales that corrected previous publications and enabled readers to study the compositional techniques and changes made by the brothers in the first publication of 1812/15.[3] His work has been complemented by Lothar Bluhm, who published an important collection of historical-philological essays, *Grimm-Philologie* (1995), and edited *Romantik und Volksliteratur* (1998), with articles by critics who have worked on various aspects of folk and fairy tales. Almost all the research by Rölleke, Bluhm, Bernhard Lauer, Dieter Hennig, and other scholars who have been associated with projects of the Grimm-Gesellschaft in Kassel, such as the editions of the letters by Holger Ehrhardt and Ewald Grothe, or of the *Enzyklopädie des Märchens* in Göttingen under the direction of Rolf Wilhelm Brednich and other eminent folklorists such as Hermann Bausinger, Wolfgang Brückner, Helge Gerndt, Lutz Röhrich, Klaus Roth, and Rudolf Schenda [4] has focused on: establishing the text corpus of the tales and the sources and informants; publishing the enormous amount of correspondence in the Grimms' posthumous papers; providing more biographical data about the Grimms and their relatives and correspondents; reevaluating the connections of the Grimms' tales to the oral tradition; reassessing their artistic achievements; and tracing connections to other folklorists and international folklore. Without the meticulous and scrupulous work of what I would call the historical-philological school and the cultural ethnographical work of folklorists in Germany, it would be impossible for other researchers to accomplish their goals.

Perhaps "impossible" is the wrong word, for there are still numerous critics and analysts like Verena Kast, Eugen Drewermann, and Carl-Heinz Mallet, who pursue psychological approaches either from a Jungian or Freudian perspective, and have little regard for history or textual matters. In their work the Grimms' tales are appreciated largely for their therapeutic value, and the interpretations of the tales depend on the manner in which the critics want to apply a particular psychological or psychoanalytical theory.[5] In a strange but different way, the same can be said of the works of the Europäische Märchengesellschaft (European Fairy-Tale Society). The adjective "European" is very misleading because most of the members of the society are German and most of the publications mainly include German authors. For instance, *Märchen und Schöpfung* (Fairy Tales and Creation, 1993) and *Zaubermärchen: Forschungsberichte aus der Welt der Märchen* (Magic Fairy Tales: Research Reports from the World of Fairy Tales, 1998), both edited by Ursula and Heinz-Albert Heindrichs, contain contributions only by German, Swiss, or Austrian scholars, and almost all their scholarly references are to other German works. Most of the essays in the books, while well-founded, are self-evident and lack a critical analytical understanding of creation, magic, and fantasy, largely because these scholars have failed to look beyond their borders to France or England, nor have they gazed across the ocean.[6] But the major point I should like to make is that, despite the great accomplishments of the historical-philological school and the cultural anthropology of folklorists in Göttingen, there is very little exchange with scholars who have developed new approaches and theses in the United Kingdom and United States, where feminists, folklorists, cultural anthropologists, and literary critics, some influenced by French critical theory, have made major gains in interpreting the Grimms' tales and the entire genre of fairy tales.[7] In both the United States and United Kingdom, the rise of cultural studies during the past 15 years has played a major role in the way American and British critics approach the Grimms and their tales.

Among the more important scholars who paved the way for fairy-tale research with a special emphasis on the Grimms, Maria Tatar and Ruth (Sue) Bottigheimer should be mentioned first of all. Tatar produced an outstanding historical-psychological book, *The Hard Facts of the Grimms' Fairy Tales*, in 1987, and it was matched by Bottigheimer's important feminist study, *Grimms' Bad Girls and Bold Boys: The Moral and Social Vision of the Tales*, in the same year. These two books, among others, generated a broad and international discussion about the social, political, racist, and sexist nature of fairy tales that has been lacking in Germany.[8] In addition, there are numerous important essays that have appeared in *Marvels & Tales*, such as Rachel Freudenberg's "Illustrating Childhood—'Hansel and Gretel'" (1998) and Hayley Thomas' "Undermining a Grimm Tale: A Feminist Reading of 'The Worn-Out Dancing Shoes' (KHM 133)" (1999), and in other American and British, not to mention European, journals, rarely considered by German scholars in their work on the Grimms' fairy tales. This is not to say that German scholarship on the Grimms' fairy tales has suffered or has gone astray, so to speak, or that the Americans and British are more cosmopolitan. But the Americans and the British, and to some extent the French, have paid more attention to developments in Germany than the Germans have looked beyond their own borders. As I have emphasized, the accomplishments of the historical-philological school and the German folklorists and ethnologists provide a firm basis for the understanding of the Grimms' tales and their heritage, but in my opinion, more critical reflection and analysis and exchange with other researchers would open up vistas to the reception and relevance of the Grimms' tales today.

One book that has been somewhat neglected, not only in Germany, but also in the United States, is Christa Kamenetsky's study, *The Brothers Grimm and Their Critics: Folktales and the Quest for Meaning* (1993). Though she is critical of my approach to the Grimms' tales and tries to defend the Grimms much too much from critiques and studies that explore the manner in which they "contaminated" the tales and were very bourgeois and religious in their ideology, her book is one of the most thorough and dependable studies of the Grimms' work in English. Moreover, she has a comprehensive knowledge of the historical development of the Grimms' tales and has traced their reception, with reliable commentary, up to 1990.

My revisions of the present volume, *The Brothers Grimm: From Enchanted Forest to the Modern World*, owe much to her questioning of my original theses. In fact, all of the essays in my book have been thoroughly reexamined, expanded, and altered in substantial ways. Given the fact that many more letters and more information about the Grimms' lives have become available since 1989, I have added much more biographical data to the original chapter 1, which has been divided into two chapters: "Once There Were Two Brothers Named Grimm: A Reintroduction" and "The Origins and Reception of the Tales." Chapter 2 in the first edition, "Dreams of a Better Bourgeois Life: The Psycho-Social Origins of the Tales," has been deleted because much of the material from that chapter is now in the new chapter 2. The final chapter in the present volume, "The Struggle for the Grimms' Throne: The Legacy of the Grimms' Tales in East and West Germany since 1945," which originally appeared in Donald Haase's *The Reception of the Grimms' Fairy Tales*, is new and has been radically changed, especially since it takes into consideration the fall of the Berlin Wall in 1989 and includes remarks on the legacy of the Grimms' tales since 1990.

The Brothers Grimm were truly great scholars and men of impeccable integrity. But they were also extraordinary artists, prone to mythopoeia, and intensely devoted to an ideal Germany that did not exist and did not come into existence. What interests me most is their artistry and ideology, how their art and political views have been passed down to us through the ages, and how their art and ideas have been appropriated by modern and post-modern writers and filmmakers such as Walt Disney, Jim Henson, and others. It is not by chance that Simon Bronner has a chapter titled "The Americanization of the Brothers Grimm" in his recent book, *Following Tradition: Folklore in the Discourse of American Culture* (1998), and that Jane Wasko pays great attention to the way Disney appropriated the Grimms' tales and other tales in *Understanding Disney: The Manufacture of Fantasy* (2001). Whatever forms the Grimms' tales take and whatever myths are spread about their lives and work, they will be with us well into the twenty-first century and beyond. Their hope for themselves and their people in the once upon a time of their fairy tales is the hope that has inspired my own work, and despite the critical and skeptical attitude I maintain in studying their work and legacy, it is their fairy-tale hope that keeps me going.

I want to express my sincere gratitude to Kristi Long, who not only encouraged me to produce a second edition of *The Brothers Grimm*, but who also made many valuable suggestions to improve the book. In addition, I am deeply grateful to Bruce Murphy for the careful copyediting of the new manuscript.

Jack Zipes
Minneapolis, June 7, 2002

PREFACE TO THE 1988 EDITION

Four years ago, as the bicentennial celebration of the birthdays of the Brothers Grimm approached, I began planning a critical study of their fairy tales. What particularly interested me at the time was the question of the tales' enduring power and the effect of the tales in modern society. My plans were somewhat altered, however, when LuAnn Walther, then with Bantam Books, asked me to do a completely new translation of the Grimms' tales. At first I refused, for this was not the project I had in mind. But then I began to reconsider, and it occurred to me that the process of translating might enable me to understand the Grimms' methods of recording their tales and their concepts of folklore more clearly. So I decided to undertake the translation, and I shifted the focus of my study to concentrate on textual matters and the history of the Grimms' mode of collecting and revising their tales. As I began to translate the narratives, I returned to questions about the production and reception of oral tales and their transformations through literature from the eighteenth century up to the present.

Questions kept arising in my mind—questions that I had been trying to answer for some years in other studies but never quite to my satisfaction: Why and how did the Grimms revise the oral and literary tales they collected? Why were they so successful in establishing the tales as a literary genre and virtually transforming that genre into an institution? (There were, after all, other writers and collectors of oral and literary tales before them.) What is the tradition of the Grimms' tales? Is this tradition a kind of cultural heritage and is there something specifically Germanic about it? Why are the tales so popular throughout the world today, and what shape do they take in various countries? Must we resort to psychology to clarify our disposition and responsiveness to the Grimms' tales and fairy tales in general?

In 1985 and 1986, I was invited to various bicentennial conferences honoring the Grimms, and I delivered talks concerned with these questions. At the same time, I continued working on the translation and analyzing the philological aspects of the Grimms' texts. Once the translation was completed in 1987, I began revising my conference talks with the aim of turning them into the full-length study I had been planning for the past several years. The result is this book—one that endeavors to treat the above questions and also to correct numerous misconceptions about the Grimms and their tales by placing their work in a sociohistorical context. My primary focus is on the factors of production and reception that led to the institutionalization of the Grimms' tales and other literary fairy tales and to the formation of the parameters for their continuous use and interpretation.

The Grimms' tales are "contagious." And to borrow a metaphor used by my friend Dan Sperber, we actually need an "epidemiology" of the Grimms' tales to understand fully why their tales are so memorable and catching. Sperber is more concerned with general questions of representations, which he understands as concrete, physical objects located in space and time. In this regard, distinctions must be made between two types of representations: "There are representations internal to the information processing device—*mental representations;* and there are representations external to the device and which the device can process as inputs—that is, *public representations.*"[1] For Sperber, an epidemiology of representations is a study of the causal chains in which these mental and public representations are involved: the construction or retrieval of mental representations may cause individuals to modify their physical environment, for instance to produce a public representation. These modifications of the environment may cause other individuals to construct mental representations of their own; these new representations may be stored and later retrieved, and, in turn cause the individuals who hold them to modify the environment, and so on.

If we look at the Grimms' tales as types of public representations (that is, as speech utterances formed through intrasubjective processes of thought and memory), we can begin to evaluate how they affect us and our environment and determine why they have become "contagious" in both a positive and negative sense. It appears that we have developed a disposition and susceptibility to receiving and transmitting the Grimms' tales and other fairy tales, and by considering the tales as part of a process of mental and public representation, we can begin to assess their cultural relevance.

We are still only at the beginning of this assessment, and by no means have I written an epidemiology of the Grimms' tales. Yet, it is with questions emanating from the need for such an epidemiology that I wrote my study. The first chapter, "Once There Were Two Brothers Named Grimm: A Reintroduction," appeared first in my translation *The Complete Fairy Tales of the Brothers Grimm*, and it has undergone extensive revision and enlargement. My new, more scholarly essay assumes that the Grimms and their work need a "reintroduction" because so many myths have been spread about them, and it provides a general overview of the Grimms' lives and fairy-tale research. Chapter Two, "Dreams of a Better Bourgeois Life: The Psycho-Social Origins of the Tales," was held as a talk at the International Conference on the Brothers Grimm in the spring of 1986 at the University of Illinois. It explores some of the underlying psychological factors that led the Grimms to begin their work in folklore. Chapter Three, "Exploring Historical Paths," was held as a talk at the International Grimm Symposium at Columbia University in November 1985 and then published in *The Germanic Review* in the spring of 1987. It has been vastly changed and expanded here to address the nature of the sociohistorical approach in light of the Grimms' soldier and tailor tales. Chapter Four, "From Odysseus to Tom Thumb and Other Cunning Heroes: Speculations about the Entrepreneurial Spirit," was a talk that I delivered at the annual MLA Meeting held in Chicago in December 1985. It is a theoretical endeavor to understand the appeal of the male heroes in the Grimms' tales from ideas developed by Theodor Adorno and Max Horkheimer in *Dialectic of Enlightenment.* Chapter Five, "The German Obsession with Fairy Tales," is a revision of the chapter that I contributed to Ruth B. Bottigheimer's book, *Fairy Tales and Society*, and it develops the notion of fairy tale as institution while trying to grasp the "Germanic" involvement in this institution.

Chapter Six, "Henri Pourrat and the Tradition of Perrault and the Brothers Grimm," was a talk delivered in June 1987 at the centennial celebration of Pourrat's birthday held in Clermont-Ferrand. It discusses the nature of the connections between Charles Perrault, the Brothers Grimm, and Henri Pourrat, in view of Mikhail M. Bakhtin's notion of speech genres. Chapter Seven, "Recent Psychoanalytical Approaches with Some Questions about the Abuse of Children," was a talk I delivered at the annual MLA Meeting in December 1986 in New York. It summarized recent West German scholarship on the Brothers Grimm and suggested that psychological and psychoanalytical approaches to the Grimms' tales might profit from the ideas of Alice Miller and more interdisciplinary considerations. Chapter Eight, "Semantic Shifts of Power in Folk and Fairy Tales," was a talk delivered at the annual MLA Meeting in December 1984, held in Washington D.C. It focuses on the patriarchalization of fairy tales with particular attention paid to the Cinderella cycle of tales. "Fairy Tale as Myth/Myth as Fairy Tale" appeared first in the catalogue of an art exhibition entitled "The Fairy Tale: Politics, Desire, and Everyday Life" that took place October 30–November 26, 1986 at the Artists Space in New York City. As chapter Nine, the essay has been greatly revised and lengthened to focus on "Sleeping Beauty" and its mythic ramifications in light of Roland Barthes' radical concept of myth.

All of the chapters have undergone extensive changes and revisions during the past year, and I am indebted to a number of friends and colleagues who have made suggestions to improve my work. In particular I would like to thank: Jacques Barchilon, Bernadette Bricout, Alan Dundes, Hilary Kliros, Wolfgang Mieder, Jim McGlathery, and Heinz Rölleke, all of whom have helped me either through discussions or ideas developed in their own essays and books. In conducting some of my research at the Brothers Grimm Archives in Kassel, I received generous support and advice from Dieter Hennig and his entire staff, and I am most appreciative for the 1987 Graduate School Summer Research Grant from the University of Florida at Gainesville, which enabled me to complete my book by the winter of 1987. Finally I would like to express my gratitude to Diane Gibbons and Bill Germano for their helpful editorial suggestions and advice that enabled me to put the final "modern" touches on the book.

CHAPTER ONE

ONCE THERE WERE TWO BROTHERS NAMED GRIMM

A Reintroduction

Many are the fairy tales and myths that have been spread about the Brothers Grimm, Jacob and Wilhelm. For a long time it was believed that they had wandered about Germany and gathered their tales from the lips of doughty peasants and that all their tales were genuinely German. Although much of what had been believed has been disproved by recent scholarship,[1] new rumors and debates about the Grimms keep arising. For instance, one literary scholar has charged them with manufacturing the folk spirit of the tales in order to dupe the general public in the name of nationalism.[2] Other critics have found racist and sexist components in the tales that they allege need expurgation,[3] while psychologists and educators battle over the possible harmful or therapeutic effects[4] of the tales. Of course, mention must be made of the feminist critiques of the Grimms, who allegedly skewed the tales to fit patriarchal expectations and offered very few alternatives to stereotypes of passive women.[5] Curiously, most of the critics and most of the introductions to the English translations of the Grimms' tales say very little about the brothers themselves or their methods for collecting the tales—as though the Grimms were incidental to their tales.[6] Obviously, this is not the case, and there is a story here worth telling.

Just who were the Brothers Grimm and how did they discover those tales, which may be the most popular in the world today?

A fairy-tale writer could not have created a more idyllic and propitious setting for the entrance of the Brothers Grimm into the world. Their father, Philipp Wilhelm Grimm, a lawyer, was ambitious, diligent, and prosperous, and their mother, Dorothea (née Zimmer), daughter of a city councilman in Kassel, was a devoted and caring housewife, even though she tended at times to be melancholy. Initially they settled in the bustling town of Hanau, and it appeared that the Grimms were set to lead a charmed life. As Ruth Michaelis-Jena remarks:

> Hanau had survived the ravages of wars and invasions, and was in the late eighteenth century enjoying a period of peace. New houses, new bridges and new roads were built, while the town's rulers, like other German princes, followed the French fashion in creating "Turkish" gardens, grottoes and follies around their spacious residences. The burgher's course of life was slow and measured, with everyone having a settled place in a firmly established social order.
>
> The Grimms' home was a typical *Bürgerhaus*, roomy, comfortable, unpretentious. Tastes were simple, and family ties close, even by the standards of an age which accepted emotional display and strong sentimental attachment to one's kith and kin. Relations were happy, and Jacob and Wilhelm were to remember their childhood affectionately in copious letters and notes, and in the autobiographies which they prepared in middle life for Karl Wilhelm Justi's biographical dictionary of Hessian scholars.
>
> From them a picture evolves of security and domestic bliss.[7]

During the first 12 years of their parents' marriage, 9 children were born, of which 6 survived: Jacob Ludwig Grimm (1785–1863),

Wilhelm Carl Grimm (1786–1859), Carl Friedrich Grimm (1787–1852), Ferdinand Philipp Grimm (1788–1844), Ludwig Emil Grimm (1790–1863), and Charlotte Amalie (Lotte) Grimm (1793–1833). By 1791 the family had moved to Steinau, near Kassel, where Philipp Grimm had obtained an excellent position as district magistrate *(Amtmann)* and soon became the leading figure of the town. He and his family lived in a spacious dwelling and had servants to help with the domestic chores. As soon as the children were of age, they were sent to a local school, where they received a classical education. They also received strict religious training in the Reform Calvinist Church. In his autobiography Jacob observed:

> We children were all raised strictly Reformed mainly through deed and example, not that we made much about this. I used to regard the Lutherans, who lived right among us in our little country town, as strangers. Even though they were in the minority, I thought they were people whom I should not really trust. As far as the Catholics were concerned, they used to travel through our town from Salmünster, about an hour away, and could generally be identified by their more colorful clothing, and I formed some strange and fearful views of them. To this day it seems as if I can only be completely devout if I am in a church furnished in Reformed style. This is how closely all faith is tied to the first impressions of childhood. Indeed, the imagination also knows how to decorate and enliven bare and empty places. Never was greater devotion ignited in me as on the day of my confirmation, after I had just received Holy Communion, when I watched my mother walking toward the altar of the church in which my grandfather had once stood in the pulpit.[8]

Both Jacob and Wilhelm were bright, hardworking pupils and were distinctly fond of country life. Their familiarity with farming, nature, and peasant customs and superstitions would later play a major role in their research and work in German folklore. At first, though, both boys appeared destined to lead comfortable lives and to become lawyers, following in the footsteps of their father, whose seal was *Tute si recte vixeris*—"honesty is the best policy in life." To be sure, this was the path that Jacob and Wilhelm took, but it had to be taken without the guidance of their father.

Philipp Grimm contracted pneumonia and died suddenly in 1796 at the age of 44, and his death was traumatic for the entire family. Within weeks after his funeral, Dorothea Grimm had to move out of the large house and manage the family of six children without servants or much financial support. From this point on, the family was totally dependent on outside help, particularly on Johannes Hermann Zimmer, the Grimms' grandfather, and Henriette Zimmer, their aunt. Jacob was compelled to assume the duties of head of the family, and both he and Wilhelm "lost their childhood," so to speak, because of their heavy responsibilities. For instance, right after the father's death, Jacob wrote the following letter to his Aunt Henriette Zimmer, his mother's sister and first lady-in-waiting at the prince's court in Kassel:

> I commend myself to your love and care with my four brothers and sister, and I am convinced that this is not a vain request. I know how deeply concerned you are about our great loss so that I should like to call on you and tell you personally about all matters that are close to my heart. How much there is to tell you about my dear suffering mother! I am sure you will console me and give me good advice.[9]

The loss of the father could have meant great deprivation for the Grimm family and disintegration if a "good fairy" like Henriette Zimmer, their grandfather, and other relatives and friends had not offered financial assistance and emotional support. Their correspondence with their grandfather and aunt between the ages of 11 and 13 reflects a remarkable degree of maturity and seriousness.[10] Clearly, they were under great pressure to succeed in all their endeavors for the sake of the family and its reputation. For instance, by 1798 their Aunt Henriette arranged for Jacob and Wilhelm to study at the prestigious Lyzeum (high school) in Kassel and obtained provisions and funds for the family. On this occasion, their grandfather wrote:

> I cannot repeat enough to you to keep in mind the reason for which you are in your present position. This means that you should apply yourselves as industriously as possible in and outside the classroom so that you may prepare your future welfare, gain honor, and provide pleasure for your mother, me, and the

> entire family. Therefore, avoid bad company, try to associate with reasonable men from whom you can always gain some profit, and above all, fear God, who is the beginning and end of all wisdom.[11]

The move to Kassel brought about a momentous change in the lives of the Brothers Grimm. Not only did it mean the final abandonment of an idyllic childhood in the country, but their initiation into manhood was also complicated by the absence of a primary male protector—their father, a lawyer, who could have explained the class system and codes that set arbitrary obstacles hindering their education and their development. Moreover, they would not have been in the situation they were—susceptible to insults and degradation. The result was that the Grimms became acutely aware of class injustice and exploitation. To compound matters, just as they entered the Lyzeum and were about to prove themselves as gifted students, their grandfather, whom they had greatly admired, died, and they were virtually left to themselves to determine their future and that of their family. Although the brothers were different in temperament—Jacob was more introverted, serious, and robust; Wilhelm was outgoing, gregarious, and asthmatic—they were inseparable and totally devoted to each other. They shared the same room and bed and developed the same work habits: in high school the Grimms studied more than 12 hours a day and were evidently bent on proving themselves to be the best students at the Lyzeum. That they were treated by some teachers as socially inferior to the other "highborn" students only served to spur their efforts. Moreover, they wanted to live up to their dead father's expectations and to pursue their studies at the university to become lawyers. The four years of rigorous schooling in Kassel did not have a negative effect on Jacob's health and constitution. Instead, the training strengthened his resolve to succeed and to help his mother bring up the other children in a proper fashion corresponding to their religious beliefs and social class. For Wilhelm, whose physical stamina was weaker than Jacob's, the pace brought about an attack of scarlet fever and asthma, from which he suffered the rest of his life, and he had to postpone his studies at the university for one year.

Although each brother graduated from the Lyzeum at the head of his class, Jacob in 1802 and Wilhelm in 1803, they both had to obtain special dispensations to study law at the University of Marburg because their social standing was not high enough to qualify them for automatic admission. Once at the university, they had to confront yet another instance of injustice, for most of the students from wealthier families received stipends, while the Grimms had to pay for their own education and live on a small budget. This inequity made them feel even more compelled to prove themselves at Marburg, which at that time was a small university with 200 students, most of whom were more interested in the social activities at fraternities and taverns than their studies.

Indicative of Jacob's attitude and also of his concept of what it meant to be *German* is this passage from his autobiography:

> In Marburg I had to live modestly. Despite all kinds of promises, we never succeeded in obtaining the slightest support, even though our mother was the widow of a magistrate and raised five sons for the state. The most profitable stipends were distributed to my schoolmates like Malsburg, who belonged to the distinguished Hessian aristocracy, and even to one who became the richest landowner of the region. However, all this never hurt me. Instead, I often felt the happiness and freedom of moderate financial circumstances. Sparseness spurs a person to industriousness and work, keeps one from many a distraction and infuses one with noble pride that keeps one conscious of self-achievement in contrast to what social class and wealth provide. I would like to generalize even more by asserting that a great deal of what Germans have achieved overall should be attributed to the fact that they are not a rich folk. They work themselves up from the bottom and break through by taking unusual and particular paths while other people walk on a wide paved main street.[12]

The identification with the common hard-working folk and the great desire to prove his individual worth were major factors in Jacob's later success and also figured in his idealization of the German folk. These were also the factors that drove Wilhelm, who shared Jacob's reverence for the simple German people and the ascetic life.

Jacob spent his first year acquainting himself with the university routine and the best professors, and he continued to apply himself "industriously" in a manner that would make his father and dead grandfather proud of him, as did Wilhelm when he arrived in Marburg. By this time Jacob's intellectual prowess and keen mind had drawn the attention of Professor Friedrich Carl von Savigny, the genial founder of the historical school of law, who was to exercise a profound personal and professional influence on the brothers throughout their lives. Savigny argued that the spirit of a law can be comprehended only by tracing its origins to the development of the customs and language of the people who share them, and by investigating the changing historical context in which laws developed. Ironically, it was Savigny's emphasis on the historical-philological aspect of law that led Jacob and Wilhelm to dedicate themselves to the study of ancient German literature and folklore. During their early school years at Kassel, the brothers had already become voracious readers, particularly of chapbooks, novels, and romances, and had begun collecting books in an endeavor to classify literature according to aesthetic and historical standards. At Marburg, they learned from Savigny how a historical method can help determine the origins not only of law, but of literature as well, in relation to the culture of a particular nation. Moreover, he also allowed them to use his vast personal library for their research and pleasure. In his autobiography, Wilhelm remarked that "the ardor with which we pursued the studies of Old German helped us overcome the spiritual depression of those days. Without doubt, world events and the need to retire into the space of research, contributed to the re-discovery of this long-forgotten literature. Not only did we seek some consolation in the past, but it was also natural for us to hope that the course we were taking would add something toward the return of better days."[13]

The wish for "better days" was also coupled with a wish for unification of Germany and the defeat of the French, and in this regard Germany's medieval past became a utopian symbol for the Grimms—the recovery of the "natural essence" of Germans was the foundation on which they hoped to build a more authentic Germany. It is important to remember that there was no such thing as a modern unified German state at that time. There were over 200 German principalities, often at war with one another.

Many rulers were petty tyrants who still believed in the principles of absolutism. Some of the principalities were religious domains that were beholden to the Catholic or Protestant Church. The more progressive thinkers of the late eighteenth century sought to overcome the divisions between the German principalities and envisioned more peaceful conditions and some kind of unified state, similar to England or France. Such visions were shared by the circle of friends around Savigny, who introduced the brothers to the poet Clemens Brentano and his wife, Sophie Merau, as well as to Achim von Arnim, who married Brentano's sister Bettina. All of these gifted artists and intellectuals had been stimulated by the works of Johann Georg Hamann and Johann Gottfried Herder, who called for a rediscovery of *Volkspoesie*, the natural and genuine literature of the people. It was in this "romantic" atmosphere that the Grimms pursued their study of law and literature.

In 1805 Savigny invited Jacob to accompany him to Paris as his assistant on a project concerned with the history of Roman law. It is interesting to note how emotionally close the brothers were and remained throughout their lives. Soon after Jacob's departure, Wilhelm wrote:"I don't know anything to tell you about the first days except to say that I was very sad and am still now melancholy and want to cry when I think that you have gone. When you left, I thought my heart would tear in two. I couldn't stand it. You certainly don't know how much I love you. In the evenings when I was alone, I thought you might come out of a corner at any moment."[14] These effusive sentiments were shared by Jacob; in fact, they are indicative of the kind of "romantic" bonding common among friends, male and female, during this period. Not only did the Grimms form strong family ties, but also close friendships, throughout their lives. Consequently, they constantly wrote letters to one another and to friends, even if they were in a nearby city.

While in Paris, Jacob sent numerous letters to Wilhelm while he collected documents and materials that were related to German customs, law, and literature, and recorded how he felt more drawn to the study of ancient German literature than anything else. It was also difficult for him to be away from Wilhelm and his family, and he reiterated in letters how much he wanted to live a simple life and devote himself to his research on ancient literature and customs. Upon returning to Germany in 1806, Jacob made the final decision to abandon the study of law to see if he could somehow earn a livelihood as a scholar of philology and literature. He left the university and rejoined his mother, who in the meantime had moved to Kassel. Given the pecuniary situation of the family, it was Jacob's duty, he believed, as head of the family, to support his brothers and sister, and he found a position as secretary for the Hessian War Commission, which made decisions pertaining to the war with France. Fortunately for Jacob, he was able to pursue his study of old German literature and customs on the side while Wilhelm remained in Marburg to complete his legal studies.

The correspondence between Jacob and Wilhelm during this time reflects their great concern for the welfare of their family.[15] With the exception of Ludwig, who later became an accomplished painter and professor of art and also illustrated some of the fairy tales, the other children had difficulty establishing careers for themselves. Neither Carl nor Ferdinand displayed the intellectual aptitude of the two oldest brothers or the creative talents of Ludwig. Carl eventually tried his hand at business and ended up destitute as a language teacher, while Ferdinand tried many different jobs in publishing and later died in poverty. All three of the younger brothers were soldiers during the Napoleonic Wars, and Jacob and Wilhelm were always preoccupied about their welfare. Lotte's major task was to assist their mother, who died in 1808. After that, Lotte managed the Grimm household until she married a close friend of the family, Ludwig Hassenpflug, in 1822. Hassenpflug became an important politician in Germany and eventually had a falling out with Jacob and Wilhelm because of his conservative and opportunistic actions as statesman.

During their youth, Ludwig, Carl, Ferdinand, and Lotte were chiefly the responsibility of Jacob, who looked after them like a stern but caring father. Even Wilhelm regarded him as such and acknowledged his authority, not only in family matters, but also in scholarship. It was never easy for Jacob to be both brother and father to his siblings—especially after the death of their mother, when they barely had enough money to clothe and feed themselves properly. They were all virtually teenagers or in their early twenties. It was during the period 1806 to 1810, when each of the siblings was endeavoring to make a decision about a future career and concerned about the stability of their home, that Jacob and Wilhelm began systematically gathering folk tales and other materials related to folklore.

In the fall of 1805 Achim von Arnim and Clemens Brentano, who had become good friends of the Grimms, had published the first volume of *Des Knaben Wunderhorn* (*The Boy's Wonder Horn*), a collection of old German folk songs, and Brentano wanted to continue his work in this field by publishing folk tales. Therefore, he requested that the Grimms help him collect oral tales for a volume that he intended to publish some time in the future. The Grimms responded by selecting tales from old books and recruiting the help of friends and acquaintances in Kassel to tell them tales or to gather them from acquaintances. In this initial phase, the Grimms were unable to devote all their energies to their research and did not have a clear idea about the significance of collecting folk tales. However, they were clearly devoted to uncovering the "natural poetry" of the German people, and all of their research was geared toward exploring the epics, sagas, and tales that contained essential truths about the German cultural heritage.

What fascinated or compelled the Grimms to concentrate on old German literature was a belief that the most natural and pure forms of culture—those which held the community together—were linguistic and were to be located in the past. Moreover, modern literature, even though it might be remarkably rich, was artificial and thus could not express the genuine essence of *Volk* culture that emanated naturally from the people's experience and bound the people together. In their letters between 1807 and 1812, and in such early essays as Jacob's "Von der Übereinstimmung der alten Sagen" ("About the Correspondences between the Old Legends," 1807) and "Gedanken wie sich die Sagen zur Poesie und Geschichte verhalten" ("Thoughts about the Relationship between the Legends and Poetry," 1808) and Wilhelm's "Über die Entstehung der deutschen Poesie und ihr Verhältnis zu der norddeutschen" ("About the Origins of German Poetry and its Relationship to Nordic Poetry," 1809), they began to formulate similar views about the origins of literature based on tales and legends or what was once oral literature. The purpose of their collecting folk songs, tales, proverbs, legends, and documents was to write a history of old German *Poesie* and to demonstrate how *Kunstpoesie* (cultivated literature) evolved out of traditional folk material and how *Kunstpoesie* had gradually forced *Naturpoesie* (natural literature such as tales and legends) to recede during the Renaissance and take refuge among the folk in an oral tradition. According to the Grimms, there was a danger in this development, in that the natural forms would be forgotten and neglected. Thus, the brothers saw it as their task as literary historians to preserve the pure sources of modern German literature and to reveal the debt or connection of literate culture to the oral tradition. In two important letters to Achim von Arnim, Jacob stated his position on this matter most clearly—one that was shared wholeheartedly by Wilhelm:

> Poesie is that which only emanates from the soul and turns into words. Thus it springs continually from a natural drive and innate ability to capture this drive—folk poesie stems from the soul of the entire community (*das Ganze*). What I call cultivated poetry (*Kunstpoesie*) stems from the individual. That is why the new poetry names its poets; the old knows none to name. It was not made by one or two or three, but it is the sum of the entire community. We cannot explain how it all came together and was brought forth. But it is not any more mysterious than the manner in which water gathers in a river in order to flow together. It is inconceivable to me that there could have been a Homer or author of the Nibelungen. . . . The old poesie is completely like the old language, simple and only rich in itself. In the old language there is nothing but simple words, but they are in themselves so capable of such great reflection and flexibility that the language performs wonders. The new language has lost innocence and has become richer outwardly, but this is through synthesis and coincidence, and therefore it sometimes needs greater preparation in order to express a simple sentence. . . . Therefore, I see in cultivated poetry, or whatever you want to call it, what I designate as preparation, even though the word is good and does not refer to anything dead or mechanical. In the nature poesie there is something that emanates from itself. May 20, 1811[16]
>
> All my work, this is what I feel, is based on learning and showing how great narrative poetry (*epische Poesie*) has lived and held sway all over the earth, how the people have gradually forgotten and neglected it, perhaps not entirely, but how the people are nourished by it. In this way, a history of poetry is for me

> based on something unfathomable, something that cannot be entirely learned, and something that provides real pleasure.
>
> October 19, 1812[17]

Between 1802 and 1812, the Grimms knew they had to establish careers for themselves as quickly as possible to look after the rest of the family. It would seem that out of a sense of dedication to their father (the old German tradition) they became absorbed by a quest to reconstitute German culture in its oral and written forms so that it would not fade from the memory of the German people. Put more positively, the Grimms saw old German literature as the repository of valid truths concerning German culture. In particular, they believed that a philological understanding of old German literature would enable Germans to grasp the connections between the customs, laws, and beliefs of the German people and their origins. In addition, by comparing the motifs and themes in the German tales and legends with those from other countries, they hoped to learn more about the distinctive qualities of German culture. Such a desire to reconstitute the old German tradition in its "pure" form, though idealistic and virtually impossible, was—I would like to emphasize—based on a desire to regain a lost, untarnished home or realm and possibly to resurrect the principles of their paternal heritage. Simultaneously, this pure, innocent realm was implicitly upheld as better than the artificial realm of the ruling class. The quest to uncover the truths of the old German tradition was unconsciously a desire to prove the worth of the Grimms' personal ethics and bourgeois culture in general. Their values were based to a great extent on the Reformed Calvinist religion, the faith in which they were raised. Recently, G. Ronald Murray has argued strongly for reconsidering the religious component in the Grimms' reworking of their collection of tales, especially Wilhelm's contribution:

> He collected and reexpressed the religious faith found in the poetic tales primarily of three ancient traditions: Classical Greco-Roman, Norse-Germanic, and Biblical. In all three he was at home as a fluent reader, student and storyteller, and in one of them, Christianity, he was a devout believer. His personal style of Johannine spirituality with its emphasis on love as the divine

> and life-giving form of faith, enabled him to have a serene reverence for pre-Christian, pagan religious awareness in Germanic and Greek forms, especially insofar as they too spoke of the primacy of love and the tragic and violent nature of its violation. To do justice to Wilhelm Grimm's retelling of the tales it is not enough to treat them as narratives that ignore the spiritual feelings of the past and integrate only the middle-class morals of the nineteenth century as some scholars seem to maintain.
>
> Through many editions over the years the preface to the brothers' collection of fairy tales always ends with a religious thought parallel to that at the beginning: the tales enable a blessing.[18]

Certainly it was in part due to their religious beliefs and upbringing that they stressed diligence, industry, honesty, order, and cleanliness as the ingredients necessary for success. Indeed, the Grimms were success-oriented; their value system, based on the Protestant ethic, favored a utilitarian function within the formation of the German bourgeois public sphere, as described by Jürgen Habermas in *Strukturwandel der Öffentlichkeit.*[19] Therefore, their ethics assumed the form of a self-validation that was also a validation of patriarchy in the family and male domination in the public realm. To this extent, the elaboration of their ethics in the tales has left us with problems in socialization through literature that still have to be resolved. How have they effected young and old readers over the years in homes and schools? While the tales exhibit a moral preference for underdogs and acts of kindness, they also reinforce notions of rightful male domination and monarchical rule. In short, the justification of patriarchy is unjust, no matter what religious persuasion one might be, and in the Grimms' time, it was second nature to assume that male domination was religiously justifiable.

As I have tried to show, the merging of the personal and the political (including the religious) in the Grimms' work on folk and fairy tales can be attributed to various circumstances that affected their lives from 1802 to 1812. And there is more to be considered here.

It was during this same period, in 1807, that Jacob lost his job on the War Commission. Kassel was invaded by the French and became part of the Kingdom of Westphalia under the rule of

Jérome Bonaparte. Without anyone fully employed—Jacob was 23, Wilhelm 22—the family was practically destitute and relied on the help of their Aunt Henriette Zimmer. It was imperative that Jacob find some new means of supporting the family. Although he had a strong antipathy to the French, he applied for the position of King Jérome's private librarian in Kassel and was awarded the post in 1808. This employment enabled him to pursue his studies and help his brothers and sister. Meanwhile, Wilhelm had to travel to Halle to undergo a cure for asthma and a rare heart disease. Ludwig began studying art at the Art Academy in Munich, and Carl began working as a businessman in Hamburg, while Ferdinand was looking for a job.

It was thanks to Jacob's employment that Wilhelm, who was at times on the verge of death, could travel to Halle in April of 1809 and remain there several months. It is not widely known that Wilhelm, who took great pleasure in providing the world with hopeful fairy tales, suffered from various ailments throughout most of his life. In his autobiography, he noted:

> After my mother's death (1808) the poor state of my health became increasingly worse. In addition to the shortness of breath, which made climbing even a few steps a great burden, and the constant fierce pains in my chest, there was now a heart condition. The pain, which I could only compare to the sensation of a flaming arrow being shot through my heart from time to time, left me with a constant feeling of anxiety. Sometimes my heart began to beat violently and suddenly, without an obvious cause, and it would end abruptly the same way. Several times I experienced this uninterruptedly for twenty hours, and I was left in extreme exhaustion. It was not without cause that I felt death was very near. I spent many a sleepless night upright, without moving, waiting for the dawn to arrive. . . . It is incredible how much one can endure physically for years, without losing the joy of life. The feeling of youth may have helped, for I was not completely cast down by my illness, and when things were bearable, I continued working, even with pleasure. I did not deceive myself about my condition, and every day that I continued to live I considered it a gift of God.[20]

The letters that the young Grimms exchanged at this time are highly revealing, for many of their differences and personal conflicts were aired in them. Worried about money, Jacob at one time felt that Wilhelm was not as seriously ill as he seemed to be, and Wilhelm felt offended that Jacob did not trust him. Wilhelm also differed with Jacob somewhat about revising folk tales and felt closer to Clemens Brentano than did Jacob. What is most striking in their letters is the openness with which they discussed their feelings for one another while at the same time they recorded information about their research and developed all kinds of collaborative projects. In particular, there is one letter written by Jacob on June 25, 1809 that is worth quoting at length because it reveals so much about their relationship and Jacob's desires and plans, which were shared by his brother:

> I was extremely happy to hear the good news about your health that was confirmed by Luise. I'm really sorry that you have to be cared for by strange people, and that we ourselves cannot help you get well and cannot contribute anything, especially since we love you more than anyone else. That's why you have to form a kind of attachment to Halle as a home. I'd love to leave Kassel. The only reason I'm fond of it is because mother lies buried here.
>
> I wish you and I could live in a small city of about 2,000–3,000 people. I'd like to know how things are going to develop for me here because I find so many things so repulsive right now that I know that I shall not remain, even though I feel quite calm and settled. If only God could help us so that we could have a moderate income and yet be independent from working just for the sake of making money! Indeed, I believe that one can gradually become accustomed to living a fine rich life but at the cost of not living so purely any more. And everything that comes from a certain solitude and homeliness would be basically contaminated—I don't mean that one should always stay at home. I have nothing against traveling since there is always a return, or rather a homecoming. . . . I would love very much to travel for some years because I know how much further it would bring our studies. Isn't that the reason why Savigny has also traveled? For the old poetry there are even 100 reasons more, and if we don't, there is much that we shall not be able to accomplish! Perhaps you will be able to do all this sooner than I provided that your health is restored and that traveling does not endanger it and put you at risk. In any event there must first be

> peace in Germany. May God give us peace and quiet. I am convinced that most people in Germany pray for peace and are devoted to it. I could give up everything for it and let everything go, and I often think how is it possible not to think about peace and that it is sinful that people prefer to do something else while there is turmoil. If only the misfortune would stop, how different things would be for us![21]

Despite the wars and Jacob's great concerns and anxiety, there was a period of relative stability and security for the Grimm family from 1809 to 1813, and Jacob and Wilhelm finally began publishing the results of their research on old German literature: Jacob wrote *Über den altdeutschen Meistergesang* (*On the Old German Meistergesang*), and Wilhelm, *Altdänische Heldenlieder, Balladen und Märchen* (*Old Danish Heroic Songs, Ballads, and Tales*), both in 1811. Together they published in 1812 *Die beiden ältesten deutschen Gedichte aus dem 8. Jahrhundert: Das Lied von Hildebrand und Hadubrand und das Wessobrunner Gebet*, a study of the *Song of Hildebrand* and the *Wessobrunner Prayer.* They had also reached an agreement with Clemens Brentano by 1810 that they would be allowed to publish the tales they had been collecting for him. So the first volume of the *Kinder- und Hausmärchen* (*Children's and Household Tales*) appeared, with scholarly annotations, in 1812. They had never planned to publish such a volume when they had begun collecting the tales, and they were not at all intended for children. The volume was simply part of their grand project to excavate the natural poetry of the German people. Without seeking fame, the Grimms gradually began to make a name for themselves among philologists not only in Germany but throughout Europe.

However, the Napoleonic Wars and the French invasion of the Rhineland were most disquieting for both Jacob and Wilhelm, who were dedicated to the notion of German unification. These wars, caused in large part by Napoleon's quest to create a French empire, had begun in 1798 and lasted until 1815, and they had a direct impact on the Grimms' lives. Their brothers fought for the German side, and they themselves were witnesses to the devastation that the wars caused. Neither Jacob nor Wilhelm wanted to see the restoration of oppressive German princes, but they did feel a deep longing to have the German people united in one nation through customs and laws of their own making. Thus, in 1813 they were relieved when the French withdrew from Kassel and the French armies were defeated in battles throughout Central Europe. In 1814, despite his disinclination to travel when the travel was not connected to his research, Jacob was appointed a member of the Hessian Peace Delegation and served as a diplomat in Paris and Vienna. As usual, he was also able to make use of his time to gather significant books and papers for the work that he and Wilhelm were doing on ancient German literature and customs. During his absence Wilhelm managed to procure the position as secretary to the royal librarian in Kassel, and concentrated on bringing out the second volume of the *Children's and Household Tales,* fully annotated, in 1815. When the peace treaty with the French was concluded in Vienna, Jacob, who had been writing political articles for a journal criticizing the petty disputes among the German princes, returned home and was further disappointed to find that the German sovereigns were seeking to reestablish their narrow, vested interests in different German principalities and had betrayed the cause of German unification.

After securing the position of second librarian in the royal library of Kassel, Jacob joined Wilhelm in editing the first volume of *Deutsche Sagen* (*German Legends*) in 1816. During the next 13 years, the Grimms enjoyed a period of relative calm and prosperity. Their work as librarians was not demanding, and they could devote themselves to scholarly research and the publication of their findings. Together they published the second volume of *German Legends* (1818), while Jacob wrote the first volume of *Deutsche Grammatik* (*German Grammar,* 1819) and *Deutsche Rechtsaltertümer* (*Ancient German Law*, 1828) by himself, and Wilhelm produced a translation of *Irische Land- und Seemärchen* (*Irish Elf Tales,* 1826) and *Die deutsche Heldensage* (*The German Heroic Legend,* 1829).

Ironically, the book that was to establish their international fame, *Children's and Household Tales,* had not been an overwhelming success, even after the second edition in 1819, and their growing reputation was due more to their philological studies than their collection of folk and fairy tales. For instance, Jacob's publication of the *German Grammar,* dedicated to Savigny, was much more important in 1819 than the second edition of the tales. As Ruth Michaelis-Jena remarks,

> the publication of the grammar brought an immediate favourable reaction from scholars at home and abroad. Marburg University conferred honorary degrees on both brothers, and they were made members of more and more learned societies. Possibly for the first time a grammar became a best-seller. The first volume was out of print a year after publication. Ties to fellow philologists became closer, particularly to the professors Lachmann of Königsberg and Benecke of Göttingen. Even Schlegel praised where he had formerly scorned. Jacob's work was giving Germanic studies a firm direction. . . . Growing fame brought the Grimms some brilliant offers, among them professorships at Bonn University. All were rejected because they wished to continue working together quietly. Lecturing to students, they feared, would mean distraction from their researches.[22]

In the meantime, there were changes in the domestic arrangement of the Grimms. Lotte moved out of the house to marry Ludwig Hassenpflug in 1822, and a few years later, in 1825, Wilhelm married Dortchen Wild, the daughter of a pharmacist in Kassel. She had known both brothers for over 20 years and had been part of a group of educated storytellers who had provided the Grimms with numerous tales, often influenced by the French tradition and their wide reading. Now it became her task to look after the domestic affairs of the brothers, for Jacob did not leave the house. Indeed, he remained a bachelor for his entire life and had very little time for socializing. The Grimms insisted on a quiet atmosphere and a rigid schedule at home so that they could conduct their research and write without interruptions. Although Wilhelm continued to enjoy company and founded a family—he had three children with Dortchen—he was just as much married to his work as Jacob, and nothing could ever come between Jacob and him. Since Dortchen had been well-acquainted with the brothers before her marriage, when she assumed her role in the family she fully supported their work and customary way of living.

In 1829, however, the domestic tranquility of the Grimms was broken when Ludwig Völkel, the first librarian of the royal library, died, and his position in Kassel became vacated. Jacob, who had already become famous for his scholarly publications, had expected to be promoted to this position. But he did not have the right connections or the proper conservative politics, and his application for the vacant position, as well as Wilhelm's request for a promotion, was rejected by William I, the Elector of Kassel, who never admired their work. Moreover, he resented them because they sided with his wife when he openly began living with his mistress.[23] In reaction to this slight by the Elector, Jacob and Wilhelm resigned their posts. Since they had been courted by various universities in Germany, they were confident that they would obtain employment. Indeed, they were soon offered positions by the renowned University of Göttingen, and one year later they traveled to the small university city, where Jacob became professor of old German literature and head librarian, and Wilhelm became librarian and, eventually, professor in 1835. At that time the University of Göttingen was considered one of the finest institutions in Europe, and such noted scholars as Wilhelm Albrecht (law), Friedrich Dahlmann (political science), and Georg Gervinus (German literature) taught there and became close friends of the Grimms. Both brothers soon established themselves as stimulating and gifted teachers, Jacob less than Wilhelm, and they broke new ground in the study of German literature, which had only recently become an accepted field of study at the university.[24] Despite their warm welcome, it took some time for the Grimms to adapt to the new environment and demands on their time. They had envisioned spending the rest of their lives in Kassel, devoted to research, and neither one of them had experience as lecturers. Aside from their teaching duties and social obligations, they did, however, manage to continue writing and publishing important works: Jacob wrote the third volume of *German Grammar* (1831) and a major study entitled *German Mythology* (1835), while Wilhelm prepared the third revised edition of *Children's and Household Tales*. Though their positions were secure, there was a great deal of political unrest in Germany due to the severely repressive political climate since 1819. By 1830 many revolts and peasant uprisings had erupted, and a group of intellectuals known as Young Germany (*Jungdeutschland*) pushed for more democratic reform in different German principalities. For the most part, however, their members were persecuted and silenced, just as the peasants, too, were vanquished. Some leading writers, such as Ludwig Börne, Heinrich Heine, and Georg Büchner, took refuge in exile. The Brothers Grimm were not staunch supporters of the Young Germany movement, but they had always supported the liberal cause throughout Germany and were greatly affected by the political conflicts. Despite their workaholic tendencies, the Grimms were not ivory-tower scholars. They made political commitments and were active in local and national politics and participated in debates that pertained to their fields of inquiry and their profession.

In 1837, when King Ernst August II, a man who carried a notorious reputation with him from England, succeeded to the throne of Hannover, he revoked the constitution of 1833 and dissolved parliament. In his attempt to restore absolutism to the Kingdom of Hannover, of which Göttingen was a part, he declared that all civil servants must pledge an oath to serve him personally. Since the king was nominally the rector of the University of Göttingen, the Grimms were "legally" obligated to take an oath of allegiance, but instead they, along with five other renowned professors, led a protest against Ernst August and were summarily dismissed. In their stand for civil rights against the tyranny of the king, the "Göttingen Seven," as they were called, were strongly supported by the student body and by numerous influential people outside the Kingdom of Hannover. Nevertheless, Jacob was compelled to leave Göttingen immediately, or else he might have been imprisoned and executed.[25] He returned to Kassel, where he was joined by Wilhelm, Dortchen, and their children a few months later.

Once again, the Grimms were in desperate financial straits. Despite the fact that they received funds and support from hundreds of friends and admirers who backed their stand on academic freedom, the ruling monarchs of the various principalities prevented them from teaching at another university—either because they did not want to offend Ernst August or because they did not want to set a precedent concerning the constitutional rights of civil servants. It was during this time, to a large degree out of economic necessity, that Jacob and Wilhelm decided to embark on writing the *Deutsches Wörterbuch (German Dictionary)*, one of the most ambitious lexicographical undertakings of the nineteenth century. Though the income from this project would be meager, they hoped to support themselves through other publishing ventures as well. Indeed, the Grimms knew how to live parsimoniously, and they were content just to return to Kassel and to devote themselves to their research and immense correspondence with scholars throughout the world. In the meantime, Bettina von Arnim, a close friend and talented writer, to whom the Grimms dedicated the first edition of *Children's and Household Tales*, was trying to convince the new King of Prussia, Friedrich Wilhelm IV, to bring the brothers to Berlin.[26] She was joined by Savigny, who was now a professor of law in Berlin, and other influential friends. Finally, in November 1840, Jacob and Wilhelm received offers to become professors at the University of Berlin and to do research at the Academy of Sciences. It was not until March 1841, however, that the Grimms took up residence in Berlin and were able to continue their work on the *German Dictionary* and on other projects. In addition to the support for their research, the Prussian king also expected them to teach seminars and deliver lectures. Indeed, the Grimms played an active role in the institutionalization of German literature as a field of study in Berlin and at other universities. Nor did they shy away from political debates, despite the traumatic experiences in Göttingen.

During the initial years in Berlin (1841–1848), the Grimms were much more active than they had anticipated or desired. As Michaelis-Jena reports, "it took a while to get used to it all. The solitary Jacob disliked the many social distractions, worried about public appearances, and found academy meetings and committees boring and unproductive. Wilhelm, too, hoped that in time they would find more quietness. All the same, both were grateful for the friendliness shown to them everywhere. They were well received, and to have obtained security was an overwhelming relief."[27]

Indeed, the Grimms established a comfortable household. Their desks faced one another, and they plunged into their work. At the same time, they never avoided social and political obligations and were totally devoted to their family and intimate friends. The letters exchanged among the brothers, Dortchen, and Hermann Grimm, Wilhelm's oldest son, during this time indicate how close the family was.[28] Both Wilhelm and his son Hermann, who was later to become a professor of art history and took charge of the Grimms' papers, were frail and often became seriously ill, as did Dortchen. Their compassion and concern for one another were expressed not only in letters, but through their untiring acts to assist each other and their friends in times of need. Fortunately, the Grimms were financially secure, but they were also aware of the great social and political unrest in Germany due to poor harvests, famines, unemployment, and political oppression. It was only a matter of time before there would be major uprisings, not only in Germany, but throughout Europe.

In February 1848 workers, students, farmers, and many other people gathered in Paris to demonstrate their support for parliamentary reforms and to end corruption, unemployment, and unfair labor practices. The police and military tried to suppress the demonstrators, who erected barricades and fought the government troops, and a massive uprising began throughout France. This French revolution was the spark that ignited multiple revolutions throughout Europe for more or less the same reasons—poverty, political repression, corrupt governments, and antiquated political systems. In Germany the revolts began in March, first in the south, and then spread to west and north Prussia. The German demonstrators also demanded constitutional reforms, and there was less bloodshed because the rulers yielded to most of the demands. The great difference between France, which was already one single nation-state, and Germany, still constituted by 30 or more principalities, was that the German revolutionaries wanted to create one sovereign state and to unite the different principalities. To this end they called for a National Assembly in Frankfurt am Main. The Grimms were elected to the civil parliament, and Jacob was considered to be one of the most prominent men among the representatives at the National Assembly held in Frankfurt am Main. However, the brothers' hopes for democratic reform and the unification of the German principalities dwindled as one compromise after another was reached with the German monarchs. Both brothers retired from active politics after the demise of the revolutionary movement.[29] In fact, Jacob resigned from his position as professor in 1848, the same year he published his significant study entitled *Geschichte der deutschen Sprache* (*The History of the German Language*). Wilhelm retired from his post as professor in 1852. For the rest of their lives, the Grimms devoted most of their energy to completing the monumental *German Dictionary*, but they got only as far as the letter F. Symbolically, the last entry was the word *Frucht* (fruit).

Though they did not finish the *German Dictionary*, a task that had to be left to a multitude of scholars in the twentieth century, they did produce an astonishing number of significant pioneer studies during their lifetimes: Jacob published 21, and Wilhelm, 14. They collaborated on another 8. In addition, there are 12 volumes of their essays and notes and thousands of important letters, many which have not been published. The Grimms made scholarly contributions to the areas of folklore, history, ethnology, religion, jurisprudence, lexicography, and literary criticism. Even when they did not work as a team, they shared their ideas and discussed all their projects together. When Wilhelm died in 1859, the loss affected Jacob deeply; he became more solitary than ever before. Nevertheless, he did not abandon the projects he had held in common with his brother. In addition, the more he realized that his hopes for democratic reform were being dashed in Germany, the more he voiced his criticism of reactionary trends in Germany.

> How often the sad fate of our fatherland keeps coming to my mind and makes my heart heavy and my life bitter. It is impossible to think about salvation without realizing that it will necessitate great dangers and revolts. . . . Only ruthless power can bring help. The older I have become, the more democratic my inclinations have become. If I were to sit in the National Assembly once again, I would side much more with Uhland and Schröder, for there can be no salvation if we force the constitution onto the track of the existing conditions.[30]

Both Jacob and Wilhelm regarded their work as part of a social effort to foster a sense of justice among the German people and to create pride in the folk tradition. Jacob died in 1863 after completing the fourth volume of his book, *German Precedents*. In German the title, *Deutsche Weistümer*, connotes a sense of the wisdom of the ages that he felt should be passed on to the German people.

CHAPTER TWO

THE ORIGINS AND RECEPTION OF THE TALES

Though the Grimms made important discoveries in their research on ancient German literature and customs, they were neither the founders of folklore as a study in Germany, nor were they the first to begin collecting and publishing folk and fairy tales. In fact, from the beginning their principal concern was to uncover the etymological and linguistic truths that bound the German people together and were expressed in their laws and customs. As they progressed in their research and gradually realized through their historical investigations how deep the international and intercultural connections of the tales were, they altered many of their beliefs about what the "true" folk tale meant while at the same time they laid the basis for the exploration of national folklore in other countries. The fame and influence of the Brothers Grimm as collectors of folk and fairy tales must be understood in this context, and even here, chance played a major role in their destiny.

In 1806, as I have already indicated, the talented poet Clemens Brentano sought out the Grimms to help him collect tales because the brothers were known to have a vast knowledge of old German literature and folklore, even though they were quite young and relatively unknown. But they were also considered to be conscientious and indefatigable workers. Brentano hoped to use whatever tales they might send him in a future publication of folk tales, and he was able to publish some of the songs they gathered in the second and third volumes of *Des Knaben Wunderhorn* (*The Boy's Wonder Horn*) in 1808. On their side, the Grimms believed strongly in sharing their research and findings with friends and congenial scholars. Between 1807 and 1812 they began collecting tales with the express purpose of sending them to Brentano, as well as of using them as source material for gaining a greater historical understanding of the German language and customs. In 1811 Jacob even composed an appeal, "Aufforderung an die gesammten Freunde altdeutscher Poesie und Geschichte erlassen" ("Appeal to All Friends of Old German Poetry and History"),[1] which was never sent but laid the groundwork for his later more fully developed *Circular wegen der Aufsammlung der Volkspoesie* (*Circular-Letter Concerned with the Collecting of Folk Poetry*) printed and distributed in 1815. It is worth citing the initial part of this letter because it outlines the basic principles and intentions of the Grimms:

> Most Honored Sir!
>
> A society has been founded that is intended to spread throughout all of Germany and has as its goal to save and collect all the existing songs and tales that can be found among the common German peasantry (*Landvolk*). Our fatherland is still filled with this wealth of material all over the country that our honest ancestors planted for us, and that, despite the mockery and derision heaped upon it, continues to live, unaware of its own hidden beauty and carries within it its own unquenchable source. Our literature, history, and language cannot seriously be understood in their old and true origins without doing more exact research on this material. Consequently, it is our intention to track down as diligently as possible all the following items and to write them down as faithfully as possible:
>
> 1) Folk songs and rhymes that are performed at different occasions throughout the year, at celebrations, in spinning parlors, on the dance floors, and during work in the fields; first of

all, those songs and rhymes that have epic contents, that is, in which there is an event; wherever possible with their very words, ways, and tones.

2) Tales in prose that are told and known, in particular the numerous nursery and children's fairy tales about giants, dwarfs, monsters, enchanted and rescued royal children, devils, treasures, and magic instruments as well as local legends that help explain certain places (like mountains, rivers, lakes, swamps, ruined castles, towers, stones and monuments of ancient times). It is important to pay special attention to animal fables, in which fox and wolf, chicken, dog, cat, frog, mouse, crow, sparrow, etc. appear for the most part.

3) Funny tales about tricks played by rogues and anecdotes; puppet plays from old times with Hanswurst and the devil.

4) Folk festivals, mores, customs, and games; celebrations at births, weddings, and funerals; old legal customs, special taxes, duties, jobs, border regulations, etc.

5) Superstitions about spirits, ghosts, witches, good and bad omens; phenomena and dreams.

6) Proverbs, unusual dialects, parables, word composition.

It is extremely important that these items are to be recorded faithfully and truly, without embellishment and additions, whenever possible from the mouth of the tellers in and with their very own words in the most exact and detailed way. It would be of double value if everything could be obtained in the local live dialect. On the other hand, even fragments with gaps are not to be rejected. Indeed, all the derivations, repetitions, and copies of the same tale can be individually important. Here we advise that you not be misled by the deceptive opinion that something has already been collected and recorded, and therefore that you discard a story. Many things that appear to be modern have often only been modernized and have their undamaged source beneath. As soon as one has a great familiarity with the contents of this folk literature (*Volkspoesie*), one will gradually be able to evaluate the alleged simplistic, crude, and even repulsive aspects more discreetly. In general the following should still be noted: although actually every area should be completely searched and explored, there are preferential places more deserving than the large cities and the towns, than the villages, and these are the places in the quiet and untouched woods and mountains that are fruitful and blessed. The same is the case with certain classes of people such as the shepherds, fishermen,

> miners—they have a stronger attachment to these tales, and these people are to be preferred and asked as are in general old people, women, and children, who keep the tales fresh in their memories.
>
> You have been selected to become a member of this society, my honored Sir, and to lend a helping hand in the firm conviction that you will be moved by the usefulness and emergency of our purpose, that today cannot be postponed without great harm in view of the increasing and damaging decline and closure of folk customs. We hope that you will be in a position to explore the region of ________________ according to our intention.[2]

What is striking in this circular letter is the emphasis placed on collecting natural and pure lore and bringing it together to celebrate a paternal heritage of a fatherland. The Grimms shared a sense of imaginative *nation-building*, and the Germany they thought had existed and existed during their lifetime was a Germany that they sought to create in the name of the fatherland. Indeed, they endeavored to bring together their own family and friends in much the same idealistic and reverent manner that they collected and reconstituted the tales. From the beginning, the Grimms sensed that they were doing monumental research about tales, legends, customs, proverbs, and expressions stemming from the people. All the more reason to collect and write down this material as accurately as possible before it was lost. To do this, they would need the help of friends and scholars.

Contrary to popular belief, the Grimms did not collect their tales by visiting peasants in the countryside and writing down the tales that they heard. Their primary method was to invite storytellers to their home and then have them tell the tales aloud, which the Grimms either noted down on first hearing or after a couple of hearings. Most of the storytellers during this period were educated young women from the middle class or aristocracy.[3] For instance, in Kassel a group of young women from the Wild family (Dortchen, Gretchen, Lisette, and Marie Elisabeth), and their mother (Dorothea), and from the Hassenpflug family (Amalie, Jeanette, and Marie) used to meet regularly to relate tales they had heard from their nursemaids, governesses, and servants, or tales they may have read. In 1808 Jacob formed a friendship with Werner von Haxthausen, a student at the University of Halle, who came from Westphalia and was interested in collecting folk songs. Wilhelm saw a great deal of Haxthausen in Halle when he was trying to find a cure for his heart problems in 1809. Then, in 1811 Wilhelm visited the Haxthausen estate and became acquainted there with a circle of young men and women (Ludowine, Marianne, and August von Haxthausen, and Jenny and Annette von Droste-Hülfshoff), whose tales he noted down. Still, the majority of the storytellers came from Hessia: Dorothea Viehmann, a tailor's wife from nearby Zwehrn who used to sell fruit in Kassel, would visit the Grimms and told them a good many significant tales; and Johann Friedrich (*Wachtmeister* or sentinel) Krause, an old retired soldier, gave the brothers tales in exchange for some of their old clothes.[4] Many of the tales that the Grimms recorded were of French origin because the Hassenpflugs were of Huguenot ancestry and spoke French at home. Most of the brothers' informants were familiar with both the oral tradition and literary tradition of tale-telling and would combine motifs from both sources in their renditions. In addition to the tales of these storytellers and others who came later, the Grimms took tales directly from books, journals, and letters and edited them according to their taste, preference, and familiarity with different versions.

While they were still collecting tales, Brentano requested in 1810 that the Grimms send him their collection, and the Brothers had copies made and sent 49 texts to him. They had copies made because they felt Brentano would take great poetic license and turn them into substantially different tales, whereas they were intent on using the tales to document basic truths about the customs and practices of the German people and on preserving their authentic ties to the oral tradition. Actually, the Grimms need not have worried about Brentano's "mistreatment" of their tales, for he never touched them, but instead abandoned them—the exact date is uncertain—in the Ölenberg Monastery in Alsace without ever informing anyone that he had done this. Only in 1920 were the handwritten tales rediscovered, and they were published in different editions in 1924, 1927, and 1974. The last publication, by Heinz Rölleke, is the most scholarly and useful, for he has carefully shown how the Grimms' original handwritten manuscripts can help us to document their sources and reveal the great changes the brothers made in shaping the tales.[5]

As it happened, after the Grimms sent their collected texts to Brentano, who was unreliable and was going through great personal difficulties, they decided to publish the tales themselves and began refining them and preparing them for publication. They also kept adding new tales to their collection. Jacob set the tone, but the brothers were very much in agreement about how they wanted to alter and stylize the tales. This last point is significant because some critics have wanted to see major differences between Jacob and Wilhelm. These critics have argued that there was a dispute between the brothers after Wilhelm assumed major responsibility for the editing of the tales in 1815 and that Wilhelm transformed them against Jacob's will. There is no doubt that Wilhelm was the primary editor after 1815, but, as Gunhild Ginschel has clearly shown,[6] Jacob established the framework for their editing practice between 1807 and 1812 and even edited the majority of the tales for the first volume. A comparison of the way Jacob and Wilhelm worked both before and after 1815 does not reveal major differences, except that Wilhelm did take more care to refine the style and make the contents of the tales more acceptable for a children's audience—or, really, for adults who wanted the tales censored for children. Otherwise, the editing of Jacob and Wilhelm exhibits the same tendencies from the beginning to the end of their project: the endeavor to make the tales stylistically smoother; the concern for clear sequential structure; the desire to make the stories more lively and pictorial by adding adjectives, old proverbs, and direct dialogue; the reinforcement of motives for action in the plot; the infusion of psychological motifs; and the elimination of elements that might detract from a rustic tone. The model for a good many of their tales was the work of the gifted romantic artist Philipp Otto Runge, whose two stories in dialect, "The Fisherman and His Wife" and "The Juniper Tree," represented in tone, structure, and content the ideal narrative that the Grimms wanted to create. But even more important for all their work was Brentano, whom they often dismissed as too free with poetic additions; and yet, they were more indebted to him than many scholars have assumed. In fact, Heinz Rölleke indicates that they were very close to him in their "contamination" and "stylization" of their tales:

> Brentano was originally responsible for the interest of the Brothers Grimm in the phenomenon of the folk tale. He stamped their ideal style decisively through his references to useful old sources and references to oral traditions, and above all through his high admiration for Runge's fairy-tale style as well as through his tendencies to adapt narratives in his own publications of "The Little Mouse," "The Story about the Little Chicken," and "Bearskin," among others.
>
> At first the Brothers Grimm unconditionally followed [Brentano's work] in all this. That is, they learned with and through Brentano their method of contamination of related texts, a method that they practiced so successfully, and they learned the restoration of corrupt passages and especially the reconstruction of what they assumed to be the original fairy-tale tone. Above all, however, from the beginning they followed the tracks indicated to them by Clemens Brentano in their search for tales: only texts and subject matter that corresponded to his ideal were regarded by them and were favored by them. The so-called real folk transmission of tales that distinguished themselves not least because of their abstruse, fragmentary, obscene or also rebellious qualities did not appeal to them and do not appear in their collection.[7]

When Rölleke uses the term "contamination," he does not do so in a pejorative sense. On the contrary, in folklore terms, to contaminate means to mix different variants of a known tale to form either a new variant or an ideal tale type based on different variants. On the one hand, this method of contamination makes the original pure substance of the tale impure, but on the other, it revives the tale and gives it new life. In fact, it is only through such contamination in the nineteenth century that much of folklore was preserved. So, the Grimms were not merely collectors of "pure" folk tales, they were creative "contaminators"[8] and artists. In fact, their major accomplishment in publishing their two volumes of 156 tales all together in 1812 and 1815 was to *create* an ideal type for the *literary* fairy tale, one that sought to be as close to the oral tradition as possible, while incorporating stylistic, formal, and substantial thematic changes to appeal to a growing middle-class audience. What concerned them most was to create a facsimile in High German of the folk manner and tone of storytelling without losing the substance of the tales. Their historical and synthetic reproduction of the oral tales became a model for the majority of European collectors in the nineteenth century.[9] By 1819, when the second edition of the tales, now in one volume and including 170 texts, was published, and Wilhelm assumed complete charge of the revisions, the brothers had established the form and manner through which they wanted to preserve, contain, and present to the German public what they felt were profound truths about the origins of German culture and European civilization. Indeed, they saw the "childhood of humankind" as embedded in customs that Germans had cultivated, and the tales, as samples of *Naturpoesie* (natural poetry), were to serve as reminders of such a rich, genuine culture.

After 1819 there were 5 more editions and eventually 39 new texts added to the collection and 8 omitted. By the time the seventh edition appeared in 1857, there were 211 texts in all. Most of the additions after 1819 were from literary sources, and the rest were either sent to the brothers by informants or recorded from a primary source. Indeed, the chief task after 1819 was largely one of refinement, selection, and combination: Wilhelm often changed the original texts by comparing them to different versions that he had acquired. While he evidently tried to retain what he and Jacob considered the essential message of the tale, he tended to make the tales more proper and charming for bourgeois audiences. Here he differed somewhat from Jacob insofar as he was more florid, while the older brother was more "scientific." Both insisted on "accuracy," that is, the approximation of what they believed to be the historical "truth" of the tale, even though they were fully aware that this could not be accomplished. Paradoxically, they sought to recapture truths by changing and synthesizing different versions they collected over time. In this regard their truthful representation of a narrative was closely connected to an idealization of what they sincerely believed to be the original messages of the tales. Thus it is crucial to be aware of the changes both brothers made between the original handwritten manuscript and the last edition of 1857, for there are subtle shifts of meanings and contradictions in their work. Compare the following, for example:

"Snow White"—Ölenberg Manuscript

When Snow White awoke the next morning, they asked her how she happened to get there. And she told them everything, how her mother, the queen, had left her alone in the woods and gone away. The dwarfs took pity on her and persuaded her to remain with them and do the cooking for them when they went to the mines. However, she was to beware of the queen and not to let anyone into the house.[10]

"Snow White"—1812 Edition

When Snow White awoke, they asked her who she was and how she happened to get into the house. Then she told them how her mother had wanted to have her put to death, but the hunter had spared her life, and how she had run the entire day and finally arrived at their house. So the dwarfs took pity on her and said, "If you keep house for us and cook, sew, make the beds, wash and knit, and keep everything tidy and clean, you may stay with us, and you will have everything you want. In the evening, when we come home, dinner must be ready. During the day we are in the mines and dig for gold, so you will be alone. Beware of the queen and let no one into the house."[11]

"Rapunzel"—1812 Edition

At first Rapunzel was afraid, but soon she took such a liking to the young king that she made an agreement with him: he was to come every day and be pulled up. Thus they lived merrily and joyfully for a certain time, and the fairy did not discover anything until one day when Rapunzel began talking to her and said, "Tell me, Mother Gothel, why do you think my clothes have become too tight for me and no longer fit?"[12]

"Rapunzel"—1857 Edition

When he entered the tower, Rapunzel was at first terribly afraid, for she had never laid eyes on a man before. However, the prince began to talk to her in a friendly way and told her that her song had touched his heart so deeply that he had not been able to rest until he had seen her. Rapunzel then lost her fear, and when he asked her whether she would have him for her husband, and she saw that he was young and handsome, she thought, he'll certainly love me better than old Mother Gothel. So she said yes and placed her hand in his.

"I want to go with you very much," she said, "but I don't know how I can get down. Every time you come, you must bring a skein of silk with you, and I'll weave it into a ladder. When it's finished, then I'll climb down, and you can take me away on your horse."

They agreed that until then he would come to her every evening, for the old woman came during the day. Meanwhile, the sorceress did not notice anything, until one day Rapunzel blurted out, "Mother Gothel, how is it that you're much heavier than the prince? When I pull him up, he's here in a second."[13]

"The Tale about the Nasty Spinning of Wax"—1812 Edition

In olden times there lived a king who loved flax spinning more than anything in the world, and his queen and daughters had to spin the entire day. If he did not hear the wheels humming, he became angry. One day he had to take a trip, and before he departed, he gave the queen a large box with flax and said, "I want this flax spun by the time I return."[14]

"The Three Spinners"—1857 Edition

There once was a lazy maiden who did not want to spin, and no matter what her mother said, she refused to spin. Finally, her mother became so angry and impatient that she beat her, and her daughter began to cry loudly. Just then the queen happened to be driving by, and when she heard the crying, she ordered the carriage to stop, went into the house, and asked the mother why she was beating her daughter, for her screams could be heard out on the street. The woman was too ashamed to tell the queen that her daughter was lazy and said, "I can't get her to stop spinning. She does nothing but spin and spin, and I'm so poor that I can't provide the flax."

"Well," the queen replied, "there's nothing I like to hear more than the sound of spinning, and I'm never happier than when I hear the constant humming of the wheels. Let me take your daughter with me to my castle. I've got plenty of flax, and she can spin as much as she likes."[15]

"Good Bowling and Card Playing"—1812 Edition

Once upon a time there was an old king, who had the most beautiful daughter in the world. One day he announced: "Whoever can keep watch in my old castle for three nights can have the princess for his bride."

Now there was a young boy from a poor family who thought to himself: 'I'll risk my life. Nothing to lose, a lot to win. What's there to think about?'

So he presented himself to the king and offered to keep watch in the castle for three nights.

"You may request to take three things into the castle with you, but they have to be lifeless objects," the king said.

"Well, I'd like to take a carpenter's bench with the knife, a lathe, and fire."

All of these things were carried into the castle for him. When it began to get dark, he himself went inside. At first everything was quiet. He built a fire, placed the carpenter's bench with the knife next to it, and sat down on the lathe. Toward midnight, however, a rumbling could be heard, first softly, then more loudly:

"Bif! Baf! Hehe! Holla ho!"

It became more dreadful, then it was somewhat quiet. Finally a leg came down the chimney and stood right before him.

"Hey there!" the young man cried. "How about some more? One is too little."

The noise began once again. Another leg fell down the chimney and then another and another until there were nine.

"That's enough now. I've got enough for bowling, but there are no balls. Out with them!"

There was a tremendous uproar and two heads fell down the chimney. He put them in the lathe and turned them until they were smooth. "Now they'll roll much better!"

Then he did the same with the legs and set them up like bowling pins.

"Hey, now I can have some fun!"

Suddenly, two large black cats appeared and strode around the fire. "Meow! Meow!" they screeched. "We're freezing! We're freezing!"

"You fools! What are you screaming about? Sit down by the fire and warm yourselves."

After the cats had warmed themselves, they said, "Comrade, we want to play a round of cards."

"All right," he replied, "but first show me your paws. You have such long claws. First I've got to give them a good clipping."

Upon saying this, he grabbed them by the scruffs of their necks and lifted them to the carpenter's bench. There he fastened them to the vise and beat them to death. Afterward he carried them outside and threw them into a pond that lay across from the castle. Just as he returned to the castle and wanted to settle down and warm himself by the fire, many black cats and dogs came out of every nook and cranny, more and more so that he could not hide himself. They screamed, stamped on the fire and kicked it about so that the fire went out. So he grabbed his carving knife and yelled, "Get out of here, you riff-raff!"

And he began swinging the knife. Most of the cats and dogs ran away. The others were killed, and he carried them out and threw them into the pond. Then he went back inside to the fire and blew the sparks so that the fire began again and he could warm himself.

After he had warmed himself, he was tired and lay down in a large bed that stood in a corner. Just as he wanted to fall asleep, the bed began to stir and raced around the entire castle.

"That's fine with me. Just keep it up!"

So the bed drove around as though six horses were pulling it over stairs and landings: "Bing-bang!"

It turned upside down, from top to bottom, and he was beneath it. So he flung the blankets and pillows into the air and jumped off.

"Whoever wants to have a ride can have one!"

Then he lay down next to the fire until it was day.

In the morning the king came, and when he saw the young man lying asleep, he thought the boy was dead and said, "What a shame."

But when the young man heard the words, he awoke, and when he saw the king, he stood up. Then the king asked him how things had gone during the night.

"Quite good. One night's gone by, the other two will also be gone."

Indeed, the other nights were just like the first. But he knew already how to handle them, and on the fourth day he was rewarded with the beautiful king's daughter.[16]

"A Tale about the Boy Who Went Forth to Learn What Fear Was"—1857 Edition

A father had two sons. The older was smart and sensible and could cope in any situation, while the younger was stupid and could neither learn nor understand anything. Whenever people encountered him, they said, "He'll always be a burden to his father!"

If there were things to be done, the older son was always the one who had to take care of them. Yet, if the father asked the older son to fetch something toward evening or during the night, and if that meant he would have to pass through the churchyard or some other scary place, he would answer, "Oh, no, Father, I won't go there. It gives me the creeps!" Indeed, he was afraid.

Sometimes stories that would send shivers up your spine were told by the fireside at night, and the listeners would say: "Oh, it gives me the creeps!" Often the younger son would be sitting in the corner and listening, but he never understood what they meant. "They're always saying 'It gives me the creeps! It gives me the creeps!' But it doesn't give me the creeps. It's probably some kind of a trick that I don't understand."

One day his father happened to say to him, "Listen, you over there in the comer, you're getting too big and strong. It's time you learned how to earn your living. Look how hard your brother works, while you're just a hopeless case."

"Oh, no, Father," he responded. "I'd gladly learn something. If possible, I'd like to learn how to get the creeps. That's something I know nothing about."

When the older son heard that, he laughed and thought to himself, 'Dear Lord, my brother's really a dumbbell! He'll never amount to anything. You've got to start young to get anywhere.'

The father sighed and answered, "You're sure to learn all about getting the creeps in due time, but it won't help you earn a living."

Shortly after this, the sexton came to the house for a visit, and the father complained about his younger son, that he was incapable of doing anything, much less learning and knowing anything. "Just think, when I asked him what he wanted to do to earn a living, he actually said he wanted to learn how to get the creeps."

"If that's all he wants," the sexton replied, "he can learn it at my place. Just hand him over to me, and I'll smooth over his rough edges."

The father was pleased to do this because he thought, 'the boy needs some shaping up.'

So the sexton took him to his house, where the boy was assigned the task of ringing the church bell. After a few days had passed, the sexton woke him at midnight and told him to get up, climb the church steeple, and ring the bell.

'Now you'll learn what the creeps are,' the sexton thought, and secretly went up ahead of him. When the boy reached the top and turned around to grab hold of the bell rope, he saw a white figure standing on the stairs across from the sound hole.

"Who's there?" he cried out, but the figure did not answer, nor did it move an inch. "Answer me," the boy shouted, "or get out of here! You've no business being here at night."

However, the sexton did not move, for he wanted to make the boy think he was a ghost. The boy shouted a second time, "What do you want? If you're an honest man, say something, or I'll throw you down the stairs!"

'He really can't be as mean as that,' the sexton thought, and he kept still, standing there as if he were made of stone.

The boy shouted at him a third time, and when that did not help, he lunged at the ghost and pushed him down the stairs. The ghost fell ten steps and lay in a corner. The boy then rang the bell, went home, got into bed without saying a word, and fell asleep. The sexton's wife waited for her husband for a long time, but he failed to return. Finally, she became anxious, woke the boy, and asked, "Do you know where my husband is? He climbed the steeple ahead of you."

"No," replied the boy. "But someone was standing across from the sound hole. When he refused to answer me or go away, I thought he was some sort of scoundrel and pushed him down the stairs. Why don't you go and see if it was him? I'd feel sorry if it was."

The wife ran off and found her husband, who was lying in a corner and moaning because of a broken leg. She carried him down the stairs and then rushed off to the boy's father screaming as she went.

"Your boy has caused a terrible accident!" she cried out. "He threw my husband down the stairs and made him break a leg. Get that good-for-nothing out of our house!"

The father was mortified and ran straight to the sexton's house, where he began scolding the boy. "What kind of godless tricks have you been playing? The devil must have put you up to it!"

"Father," he replied, "just listen to me. I'm completely innocent. He was standing there in the dark like someone who had evil designs. I didn't know who he was and warned him three times to say something or go away."

"Ah," said the father, "you'll never be anything but trouble for me! Get out of my sight. I don't want to see you anymore."

"All right, Father. Gladly. Just give me until daylight, and I'll go away and learn how to get the creeps. Then I'll know a trick or two and be able to earn a living."

"Learn what you want," the father said. "It's all the same to me. Here's fifty talers. Take them and go out into the wide world, but don't tell anyone where you come from or who your father is because I'm ashamed of you."

"Yes, Father, as you wish. If that's all you desire, I can easily bear that in mind."

At daybreak the boy put the fifty talers in his pocket, went out on the large highway, and kept saying to himself, "If I could only get the creeps! If I could only get the creeps!"

As the boy was talking to himself, a man came along and overheard him. When they had gone some distance together, they caught sight of the gallows, and the man said to him, "You see the tree over there. That's where seven men were wedded to the ropemaker's daughter. Now they're learning how to fly. Sit down beneath the tree and wait till night comes. Then you'll certainly learn how to get the creeps."

"If that's all it takes," the boy responded, "I can do it with ease. And, if I learn how to get the creeps as quickly as that, you shall have my fifty talers. Just come back here tomorrow morning."

The boy went to the gallows, sat down beneath it, and waited until evening came. Since he was cold, he made a fire. Nevertheless, at midnight the wind became colder, and he could not get warm in spite of the fire. When the wind knocked the hanged men against each other and they swung back and forth, he thought, 'If you're freezing down here by the fire, they must really be cold and shivering up there.' Since he felt sorry for them, he took a ladder, climbed up, untied one hanged man after the other, and hauled all seven down to the ground. Then he stirred the fire, blew on it, and set them all around it so they might warm themselves. However, they sat there without moving, and their clothes caught on fire.

"Be careful," he said, "otherwise I'll hang you all back up there."

The dead men did not hear. Indeed, they just remained silent, and their rags continued to burn. Then the boy became angry and said, "If you won't take care, I can't help you, and I surely won't let you burn me."

So he hung them up again, all in a row, sat down by his fire, and fell asleep. Next morning the man came and wanted his fifty talers.

"Well," he said, "now you know what the creeps are, don't you?"

"No," answered the boy. "How should I know? Those men up there didn't open their mouths. They're so stupid they let the few old rags they're wearing get burned."

The man realized he would never get the fifty talers that day. So he went off saying, "Never in my life have I met anyone like that!"

The boy also went his way, and once again he began talking to himself. "Oh, if I could only get the creeps! If I could only get the creeps!"

A carter, who was walking behind him, overheard him and asked, "Who are you?"

"I don't know," answered the boy.

"Where do you come from?" the carter continued questioning him.

"I don't know."

"Who's your father?"

"I'm not allowed to tell."

"What's that you're always mumbling to yourself?"

"Oh," the boy responded, "I want to get the creeps, but nobody can teach me how."

"Stop your foolish talk," said the carter. "Come along with me, and I'll see if I can find a place for you to stay."

The boy went with the carter, and in the evening they reached an inn, where they intended to spend the night. As they entered the main room, the boy spoke loudly once more. "If I could only get the creeps! If I could only get the creeps!"

The innkeeper heard this and laughed. "If that's what you desire," he remarked, "there'll be ample opportunity for you to get it here."

"Oh, be quiet!" the innkeeper's wife said. "There have already been enough foolish fellows who've lost their lives. It would be a mighty shame if that boy with such pretty eyes never saw the light of day again."

But the boy said, "It doesn't matter how hard it may be. I want to get the creeps. That's why I left home." He kept bothering the innkeeper until the man told him about the haunted castle nearby, where one could really learn how to get the creeps. All he had to do was to spend three nights in it. The king had promised his daughter to anyone who would undertake the venture, and she was the most beautiful maiden under the sun. There were also great treasures in the castle guarded by evil spirits. Once the treasures were set free, they would be enough to make a poor man rich. Many men had already gone into the castle, but none had ever come out again.

The next morning the boy appeared before the king and said, "If I may have your permission, I'd like to spend three nights in the haunted castle."

The king looked at him and found the boy to his liking, so he said, "You may request three things to take with you into the castle, but they must be lifeless objects."

"Well then," he answered, "I'd like to have a fire, a lathe, and a carpenter's bench with a knife."

The king had these things carried into the castle for him during the day. Just before nightfall the boy himself went up to the castle, made a bright fire in one of the rooms, set up the carpenter's bench with the knife next to it, and sat down on the lathe.

"Oh, if I could only get the creeps!" he said. "But I don't think I'll learn it here either."

Toward midnight he wanted to stir the fire again, but just as he was blowing it, he suddenly heard a scream coming from a corner. "Meow! Meow! We're freezing!"

"You fools!" he cried out. "What are you screaming for? If you're freezing, come sit down by the fire and warm yourselves."

No sooner had he said that than two big black cats came over with a tremendous leap, sat down beside him, and glared ferociously at him with their fiery eyes. After a while, when they had warmed themselves, they said, "Comrade, let's play a round of cards."

"Why not?" he responded. "But first show me your paws."

They stretched out their claws.

"My goodness!" he said. "What long nails you have! Wait, I've got to give them a good clipping."

Upon saying that, he grabbed them by the scruffs of their necks, lifted them onto the carpenter's bench, and fastened their paws in a vise.

"I was keeping a sharp eye on you two," he said, "and now I've lost my desire to play cards."

Then he beat them to death and threw them into the water. But, after he had put an end to those two and was about to sit down at his fire again, black cats and black dogs on glowing chains came out of all the nooks and crannies, and they kept coming and coming so it was impossible for him to flee. They made a gruesome noise, stamped on his fire, tore it apart, and tried to put it out. He watched them calmly for a while, but when it became so awful that he could no longer stand it, he grabbed his knife and yelled, "Get out of here, you lousy creatures!" And he started swinging the knife. Some of them ran away while he killed the rest and threw them into the pond. When he returned to his place, he built up his fire again by blowing on the sparks and proceeded to warm himself. As he was sitting there, his eyelids grew heavy, and he felt a strong desire to sleep. Then he looked around and saw a large bed in the corner.

"That's just what I was looking for," he said and lay down on it. But just as he was about to shut his eyes, the bed began to move by itself and raced all around the castle.

"Keep it up," he said. "But go a little faster."

The bed sped on as though it were being draw by six horses. It rolled through doorways and up and down stairs. Then all of a sudden—*Bing-bang!* It turned upside down and lay on top of him like a mountain. But he flung the blankets and pillows in the air, climbed out, and said, "Now, anyone else who wants a ride can have one." He lay down by the fire and slept until it was day.

In the morning the king came, and when he saw the boy lying on the ground, he thought that he was dead and that the ghosts had killed him.

"What a pity! He was such a handsome fellow," the king said.

Upon hearing this the boy sat up and said, "It's not over yet!"

The king was astonished but also glad and asked him how things had gone.

"Very well," he answered. "One night's over and done with. The other two will also pass."

Then he went to the innkeeper, who gaped at him in amazement.

"I never expected to see you alive again," he said. "Have you learned now what the creeps are?"

"No," he said. "It's no use. If only someone could tell me!"

The second night he went up to the old castle, sat down at the fire, and repeated his old refrain. "If I could only get the creeps!"

Toward midnight he heard a lot of noise and rumbling, first softly, then louder and louder. Soon it became quiet for a while until suddenly, with a loud cry, half a man came tumbling down the chimney and fell right at his feet.

"Hey there!" cried the boy. "There's a half missing. This isn't enough."

Once again the noise began. There was a roaring and howling, and the other half came tumbling down.

"Wait," the boy said. "I'll just give the fire a little stir for you."

After he had done that, he looked around and saw that the two pieces had joined together to form a gruesome-looking man who was now sitting in his place.

"That wasn't part of the bargain," said the boy. "The bench is mine."

The man tried to push him away, but the boy did not let him. Instead, he gave the man a mighty shove and sat back down in his place.

Suddenly more men came tumbling down the chimney, one after the other, and they brought nine dead men's bones and two dead men's skulls, set them up, and began to play a game of ninepins.

The boy felt a desire to play as well and asked, "Hey, can I play too?"

"Yes, if you have money."

"Money enough," he answered, "but your balls aren't round."

He took the skulls, put them in the lathe, and turned them until they were round.

"Now they'll roll much better," he said. "Hurray! Let's have some fun!"

He joined their game and lost some of his money, but when the clock struck twelve, everything disappeared before his eyes, and he lay down and fell asleep in peace.

The next morning the king came to inquire about him, and he asked, "How did things go for you this time?"

"I played a game of ninepins," he said, "and I lost a few hellers."

"Didn't you get the creeps?"

"Not at all!" he responded. "I had a lot of fun. If I only knew what the creeps were!"

The third night he sat down on his bench again and said quite sadly, "If I could only get the creeps!"

When it grew late, six huge men came in carrying a coffin. Then he said, "Aha, that must be my cousin who died just a few days ago." He signaled to them with his finger and cried out, "Come here, little cousin, come here!"

They set the coffin on the ground, and he went over and lifted the lid. There was a dead man lying inside, and the boy felt his face, which was as cold as ice.

"Wait," he said. "I'll warm you up a bit."

He went to the fire, warmed his hand, and placed it on the dead man's face, but it remained cold. So he took the dead man out and set him near the fire, then put him on his lap and rubbed his arms until his blood began circulating again. When that did not work either, the boy recalled that two people can warm each other up when they lie in bed together. So he brought the man to the bed, covered him, and lay down beside him. After a while the dead man got warm and began to move.

"You see, cousin," said the boy. "What if I hadn't warmed you?"

But the dead man shouted, "Now I'm going to strangle you!"

"What?" the boy responded. "Is that my thanks? I'm going to put you right back into your coffin."

He lifted him up, tossed him inside, and shut the lid. Then the six men returned and carried the coffin away.

"I can't get the creeps," the boy said. "I'll never learn it here no matter how long I live."

Just then a ghastly-looking man entered. He was old and larger than the others and had a long white beard.

"Oh, you scoundrel!" The man cried out. "Now you'll learn what the creeps are, for you're about to die."

"Not so fast!" said the boy. "If I'm about to die, you'll have to get me first."

"Don't worry, I'll get you," said the monster.

"Easy does it. Don't talk so big! I'm just as strong as you are if not stronger."

"We'll see about that," said the old man. "If you're stronger than I am, I'll let you go. Come, let's give it a try."

He led the boy through dark passages to a smithy, picked up an ax, and drove an anvil right into the ground with one blow. "I can do better than that," the boy said, and he went to the other anvil. The old man, with his white beard hanging down, drew near him to watch. The boy grabbed the ax, split the anvil in two with one blow, and wedged the old man's beard in the middle.

"Now I've got you!" the boy said. "It's your turn to die!"

He seized an iron and beat the old man until he whimpered and begged the boy to stop and promised to give him great treasures. The boy pulled out the ax and let him go. The old man led him back into the castle and showed him three chests full of gold in a cellar.

"One of them," he said, "belongs to the poor, the second to the king, and the third is yours."

Just then the clock struck twelve, and the ghost vanished, leaving the boy standing in the dark.

"I'll find my way out of here all the same," he said, and groped about until he found the way back to his room, where he fell asleep by the fire.

In the morning the king came and said, "Now you must have learned what the creeps are."

"No," he answered. "What are they? My dead cousin was here, and a bearded man came. He showed me a great deal of money down in the cellar but nobody told me what the creeps are."

> Then the king said, "You've saved the castle and shall marry my daughter."
>
> "That's all fine and good," he answered, "but I still don't know what the creeps are."
>
> Now the gold was brought up from the cellar, and the wedding was celebrated. The boy loved his wife dearly and was very happy, but he still kept saying, "If I could only get the creeps! If I could only get the creeps!"
>
> After a while his wife became annoyed by that, but her chambermaid said, "Don't worry. I'll make sure he gets to know what the creeps are."
>
> She went out to a brook that ran through the garden and fetched a pocket full of minnows. That night, when the young king was sleeping, his wife pulled the covers off him and poured the bucket full of cold water and minnows on him. Then the little fish began flapping all over him, causing him to wake up and exclaim, "Oh, I've got the creeps! I've got the creeps! Now I know, dear wife, just what the creeps are."[17]

As is evident from the above examples, the Grimms made major changes while editing the tales. They eliminated erotic and sexual elements that might be offensive to middle-class morality, added numerous Christian expressions and references, emphasized specific role models for male and female protagonists according to the dominant patriarchal code of that time, and endowed many of the tales with a "homey" or *biedermeier* flavor by the use of diminutives, quaint expressions, and cute descriptions. The examples of "Good Bowling and Card Playing" and the "Tale about the Boy Who Went Forth to Learn What Fear Was" have been provided in full to show just how carefully the Grimms artistically "contaminated" their tales.[18] What was originally a short story that featured a resolute young boy from a peasant family was transformed by Wilhelm into a comic fairy tale about a bumbling boy, who stumbles into wealth and a propitious marriage. The language is embellished, and the sequences are expanded to flow more smoothly, while the entire meaning of the tale is changed. Although children might have liked and might still like both versions, the "Tale about the Boy Who Went Forth to Learn What Fear Was" was not included in the *Small Edition* of the brothers and was never specifically intended for children. This is an important point to stress.

Though the collection was not originally printed with children in mind as the primary audience—the first two volumes had scholarly annotations, which were later published separately—Wilhelm made all the editions from 1819 on more appropriate for children, or rather, conform to what he thought would be proper for children to learn. Indeed, some of the tales, such as "Mother Trudy" and "The Stubborn Child," are intended to be harsh lessons for children. Such didacticism did not contradict what both the Grimms thought the collection should be, namely an *Erziehungsbuch*, an educational manual. The tendency toward attracting a virtuous middle-class audience is most evident in the so-called *Kleine Ausgabe* (*Small Edition*), a selection of 50 tales from the *Grosse Ausgabe* (*Large Edition*). The *Small Edition* was first published in 1825 in an effort to popularize the larger work and to create a best-seller. Interestingly, the Grimms based this edition on the successful translation of Edgar Taylor's *German Popular Tales* (1823) with illustrations by George Cruikshank. This collection was produced explicitly for children, and though the translations have a fresh, colloquial style, they are also tendentious and moralistic. In this regard, Wilhelm was somewhat influenced by Taylor in his endeavor to cater to a wider audience. There were ten editions of this *Kleine Ausgabe* from 1825 to 1858, which contained the majority of the *Zaubermärchen* (magic fairy tales). With such tales as "Cinderella," "Snow White," "Sleeping Beauty," "Little Red Riding Hood," and "The Frog King," all of which underline morals in keeping with the Protestant ethic and a patriarchal notion of sex roles, the book was bound to be a success.

The magic fairy tales were the ones that were the most popular and acceptable in Europe and America during the nineteenth century, but it is important to remember that the Grimms' collection also includes unusual fables, legends, anecdotes, jokes, and religious tales. The variety of their tales is often overlooked because only a handful have been selected by parents, teachers, publishers, and critics for special attention to form what we might consider today the Grimm canon. This selection process is generally neglected when critics talk about the effects of the tales and the way they should be conveyed or not conveyed to children.

As I have shown, given the scholarly apparatus and the original intention of the Grimms to reproduce genuine folklore for adult readers, the Grimms' collection *Children's and Household Tales* was not an immediate success in Germany. In fact, Ludwig Bechstein's later book *Deutsches Märchenbuch* (*German Book of Fairy Tales,* 1845), modeled on the work of the Grimms, was more popular for a time because of its overtly "folksy" and didactic appeal to children. However, the Grimms' collection held its own, and each edition was sold out. By the 1870s the Grimms' tales had been incorporated into the teaching curriculum in Prussia and other German principalities, and they were also included in primers and anthologies for children throughout the western world. By the beginning of the twentieth century, the *Children's and Household Tales* was second only to the Bible as a best-seller in Germany, and it has continued to hold this position. For instance, the celebration of the Grimms' two hundredth birthdays in 1985 and 1986 saw an astounding proliferation of the Grimms' collection of tales in all German-speaking countries, where more than 50 different illustrated editions of the Grimms' fairy tales were issued.[19] Furthermore, there is no doubt that the Grimms' tales, published either together in a single volume or individually as an illustrated book, continue to enjoy the same popularity throughout the world.

Such popularity has always intrigued critics, and advocates of various schools of thought have sought to analyze and interpret the "magic" of the Grimms' tales. Foremost among the scholars are the folklorists, educators, psychologists, and literary critics of different persuasions, including structuralists, literary historians, semioticians, and Marxists. Each group has made interesting contributions to the scholarship on the Grimms' tales, although there are times when historical truths about the Grimms' work are discarded or squeezed to fit into a pet theory.

The efforts made by folklorists to categorize the Grimms' tales after the nineteenth century were complicated by the fact that numerous German folklorists used the tales to explain ancient German customs and rituals, under the assumption that the tales were authentic documents of the German people.[20] This position, which overlooked the French and other European connections, led to an "Aryan," or nationalist, approach during the 1920s, 1930s, and 1940s, which allowed many German folklorists to interpret the tales along racist and elitist lines[21]—something that would have been antithetical to the Grimms' perspective. Though some folklorists outside Germany contributed to such a misconception of the tales by relating them to primordial myths and German mythology, the overall tendency of international folklore research in the latter part of the twentieth century has been to view the tales as part of the vast historical development of the oral tradition, wherein the Grimms' collection is given special attention because of its unusual mixture of oral and literary motifs. These motifs have been related by folklorists to motifs in other folk tales in an effort to find the origin of a particular motif or tale type and its variants. By doing this kind of research, folklorists have been able to chart distinctions in the oral traditions and customs of different countries.

Educators have not been interested in motifs so much as in the morals and the types of role models in the tales. Depending on the country and the educational standards in a particular historical period, teachers and school boards have often dictated which Grimms' tales are to be used (or abused). Generally speaking, such tales as "The Wolf and the Seven Young Kids," "Cinderella," "Little Red Cap," and "Snow White" have always been deemed acceptable because they instruct children through explicit warnings and lessons, even though some of the implicit messages may be harmful to children.[22] Most of the great pedagogical debates center around the brutality and cruelty in some tales, and the tendency among publishers and adapters of the tales has been to eliminate the harsh scenes. Consequently, Cinderella's sisters will not have their eyes pecked out; Little Red Cap and her grandmother will not be gobbled up by the wolf; the witch in "Snow White" will not be forced to dance in red-hot shoes; and the witch in "Hansel and Gretel" will not be shoved into an oven.

Such changes have annoyed critics of various psychological and psychoanalytic orientations because they believe that the violence and conflict in the tales derive from profound instinctual developments in the human psyche, and hence represent symbolical modes by which children and adults deal with sexual problems.[23] Most psychoanalytic critics take their cues from Freud, even if they have departed from his method and have joined another school of analysis.[24] One of the first important books about the psychological impact of the Grimms' tales was Josephine Belz's

Das Märchen und die Phantasie des Kindes (*The Fairy Tale and the Imagination of the Child*, 1918),[25] in which she tried to establish relevant connections between children's ways of fantasizing and the symbols in the tales. Later, Géza Roheim[26] and Carl Jung[27] wrote valuable studies of fairy tales that sought to go beyond Freud's theories. In the period following World War II, Aniela Jaffé,[28] Joseph Campbell,[29] Marie von Franz,[30] and Verena Kast[31] charted the links between archetypes, the collective unconscious, and fairy tales, while Erich Fromm,[32] Julius Heuscher,[33] and Bruno Bettelheim[34] focused on Oedipal conflicts from neo-Freudian positions in their analyses of some Grimms' tales. Finally, André Favat published an important study, *Child and Tale* (1977),[35] which uses Piaget's notions of child development, interests, and stages of understanding to explore the tales and their impact. Although the various psychoanalytic approaches have shed light on the symbolic meanings of the tales from the point of view of particular schools of thought, the tales have often been taken out of context to demonstrate the value of a psychoanalytic or psychological theory rather than to render a cultural and aesthetic appreciation and evaluation of the text.

Literary critics have reacted to the psychoanalytical approach in different ways. Influenced by the theories of Vladimir Propp (*Morphology of the Folktale*, 1968)[36] and Max Lüthi (*Once Upon a Time*, 1970),[37] formalists, structuralists, and semioticians have analyzed individual texts to discuss the structure of the tale, its aesthetic components and functions, and the hidden meanings of the signs. Literary historians and philologists such as Ludwig Denecke,[38] Heinz Rölleke,[39] and Lothar Bluhm[40] have tried to place the Grimms' work in a greater historical context in order to show how the Brothers helped develop a mixed genre, often referred to as the *Buchmärchen* (book tale), combining aspects of the oral and literary tradition. Sociological and Marxist critics such as Dieter Richter and Johannes Merkel,[41] Christa Bürger,[42] and Bernd Wollenweber[43] have discussed the tales in light of the social and political conditions in Germany during the nineteenth century and have drawn attention to the racist and sexist notions in the tales. In the process, they have added fuel to the debate among educators, psychologists, folklorists, and literary critics in regard to the use and relevance of the Grimms' tales.

The reception of the Grimms' tales, like the reception of classical literary works including the Bible and ancient Greek and Roman literature, is crucial in western civilization because the appreciation, evaluation, and use of these works determine our cultural heritage. We do not simply inherit major works of art and treat them as models that we want to emulate. Rather, we periodically select works of art from the past and preserve them in new ways (sometimes critically, sometimes uncritically) because we believe that they continue to speak to our present habits, customs, needs, wishes, and hopes. Not all the works that constitute our cultural heritage are "classical" or so-called works of high art. Some are fairy tales, folk songs, nursery rhymes, comic strips, or so-called popular or minor works of art, but they contain what Ernst Bloch, the German philosopher of hope, has designated a utopian surplus or an anticipatory illumination of a better life.[44] That is, there is always something "left over" in them, something indelible that provides glimpses into our universal struggles and suggests alternatives to our present personal and social situation. These artworks form part of our cultural heritage because they are also historical documents of how we endeavor to mark the world, to provide significance to our lives, which we want to endow with reason. Such reason is not always demonstrably rational, and thus we thrive on the symbolic—for it is only through our imagination and art that pictures of our struggles are recorded and wish-landscapes of a different world are projected.

Naturally, one could argue that almost all art, ranging from classical to rock music, the well-made play to happenings and improvisational theater, is utopian and contains images of a different world, sparks of anticipatory illumination. However, not all art remains indelible because the forms, contours, signs, sounds, colors, tones, and ideas must be fused by the artist in such a way as to convince us that there is something special and unique, something we cannot find anywhere else, something that will help us survive with the hope that life is not just a question of survival.

What is unique, what "deserves" to be preserved—whether it be high, middle, or low art—depends on the "cultivators" of culture. Since culture has always been a class matter, its cultivators have always been part of a consortium of the ruling social groups in history, like the aristocracy, the church hierarchy, the bourgeoisie, and today, the corporate managers of huge consortiums in collusion with politicians. These are the dominant groups that employ, support, and encourage artists, architects, writers, publishers, editors, librarians, conductors, composers, museum directors, theater managers, teachers, movie directors, television producers, advertisers, educators, and so on. Throughout history, dominant groups have co-opted and appropriated art works, including those that "arise from the masses" or have their origins in "low" art forms, and made them part of our ongoing cultural heritage. But co-optation and appropriation do not necessarily mean, as Max Horkheimer and Theodor Adorno have suggested,[45] that most contemporary artworks are homogeneous and lack quality and originality. In fact, our cultural heritage is an incalculable process of determination, and there is a constant dialogue and debate concerning the determination of this process. The dominant cultural parameters have long been set in the West by "bourgeois" institutions operating in a public sphere in which the manipulation of dialogue and debate is a major concern of different social groups and vested interests within these social groups—what Pierre Bourdieu has called "the site of struggles in which what is at stake is the power to impose the dominant definition of the writer and therefore to delimit the population of those entitled to take part in the struggle to define the writer."[46] But despite class hegemony, there is not and never has been absolute unanimity within Western bourgeois institutions regarding the preservation of particular artworks and the determination of a "canon" on which to build for the future. Each subgroup within each generation of the dominant classes of a particular society reinterprets and reevaluates its cultural heritage, rediscovers works, discards works, and outlines plans and projects for a future that it deems will bring about a "happy end" for all the constituents of that particular culture.

In the case of the Brothers Grimm and their fairy tales, we are certainly dealing with "bourgeois appropriation" and the institutionalization of a "bourgeois genre," one that has great ramifications for our "happy-end" narratives. To avoid misunderstandings, I want to clarify the terms "bourgeois," "appropriation," and "institutionalization," since they are crucial for grasping the reception of the Grimms' tales.

In the significant study, *Bürger und Bürgerlichkeit im 19. Jahrhundert*, edited by Jürgen Kocka,[47] several leading German historians, folklorists, and literary critics sought to redefine and reconsider the categories of "bourgeois" and "bourgeoisie" in light of German history. The consensus reached by most of these critics is that the bourgeoisie underwent various transformations as an estate and class in the seventeenth, eighteenth, and nineteenth centuries, so that it is extremely difficult to define it as an entity. For instance, in Germany the bourgeoisie consisted at first of town or city dwellers, who formed a legal estate that gave them certain privileges within the feudal system of a German principality. One could only become a burgher through inheritance or through procurement of the title by fulfilling specific conditions. Most of the early German burghers were artisans, shopkeepers, and merchants. Toward the end of the eighteenth century, the term "bourgeois" (*bürgerlich*) was expanded to include the owners and directors of factories, publishing houses, industrial firms, and banks; and professors, educated bureaucrats, intellectuals, and even artists, especially musicians and painters. In other words, "bourgeois" or "burgher" was no longer limited to a legal status, but began to represent a class of people who believed in the ideas of the Enlightenment, and who felt that they, as rational subjects, should be able to participate in the government of a civil society. However, given the social and industrial changes in German society by 1800, it was difficult even then to define the bourgeoisie as one class. The dominant bourgeois forces were the new financial and industrial entrepreneurs and the educated professionals (*Bildungsbürger*) who were the decision makers in such middle-class institutions as schools, universities, hospitals, legal systems, publishing, and commerce. The old burgher class, which included the artisans and shopkeepers, was now considered to be part of the petit bourgeoisie; and there were also major differences between the burgher from large cities and small cities and from different regions of Germany. The definition of bourgeois could no longer be determined by estate or class status. Rather, as Kocka suggests, the term was defined by a common value system, mentality, and style of life:

> Considered from this perspective, the bourgeoisie and *Bildungsbürgertum* shared an especially high regard for individual

> achievement in the most various realms of life (not only, but also in the business world) and based their claims for economic reward, social prestige, and political influence on this. Connected to this notion was a positive basic stance in favor of routine work and a typical inclination toward rationality and methodology in leading one's life. In this perspective it was considered definitely bourgeois to strive for the independent shaping of one's individual and common tasks. The latter were to be accomplished through clubs and associations, corporations and self-administration (instead of through official channels of authority). The emphasis on education (instead of religion or in connection with a variant of religion that was educationally compatible) designated the self-understanding of the bourgeois and their understanding of the world. Education belonged simultaneously to the common ground for their associating with one another and for setting themselves off from others (for example, through quoting and the ability to converse). A close relationship—one that was considered relatively autonomous by the bourgeoisie—to aesthetic culture (art, literature, music) characterized the bourgeoisie just as much as respect for economics.[48]

Crucial for the development of this bourgeois culture was the family, which was regarded as a communal unit that decided its own purpose and was united by emotional bonds rather than by utilitarian and competitive relations in the public sphere. The family was the primary socializing agent of bourgeois culture, in which table manners, social conventions, proper taste in matters of art, codes of dress, correct speech such as high German, morals, and ethics were learned. It is not by chance that a certain type of novel, generally referred to as the *Bildungsroman* and exemplified by Goethe's *Wilhelm Meisters Lehrjahre* (1795/96), was conceived toward the end of the eighteenth century and became a staple of German bourgeois reading audiences in the nineteenth century. Even today a well-educated German is not really "educated" unless he or she has read Goethe's *Wilhelm Meister* or Thomas Mann's *The Magic Mountain* (1924) and can quote the works. More to the point, there are few contemporary middle-class Germans who have not read or been introduced to the Grimms' fairy tales—and this holds true for the middle classes of North America, Europe, and the United Kingdom. If they have not read or heard the tales, they will at one point in their lives feel obliged to become acquainted with them.

The Grimms were eminent representatives of the German *Bildungsbürgertum.* After the social decline of the family due to their father's death, they re-ascended the social ladder through education and the acquisition of the proper credentials and social skills that would contribute to their standing and prestige. They were devout Christians; industrious, moral, dedicated to their family, methodological, highly disciplined, and law-abiding; believed in the principles of the Enlightenment; cultivated their manners, speech, and dress, which made them acceptable among others members of the bourgeois class as well as the aristocracy; and cared a great deal about maintaining the good name of the Grimm family. Time and again, in their letters and their scholarly writings, one comes across the terms *Fleiß* (industriousness) and *Sitte* (norm or custom) as values to be cherished both within the family and society. As Paul Münch, in a collection of texts and documents about bourgeois virtues, has pointed out,[49] the qualities of *Ordnung* (order), *Fleiß*, and *Sparsamkeit* (thrift) were extolled in bourgeois families and had interestingly emanated from fifteenth- and sixteenth-century notions about proper household management that had cut across all social classes. What made for good economy in a house was mediated by the Christian Church and bourgeois class to legitimize particular interests. And it was in the house and through *household* items that bourgeois character was to be developed.

The Grimms were typical if not exemplary *Bildungsbürger,* and consequently, they sought to shape the character of their family often in opposition to the ruling class and government—for it was within the family that they were free to cultivate a style of life that was more true to their religious beliefs and to an ideal notion of the German fatherland than the life style of the aristocracy and governmental leaders. Thus there was always a notion of righteousness in the actions of the Grimms and the German bourgeoisie. They believed they knew and could prove that right and justice were on their side. They also thought they deserved everything they achieved and that they could conceive more equitable and rational forms of government. It is with the German bourgeoisie (as was also the case in England and France) that idealistic conceptions of a single nation-state developed. The bourgeoisie experimented with speech, forms of behavior, conventions, habits, customs, and codes, in order to distinguish itself from the aristocracy and point the right direction toward a more democratic if not utopian society.

In seeking to establish its rightful and "righteous" place in German society, the bourgeoisie, due to its lack of actual military power and unified economic power, used its "culture" as a weapon to push through its demands and needs. In the process, the middle classes mediated between the peasants and the aristocracy, and later between the aristocracy/high bourgeoisie and workers, through institutions that were of their own making and served their interests. One mode used by the bourgeoisie to create its own institutions and conventions was that of appropriation—taking over and assuming ownership of the property, goods, and cultural forms of lower classes and refining them to suit the sensibility and wants of bourgeois culture. (One could also speak of the bourgeois appropriation or imitation of aspects of aristocratic culture.) Of course, appropriation is not peculiar to the bourgeoisie, for ruling classes and colonialists throughout history have always expropriated the people they have governed or conquered. What was different in the case of the bourgeoisie—particularly in regard to orality and literacy, oral art forms, and literature—was that technological advancement enabled the middle classes to secure their art forms and modes over and against the peasants (and to a certain extent the aristocracy) through the printed word and sophisticated codes that only literate initiates of the bourgeoisie could grasp and use effectively because of their privileged training. Through education and literacy, bourgeois ideas and practices were disseminated and institutionalized so that they became accepted in the life of each individual after a period of years as second nature; and especially as manifested in speech and writing, they had become the standards of behavior for other social classes.

For instance, it became "second nature" to begin a fairy tale with "once upon a time." It became second nature to structure a fairy tale according to a functional scheme that enables an individual to prove his merits, rise in social status, and achieve success through cunning and industriousness. What appears to be natural in the Grimms' tales was not natural in the oral folk tradition: The oral tales were not, nor are they today, as eloquently structured and thematically oriented around bourgeois values until literate members of the aristocracy and bourgeoisie began accepting them and adapting them for the printed page and for educated audiences. The bourgeois and Christian appropriation of folk tales began in the fourteenth and fifteenth centuries, if not before, when such writers as Geoffrey Chaucer, Giovanni Boccaccio, and Giovan Francesco Straparola, among others, began making great use of them, and when priests and ministers incorporated them into their sermons and religious texts for the masses.[50] Such appropriation did not mean, nor does it mean now, that the folk, the common people, were robbed of their voices and "cultural goods," for as the literary tales were printed and distributed for amusement and instruction, they were often reworked by nonliterate storytellers, who retold them in their own language with a different emphasis. There is a reciprocal interaction between the oral folk tale and literary fairy tale, a dialogue that continues in various ways up through the present. Whenever a literary writer of a fairy tale sits down to write out a fairy tale, he or she carries on a dialogue with the oral tradition that forms a portion of what has become institutionalized as genre today.[51]

Still, despite the continuous dialogue, it is the literary fairy tale that eventually became "classical" in the process of civilization dominated by bourgeois culture. Given our emphasis on literacy, the literary fairy tale had to become exemplary as a genre, and consequently, the appropriation of the oral tradition led gradually to an institutionalization of the genre. By institutionalization I mean the manner in which a certain type of literature develops conventional narrative motifs, themes, semantic codes, and character types that are easily recognizable (despite variations); creates specific audience expectations through these conventions; sets up a customary social system that calls for its use in socializing and amusing children in schools or at nighttime and in providing pleasure for adults, who can recall childhood experiences or experiment with more complicated versions of the genre; and engenders a production and distribution system that responds to market conditions. Such institutionalization was not really possible until the bourgeoisie needed it and had created the technology and other supporting institutions that would make the fairy tale a vital component in the socialization of children through literature. As oral folk tale, the narrative forms and themes had been too coarse and rough aesthetically and ideologically to gain acceptance by the bourgeoisie, a bourgeoisie that was seeking extremely didactic stories for children. Thus, at first there was a debate in the seventeenth and eighteenth centuries about the use of the printed versions of folk tales (i.e., literary fairy tales) for children that lasted well into the nineteenth century throughout Europe and North America. Yet, by the time the Grimms had begun publishing their tales, the debate had swung in favor of the appropriators and adapters of folk tales for children, for the metaphorical fantasy and magic of the tales were being tailored to suit the norms of bourgeois culture. In this regard, the tales of Hans Christian Andersen were more important and more popular than those of the Grimms in nineteenth-century England and America.

Upon meeting Hans Christian Andersen—the Danish contemporary of the Grimms, whose tales are almost as popular today as those of the brothers—Heinrich Heine, the great ironic German poet, remarked with caustic wit that Andersen resembled more a petit-bourgeois tailor than a writer, and he felt that the self-deprecating demeanor of Andersen was more suited to pleasing monarchs than anything else. The Grimms, who stood up to monarchs even though they respected the system of constitutional monarchy, were not at all like the obsequious Andersen. Yet they, too, were like tailors, for they kept mending and ironing the tales they collected so that they would ultimately fit the patriarchal and Christian code of bourgeois reading expectations and their own ideal notion of pure, natural German culture. By tailoring the tales, they intervened in their cultural heritage and actually projected their own present and their future hopes onto the past. They anticipated forms of social relations and utopian conditions. All this in a male-dominated discourse that has had social and ideological ramifications for the civilizing process in the West.

Though we tend to think of fairy tales as part of the female domain, as belonging to the household and child rearing, the "tailors" are the ones who have reigned in the fairy-tale tradition. To be sure, there were some remarkable female writers of fairy tales from the beginning such as Mme. d'Aulnoy, Mlle. Lhéritier, Mme.

Lubet, Mme. de Villeneuve, and Mme. Leprince de Beaumont.[52] But by and large, the development of the literary genre has taken place within a discourse established by male writers: Giovan Francesco Straparola, Giambattista Basile, Charles Perrault, the Brothers Grimm, Wilhelm Hauff, Hans Christian Andersen, Ludwig Bechstein, George MacDonald, Lewis Carroll, Oscar Wilde, Andrew Lang, Joseph Jacobs, Carl Ewald, Henri Pourrat, L. Frank Baum, A. A. Milne, C. S. Lewis, J. R. R. Tolkien, Italo Calvino, Michael Ende—these are just some of the major names of collectors and writers of fairy tales, who have influenced our thinking about what a fairy tale should be. The male domination of the genre does not mean that women writers have been without influence, especially within the last forty years; rather, it means that the genre as an institution operates to safeguard basic male interests and conventions against which various writers, male and female, have often rebelled.[53] The dialogue remains open, but only under certain institutionalized conditions that have largely been set by men of bourgeois culture.

To demonstrate how strongly male fantasizing about women and power are still entrenched in the fairy-tale genre, we must turn briefly to the Walt Disney industry. As is well known, Disney, the person, was responsible for producing four feature-length fairy-tale films: *Snow White and the Seven Dwarfs* (1937), *Pinocchio* (1940), *Cinderella* (1951), and *Sleeping Beauty* (1959). The fact that these films became classics during Disney's own lifetime has a great deal to do with the institutionalization of the literary genre and the extreme popularity of the Grimms' texts within the genre. However, there are other factors that are important to consider, for Disney "Americanized" the Grimms' texts. As Simon Bronner has incisively remarked:

> The Grimms' tales have been translated into 140 languages and are indeed known worldwide, but they have a special American impact because of Hollywood's recontextualization of Grimms' tales into mass culture. As Walt Disney and countless children's authors re-created Grimms' fairy-tale figures for popular consumption, the German quality of the original has given way to media fantasy. They have become stylized vehicles for popular entertainment of romance, music, and comedy

> rendered gleefully through cineramic animation. Indeed, they have become Americanized, given a cheery message and romantic core, and thereby globalized. If there is a German connection within mass culture, it is in the Grimm reference to the German peasantry as the quintessential folk. Assumed to be old and of earthy appearance, isolated and communally rural, poor yet socially content, peasants are depicted as usually telling stories, often for children, and being fairy tales unto themselves.[54]

In addition to the transformation of the tales into entertainment commodities, Disney brought about significant changes by celebrating the virile innocence of male power; emphasizing the domestication of sweet, docile pubescent girls; and extolling the virtues of clean-cut, all-American figures and the prudent, if not prudish life. If we recall the *Grimms' texts*—with the exception of Collodi's *Pinocchio*—the male hero is practically incidental to "Snow White," "Sleeping Beauty," and "Cinderella," for these tales are primarily about struggles between women. The hero appears at the end of each narrative and is necessary only for the closure, to bring about the salvation of the female and the eventual marriage. He is barely described, and it is obvious that his function, though important, is limited. On the other hand, in the Disney cinematic versions (the scenarios of which were first drawn up by Walt Disney himself and then scripted), the male hero is given an enormous role—particularly in *Sleeping Beauty*, in which he is introduced very early in the narrative and eventually assumes the dominant role by fighting a witch. In *Snow White*, too, the prince appears early in the narrative, and though he does not kill the witch—the infantile but manly dwarfs manage that—he does restore Snow White to life. In each and every case, the female protagonist is reduced to singing a version of "some day my prince will come" and is characterized by waiting, suffering, helplessness, and sweetness. The rugged male hero is, of course, daring, resourceful, polite, chaste, and the conqueror of evil. This evil is always associated with female nature out of control—two witches and a bitchy stepmother with her nasty daughters. The ultimate message of all three films is that, if you are industrious, pure of heart, and keep your faith in a male god, you will be rewarded. *He* will find you and carry you off to the good kingdom that isn't threatened by the wiles of female duplicity. Wild nature can be tamed, and the depiction of nature in the films reveals to what extent *man* can arrange everything in harmonious order and in agreeable pastel colors to create the perfect American idyll.

Snow White and the Seven Dwarfs was made during the Depression of the 1930s, and *Sleeping Beauty* and *Cinderella* were created during the Cold War period. In celebrating the moral innocence of the white Anglo-Saxon male, made in America, Disney projected his ideological vision of an orderly society that could only sustain itself if irrational and passionate forces are held in check, just as his amusement parks today demonstrate. Instead of associating evil with the oppressive rule of capitalist or fascist governments or with inegalitarian socioeconomic conditions, it is equated with the conniving, jealous female, with black magic and dirty play, with unpredictable forces of turbulence that must be cleaned and controlled. Though the intention was not malevolent, the Disney films *were meant* to distract viewers from grasping the evil they confronted in their daily lives, and pointed to illusory possibilities for happiness and salvation. In this sense the utopian nature of the original Grimms' tales in their times has become perverted in ours, for the corpus of the Grimms' tales contains clear indications of class injustice and familial problems that enable readers to focus on both historical and psychological causes of repression with hope for change.

Admittedly, my reading of the Disney films is narrow and exaggerated,[55] but I have done this to make a point about how the institutionalization of the fairy tale, particularly the Grimms' tales, continues to take place within a male-dominated discourse. One need only study other cinematic and video productions of fairy tales, such as Shelley Duvall's films in the Faerie Tale Theatre series or *The Princess Bride* (1987), to recognize that the production and reception of fairy tales are limited by the conditions of institutionalization; and that even women continue to subscribe to male myths about their appropriate social roles and biological nature.

Why worry about this institutionalization? What is so important about the sociohistorical development of the fairy tale? Aren't fairy tales just wonderful, harmless tales that provide pleasure for young and old?

their oral, literary, and mass-mediated forms ...en and adults to conceive strategies for placing ... the world and grasping events around them. Im... and learned in infancy, fairy tales provide the means for structuring and giving shape to people and incidents that children encounter on a daily basis. The acquisition of words and the capacity to narrate endow children with a powerful feeling that they can determine the course of their lives. Encountering obstacles in reality, children play and create their own plots to fulfill their desires and needs. Obviously, fairy tales are not the only stories children are told or read, but fairy tales—particularly the classical Grimms' tales—are more readily learned because their formulaic structure can be easily memorized, because the structure and themes are affirmed by their parents and other authority figures, because the metaphorical language frees children to project themselves into different situations that can be varied slightly in their own minds, and because we have phylogenetically acquired a susceptibility to the utopian nature of the tales. A common plot line in a Grimms' fairy tale is: (1) the departure of the protagonist to explore the great wide world; (2) several encounters (generally three) in which the protagonist either helps needy creatures or obtains gifts from strange but helpful people; (3) an encounter with a powerful person or ogre who threatens to deprive the protagonist of obtaining success and happiness; (4) the demonstration by the protagonist that he or she is resourceful by using the gifts obtained or by calling upon the needy creatures that he or she had once helped; (5) the reward in the form of wealth or a perfect union with someone else.

Though magic and the supernatural are involved in this plot line, there is something eminently rational and methodological about the structure, and the emphasis on the capability of an individual to achieve success despite overwhelming odds corresponds to a basic bourgeois notion of progressive Enlightenment thinking. That is, characteristic of the literary fairy tale, as it has taken shape over the past three hundred years, is its enlightening and didactic function that has always been associated with utopian desire: The fairy tale provides us with the verbal power and narrative skills to inscribe our hopes and wishes in the world. It conceals and simultaneously reveals our underlying motives and drives that we cannot articulate in a totally rational manner; dressed in symbolic form, these discursively linked motives and instincts appear special and reasonable to us. That is why we continually listen to fairy tales and create them throughout our lives.

Unlike any other art form, the fairy tale stays with us from infancy into old age. We receive it as children; play and experiment with it as children; use it in different ways as adolescents, and may be attracted to other types of literature that incorporate fairy-tale motifs such as comics and romances; and return to it as adults with secret yearnings, especially if we have children. Psychologists use the tales in helping children uncover the causes of their disturbances and conflicted feelings. We encounter fairy-tale motifs constantly in our daily lives, in advertisements, television serials, rock videos, movies, on the internet, and so on. Who is that ninety-pound weakling who can hit a home run or make an impression on a beautiful young girl as soon as he drinks that magic potion of Coca Cola? Who is that worn-out housewife who cannot get her floors and bathrooms clean until a friendly, clean-cut giant gives her a magic powder that makes everything spic and span? Who are those drab young men and women whose messy, dry, and dandruffed hair gives them so much trouble, until they use the magical shampoo that makes them amazingly attractive? Who are those colorless teenagers who do not attract admiration or friends until they wear those super jeans that make them bulge in the right places, or those super sport shoes that make them fly through the air or dance like a godlike figure? Who is that daring young woman in a red cape whose perfume overwhelms a wolf before he realizes what is happening?

Fortunately or unfortunately, we tend to structure our lives according to fairy tales. Young boys want to become like princes when they grow up, and young girls want to become like princesses. Though there are signs that many men and women are dissatisfied with fairy-tale types and schemes when they grow up, the fairy tale still plays a vital role in our phylogenetic and ontogenetic development and in socialization processes. Thus have the Grimms' fairy tales been institutionalized as part of our cultural heritage. The remainder of the essays in this book will probe different aspects of this institutionalization in an effort to clarify what is genuinely utopian in our modern-day efforts to preserve the fairy-tale tradition. The Grimms' tales reflect the concerns and contradictions of different civilizing processes, and despite the atavistic aspects and patriarchal discourse, their tales still read like innovative strategies for survival. Most of all, they provide hope that there is more to life than mastering the art of survival. Their "once upon a time" keeps alive our longing for a better modern world that can be created out of our dreams and actions.

CHAPTER THREE

EXPLORING HISTORICAL PATHS

Inevitably they find their way into the forest. It is there that they lose and find themselves. It is there that they gain a sense of what is to be done. The forest is always large, immense, great, and mysterious. No one ever gains power over the forest, but the forest possesses the power to change lives and alter destinies. In many ways it is the supreme authority on earth and often the great provider. It is not only Hansel and Gretel, who get lost in the forest and then return wiser and fulfilled.

> Once upon a time there was a prince who was overcome by a desire to travel about the world, and the only person he took with him was his faithful servant. One day he found himself in a great forest when evening came. He had not found a place to spend the night and did not know what to do. Then he noticed a maiden going toward a small cottage, and when he came closer, he saw that she was young and beautiful. ("The Riddle")[1]

❊ ❊ ❊

> The boy set out with this letter but lost his way, and at night he came to a great forest. When he saw a small light in the darkness, he began walking toward it and soon reached a little cottage.

Upon entering, he discovered an old woman sitting all alone by the fire. ("The Devil with the Three Golden Hairs," 110–111)

❋ ❋ ❋

The little tailor traveled on and came to a forest. There he met a band of robbers who planned to steal the king's treasure. ("Thumbling's Travels," 164)

❋ ❋ ❋

Once upon a time a forester went out hunting in the forest, and as he entered it, he heard some cries like those of a small child. ("Foundling," 189)

❋ ❋ ❋

Meanwhile, the poor child was all alone in the huge forest. When she looked at all the leaves on the trees, she was petrified and did not know what to do. Then she began to run, and she ran over sharp stones and through thorn bushes. Wild beasts darted by her at times, but they did not harm her. She ran as long as her legs could carry her, and it was almost evening when she saw a little cottage and went inside to rest. ("Snow White," 197)

❋ ❋ ❋

Once upon a time there was a man who had mastered all kinds of skills. He had fought in the war and had conducted himself correctly and courageously, but when the war was over, he was discharged and received three pennies for traveling expenses. "Just you wait!" he said. "I won't put up with that. If I find the right people, I'll force the king to turn over all the treasures of his kingdom to me." Full of rage, he went into the forest, and there he saw a man tearing up six trees as if they were blades of wheat. ("How Six Made Their Way in the World," 274)

❋ ❋ ❋

When the rooster was ready, Hans My Hedgehog mounted it and rode away, taking some donkeys and pigs with him, which he wanted to tend out in the forest. Once he reached the forest, he had the rooster fly up into a tall tree, where he sat and tended the donkeys and pigs. He sat there for many years until the herd was very large, and he never sent word to his father of his whereabouts. ("Hans My Hedgehog," 394)

❋ ❋ ❋

There was once a poor servant girl who went traveling with her masters through a large forest, and as they were passing through the middle of it, some robbers came out of a thicket and murdered all the people they could find. Everyone was killed except the maiden, who had jumped from the carriage in her fright and had hidden behind a tree. ("The Old Woman in the Forest," 440)

❋ ❋ ❋

Let no one ever say that a poor tailor cannot advance far in the world and achieve great honors. He needs only to hit upon the right person and, most important, to have good luck. Once there was such a tailor, who was a pleasing and smart apprentice. He set out on his travels and wandered into a large forest, and since he did not know the way, he got lost. ("The Glass Coffin," 522–523)

❋ ❋ ❋

Once the guardian angel pretended not to be there, and the girl could not find her way back out of the forest. So she wandered until it became dark. When she saw a light glowing in the distance, she ran in that direction and came upon a small hut. She knocked, the door opened, and she entered. Then she came to a second door and knocked again. An old man with a beard white as snow and a venerable appearance opened the door. ("Saint Joseph in the Forest," 634)

A prince, a foundling, a miller, a miller's daughter, Thumbling, a sorcerer, a brother, a sister, a king, a forester, a princess, three poor brothers, a blockhead, a discharged soldier, a miller's apprentice, a tailor and a shoemaker, a hedgehog/human, a hunter, a poor servant girl, a poor tailor, a pious, good little girl, St. Joseph, a hermit, a man, a poor tailor, and the Virgin Mary.[2] These are just a few of the characters in the Grimms' tales whose fates are decided in the forest, and it is interesting to note that the forest is rarely enchanted though enchantment takes place there. The forest allows for enchantment and disenchantment, for it is the place where society's conventions no longer hold true. It is the source of natural right, thus the starting place where social wrongs can be righted. In a letter to Wilhelm on April 18, 1805, Jacob stated:

> The only time in which it might be possible to allow an idea of the past, an idea of the world of knights, if you will, to blossom anew within us is when it is transformed into a forest in which wild animals roam about (for example, wolves with which one must howl if only to be able to live with them). This is the only way to break away from the norms (*Sitten*) that have restricted us until now and shall continue to do so. I believe that I would have been naturally inclined to do this. A constant warning against this and my drive to be obedient have fortunately suppressed this inclination. I can only be happy about this since one or just a few individuals would not be able to achieve anything worthwhile by doing this, and I would have easily gone astray.[3]

The forest as unconventional, free, alluring, but dangerous. The forest loomed large metaphorically in the minds of the Brothers Grimm. In 1813 they published a journal entitled *Altdeutsche Wälder* (*Old German Forests*), intentionally recalling the title of Johann Gottfried Herder's *Kritische Wälder* (*Critical Forests*, 1769)—Herder being the man who was responsible for awakening the interest in German folklore of the romantics. This journal was to contain traces, indications, signs, and hints with regard to the origins of German customs, laws, and language. It was as though in "old German forests" the essential truths about German customs, laws, and culture could be found—truths that might engender a deeper understanding of present-day Germany and might foster unity among German people at a time when the German principalities were divided and occupied by the French during the Napoleonic Wars. The *Volk*, the people, bound by a common language but disunited, needed to enter old German forests, the Grimms thought, to gain a sense of their heritage and to strengthen the ties among themselves.

In her critical biography of the Brothers Grimm,[4] Gabriele Seitz sees both the *Kinder- und Hausmärchen* (*Children's and Household Tales*, 1812, 1815) and the journal *Altdeutsche Wälder* as part of a political program conceived by the Grimms to reactivate interest in the customs, laws, and norms that bound German people together through language. And, to a certain extent, one could look upon the Grimms' act of developing and collecting the tales as the cultivation of an "enchanted forest," a forest in which they were seeking to capture and contain essential truths that were expressive and representative of the German people—truths that the German people shared with other peoples, for the tales were considered by the Grimms to be Indo-Germanic in origin and to possess relics of the prehistoric past. If one studies the notes to the tales that the Grimms compiled, it is apparent that they wanted to stress the relationship of each tale to an ideal *Urvolk* (primeval people) and *Ursprache* (primeval language), recognizing their universality and international ties while at the same time focusing on German tradition with the express purpose of discovering something new about the origins of German customs and laws. Historically, the Grimms did indeed succeed in creating a monument in honor of the German cultural heritage, bringing fame and renown to Germany through their tales. But perhaps they succeeded more than they would have liked in the creation of a peculiar German monument—for the tales have been the subject of ideological debate, attracting both ultraconservative scholars such as Josef Prestel and Karl Spiess, who used them to promote a racist ideology, and radical critics such as Ernst Bloch, Walter Benjamin, and even Antonio Gramsci, who sought to grasp their revolutionary appeal.[5] Furthermore—and perhaps this is the most questionable aspect of the Grimms' success from their own original viewpoint—their enchanted forest, created to illuminate and celebrate basic truths about German culture, was turned into and still is a pleasure park, where people stroll and pluck their meanings randomly, with complete disregard for the historical spadework of the Grimms.[6] Certainly the personal, or subjective, approach and sampling of the tales is a legitimate way of appreciating the tales, but often they have been endowed with more "magical power" than they possess and have been appropriated in a manner that makes them appear unhistorical and juvenile, in the more pejorative sense of juvenile.

To counter the general tendency of dehistoricizing the Grimms' tales, I want to demonstrate how deeply they are entrenched in central European history of the late eighteenth and early nineteenth centuries. My purpose is not "historicist" in a narrow philological sense, that is, I do not want to treat the tales as historical texts of a particular epoch whose authorship, chronology, composition, and "truth value" need to be documented. Rather, I am more interested in the complex levels of historical representation that reveal the sociopolitical relations of a period in a symbolical manner. By reexamining the tales critically as social commentaries that represent aspects of real experience of the past, we can learn to distinguish social tendencies in our own culture and times more clearly and perhaps comprehend why we are still drawn to the Grimms' tales. Some historians, like Eugen Weber[7] and Robert Darnton,[8] have already taken a step in this direction by arguing that the tales are repositories of peasants' social and political living conditions. In particular, Darnton has reconstructed the way French peasants saw the world under the Old Regime by asking what experiences they shared in everyday life and then interpreting the tales as direct expressions of their experiences. Though his interpretations are valid to a certain degree, Darnton simplifies the problem of symbolic representation by assuming that the oral tales of the seventeenth, eighteenth, nineteenth, and early twentieth centuries were direct expressions of the common people and not mediated by literate collectors, editors, and publishers who always played a role in the transmission by altering style and themes. Moreover, he does not even mention that many of the tales that were in the oral tradition between 1700 and 1900 were actually taken from church sermons, writings by educated travelers, and plays written by educated people of a different class.[9] It became customary during the baroque period for priests and preachers to include folk tales as exemplary stories in the vernacular when they delivered sermons to the peasants, just as it was customary for educated travelers to read stories or tell tales about their travels to peasants and artisans gathered in an inn. To be sure, the tales were remembered by their listeners and retold in a different way but not always—and they were not always altered drastically. Thus, the peasants were not always the preservers of the oral tradition. To assume that the viewpoint of a folk tale always equals the viewpoint of the "average" French or German peasant is misleading, especially since there were major differences among the peasants themselves. Moreover, it was customary in the eighteenth and early nineteenth centuries for people of the aristocracy and middle classes to read aloud and to gather in circles to listen to tales. In short, the "folk" ways were often shared by different social classes, and it is important to avoid generalizations and idealizations of the folk.

For instance, there is a mistaken assumption about the folk that undermines an otherwise interesting historical study entitled "Hessian Peasant Women, Their Families, and the Draft: A Social-Historical Interpretation of Four Tales from the Grimm Collection," by Peter Taylor and Hermann Rebel.[10] They begin their article by recounting the history of the Hessian draft system and the attitudes of the peasants toward the draft at the end of the eighteenth century. Their intention is to show that some of the Grimms' tales reveal more about the common people's dispositions toward the military and family relations than do contemporary documents. They argue that

> a more fruitful approach to fairy tales is to see them in connection with actual social life and social institutions, as a popular (and not elite) ideological product focused on the inherently imperfect and conflicting workings of a given social order. . . . Fairy tales are indeed ideological creations emerging from the folk and often do address themselves to the psycho-social strains in an historically evolving social system; the crucial difference in approach is not to see the tales and their contents as expressions of strain but as objective linguistic and conceptual materials—"symbolic templates"—by which members of a population fashioned for themselves analyses that continually interpreted and reinterpreted their social politics. (352)

So far, so good. However, as we shall see, their next step in their approach is a wobbly one. On the basis of four tales from the Grimms' collection ("The Twelve Brothers," "Brother and Sister," "The Seven Ravens," and "The Six Swans"), they argue that there is a social development in the pattern of these tales that can be related to ultimogeniture and the attitude of sisters toward brothers who were drafted into the army. They stress the importance of the female peasant storytellers, "Old Marie" and Dorothea Viehmann, who were allegedly the sources of the tales, for they certainly represent popular viewpoints and were custodians of popular culture. Given the folk origins of the tales, Taylor and Rebel assume that they express a peasant view from below and show how each one, with certain variations, involves brothers who are dispossessed because of their younger sister, sent into exile, transformed into animals, and rescued by their courageous sister, who helps them resolve the question of dispossession. Next, Taylor and Rebel supply the historical basis for interpreting the patterns of the tales as they do: Ultimogeniture was a common practice in Hessia at the end of the eighteenth century and the beginning of the nineteenth century, and, they argue, the tales represent the defense of a new nonpatrimonial inheritance system in which the youngest daughter is allowed to inherit the family property and maintain it in the family's interests. Taylor and Rebel claim that the

> themes of sexual exchange must be tied to the changing social circumstances of inheritance. Here the tales portray strategies that contradict conflicts over narrowly defined access to patrimony, whether matriarchal or patriarchal; they advocate (if indeed they advocate anything) strategies of inheritance that neither dispossess male siblings nor force them from the social framework of family life into a world of outlawry and military violence. (367)

Some questions arise. Why was there a change in inheritance practices in Hessia? Why did they become more nonpatrimonial? Why, according to the tales, did the youngest sister, who benefitted from the new system, want to help her brothers? Taylor and Rebel demonstrate that Hessia had made a business of drafting and selling peasant soldiers to other nations, and that the military was run as a kind of state business. Given the fact that many sons of peasants were obliged to serve in the army and could earn a living through the military, the fathers often preferred to leave their property or the bulk of their property to daughters, whom they could influence. In addition, the laws of preferential partibility allowed the father to control the reconstitution of the property and the services of the son-in-law. So it would seem that daughters in Hessian peasant families might rejoice in becoming the sole heirs of property. However, Taylor and Rebel argue, by inheriting property they were placed under greater stress to follow their fathers' dictates by marrying the right kind of man (if they could find a man in Hessia, for so many were drafted) and producing the right kind of children in accordance with inheritance strategies. Evidence shows that women balked at becoming heirs because of the pressures and because they did not want to remain in Hessia, where it was difficult to find husbands and live under restricted circumstances. Many Hessian women chose migration rather than stay in Hessia, and Taylor and Rebel claim that the four Grimms' tales they selected for analysis provide some explanations for social conditions and changes in Hessia:

> In all four tales examined, the sisters sought to bring their brothers back into the world of people, into the social world of families; and to reject the role of "advantaged heir" to accomplish this. In all but one of the tales—in which the simple act of renunciation suffices—reconnection is accomplished by emigrating with a husband through whose family the brothers reacquired their human social shape. If these tales have social validity, then some of the observed female outmigration represents the effort by an unknown number of Hessian women to marry outside the state in order to offer their brothers a place of refuge, a family to which they could attach themselves to escape the calculated and dehumanizing meshes of preferential partibility and the draft. (375)

In conclusion, Taylor and Rebel maintain that, though the tales may have represented other things for the audiences of the early nineteenth century, they

> were also symbolic analyses which held up to view the negative social consequences of the existing social and military systems. They were passionate and often violent polemics that not only expressed and took a stand against the dehumanizing and painful experiences arising from a narrow system of property devolution working in conjunction with a draft state; they also advocated alternative action for women. The tales demonstrate a relatively sophisticated but non-revolutionary social consciousness in their advocacy of the riskier path of emigration, one that consciously rejected a system where security and profit were gained at the cost of dispossession and of the destruction of family relations. (375–376)

As I mentioned before, this "historical" interpretation is certainly interesting, if not ingenious, but it is highly flawed because the historians have not done their historical homework. First of all, there is the problem of narrative perspective. Taylor and Rebel claim that the original sources were two peasant women, "Old Marie" and Dorothea Viehmann. Yet in reality, none of the tales was told to the Grimms by these women. "The Twelve Brothers" was supplied by the sisters Julia and Charlotte Ramus, daughters of a French pastor; "Brother and Sister" was provided by Marie Hassenpflug, who came from a middle-class family with French origins; "The Seven Ravens" also came from the Hassenpflug family; and "The Six Swans" was obtained from Dortchen Wild, daughter of a pharmacist and the future wife of Wilhelm. In other words, not one of the tales emanated directly from the peasantry, and certainly not from the sources given by Taylor and Rebel. Indeed, "The Six Swans" had already appeared in print in an anthology of literary fairy tales before the brothers had collected it.[11]

Even if one were to give Taylor and Rebel the benefit of the doubt and assume that the tales, despite the bourgeois origins of their informants, were told to the middle-class women by peasant women, there is the problem of changes and transformations by the Brothers Grimm. In fact, it is easy to show a certain disposition on the part of the Brothers to collect and alter the tales according to their ideal sense of family. Interestingly, some of the remarks made by Taylor and Rebel reveal that there was possibly a shared feeling on the part of Hessian women about maintaining family cohesion—but the vision of family in the Grimms' tales becomes more and more "bourgeoisified" from 1812 to 1857. This transformation is made eminently clear in Lothar Bluhm's cogent and critical response to Taylor and Rebel:

> There are at least two other factors that should at least be mentioned because they have had an influence on the character of the Grimms' tales, that is, on how the brothers consciously and unconsciously edited the tales. The first factor is the Protestant prudery of the Grimms in a narrow sense of the term, typical for the times, that led to the elimination of all offensive passages in consideration of young readers, and excluded smut from the very beginning. (By doing this the actual spectrum of orally transmitted folk stories was definitively limited.) The second factor is the familiarity of most contributors with the literary tradition of the French *contes de fées*, and this familiarity can be documented in a series of texts down to their very literal formulations borrowed from the *contes*. Therefore, a differenti-

> ated social-historical study must not misinterpret the *Children's and Household Tales* as a document of an oral narrative tradition in which the social experiential world of agrarian lower classes has found its manifest expression. Even stories, which can be traced back to peasant sources, must be understood in their published narrative shape and in their manifold revised form, also in regard to the narrative content, more as documents of (educated) bourgeois conceptions of the experiential world of this social stratum.[12]

Unfortunately, Taylor and Rebel do not take this into account. Finally, from a folklorist viewpoint, the four tales they discuss are tale types that can be found in many different countries and are hundreds of years old.[13] They are not peculiarly Hessian, and it is most unclear what they have to do with the draft system in Hessia. They show signs of matrilineal inflation and marital rites that may be pre-Christian. Undoubtedly they were changed over the years and could be connected to the Hessia of 1800, but not in the unhistorical and unscholarly manner in which Taylor and Rebel have worked.

In another flagrantly unhistorical endeavor to reclaim the Grimms' tales for the oral tradition and German peasantry, Rebel vehemently (and to my mind, mistakenly) criticizes Heinz Rölleke for seeking to eliminate an alleged informant by the name of "Old Marie" Müller from the original storytellers:

> The view that the tellers' authorship is not as important as the unchanging substance of the tales is also shared by Heinz Rölleke with regard to the Grimm collection. There, however, this idea has become part of a much more direct route towards denying the importance of lower-class origins of the tales; Rölleke's assertion is simply that the Grimms not only did not have direct access to lower-class sources but that one of the most important pantheons of their contributors, Old Marie, the housekeeper in the apothecary Wild's household, did not even exist. This startling and radical rejection of what has for so long been assumed as certain knowledge needs to be examined very closely before it can be accepted as the new conventional wisdom, as the new password that seems to meet a present need in the historical representation of German popular culture.[14]

Why Rebel makes such misleading claims is difficult to understand. Rölleke never sought to diminish the role of the storytellers or to dispute the lower-class origins of the tales but to clarify with great philological exactitude who the Grimms' informants really were. Nor did he ever argue that Marie Müller did not exist. What he has done in all his editorial work has been to demonstrate that previous assumptions about the informants and origins of the texts had to be questioned and altered. Moreover, he has consistently argued for understanding the Grimms' texts as "contaminated texts" or *Buchmärchen* (book fairy tales) because there are so many strands of tales from different informants in them. In this regard, our historical perspective on the Grimms' texts has had to undergo shifts. In fact, Rölleke has demystified certain "Aryan" myths about the pure Germanic tradition of the tales, while ironically, Rebel, in seeking to defend the lower classes and their contribution to folklore, has miscast them as victims and cast aspersions on the credible work of leading philologists in Germany.[15]

In approaching the Grimms' tales from a sociohistorical and ideological perspective, we must constantly bear in mind that we are dealing with multiple representations and voices within the narrative structure of each tale. First, depending on the tale, there is the viewpoint of the informant, often an educated female, who had memorized a tale probably told by a peasant or read in a book. Next, there is the viewpoint of Jacob or Wilhelm, who revised the oral or literary tale that was collected. Not to be forgotten, there is the viewpoint of the submerged creator of the tale—probably a peasant, artisan, soldier, or journeyman who sought to represent his or her experience through a symbolic narrative at a given time in history. And finally, there are the viewpoints of intervening tale tellers who pass on the narrative from author to listeners and future tellers. By conserving the material according to narrative formulae that had been cultivated in both an oral and literary tradition in central Europe, the Grimms were maintaining a dialogue about social experience with the anonymous original creator, intervening tellers of the tales, the direct source of the informant, and the informant. In so doing, they contributed to the institutionalization of discursive genres such as the fable, the anecdote, the legend, and the magic fairy tale, all of which were in the process of being conventionalized.

It is difficult to define just what a Grimms' tale or *Märchen* is, for there is very little unanimity among folklorists, literary critics, ethnologists, psychologists, and historians as to what exactly an oral folk tale or a literary fairy tale is. However, among the different endeavors to create a working definition, it appears to me that Dietz-Rüdiger Moser has summarized the major characteristics of the folk tale with clear categories that can enable us to grasp the historical signification of the Grimms' tales. According to Moser,

> the fairy tale is a narrative work of fiction that is complete in itself. Since it is transmitted, it is, therefore, conservative. [In other words, it tends to conserve] and contains typical figures, properties, situations, and aspects of action that serve the portrayal of how conflicts are solved on the basis of fixed moral notions. Those events that are described in it can leave the immediate realm of experience. Yet, the conflict that it treats is continually anchored in this realm.[16]

Moser emphasizes that the manner "of how conflicts are solved must be recognized as the dominant concern of the genre, and the portrayal is realized in a consequent and uniform way. Accordingly, the analysis must distinguish between the immediate initial and internal conflicts that are effective for the action and the central conflict that is constitutive for the particular total message."[17]

Though the Grimms' collection contains numerous tales that cannot be considered fairy tales (such as anecdotes, fables, and legends), the majority of them do fit Moser's definition: They are definitely concerned with the solution of conflicts, and they contain a moral viewpoint that the Grimms modified according to their own principles. Due to the fact, however, that the Grimms did not always alter the viewpoint of the informants, there are sometimes ambivalent solutions and viewpoints because of the gap between the Grimms and their informants. Most important is that the conflicts represented and the attitudes assumed by the Grimms and by their informants toward the resolution of the conflicts reveal the social and political relations of particular social types in the culture of a nation during a certain historical stage of development.

Given their legal training under the guidance of Friedrich Carl von Savigny, the Grimms were particularly sensitive toward social types and the theme of justice in their tales, and they tried to connect these types to German customs and law.[18] Though the Grimms never categorized their tales according to social roles and functions, it is certainly possible to elicit a sociological typology from them. Such a typology can help reveal more than we already know about the social and political purpose behind the Grimms' shaping and revising of their tales. If we were to catalogue the tales according to social types—that is, examine the tales as representative of customary attitudes and patterns peculiar to the major protagonist who carries the action—we would find the following principal types:[19]

prince (17)	princess (12)
tailor (10)	soldier (9)
servant (8)	huntsman (4)
miller's daughter (4)	miller's apprentice (4)
daughter of a rich man (2)	fisherman (2)
God (2)	Jew (2)
magician (2)	shepherd (2)
thief (2)	Thumbling (2)
Virgin Mary (2)	woodcutter's daughter (2)
army surgeon (1)	blacksmith (1)
cook (1)	drummer (1)
elf (1)	foundling (1)
gambler (1)	goldsmith (1)
hermit (1)	journeyman (1)
king (1)	merchant (1)
musician (1)	shoemaker (1)
son of a rich man (1)	St. Joseph (1)
water nixie (1)	woodcutter's son (1)

In addition, there are 78 tales in which farmers, poor people, sons and daughters of poor people, and peasants play major roles. Then there are 27 tales about animals. In keeping with the oral tradition, the Grimms referred to their characters in terms of their social class, family standing, or profession. Here and there they used typical names such as Hans, Heinz, Lise, Else, and Gretel to stress the common quality of their protagonist as a type of simple person, everyman, or lazy person.

The Grimms were eager to understand and trace commonalities and peculiar characteristics of their types—both the social and tale types—and so they very rarely accepted and printed tales that were too similar in theme and structure. Whenever they collected several versions of the same tale type, they would either combine these versions into one or alter the best of the versions—in any event, creating their own synthetic tale. By synthesizing social and tale types, the Grimms hoped to reveal customary behavior, and thereby enable readers to learn about general folk attitudes and draw conclusions about the right way to behave in given circumstances.

In light of their empirical-ethical bias, it is interesting to see how the forest serves in a majority of the tales as a kind of topos: It is the singular place that belongs to all the people; it levels all social distinctions and makes everyone equal. The forest allows for a change in the protagonist's destiny and enables the social type to distinguish him or herself.

The importance of concentrating on social types rather than on, for instance, tale types and motifs (in the manner often done by folklorists using the Aarne-Thompson type classification[20] and the Thompson motif index[21]), is that doing so brings us closer to the historical reality of the Brothers Grimm and enables us to learn more about their personal proclivities in collecting, selecting, and rewriting the tales. Furthermore, it may also help us learn something about the life of particular social types during the eighteenth and nineteenth centuries, conditions surrounding the type, and different attitudes toward the type. The Grimms spent their early childhood in the country and were strongly attached to the agrarian customs and ways of life that they began studying closely when they were young. Class and legal distinctions were made clear in their home, especially by their magistrate father. The Grimms' tales are filled with depictions of agrarian types, artisans, and townspeople, and their idiomatic expressions and proverbs were noted down by the Grimms and incorporated into the tales.[22] In general, then, their tales tend to blend their ideal notions of the people, their trust in a monarchical constitutional state, and their empirical findings about customs and law that reveal what they believed were basic truths about the origins of language and *Gemeinschaft* (community).

To illustrate how they worked with social types and the significance of these types for their tales, I want to concentrate on two different tale cycles that focus on the soldier and the tailor, as well as the normative patterns that evolve from the action of the tales.

Often it is obvious that the original teller of the tale must have been a soldier or tailor or someone who shared their experiences, and that their representations formed the basis of the later work done by other storytellers and, eventually, the Grimms. However, I shall not focus on the relationship of the original storyteller or the source of the text, as Rölleke often does. This choice of emphasis is not because I dismiss this approach but because I feel that the changes, stylization, and subjective selection process of the Grimms is more important for a comprehension of the total meaning of the tales in their sociohistorical context. As I have already remarked, the Grimms were more than just midwives; they conceptualized many of the tales and lent them their indelible substantive mark.

❖ ❖ ❖

There are ten soldier tales in the *Children's and Household Tales:*[23] "The Three Snake Leaves," "How Six Made Their Way in the World," "Brother Lustig," "Bearskin," "The Devil's Sooty Brother," "The Blue Light," "The Devil and his Grandmother," "The Worn-Out Dancing Shoes," "The Boots of Buffalo Leather," and "The Grave Mound."[24] The sources for these tales vary greatly: Johann Friedrich Krause, a former soldier; Dorothea Viehmann, a peasant woman; the von Haxthausens, a landed-gentry family; and books published by Friedmund von Arnim and Philipp Hoffmeister. The original sources of all ten tales were evidently soldiers themselves, and the relatively high percentage of soldier's tales in the Grimms' collection is most likely a direct result of the Napoleonic Wars and the vast increase of soldiering as a profession in the European population.

After standing armies became widespread in the seventeenth century, more and more men from the peasantry and lower classes were recruited as common soldiers.[25] By the eighteenth century, there had been a definite shift in the social and economic structure of the German principalities due to the rise of the military as a dominant political force. To keep standing armies and increase their power, the German sovereigns had to levy taxes on the populace at large. As the officer corps developed and played a role in the administration of different regions, the army elite formed a caste that exercised great influence in domestic and foreign policies. Moreover, the code of discipline and punishment and the actual regimentation within the army anticipated the type of control that would be utilized in schools, prison systems, insane asylums, and factories, as society became more rationalized and institutionalized. The common soldier's lot was miserable.

As a member of the standing army, the common soldier had few rights and had to undergo long periods of strict drilling and guard duty during peacetime. Although soldiers were allowed to have another trade on the side, their first obligation was to the army, and they were under constant surveillance by the officers to make sure that they would not desert. Corporal punishment was the rule for any offense, and death sentences were common for desertion, and even at times for disobeying orders. The leisure time of soldiers was generally spent drinking and frequenting taverns where camp followers and easy women were to be found. During wartime, the soldiers suffered immensely because their food and clothing were scant; they were treated more like cannon fodder than human beings. In a letter to Wilhelm on March 24, 1814, a time when the three younger Grimm brothers were in the army, Jacob remarked:

> It's imperative that one look closely at what a soldier must stand. Sickness, hospital and prison are the most terrible. Some days ago I saw a young Austrian near Combeaufontaine lying on the main road. Most everyone had to go around him while he continued to die. Others just walked indifferently right by him, and so he just died under the open sky without anyone knowing whether he would be buried. In Bar sur Aube the unburied corpses are said to have caused a pestilent plague. There are now only 30 to 40 inhabitable houses in this unfortunate city.[26]

Since the peasantry and the bourgeois town and city dwellers were obligated to house the soldiers and pay for their maintenance, there was a distinct antipathy toward both the military establishment and the soldiers, often considered the dregs of society. Indeed, even the so-called "dregs," the common soldiers, did not like to serve in the army and did not think highly of their military commanders. As soon as a soldier found a good reason to resign or desert, he did. Very rarely did a common soldier have anything good to say about the army as an institution. The major factors that kept most soldiers in a standing army were money (even if it was not much) and the threat of punishment.

Given these general conditions, it is not by chance that most of the Grimms' tales reveal the common soldier's dissatisfaction with the treatment he received from his superiors. Moreover, the tales also incorporate the general antimilitary sentiment common among the peasants and the bourgeoisie. Of the ten tales that focus on the soldier, eight of them deal with discharged or ex-soldiers, who are down and out and want to gain revenge on the king or their former officers. One tale deals with a poor farmer who enlists and becomes a hero for the fatherland (perhaps a reference to the Napoleonic Wars) while another depicts three soldiers who desert. The general purpose in all these tales, the motive of the protagonists that stamps the action, is the struggle to overcome a desperate situation. The ex-soldier wants to survive a bad experience as soldier. None of the protagonists starts with an idealistic goal. The last thing on their minds is rescuing or marrying a princess (although that might occur). On the contrary, the ex-soldiers all want simply to get by and, obviously, raise their social status if possible. They have nothing to lose, and this is the reason that the soldier protagonist is, without exception, fearless. Yet, bravery is not what society demands from a soldier if he wants to be reintegrated and accepted—especially when that society is hostile toward the military and expects correct behavior according to the Protestant ethic. So a soldier's integrity must be tested, and often the forest plays a role in determining his destiny, for it is here that the soldier is not only tempted by evil forces but also given an equal chance to be recognized.

For instance, it is in the forest that the discharged soldier in "How Six Made Their Way in the World" becomes "full of rage" against the king and then finds the extraordinary companions who help him gain vengeance on the king. The two discharged soldiers in "The Devil's Sooty Brother" and "Bearskin" meet the devil in the forest, and he enables them to procure money and marry well. The discharged soldier in "The Blue Light" meets a witch in the forest who facilitates his discovery of the light that, in turn, helps him marry a king's daughter and punish the king. One of the soldiers in "The Devil and his Grandmother" must go into the forest to visit the devil's grandmother to solve the devil's riddles and save their souls. The soldier in "The Boots of Buffalo Leather" gets lost in the forest, helps a king overcome robbers, and is rewarded for his fearlessness.

If it is not the forest where the soldiers must prove themselves, then it will still be outside, in the fields or a graveyard. With the exception of "The Three Snake Leaves," in which the enlisted soldier fights for the fatherland, all the soldier tales depict ex-soldiers, who must go outside society and make pacts with unconventional figures such as the devil, the devil's grandmother, or a witch to attain their goals. Even in "The Three Snake Leaves," the enlisted soldier, who marries a king's daughter, is murdered by her and can only gain justice through the magic of the snake leaves. Despite the pacts with suspicious creatures, the ex-soldiers, always fearless, remain their own men; that is, they never lose their souls to the devil or witch but outsmart them.

If we were to draw a composite picture of the common soldier in the Grimms' tales, he would be fearless, cunning, virtuous, generous, honest, opportunistic, and ambitious. An exception here is Brother Lustig, in the tale named after him, who nevertheless possesses many of the above attributes. These attributes are always manifested in a manner that allows the soldier to gain retribution for the mistreatment he received in the army. On one level, it would be possible to argue that the Grimms favored the soldier tales because of the slights they themselves experienced in a rigid class society and because they understood from first-hand experience what the soldiers had to endure. From a psychological point of view, it would he interesting to study their fondness for the soldier tales as compensatory narratives; this interpretation would also work on a more social level, for certainly the tales were socially symbolic acts of creation by the original narrators, and they contained their wish-fulfillments to gain revenge against their superiors, even if this meant metaphorically aligning themselves temporarily with the devil. That the soldiers are good, if not better, men than their kings and superiors is proven by the way in which the soldiers keep their hearts pure. (It is this basic innocence or purity of heart that permits even Brother Lustig to gain a place in heaven.)

The depiction of the common lot of the soldiers in the Grimms' tales indicates a definite sympathy for their social condition and the need to improve their treatment, both in the army and in society. After all, they had served their king and country and should have been rewarded. Unlike women, who are rarely encouraged in the tales to assume an active role in determining their destiny, the soldiers, as men, are expected to become socially useful and fight for their goals. Heroines are generally portrayed as domestic figures or figures who need domestication. Heroes are generally adventurers who need experience and a touch of respectability to become successful as public figures. Here the soldier tales reflect the clear nineteenth-century patriarchal notions about gender roles that the Grimms shared with their society at large: The male hero must prove himself by asserting himself and showing through his behavior to what extent he is graced by God. Implicit in the normative behavior of the "good" soldier is a patriarchal reinforcement of the Protestant ethic.

⌘ ⌘ ⌘

The tales about tailors also exemplify the Grimms' social and religious creed and are closely related to the soldier tales. There are 11 such narratives in all: "The Brave Little Tailor," "The Tailor in Heaven," "The Magic Table, The Gold Donkey, and the Club in the Sack," "Thumbling's Travels," "The Two Travelers," "The Clever Little Tailor," "The Bright Sun Will Bring It to Light," "The Glass Coffin," "Sharing Joys and Sorrows," "The Gifts of the Little Folk," and "The Giant and the Tailor."[27] Here again the sources used by the Grimms ranged greatly from the Hassenpflug family to publications by Franz Ziska, Emil Sommer, and Jakob Frey. Originally all of the tales were told by journeymen and townspeople. Almost all the tailors in the tales are journeymen or apprentices; none are master tailors.[28] Unlike the soldiers, who are generally portrayed as sympathetic and admirable figures, the tailors are more differentiated as protagonists. On the one hand, they appear to be shifty and dubious characters, reflecting the attitudes of townspeople toward men who were often out of work and wandered from town to town. (Ever since the Middle Ages the profession of tailoring had not been highly regarded because it did not

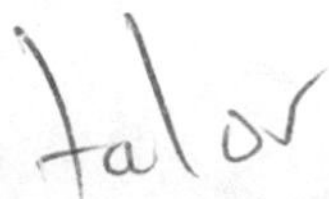

demand much skill or material. Nor did one have to be exceptionally strong, so that the weaker sons were generally apprenticed to master tailors. In addition, there were so many tailors that a tailor's life was generally one of poverty.[29]) On the other hand, the tales also depict some industrious tailors bent on overcoming difficult obstacles and desirous of becoming respected citizens in society. These characters use their wit and skills to try to become master tailors and win admiration for their shrewdness.

Although some of the Grimms' sources date back to the fifteenth century, there is little doubt that the tales tend to characterize the hazards and vicissitudes in the lives of the tailors as they traveled from town to town and job to job in the eighteenth and nineteenth centuries. The eighteenth century saw a change in the structured lives of tailors.[30] Formerly the guilds had exercised great control over employment, prices, and conditions in the trade; but with the growth of manufacturing, the establishment of clothing shops, and the expansion of cities, there was a gradual shift, leading to a loss of power. This development meant that many apprentices and journeymen did not have to join a guild to find employment. The trade succumbed to the free market and brutal competition for customers. Whereas the guild masters (*Zunftmeister*) of each town or locality had customarily divided the work among themselves and had provided training and housing for apprentices and journeymen, this system was becoming obsolete by the beginning of the nineteenth century. As Wolfgang Renzsch points out:

> A very small group of well-to-do important master tailors faced a large number of tailors who could only make a miserable living. To be sure it was relatively easy to establish oneself as a master tailor because the trade did not demand much of an initial capital investment. But the leap from a type of proletarian existence as craftsman must have been enormously difficult. The medium-sized shops—shops with approximately three to five journeymen—were very scarce.[31]

In fact, since it was so difficult to make a decent living as a master tailor, most apprentices remained journeymen for the majority of their lives, and they were constantly looking for better situations. Given the hardships tailors endured, it is no surprise to find them cutting corners and resorting to dubious means to make a profit or to make a living. Consequently, there is an underlying attitude of suspicion toward tailors in the Grimms' *Children's and Household Tales:* The tailor is not to be trusted. He is often boastful, tricky, and sly. On the other hand, there are also the good souls, the industrious tailors, who uphold the good name of their craft and demonstrate that they can do solid work. Yet, whether the tailor be cunning, carefree, or hardworking, he is more often than not portrayed as a wanderer, someone in search of a better situation than tailoring. Almost all the tales begin with the tailor either on his journey or about to set out on a journey. The plucky fellow in "The Brave Little Tailor" starts out to show the world how brave he is right after he has revealed how stingy he is in his dealings with an old peasant woman. The tailor's sons in "The Magic Table, The Gold Donkey, and the Club in the Sack" must leave their father's house under duress and learn other (certainly more profitable) trades. Once they learn another skill and are rewarded for their hard work, they ultimately free their father from tailoring. The tiny fellow in "Thumbling's Travels" goes out into the world and learns how difficult it is to work as a tailor's apprentice. The tailor in "The Two Travelers" comes to realize that he must give up the carefree life and settle down if he is to be happy and successful. The simpleton tailor in "The Clever Little Tailor" is the one who solves the riddle of the princess and abandons tailoring to marry her. In "The Bright Sun Will Bring It to Light," a starving tailor's apprentice kills a Jew on the road so he can establish himself in a nearby town. A lucky young tailor in "The Glass Coffin" gets lost in a forest and eventually rescues a princess, who becomes his wife. In "The Gifts of the Little Folk," another tailor has luck on a journey and is rewarded with gold by the little folk. Finally, a boastful tailor in "The Giant and the Tailor" leaves his workshop to see what he can see in the forest and is eventually cast out by a giant because he is such a nuisance. There are two basic related motifs in these tales: (1) either the tailor wants to abandon his trade and move on to something better because the trade (perhaps like spinning) is unprofitable and dreary; or, (2) the protagonist learns how to settle down and become an established, more responsible tailor. Here again the forest or the great wide world is the domain where the tailor is given a chance to change and where his fate is decided. For instance, the brave little tailor meets the giant in the forest, demonstrates his skills and courage, and later performs amazing feats in the forest to become king. The tailor's three sons in "The Magic Table, the Gold Donkey, and the Club in the Sack" and Thumbling have adventures in the forest and outside world that test their valor and cunning before they settle down. This is also the case with the tailor in "The Two Travelers," who is sorely tested and loses his eyesight in the forest. It is through the loss of sight that he regains a sense of priorities, and it is in the forest that he learns to see again. The forest also appears in "The Glass Coffin," "The Gifts of the Little Folk," and "The Giant and The Tailor" as the place where the tailors can attain a sense of themselves and acquire fortune if they put their talents to good use. If they fail, as in the case of the tailor in "The Giant and the Tailor," they are severely punished. "The Tailor in Heaven," "The Bright Sun Will Bring It to Light," and "Sharing Joys and Sorrows" are all about tailors who are either cocky or cunning and endeavor to make their way through the world by tricking and exploiting others.

As in the soldier's tales, there is a normative behavior pattern established by the protagonist's comportment. The good tailor is indeed cunning, but also compassionate, hardworking, generous, and brave. More often than not he is searching for a secure place in society and must prove he is worthy enough to meet society's demands and win this place—one that is generally above his station. The good tailor is one who becomes a king or gets rich because he makes the best of his talents. The bad tailor is the drunk or the murderer. He is an arrogant man who lacks compassion and disregards the rights of his fellow human beings.

The appeal of the male protagonists, whether they be tailors or soldiers, is that they demonstrate a distinct willingness to rectify social injustices, particularly when they are class-related. Although the Grimms did believe in a class society and in maintaining distinctions among different groups of people, they also believed in social mobility and universal respect for a person's qualities—no matter what the person's class was or what trade a person plied. In fact, as time passed, their sentiments against class distinctions and the aristocracy grew more radical.[32] Such a progressive turn in their politics was merely the logical outcome of their democratic sentiments which were embedded in their folklore projects from the beginning. This is why the forest as a topos is so important in their tales; it also was evidently important in the minds of the oral narrators, especially when they depicted the soldier or tailor in need of overcoming prejudices or searching for some magical help to bring about a new sense of social justice.

In 1852, Wilhelm H. Riehl, a remarkable political thinker and folklorist,[33] who was a contemporary of the Grimms, wrote a book entitled *Land und Leute*, in which he discussed the significance of the forest for the German people:

> In the opinion of the German people the forest is the only great possession that has yet to be completely given away. In contrast to the field, the meadow, and the garden, every person has a certain right to the forest, even if it only consists in being able to walk around it when the person so desires. In the right or privilege to collect wood and foliage, to shelter animals, and in the distribution of the so-called *Losholz* (free wood) from communal forests and the like, there is a type of communist heritage that is rooted in history. Where is there anything else that has been preserved like this other than the forest? This is the root of genuine German social conditions.[34]

Further on, Riehl stated:

> It is generally known that the notion of privately owned forests developed only very late with the German people, and this was a gradual development. Forest, pasture, and water are according to ancient German basic law to be open to common use of all the people in the region (*Markgenossen*). The saying of *Wald, Weide und Wasser* (forest, pasture, and water) has not yet been entirely forgotten by the German people.[35]

Despite the ideological tendentiousness in the above remarks and also in some of Riehl's other studies of social customs, everyday life, and social classes of the German people, he draws our attention here to the manner in which the Grimms accepted and portrayed the forest in their tales and also the manner in which various social types related to the forest. As *Urwald* (primeval forest), the forest is the seat of tradition and justice; the heroes of the Grimms' tales customarily march or drift into the forest and they are rarely the same people when they leave it. The forest provides them with all they will need, if they know how to interpret the signs.

The Grimms themselves were fascinated by the forest. Indeed, they were fascinated by all that gave rise to what constituted German culture—language, law, craftsmanship, and daily customs. They considered the tales that they collected signs and traces of the past and present that enabled them to glean essential truths about the German people. This is ultimately why the social types such as the soldier and the tailor and topoi such as the forest need further study if the Grimms' cultural investment in the *Children's and Household Tales* is to be fully grasped. After all, it was through their persistent hard work, integrity, cunning, devotion to an ideal of the German people, and their belief in the Protestant ethic that they advanced in society and provided us with an *Erziehungsbuch* (educational manual) to be used with great care. Yet, even more than an *Erziehungsbuch*, their collection is historically like an enchanted forest that can illuminate the past while providing hope for the future. We need only learn to read the signs.

CHAPTER FOUR

FROM ODYSSEUS TO TOM THUMB AND OTHER CUNNING HEROES

Speculations about the Entrepreneurial Spirit

In her introduction to the 1976 Insel edition of the Grimms' *Kinder- und Hausmärchen* (*Children's and Household Tales*), the noted ethnologist Ingeborg Weber-Kellermann states:

> The triumphal procession of the *Children's and Household Tales* succeeded only because the nurseries of bourgeois homes formed the well-disposed circle of consumers. With its strong bourgeois sense of family the nineteenth century was receptive to the Grimms' fairy tales as a book that mothers and grandmothers could read aloud and that children could read to themselves. . . . The possibilities for identification involved nationalist thought and German *Volkstümlichkeit*, and all of this was considered to be perfectly captured in the Grimms' *Children's and Household Tales.* The success of their book cannot be

> understood without studying the social history of the nineteenth century.[1]

Some years later, Heinz Rölleke, the foremost scholar of the Grimms' tales in postwar Germany, reiterated Weber-Kellermann's point in his book *Die Märchen der Brüder Grimm* (1985), with a slightly different twist:

> The bourgeoisie has continually accepted the possibilities for identification in these texts beyond national boundaries, texts which effectually represent their own virtues and ideals and can be used effectively for pedagogical purposes. The bourgeois sense of family, an entirely new and high estimation of the child as autonomous personality, a moderate *biedermeier* world-view in keeping with the European social history of the nineteenth century, but also more or less with the Japanese of the late twentieth century—these were and continue to be the significant factors for the enthusiastic reception of the Grimms' fairy tales from generation to generation. Hence, it was not the joy about the "German essence" of the tales that brought about the international success of the *Children's and Household Tales* as a book but much more the respective affinity between the social and cultural givens in a particular country with those of Germany at the beginning of the nineteenth century.[2]

Whereas Weber-Kellermann finds that the reasons for the success of the *Children's and Household Tales* are due to the growing nationalist and bourgeois climate in nineteenth-century Germany, Rölleke points to the international bourgeois reception and endeavors to discount the "German essence" of the tales. Both are in agreement, however, that the tales offer bourgeois models or narrative paradigms that reinforce social, moral, and political codes that have become common to modern nation-states. Surprisingly, neither Weber-Kellermann nor Rölleke have endeavored to explore the so-called bourgeois appeal of the tales in depth, even though the key to their reception and celebration in the modern world today lies there.

As I have demonstrated in previous chapters and also in *Fairy Tales and the Art of Subversion*,[3] there is a clear connection between the rise of the civilizing process, standards of civility and *Bildung* (education) set largely by the bourgeoisie, and the origins of the fairy tale as institution in the eighteenth and nineteenth centuries. The connection accounts for the continued appeal not only of the Grimms' tales but of most classical fairy tales that received approbation by the middle-class reading public because of the manner in which the tales constructed solutions to moral and political conflicts. As devout Calvinists dedicated to the principles of the enlightened German *Bildungsbürgertum*, the Grimms were the perfect pair to stamp the fairy-tale genre with the imprint of the Protestant ethic. If today we continue to value the tales that they collected and revised, it is because they stylistically formulated those norms and gender roles that we have been expected to internalize psychologically and ideologically, from childhood to old age. Or, to put it another way, the "contagious" charm of the Grimms' fairy tales emanates from the compositional technique and ethics developed by the Brothers Grimm to stress fundamental bourgeois values of behavior and moral principles of Christianity that served the hegemonic aspirations of the rising middle classes in Germany and elsewhere. As various critics have noted, these values and principles are also oriented toward male hegemony and patriarchy.[4] Consequently, most critical attention has been paid to sexism and female role expectations in the Grimms' tales and classical fairy tales,[5] and there has curiously been very little research on male heroes, stereotypes, and role expectations.[6] This is unfortunate, since I believe that an understanding of the different roles played by the male protagonists in the Grimms' tales might enable us to gain a deeper understanding of the bourgeois content, popular appeal, and endurance of the Grimms' tales. Let us then see what can be done here with a little speculation.

In his essay "Die Frau in den Märchen der Brüder Grimm,"[7] Rölleke has argued that there is a danger in generalizing about a gender type, for there is no single female type consistently depicted in the same manner throughout the tales. Indeed, there are many different types of women at different stages in their lives, and they have various occupations and social backgrounds. At best, one could select the dominant characteristics of heroines in the most popular tales to illustrate readers' preferences in the portrayal of acceptable female behavior. The different types of women and their various modes of action in the tales have all been leveled in the cultural *reception and use* of the tales. For instance, among the Grimms' tales there are only a few "heroines" who stand out in the public's memory today—such as Cinderella, Sleeping Beauty, Snow White, Little Red Riding Hood, Rapunzel, the miller's daughter in "Rumpelstiltskin," and the princess in "The Frog King." For the most part these heroines indicate that a woman's best place is in the house as a diligent, obedient, self-sacrificing wife. In the majority of these tales and their imitations, the male is her reward, and it is apparent that, even though he is an incidental character, he arrives on the scene to take over, to govern, and control her future. (We tend to forget the tales in which women are strong, intelligent, and brave, and outwit men. Such tales as "Clever Gretel," "The Clever Farmer's Daughter," or "The True Bride" have not become part of the fairy-tale canon.)

But what about the tales in which the male is the protagonist? What about the tales in which the male is largely concerned with his own fate? In the 211 tales of the last edition of 1857 and in the additional 28 tales that had appeared in previous editions but were omitted for various reasons at a later date, we encounter such types as the magician, drummer, thief, goldsmith, shoemaker, woodcutter, servant, Jew, shepherd, blacksmith, fisherman, huntsman, elf, gnome, dwarf, journeyman, cook, army surgeon, king, prince, hermit, soldier, tailor, giant, hedgehog, donkey, Thumbling, youngest son, and farmer/peasant. Their behavior varies according to their situation, occupation, and class; though magic and miraculous events do occur, these types all evince characteristics that correspond realistically to representative figures of the eighteenth and nineteenth centuries. Therefore, it is important to gather historical information about social conditions during these centuries if we are to grasp both differences and similarities among the heroes. As we saw in chapter 3, historical data enables us to comprehend to a certain degree why the soldiers in the Grimms' tales display a distinct dislike for the army and their superiors; we saw why they are often bent on revenge after having been mistreated and why they want nothing more to do with soldiering. We also grasped why tailors in Grimm tales are anxious to abandon their craft: because at the time the guilds were declining and tailoring was no longer profitable. Similarly, history tells us a good deal about the third or youngest son, who is denied property and inheritance due to primogeniture and must prove his worth alone in the wide world. What unites these types—the soldier, tailor, and youngest son—is the will for survival and a strong desire to improve their lot, no matter what risks they have to face.

Here the specific can be linked to the general. The male heroes in the Grimms' tales tend to be adventurous, cunning, opportunistic, and reasonable. They take "calculated" risks and expect these risks to pay off. And, for the most part, their *Fleiß* (industriousness) and aggressive behavior are rewarded. Contrary to what one might expect, the majority of the male heroes in the Grimms' tales are *not* princes—at least, not at the outset, nor can we say that their conduct is "princely" or aristocratic in any way. If anything, the majority of the male heroes reveal a definite bourgeois entrepreneurial spirit, and even the princes must toe the bourgeois line.

But what is meant by bourgeois entrepreneur? What is meant by the "bourgeois line" that the Grimms' protagonists must toe? Here I would like to turn to Theodor Adorno and Max Horkheimer for some help—two unlikely critics at first glance, and yet I believe that they open up a general view of male protagonists in western culture that may prove invaluable for the study of male behavior in the Grimms' tales and their favorable reception in Western societies up to the present.

In the second chapter of their book *Dialectic of Enlightenment*,[8] Adorno and Horkheimer discuss Homer's *Odyssey* in relation to their notion of bourgeois enlightenment and myth with the intention of showing how the struggle for self-preservation and autonomy has been linked to sacrifice, renunciation, and repression ever since the beginning of western thought. For Adorno and Horkheimer, Odysseus is the prototype of the bourgeois individual, and they analyze his struggles philosophically as representing both the general and particular form that the struggle against nature takes. Odysseus battles his way home while demonstrating what qualities one needs in order to retain control over inner and outer nature. According to Adorno and Horkheimer, Odysseus is mostly concerned with his own vested interests and self-preservation, not with the welfare of the collective. Yet, at the same time, these concerns entail the repression of his own instincts and immediate needs, for

> the nimble-witted survives only at the price of his own dream, which he wins only by demystifying himself as well as the powers without. He can never have everything; he always has to wait, to be patient, to do without; he may not taste the lotus or eat the cattle of the Sun-god Hyperion, and when he steers between the rocks he must count on the loss of the men whom Scylla plucks from the boat. He just pulls through; struggle is his survival; and all the fame that he and the others win in the process serves merely to confirm that the title of hero is only gained at the price of abasement and mortification of the instinct for complete, universal, and undivided happiness.[9]

In the eyes of Adorno and Horkheimer, each trial and test experienced by Odysseus represents a stage in self-mastery. During the course of his voyage, Odysseus learns how to dominate by developing and making instrumental a personal system of rational calculation. The authors argue that this mythic model became general and historical for Western bourgeois men by the nineteenth century. For instance, when Odysseus arrives home, he has completed a voyage or course in civilization that appears to be one of fulfillment, but it is actually the culmination of self-renunciation and self-alienation. By withstanding the forces of magic, chaos, nature, and sensuality, Odysseus acts in the name of civilizing rationality, which constitutes the very essence of the bourgeois individual. Adorno and Horkheimer continually underline how cunning leads Odysseus to mark the formation of the bourgeois entrepreneur:

> From the standpoint of the developed exchange society and its individuals, the adventures of Odysseus are an exact representation of the risks which mark out the road to success. Odysseus lives by the original constitutive principle of civil society: one had the choice between deceit and failure. Deception was the mark of the ratio which betrayed its particularity. Hence universal socialization, as outlined in the narratives of the world traveler Odysseus and the solo manufacturer [Robinson] Crusoe, from the start included the absolute solitude which emerged so clearly at the end of the bourgeois era. Radical socialization means radical alienation. Odysseus and Crusoe are both concerned with totality—the former measures whereas the latter produces it. Both realize totality only in complete alienation

> from all other men, who meet the two protagonists only in an alienated form—as enemies or as points of support, but always as tools, as things.[10]

As discussed by Adorno and Horkheimer, *The Odyssey* is about its male hero's civilizing rationality. This same kind of "bourgeois" male self-mastery, one that flowers in the Enlightenment, informs male behavior in the Grimms' tales. Here I would like to maintain that the *magic* fairy tales of the Grimms were designed by them as literary products to put an end to magic (deus ex machina, good fairies, supernatural luck, spells)—perhaps first even told by others with this end in mind—and to establish the significance of cunning and rational enlightenment. A "male" principle of literacy is at work here, for to become literate and sophisticated is to learn to exploit the distinction between word and fact and to deceive the outside world in order to conquer it. The principles of literacy in the West have been formulated largely by men in their enterprise to deceive, for men know that their principles are not based on fact or on nature but on their own vested interests for power and survival. To know the world is to conceive narratives to control cognition when it is apparent that the truth and essence of the world can never be known. Consequently, men, especially rulers and their advisers, must use their cunning to concoct words so as not to be found out—just as Odysseus does in his encounter with Polyphemus, where he pretends to be nobody. By playing with words Odysseus shows his intellectual superiority, but he is also compelled to deny his identity to escape and make his way home. The escape toward home as a realm of nonalienation is opposed to the deceitful discourse that enables the hero to succeed. The escape toward home marks the narrative purpose of most fairy tales in the Grimms' collection, and the tension in the compositional technique of fairy tales resides in the self-consciousness of the narrator, who knows that words can be used to maintain domination over nature in the interests of men but can also be employed to liberate humankind from deceitful myths that cause the enslavement of humankind. If we focus on how different male heroes in the Grimms' tales use cunning in securing their realms, we shall see that reason is used instrumentally to banish magic and establish male governance that appears to be home.

In contrast to the structural approach to fairy tales that tends to homogenize the hero according to an aesthetic function, the sociohistorical approach must try to differentiate and grasp the action of the hero in the Grimms' tales in light of his predicament—the German term *Not* (need) is often used—and social class. Moreover we must bear in mind at all times that the Grimms selected tales according to the manner in which they exemplified customary behavior and language and revealed truths about all strata of the German people and their social laws. However, as the Grimms recorded and revised the tales, there is no doubt that they framed all conflicts and normative resolutions within the general Protestant ethic and code of the bourgeois enlightenment. The quest for self-preservation in the tales—and almost all the quests are for self-preservation and the resolution of a conflict—involves adventures that show how the hero is *graced,* and how he uses his wits and reason and exhibits industriousness and valor to succeed in acquiring a fortune. Paradoxically, magic is extolled and used by the hero to ban magic. Nothing is to be left to chance at the end. Home is the overcoming of self-alienation marked by a rational closing of the narrative, which is also the rational enclosure of the future. Becoming king or prince at the end of a Grimms' tale is a socially symbolic act of achieving self-mastery—as well as mastery over outside forces that include women and nature.

How are self-mastery and mastery represented by the male heroes in the Grimms' tales? Let us glance at several examples related to one another by their rational design: resolving conflicts in a calculated way to serve the interests of male domination. The compositional strategy of the tales is closely connected to the theme of cunning and calculation.

In "The Boy Who Set Forth to Learn about Fear," a peasant boy's apparent naiveté and self-restraint enable him to survive various encounters with a ghost, hanged men on a gallows, and an assortment of ghoulish creatures in a haunted castle. It is his fearlessness along with his self-control that allow him to survive, discover a treasure, and marry a princess. Whereas the peasant boy is a "pure soul," whose curiosity and adventurous spirit are rewarded—in contrast to women, who are punished for the same tendencies—the tailor in "The Brave Little Tailor" achieves his goals through his deft use of words, first by announcing his skills (he can kill "seven with one blow"), which are deceptive because the words are ambivalent, and then by using the spoken word to get himself out of difficulties. Like Odysseus, he is a boaster who outwits giants, dangerous animals, and a king and his court to become a king himself. In "The Riddle," it is a prince this time who desires to see the world, and after escaping from a witch he uses his wits in a battle of words to pose a riddle to a princess and win her for his bride. In "The Magic Table, the Gold Donkey, and the Club in the Sack," the use of cunning again is important: The tailor's youngest son diligently learns the trade of a turner and then employs his brains to outwit the innkeeper who had stolen the magic table and donkey from his brothers. Again, it is knowing how to use words that gives the hero power over others and objects. The youngest son restores his brothers' rightful property to them, and they can now lead prosperous lives. In a variation on this theme, "The Knapsack, the Hat, and the Horn," the youngest of three poor brothers uses magic gifts and cunning to punish his brothers, a king, and the king's daughter, to become king himself. Knowing the right incantation gives him power to devastate his opponents. Most youngest sons are compelled to become facile with words and exploit their meanings in deceitful ways to set their own rules for attaining success. In "The Golden Goose," another youngest son, known as a simpleton, reveals that his naiveté merely concealed his cunning. With the help of a dwarf and the magic goose, he tricks all those around him so that he can eventually marry a king's daughter and inherit a kingdom. In "The King of the Golden Mountain," a merchant's son manages to save himself from the devil and outfoxes three giants to regain his kingdom. He becomes a ruthless, revengeful ruler at the end by commanding a magic sword to chop off all the heads of the guests at his wife's wedding—except his own, of course. The establishment of his realm is determined by his word as law. Another protagonist, the soldier in "Bearskin," also meets the devil. However, in stark contrast to the merchant's son, he displays remarkable self-control and piety for seven years by keeping his word. His reward is a bride, who exhibits patience and faithfulness, and a fortune. His self-denial and deception lead to a "cleaning up" of his own messiness followed by blessed days.

In the tales discussed thus far, we have a peasant boy, a tailor, a prince, a turner, a poor boy, a simpleton, a merchant's son, and a soldier, all of whom outwit their adversaries largely through their capacity to use words cunningly in order to deceive others and gain their objectives. The emphasis in the tales is on *cunning*, and invariably the hero orders his world and the outside world so he will not be threatened by nature, magic, or the unknown. He, the knower, who knows that he deceives through words, makes the objective world known so that he will have it at his command. In contrast to tales in which female protagonists must exhibit *silence*[11] and patience if they are to survive and wed, the male heroes must be verbally adroit and know how to use words and their wits as weapons. In most cases the protagonist as adventurer moves up in social class and improves his state of affairs. Given a chance, he uses every opportunity to economize his energies and advance himself without really giving a thought to people around him. Maria Tatar has argued that the Grimms' heroes tend to be compassionate,[12] but this is not really a striking characteristic of most heroes. They help people and animals when they believe it will be to their advantage and *expect* to be paid back in the end. More often than not, the hero is out to prove himself at all costs and to survive—and love has very little to do with his actions. (Most marriages in the eighteenth and nineteenth centuries, we should note, were based on economic arrangements and convenience.) Love and compassion are not major themes in the Grimms' tales, even though they may at times play a key role. Rather, arranging and rearranging one's life to settle down comfortably according to one's self-interests takes precedence over "noble" feelings. Survival and self-preservation—whether one is aristocrat, bourgeois, or peasant—mean acquiring, learning, and knowing how to use verbal codes to increase one's power. The tales that most attracted the Grimms as *Bildungsbürger* were those that involve the adroit use of words to gain wealth, happiness, and above all, power; these tales all show a distinct narrative bias for the underdog, the underprivileged, and those who need to display the right "civil" sense of cunning to make their way in society.

It is thus not by chance that three of the tales that captured the Grimms' imagination involved Tom Thumb: "Thumbling," "Thumbling's Travels," and "The Young Giant." In fact, Wilhelm dealt with the *Däumling* figure in a scholarly article and commented on it in the introduction to the second printing of the 1819 edition of the *Children's and Household Tales:*

> The simpleton is that person who is despised, inferior, and small, and if he becomes strong, he is only sucked up by giants. In this way he is close to Tom Thumb (*Däumling*). This figure is only as large as a thumb at birth and does not grow any more than that. But the determining factor with him is cleverness: he is completely cunning and deft so that he can get himself out of any dilemma because of his small stature, and he even knows how to use his size to his advantage. He makes a monkey out of everyone and likes to tease people in a good-natured way. In general this is the nature of dwarfs. Most likely the tales about Tom Thumb emanate from the legends about dwarfs. Sometimes he is portrayed as a clever little tailor who terrifies the giants with his incisive and quick wit, kills monsters, and wins the king's daughter. Only he can solve the riddle put before him.[13]

And the tales prove Wilhelm's point. In "Thumbling," the son of poor peasants allows himself to be sold so his father can gain some money. After numerous adventures in which he is almost swallowed and killed by different animals, Thumbling uses his brains to return safely to his parents. In "Thumbling's Travels," the protagonist is a tailor's son and goes out into the world where he works as a journeyman, becomes a thief, and works at an inn. Finally, he too returns home, cleverly avoiding the hazards of the outside world. In "The Young Giant," Thumbling is a peasant's son who is kidnapped by a giant and then becomes a giant himself (one of the few tales in which Thumbling grows). He travels about the countryside, punishes miserly masters, and fends for himself wherever he goes.

Though each one of the Tom Thumb tales differs, they all focus on the same major concerns of *The Odyssey* as discussed by Adorno and Horkheimer: self-preservation and self-advancement through the use of reason to avoid being swallowed up by the appetite of unruly natural forces. The voyage in the Thumbling tales is an apprenticeship in which the small hero learns self-control and how to control others. This is one of the reasons why Tom Thumb is related to the thief, who must become an absolute master of self-control and capable of controlling appearances and how he is seen by other people.

Theft has something to do with being deft, and the thieves in the Grimms' tales (not to be confused with the murderous robbers) are generally admired, for thievery is an art form. It involves creating an illusion, just as the Grimms, in the composition of their tales, were seeking to create an illusion—which could transform itself into an anticipatory illumination, pointing to the way the underprivileged and disadvantaged might overcome obstacles and attain happiness.

Practically all the protagonists in the Grimms' tales must learn something about the art of thievery, especially when they are confronted by ogres, giants, tyrannical kings, or witches. A classical case is the peasant boy born with a caul in "The Devil with the Three Golden Hairs," who must eventually trick the devil and a king to gain a princess and a kingdom. In the three tales that focus directly on the art of thievery, "The Thief and His Master," "The Four Skillful Brothers," and "The Master Thief," the young man is a peasant who learns his craft in order to survive and maintain himself against "legitimate" but unjust rulers. (Obviously, the craft of thievery was one that mainly lower-class men learned or had to learn, since other choices were not always available to them.) In "The Thief and His Master," a man named Jan is concerned about his son's future and is tricked by the sexton of a church into sending his son to learn the trade of thieving. Later, however, the son uses his skills of deception and transformation to make his father a rich man. Not only does thievery pay in this tale, but the son appears to be more considerate toward his father than the sexton. In "The Four Skillful Brothers," one of the sons of a poor man becomes a master thief and joins with his three gifted brothers to rescue a princess from a dragon. There is not the slightest hint of condemnation regarding the son's profession. Only in "The Master Thief" is there an indication that thieving might indicate a "crooked" upbringing, when a son returns home to his peasant parents and the father tells him that nothing good will come out of his profession. In fact, the father is wrong, for the son makes a fool of the count, his servants, and his pastor, and eventually leaves his home to wander about the world.

The Grimms' apparent admiration for cunning heroes was such that they could not bring themselves to condemn or punish a hero for being a thief. In another tale, entitled "The Robber and His Sons"[14]—which appeared in the fifth and sixth editions of *Children's and Household Tales* in 1843 and 1850, but was omitted in the final 1857 edition because it was too closely related to the Polyphemus tale in *The Odyssey*[15]—a famous retired robber/thief recounts three adventures in order to save his sons, who had disregarded his advice against becoming robbers and tried to follow in his footsteps by stealing a horse from the queen. They are captured by the queen's men, and only by telling the queen three extraordinary tales about his days as a great robber can the father gain clemency for his sons. One of the adventures concerns his entrapment in a cave by a giant (similar to Odysseus' plight with Polyphemus) and how he managed to outwit the giant by escaping in a sheepskin. Aesthetically speaking, the text as composed by Wilhelm employs a framework similar to the one used in *A Thousand and One Nights.* Here the third-person narrative shifts to the more personal first-person narrative—in effect, a strategy for emancipation, a plea. The father adroitly uses his words to conjure pictures of his unusual adventures and thereby gains the freedom of his three sons. Cunning is again exemplified in the figure of a thief as narrator, and one who is, for the Grimms, much more than a thief; for them, he represents the spirit of bourgeois entrepreneurism and civilization.

In 1857, the very year in which "The Robber and His Sons" was eliminated from *Children's and Household Tales,* Wilhelm held a talk in the Berlin Academy of Sciences entitled "Die Sage von Polyphem" ("The Legend of Polyphemus"),[16] in which he drew comparisons between ten similar legends and myths based on the Polyphemus material. The main point of the talk was to prove that, despite major differences between the versions, they all stemmed from a primeval myth, an *Urmythos,* that dealt with the origins of the world and the struggle between good and evil forces personified by a "good" dwarf or little man and an "evil" giant, whose one eye is a mark of his divine origins that he has betrayed:

> If a greater meaning is established with such references, then we can perhaps move closer toward understanding the original figure. What else do the mythical songs of primeval times celebrate but the origins of the world and, so long as the world lasts,

> the movements of powerful, inimical forces that never rest? They are the battles of the elements among themselves, of heaven and the underworld, of summer and winter, of day and night, that reflect the moral opposites of benediction and corruption, love and hate, joy and sadness. The opposition between the outer, terrifying natural forces and the quiet, concealed natural forces or the opposition in the moral connection between raw power and cunning deftness is expressed in the myths about giants and dwarfs. It is here that I find the original content and meaning of the Polyphemus legend, which is articulated most clearly in the nordic tradition.[17]

Though Wilhelm's theory cannot be proved, it does reveal something important about male protagonists in the Grimms' tales and the Grimms' compositional techniques in regard to moral order. The Thumbling, the simpleton, the thief, the youngest son, and the little man are all one and the same man, who serves the same aesthetic and thematic function. He is faced with unruly forces of nature and a world that is unjust or incomprehensible, and represents the moral principle of order based on reason and cunning. His task is to enlighten himself and enlighten the world. The embarkation on a voyage is like the initial stages of the narrative composition in the Grimms' work on their tales. The hero, like the Brothers Grimm, embarks to resolve conflicts and order the world according to his basic self-interests. In the case of the Grimms, the reassembling of the tales was completed in a dialogue with moral standards and ethical principles of the German *Bildungsbürgertum*, and the tales were to be published and institutionalized as an *Erziehungsbuch* (education manual) within the bourgeois public realm governed by male regulations. Each tale they heard was a speech utterance that they sought to reshape and designate generically as fable, legend, anecdote, magic fairy tale, joke, ditty, etc. While the Grimms consciously endeavored to work within the European tradition of oral storytelling, they also tried to improve the tales and shape them into authoritative representations of their view of the world. As Mikhail Bakhtin has pointed out,

> in each epoch, in each social circle, in each small world of family, friends, acquaintances, and comrades in which a human being grows and lives, there are always authoritative utterances

> that set the tone—artistic, scientific, and journalistic works on which one relies, to which one refers, which are cited, imitated, and followed. . . . This is why the unique speech experience of each individual is shaped and developed in continuous and constant interaction with others' individual utterances. This experience can be characterized to some degree as the process of *assimilation*—more or less creative—of others' words (and not the words of a language). Our speech, that is, all our utterances (including creative works), is filled with others' words, varying degrees of otherness, of varying degrees of "our-own-ness," varying degrees of awareness and detachment. These words of others carry with them their own expression, their own evaluative tone, which we assimilate, rework, and re-accentuate.[18]

By appropriating oral tales largely from female informants and reworking tales from books and texts that were sent to them, the Grimms chose words, expressions, and narrative forms of development that provided for rational cohesion and a reward system that justified male domination within the bourgeois public sphere. Even when a male does not figure prominently within the action of a tale like "Snow White," "Cinderella, "One-Eye, Two Eyes, and Three-Eyes," or "The Goose Girl," he brings about the proper closure by rationally, morally, or cunningly ordering her world so that it becomes *his* world. The principles of the writing of the tale and the action within the tale are the same: prudence with respect to overt sexuality, industriousness with respect to forming a new world, perseverance in seeking the right words, rationalization in championing the power of enlightenment, and equality in establishing the rights of men with the principles of enlightenment and justice.

In various kinds of dialogues with others—their informants, the legal system of their day, their national heritage, the ancient Greek and Roman tradition, the Christian faith, and between themselves—the Grimms set the tone for the development of a literary language that preferred the Odyssean principle. It is not by chance that Odysseus becomes the prototype of the bourgeois entrepreneur in the nineteenth century, and the Grimms were not the only ones to champion this spirit of rational entrepreneurism and appropriation. In the Western fairy-tale tradition there is an abundance of Tom Thumbs, Jack the Giant Killers, and swineherds—Horatio Algers, explorers, pioneers, and colonialists take center stage in bourgeois novels and stories of adventurers in the nineteenth century. What marks these adventurers is the cunning manner in which they go about their business. Women, magic, nature, and raw power are put to use to guarantee harmony in accordance with the self-interest of an individual male, whose word spoken as law appears to be the last word on justice. Ultimately, what underlies the actions of the male protagonists in the Grimms' tales is a principle of instrumental reason, and if we want to attain a fuller understanding of the bourgeois appeal of the Grimms' fairy tales, we might do well to look today at our own need for control and domination of nature, and at our manly means of fairness and order in public and private realms of action.

CHAPTER FIVE

THE GERMAN OBSESSION WITH FAIRY TALES

It is not by chance that the cover of the August 11, 1984 issue of *The Economist* portrayed a large, green-shaded picture of Hansel and Gretel with a beckoning witch under the caption, "West Germany's Greens Meet the Wicked World." Inside the magazine a special correspondent began his report:

> Once upon a time (in the late 1960s), a hostile stepmother (West Germany's Christian Democrats) and a kindly but weak father (the Social Democrats) decided that they had no room for children who thought for themselves. So they abandoned Hansel and Gretel (rebellious young West Germans) in a dense wood. Far from perishing, as their parents had expected, Hansel and Gretel became Greens. They quaked at the forest's nuclear terrors and cherished its trees. Soon they spied a glittering gingerbread house at the Bundestag in a clearing. Being hungry, they ran inside. This was their first big test. For the house belonged to the wicked witch of the establishment.[1]

The metaphorical use of a Grimm fairy tale to explain current German politics and the association of Germany with a fairy-tale realm are not new, and they are certainly not exclusive to *The Economist*. Ever since the collection of the Brothers Grimm became a household item in the nineteenth century, the Germans have repeatedly used fairy tales to explain the world to themselves. Aside from cultivating traditional folk tales, they have also developed the most remarkable literary fairy-tale tradition in the West. In fact, folk and fairy tales have been preserved and investigated by Germans with an intense seriousness often bordering on the religious, and nationalist overtones have often smothered the philosophical and humanitarian essence of the tales. Yet, despite the national solemnity, German authors have not lacked humor. Take, for example, Rudolf Otto Wiemer's poem "The Old Wolf" (1976):

The wolf, now piously old and good,
When again he met Red Riding Hood
Spoke: "Incredible, my child,
What kinds of stories are spread. They're wild.

As though there were, so the lie is told,
A dark murder affair of old.
The Brothers Grimm are the ones to blame.
Confess! It wasn't half as bad as they claim."

Little Red Riding Hood saw the wolf's bite
And stammered: "You're right, quite right."
Whereupon the wolf, heaving many a sigh,
Gave kind regards to Granny and waved good-bye.[2]

Parodies of the Grimms are common in the creative works of numerous contemporary German writers, and German critics have continually made important, innovative contributions to Grimm and fairy-tale scholarship. On the other side of the Atlantic, however, certain American academicians appear to have lost their sense of humor and perspective. They have taken Wiemer's line "the Brothers Grimm are the ones to blame" and made it into a leitmotif; and, though they have not accused them of a "dark murder affair of old," they have linked the Grimms and German folk tales to a national tradition that they believe may explain why the Germans were so receptive to fascism. In particular, both Robert Darnton and

John Ellis see dark shadows and designs behind German folk tales and the nationalist leanings of the Grimms.

In "Peasants Tell Tales: The Meaning of Mother Goose," Darnton compares various French folk tales with German ones, largely taken from the Grimms' collection, and concludes that

> allowing for exceptions and complications, the differences between the two traditions fall into consistent patterns. The peasant raconteurs took the same themes and gave them characteristic twists, the French in one way, the German in another. Where the French tales tend to be realistic, earthy, bawdy, and comical, the German veer off toward the supernatural, the poetic, the exotic, and the violent.[3]

Taking a different approach, but also accusing the Grimms of contributing to the conservative cause of German nationalism, John Ellis has written an entire book criticizing the Grimms for fabricating a false notion of the "Germanic" origins of their tales:

> The Grimms appealed strongly to German nationalism because their own motives were nationalistic; and so this factor is dominant both in the brothers' fabrications and deceit, and in the strong reluctance of later scholars to acknowledge what they had done when the evidence emerged. The Grimms wanted to create a German national monument while pretending that they had merely discovered it; and later on, no one wanted to seem to tear it down.[4]

Darnton's conclusions about the German characteristics in folk tales are of limited value because his scholarship lacks depth. He provides scant evidence that German raconteurs favored "cruel" tales in the late Middle Ages and fails to make regional distinctions. In fact, this was a time, after all, when Germany did not exist as a nation-state. Furthermore, living conditions among the French peasantry in the eighteenth and early nineteenth centuries—conditions that Darnton believes account for the types and tones of French folk tales—were quite similar to the lifestyle and experiences of German peasants and artisans in the same period. In some cases differences in living conditions between the French in the north and the south of France were greater than differences between the French and the Germans.[5] Moreover, Darnton bases many of his assumptions about German folk tales on French tales that made their way into the Grimms' collection through mediators of Huguenot descent. Finally, his depictions of the historical origins of such French tales as "Little Red Riding Hood"[6] are often misleading. There is no doubt that important discoveries about national character and nationalism can be made through ethnological and historical studies of folk tales, but not when Germans are stereotypically linked with violence and cruelty.

Ellis, too, works with stereotypes, but his general thesis is perhaps even more farfetched than Darnton's. Ellis is certainly not wrong in claiming that the Grimms knew that most of their sources for the material they used were not "older, untainted, and untutored German peasant transmitters of an indigenous oral tradition but, instead, literate, middle-class, and predominantly young people, probably influenced more by books than by oral tradition—and including a significant presence of people who were either of French origin or actually French-speaking."[7] And he is also certainly correct in demonstrating that the Grimms made numerous textual changes to improve the tales stylistically and make them more suitable for German audiences. However, there is no evidence to indicate that the Grimms consciously sought to dupe German readers and feed them lies about the German past, nor that later scholars conspired to cover up the "nationalist" designs of the Grimms. If anyone is playing with the public, it is Ellis, who relies heavily on the original research of Heinz Rölleke[8] and other German scholars, distorts their findings, and conjures a myth of the Grimms' duplicity. As Donald Ward has pointed out,

> Virtually all of Ellis's material is based upon the research of others. He apparently did not engage in any kind of primary research, did not consult archival materials nor manuscripts or letters. Even though Ellis acknowledges his secondary sources in footnotes, he often does so as a kind of afterthought, giving at least the impression that most of the research is his own. This practice is most disturbing when Ellis compares the manuscript materials with subsequent editions, something he could not have done without the splendid synoptic edition of Heinz Rölleke. Indeed, Rölleke is the author upon whose research Ellis

> relies throughout his book, a fact that does not, however, preclude him from criticizing this scholar from whose works he draws upon so liberally. The only truly original contribution Ellis has to offer is his tone of indignation at the alleged "fraud and forgery" perpetuated by the Grimms. Alas, it is in this original part of his work where Ellis goes astray."[9]

The Grimms were indeed nationalistic but not in the negative sense in which we tend to use the term today. When they began their folklore research as young men in their twenties, Germany, as we now know it, did not exist. Their "country," essentially Hesse and the Rhineland, was invaded by the French, and they were disturbed by French colonialist aspirations. Thus, their desire to publish a work which expressed a German cultural spirit was part of an effort to contribute to a united German front against the French. They also felt that they were part of the nascent national bourgeoisie seeking to establish its own German identity in a manner more democratic than that allowed by the aristocratic rulers who governed the 300 or so German principalities. In short, the issue of the relations between German nationalism and the Grimms' *Kinder- und Hausmärchen* (*Children's and Household Tales*) is a complex one.[10] The so-called lies and fabrications, which Ellis concocts, were actually deeply held beliefs and emanated from a deep devotion to the German folk. As I have sought to show in previous chapters, the Grimms believed that they were nurturing and being faithful to a German cultural tradition. Over the course of their careers, they came to view themselves as midwives who, perhaps because of a strong affection for their material and the German people, became zealous advocates not only of German nationalism but of democratic reform.

If the issue of nationalism is at the crux of the Grimms' reformations of the tales—and I believe it is—then Ellis does not pursue in his study the many exciting avenues he could have followed. For instance, he never discusses the significance of the subjective selection of the tales and the changes made in terms of the "democratic ideology" of the Grimms. (There is also the psychological factor of the Grimms' patriarchal attitudes.) Nor does he consider the major reason for the revisions made largely by Wilhelm, who felt that all the editions after 1819 should be addressed in part toward children. For Wilhelm, it was as though he were bent on regaining a lost childhood or paradise. As Wilhelm Schoof in his book about the origins of the Grimms' collection has maintained, Wilhelm Grimm

> was guided by the desire to endow the tales with a tone and style primarily for children. He created a literary art form for them through the use of rhetorical and artistic means. This form is a synthesis based on faithful and scientific reproduction and the popular (*volkstümlich*) narrative style. Given his own ability to capture the appropriate childlike tone, he created a uniform fairy-tale style which has prevailed in the course of time and has become known as the classical or Grimm fairy-tale style.[11]

Contrary to Ellis's claim, then, the Grimms were totally conscious and open about their endeavors to make their material more suitable for children and to incorporate their notion of family, their sense of a folk aesthetic, and their political ideals in the tales; they wanted to share cultural goods with like-minded people.[12] They "Germanicized" their material in order to stay in touch with the concerns and sensibility of the German people, and this is their accomplishment, not their "crime." In response, the German people have made the Grimms' collection the second-most popular book in Germany, and during the last 150 years only the Bible has exceeded it in sales.

The love affair of the German people with the Grimms and with fairy tales in general reveals a great deal about the German national character that cannot be understood by linking the Grimms and their tales to rabid nationalism. Although vestiges of archaic societies, feudalism, and patriarchy remain in the Grimms' tales, the brothers also imbued them with certain qualities that corresponded to the progressive aspirations of the German middle class and peasantry. Or, to recall Ernst Bloch's term, there is in the tales a *Vor-Schein*,[13] an anticipatory illumination of the formation of utopia, which underlies their socially symbolic discourse. To a certain extent, the Grimms made an institution out of the fairy-tale genre: They established the framework of the genre, one that has become a type of public sphere in which various writers convene to voice their personal needs and a social need for pleasure and power under just conditions. The most resilient genre in German literary history since the eighteenth century, the literary fairy tale has also been Germany's most democratic literary institution. The aesthetic nature of the symbolic discourse as consolidated by the Grimms has enabled writers of all classes to use it to voice their views without fear of reprisal; to seek to alter the dominant discourse; and to gain understanding from the discourse itself.

When folklorists and other critics discuss the *Children's and Household Tales*, it has been customary to categorize them according to the Aarne-Thompson type index.[14] They are generally classified according to such types and motifs as animal helpers, the beast-bridegroom, the enchanted mountain, the test by fire, the seven-league boots, and the lecherous father, so that parallels with other folk tales and their origins can be traced. Such typology—and there are other formalist and structuralist approaches such as those developed by Max Lüthi and Vladimir Propp—may assist in the kind of classification work done by folklorists, ethnologists, and structural-minded critics, but in dealing with the Grimms' collection, it has detracted from the social and historical meaning of their work. Here I want to propose another way to analyze the Grimms' collection in order to shed light on their major contribution to the genre as an institution and to help us gain a deeper grasp of the German obsession with the fairy tale in general.

With the publication of the final edition of the *Children's and Household Tales* in 1857, there were 211 tales. Strictly speaking, as I have already shown, they are not all folk and fairy tales. There are legends, fables, anecdotes, didactic narratives, and journeyman tales in the collection, and their mediation by educated people and then by the Grimms makes them literary products. Their variety and mediation constitute their broad democratic appeal: there are numerous voices to be heard in the collection, and they are not only of German descent. Their international and interregional flavor, however, was influenced by German conditions.[15] The tales were collected and transmitted at a time when the German principalities were at war with France. The Grimms continued to collect their tales after the initial publication of the tales in 1812. They added to the collection and altered the tales up to 1857, during a time when there was a growing conscious movement to unite the German principalities and form a constitutional state. Not only did the Napoleonic Wars influence the social attitudes of the Grimms and their mediators, but the revolts of the 1830s and the revolutions of 1848 were also significant. We must not forget that the Grimms themselves had to leave Göttingen in 1837 because they were opposed to the tyrannical rule of King Ernst August of Hannover. They continued to support democratic causes after this incident, and in 1848 Jacob was chosen to represent Berlin in the constitutional assembly that met in Frankfurt am Main. A clear relationship exists between the Brothers Grimm, their sociopolitical notions, and their audience in Germany at that time; their household tales were items largely in middle-class homes and among literate groups of people. That Wilhelm kept editing the tales to guarantee that the collection would remain a household item and that he even developed a special smaller edition (which became a bestseller), suggest that he and his brother had a distinct concept of home and socialization in collecting and rewriting the tales. The rise in popularity of the tales occurred when the middle classes in Germany also sought to constitute a new home in opposition to feudalism, and when they were struggling for a nation-state that might guarantee their rights and those of the oppressed peasants.

If we look at some of the themes and narrative components of the 211 tales collected and altered by the Grimms on the basis of their relationship to democratic ideals and the Protestant ethic, then we can make some interesting observations as to why the German bourgeoisie was initially attracted to the tales and why this class institutionalized the genre that captured the imagination of the Germans as a whole. Perhaps the most striking feature of many of the tales is that, at their beginning, the majority of the protagonists, whether male or female, are either poor, deprived, or wronged in some way. They come largely from the peasant, artisan, or mercantile class. By the end of many of the tales, these protagonists, whether male or female, experience a rise in fortune that enables them to win a wife or husband, amass a fortune and power, and constitute a new realm. Marriages are not preordained or arranged. There is an underlying notion that love can arise sentimentally and can serve as the basis for marriage, which can cut across classes and form the foundation of a happy union or realm. We should note that the constitution of a new realm is also the realization of a new home away from home. Very few protagonists return to their old home after their adventure. Very few heroes in the tales have unusual physical power or military support at their disposal to take charge of the new kingdom. Instead, they must rely on their wits. In chapter 4, I endeavored to demonstrate that the Grimms' male protagonists are generally clever, reasonable, resolute, and upwardly mobile, and this is true also of the females, even though they are more docile and domestic. They appear to know their destiny and strive diligently to realize it. It is in the name of this destiny, which celebrates upward mobility and transformation, that the narrative voices of the tales collect themselves and were collected to speak in one voice. The archaic structure of the oral folk tale is modernized through an artistic high German style, endowed with the raison d'etre of transaction and commerce, polished and pruned of moral turpitude. The succession to power of lower-class figures is legitimized by their essential qualities of industriousness, cleverness, opportunism, and frankness. The imaginary private adventure becomes an imaginary social venture for power—a fact that probably did not escape most middle-class and peasant readers in the German reality of the nineteenth century.

If a Grimm protagonist (even an animal or object) does not communicate with helpers, whether they be beasts, fairies, devils, giants, or hags, he or she is lost. The tales describe the need for communicative action that enables the protagonist to seize the possibility to right a wrong and move up in society, to overcome feudal restrictions, to conceive a more just realm. It is interesting that the Grimm protagonist is nothing alone, by him or herself, but becomes omnipotent when assisted by small creatures or outsiders—those figures who are marginal and live on the border between wilderness and civilization, between village and woods, between the earthly world and the other sacred world.

The new realm to which the Grimm protagonist succeeds is made possible through his or her own ingenuity and the help of other small creatures or outcasts. Generally speaking, the creation of the smart and successful fairy-tale hero is founded on a collective enterprise of collaborators—just as the literary institution of the Grimms' fairy tales depended on centuries of oral transmission by gifted storytellers and on the mediation of middle-class informants.

It may seem strange to view the Grimms' fairy tales and literary fairy tales in general as an institution. Yet it seems to me that the distinct German character of the tales collected by the Grimms—and perhaps their universal appeal—might become clearer if we take this view. In his essay "Institution Kunst als literatursoziologische Kategorie," Peter Bürger defines the concept of institution as comprising "the factors which determine the function of art in a particular historical period and in its social context."[16] If literature is regarded this way, Bürger maintains that the

> factors which determine the function be linked to the material and intellectual needs of the cultivators [*Träger*] and placed in a specific relationship to the *material conditions of their production and reception of art*. The differentiation of the factors that determine the function results from this, and it is mediated via aesthetic norms: in the case of the producer by the *artistic material*, in the case of the recipient by the establishment of *attitudes of reception*.[17]

Within literature itself, genres become institutionalized in such interactions: They have their own history that depends on their formal attributes, production, reception, and social function in a historical development.

For the literary fairy tale as a genre in Germany, one would have to trace its institutionalization first to the French court of Louis XIV, where it performed the function of representing and legitimizing the norms of absolutism while providing *divertissement* and even, especially for female writers, a means to air some discontent with marital arrangements and patriarchal domination. The artistic output and ingenuity of Charles Perrault, Madame d'Aulnoy, Mademoiselle Lhéritier, Madame Lubert, and a host of other writers testify to the establishment of an actual mode of fairy-tale discourse.[18] It was this French mode, along with the European peasant oral tradition, that gave rise to the German literary fairy tale as institution. In other words, toward the end of the eighteenth century the German literary fairy tale begins to break with aesthetic and social prescriptions carried by the French courtly tale and the German peasant oral tradition; it is in the manner in which it breaks and defines itself while functioning for a different audience that we can locate the significance of the German literary fairy tale as a national institution. The fairy tales of

Musäus, Wieland, Goethe, Naubert, and the romantics give rise to a bourgeois literary institution that has a distinctly new and more autonomous function than the courtly fairy tales and peasant folk tales. Instead of writing their literary fairy tales for courtly audiences or telling them orally, German writers directed their tales to a middle-class reading public in the process of forming itself and the free market. They incorporated notions of bourgeois individualism and the autonomy of art in their works, and endowed the genre with a unique secular religious quality based on the cult of genius and the great philosophical works of Kant, Fichte, Schelling, and Hegel. As Bürger remarks, "the institution is just as much in the individual as the individual work functions within the institution."[19]

To view the German literary fairy tale as a literary institution does not mean to regard it statically or hypostatize form and content. Rather, this method enables us to grasp literature as it transforms itself and is actively transformed historically by its producers in unique ways and to identify the extraliterary forces that influence the immanent development of literature. Nor does this method mean that the individual work itself becomes negligible. To study a genre of literature as an institution allows us to uncover the uniqueness of a work when measured against the norms set down by the institution, and it allows us to understand its historical function and appreciate its present impact in a more comprehensive manner. Bürger maintains that

> after religion had lost its universal validity in the course of the European Enlightenment and had forfeited its paradigm of reconciliation which, for centuries, had carried out the task of expressing criticism about society while at the same time making it practically ineffectual, art now assumed this role—at least for the privileged social classes with property and education. Art was supposed to restore the harmony of the human personality that had been destroyed by a strict, utilitarian regimented daily life. This can only happen when it is radically separated from the practical affairs of daily life and set in opposition to it as an independent realm.[20]

Such a separation can already be seen in the fairy tales of Johann Karl August Musäus and Christoph Martin Wieland, written in

Weimar during the 1780s. They reflect the French courtly influence and also German folk traditions and were the first major endeavors to create an autonomous bourgeois art form. The production of their tales and their reception in Germany constitute a shift in the nature of the literary fairy tale as institution. However, it is first with the production of Goethe's "Das Märchen" ("The Fairy Tale"), Wilhelm Heinrich Wackenroder's "Ein wunderbares morgendländisches Märchen von einem nackten Heiligen" ("A Wonderful Oriental Fairy Tale of a Naked Saint"), Novalis's "Sais-Märchen" ("The Sais Fairy Tale") and fairy tales in *Heinrich von Ofterdingen*, and Ludwig Tieck's "Der blonde Eckbert" ("Eckbert the Blond"), "Der Fremde" ("The Stranger"), and "Der Runenberg" ("The Runenberg")—all written between 1790 and 1810—along with the tales of Clemens Brentano, Joseph von Eichendorff, Justinus Kerner, Friedrich de la Motte Fouqué, Adelbert Chamisso, and E.T.A. Hoffmann that we see the literary fairy tale institutionalizing itself as an independent genre and functioning to provide confirmation of a new bourgeois aesthetic and social attitude.[21]

As a literary institution, the fairy tale assumes a secular religious purpose: It presents moral and political critiques of society at the same time as it undermines them and reconciles the distraught protagonist with society. Obviously, such projections of harmony are not to be found in all literary fairy tales. Wackenroder, Tieck, and Hoffmann, for example, often leave their heroes insane, distressed, or destroyed. Yet the norm in the literary fairy tale is based on compensatory images of reconciliation. The overall social function of the literary fairy tale as institution at the beginning of the nineteenth century is to provide aesthetic formations of social redemption. Given the Napoleonic Wars, censorship, the lack of unification of the German people, the ineffectual peasant revolts, and the gradual rise of bureaucracy, the literary fairy tale became a means for German writers and a bourgeois reading public to pose and explore more harmonious options for the creative individual experiencing the development of a free market system, while also questioning such a system and the utilitarian purposes that the incipient bourgeois institutions had begun to serve. Unlike in France, where the literary fairy tale was first and foremost courtly and had declined by the time of the

French Revolution, and unlike in England, where the literary fairy tale was more or less banned by the bourgeois revolution of 1688 and did not revive until the Victorian period (partially due to German influence), the literary fairy tale in Germany became a major mode of expression for German bourgeois writers, a means of socioreligious compensation and legitimation.

More than Goethe, Novalis, Wackenroder, Tieck, Eichendorff, Brentano, and Hoffmann, whose complex, symbolic tales were not easily accessible to a large public—nor were they widely distributed—the Grimms were able to collect and compose tales that spoke to readers of all classes and age groups. They themselves had already been influenced by Goethe, the early romantics, and Brentano and Arnim, and their work is the culmination of a folk tradition and bourgeois appropriation of the folk tale. The Grimms were able to institutionalize the literary fairy tale as a genre because they articulated the interests and needs of the German bourgeoisie and peasantry. Generally speaking, the Grimms' fairy tales assumed a function in the nineteenth century that illuminates what is quintessentially German in this institutionalization: Through socially symbolic acts of compensation, they enabled readers to gain pleasure from different depictions of power transformation. The tales celebrated the rise of seemingly ineffectual, disadvantaged individuals who were associated with such bourgeois and religious virtues as industry, diligence, cleverness, loyalty, and honesty. Moreover, the critique of unjust social and political conditions in most of the Grimms' fairy tales was realized metaphorically by magical means that reconciled the readers of their tales to their helplessness and impotence in society. Paradoxically, the result was a rationalization of unjust conditions through magic, which also provided hope that alternative ways of living were possible.

Stylistically, the Grimms combined the elegance of the simple, paratactical oral narrative with the logical, succinct, economic prose of the middle classes to establish a conventional form for fairy-tale narration, one that became a model for most fairy-tale writers and collectors in the nineteenth century—and not only in Germany. What is special about Germany is that the fairy tale as an institution became a sacred meeting place of readers from the agrarian, middle-class, and aristocratic sectors of the population, a place to which they could withdraw, a source from which they could draw succor, and through which their aspirations and wishes could be fulfilled. Within the institution of the fairy tale they could become legitimate human beings again; it was within this institution that all social classes in what was to become Germany could unite.

Historically, the Grimms' collection exercised this function in Germany and continues to do so more or less in present-day Germany. Like the Bible, however, it has also transcended its specific social function nationally to appeal to readers throughout the world. And, as we know, the tales—that is, a select group of tales such as "Cinderella," "Little Red Riding Hood," "Sleeping Beauty," and "Snow White"—have been specifically cultivated to socialize children everywhere. In each country the tales function differently, and the way they are used and received indicates something about the national character of that country. For instance, in the United States, the Grimms' tales have been "Disneyized,"—as we saw in chapter 1—and it is through the Disney industry that one can learn how most Americans receive and use the Grimms' tales and other tales.[22] In Germany, the obsession with the Grimms is actually an obsession with the fairy tale as a vital and dynamic literary institution, a national institution, that offers writers and nonliterate storytellers a means to participate in a dialogue and discourse about specific social conditions. Germans depend on this institution more than people in other Western countries because its development occurred exactly at a time when the nation was forming itself and when the bourgeoisie was achieving self-consciousness.[23] In stark contrast to the utopian literature and science fiction that emerged as more characteristic forms in France, England, and the United States, the literary fairy tale in Germany became dominant before industry was fully developed and when the people, largely influenced by agrarian lifestyles and patriarchal authoritarianism, were striving for a type of familial unification. The fairy tale as institution freed writers and readers to withdraw from the conflicts of daily life, to contemplate harmonious resolutions without actually expending energy in reality, and to guard their own private realms. The obsession with fairy tales in the nineteenth century—and perhaps today as well—expressed a German proclivity to seek resolutions of social conflicts within art, within subjectively constructed realms, rather than to oppose authorities in public.

Much has been made of German *Innerlichkeit*, the predilection of Germans to repress their feelings, to seek inner peace, to dwell in spiritual and ethereal realms, and to avoid social conflict. While there is some truth to such generalizations, and while prominent individual fairy tales (for example, those by Hermann Hesse and Michael Ende) may celebrate such *Innerlichkeit*, the actual social function of the fairy tale in Germany is different: It is the compensatory aesthetic means of communication through which Germans share, discuss, and debate social norms and individual aspirations. As an institutionalized dialogue that takes place in both written and oral form, it is maintained on many levels, but most important, the fairy tale serves as a key reference point in German culture for self-comprehension and *Weltanschauung*.

Since the Grimms' fairy tales became established as the conventional model of the fairy tale in the nineteenth century, hardly a single German has escaped being influenced by a Grimm fairy tale, a literary fairy tale by another author, or an oral folk tale. There was also an abundant number of tales written by German women during the late eighteenth and nineteenth centuries, recently collected and translated by Shawn Jarvis and Jeannine Blackwell, that reveal how widespread the interest in fairy tales was.[24] Used first as a household item, the Grimms' tales and other tales became pedagogical tools by the early twentieth century.[25] Use at home and at schools engendered numerous literary experiments, so that almost all the significant German (including Swiss and Austrian) writers from the mid-nineteenth century to the present have either written or endeavored to write a fairy tale: Bettina von Arnim, Gottfried Keller, Fanny Lewald, Theodor Storm, Wilhelm Raabe, Gisela von Arnim, Theodor Fontane, Marie von Ebner-Eschenbach, Ricarda Huch, Hugo von Hofmannsthal, Hermann Hesse, Rainer Maria Rilke, Franz Kafka, Thomas Mann, Bertolt Brecht, Ödön von Horvàth, Carl Zuckmayer, Gerhart Hauptmann, Alfred Döblin, Georg Kaiser, Joachim Ringelnatz, Kurt Schwitters, Kurt Tucholsky, Walter Hasenclever, Hans Fallada, Oskar Maria Graf, Erich Kästner, Siegfried Lenz, Helmut Heißenbüttel, Ingeborg Bachmann, Peter Hacks, Günther Kunert, Wolf Biermann, Christa Wolf, Stefan

Heym, Irmtraud Morgner, Peter Härtling, Max Frisch, Nicolas Born, Peter Handke, and Günter Grass. They have all worked within the institution of the fairy tale and have viewed it as a viable means for reaching audiences and for expressing their opinions both about the form itself and society.

It is not only German creative writers who have responded to the fairy tale as an institution, but also German critics and philosophers. The field of folklore research and fairy-tale criticism began developing in the late nineteenth century and remains prominent throughout Germany today. More interesting than the traditional scholarly approach is the manner in which various astute philosophers and cultural critics of the twentieth century—such as Walter Benjamin, Ernst Bloch, Theodor Adorno, Elias Canetti, Oskar Negt, and Alexander Kluge—have employed the fairy tale to register their insights about society and the potential of the tale itself to have a social impact. Thus, Benjamin writes: "Whenever good counsel was at a premium, the fairy tale had it, and where the need was the greatest, its aid was nearest. . . . The wisest thing—so the fairy tale taught mankind in olden times, and teaches children to this day—is to meet the forces of the mythical world with cunning and high spirits."[26] And Bloch comments:

> The cunning of intelligence is the humane side of the weak. Despite the fantastic side of the fairy tale, it is always cunning in the way it overcomes difficulties. Moreover, courage and cunning in fairy tales succeed in an entirely different way than in life. . . . While the peasantry was still bound by serfdom, the poor young protagonist of the fairy tale won the daughter of the king. While educated Christians trembled in fear of witches and devils, the soldier of the fairy tale deceived witches and devils from beginning to end—it is only the fairy tale which highlights the "dumb devil." The golden age is sought and mirrored, and from there one can see far into paradise.[27]

Finally, Elias Canetti remarks: "A more detailed study of fairy tales would teach us what awaits us still in the world."[28]

These statements are not so much significant for their unique perspectives—although they are well worth studying—as they are for the manner in which they all focus on the social function of the fairy tale as prophetic and messianic. Indeed, these critics assume that the fairy tale is an institution capable of revealing the true nature of social conditions. However, the power and communicative value which these critics attribute to the fairy tale is not typical of the way the majority of writers and thinkers outside Germany regard the genre. Undoubtedly the fairy tale as institution has its own special tradition in other countries, but outside Germany it has not become such a "sacred" convention and used as such a metaphorical medium to attain truth.

The continuities of a dialogue within the institution are astounding. If we consider just the productive side of fairy tales in Germany from the late 1960s until the present, we can grasp the significance the fairy tale as an institution has retained for Germans. In the realm of children's literature, numerous anthologies have aimed at revising the Grimms' tales, while new types of provocative tales have sought to upset the normative, traditional expectations of readers weaned on tales by the Grimms, Ludwig Bechstein, and Andersen. Among the more interesting books here are Paul Maar's *Der tätowierte Hund* (1968); Christine Nöstlinger's *Wir pfeifen auf den Gurkenkönig* (1972); Friedrich Karl Waechter's *Tischlein deck dich und Knüppel aus dem Sack* (1972) and *Die Bauern im Brunnen* (1979); Janosch's *Janosch erzählt Grimm's Märchen* (1972, revised in 1991); Michael Ende's *Momo* (1973) and *Unendliche Geschichte* (1979); Hans Joachim Gelberg's anthology *Neues vom Rumpelstilzchen* (1976), with contributions from 43 authors; Otto F. Gmelin and Doris Lerche's *Märchen für tapfere Mädchen* (1978); Wolf Biermann's *Das Märchen von dem Mädchen mit dem Holzbein* (1979); Volker Kriegel's *Der Rock'n Roll König* (1982); Uta Claus and Rolf Kutschera's *Total Tote Hose. 12 bockstarke Märchen* (1984); Heinz Langer's *Grimmige Märchen* (1984); Franz Hohler's *Der Riese und die Erdbeerkonfitüre* (1993); Dieter Kühn's *Es fliegt ein Pferd ins Abendland* (1994); and *Der fliegende König der Fische* (1996); Stefan Heym's *Märchen für kluge Kinder* (1998); and Rotraut Susanne Berner's *Märchen-Stunde* (1998). The fairy tales written and collected for adults follow more or less the same pattern. Here the following works are significant: Iring Fetscher's *Wer hat Dornröschen wachgeküßt* (1972) and *Der Nulltarif der Wichtelmänner: Märchen und andere Verwirrspiele* (1982); Jochen Jung's anthology *Bilderbogengeschichten* (1974), with contributions by 15 well-known authors; Helmut Brackert's mammoth collection *Das große deutsche*

Märchenbuch (1979), with hundreds of tales from the eighteenth century to the present; Margaret Kassajep's *Deutsche Hausmärchen frisch getrimmt* (1980); Günter Kämp and Vilma Link's anthology of political fairy tales *Deutsche Märchen* (1981), with contributions by 20 authors; Heinrich E. Kühleborn's *Rotkäppchen und die Wölfe* (1982); Peter Rühmkorf's *Der Hüter des Misthaufens: Aufgeklärte Märchen* (1983); Mathias Richling's *Ich dachte, es wäre der Froschkönig* (1984); Burckhard and Gisela Garbe's *Der ungestiefelte Kater: Grimms Märchen umerzählt* (1985); Chris Schrauff's *Der Wolf und seine Steine* (1986); Rafik Schami's *Das Schaf im Wolfspelz* (1989) and *Der Wunderkasten* (1990); and Roland Kübler's *Die Mondstein Märchen* (1988) and *Der Märchenring* (1995).

Finally, there has been a plethora of literary criticism dealing with folk and fairy tales which has matched the literary production itself. The major accomplishment of these critical works has been the elaboration of sociohistorical methods with which one can analyze the contents and forms of the tales in light of their ideological meanings and functions within the specific German and the general Western socialization process. The focus is naturally more on Germany than on the West at large. Among the best books here are: Dieter Richter and Johannes Merkel's *Märchen, Phantasie und soziales Lernen* (1974); August Nitschke's *Soziale Ordnungen im Spiegel der Märchen* (1976–1977); Werner Psaar and Manfred Klein's *Wer hat Angst vor der bösen Geiß?* (1976); Friedmar Apel's *Die Zaubergärten der Phantasie* (1978); Helmut Brackert's anthology *Und wenn sie nicht gestorben sind?* (1980), with contributions by several different critics; Heide Göttner-Abendroth's *Die Göttin und ihr Heros* (1980); Jens Tismar's *Das deutsche Kunstmärchen des 20. Jahrhunderts* (1981), revised in 1997 by Mathias Mayer; Ulrike Bastian's *Die 'Kinder- und Hausmärchen' der Brüder Grimm in der literatur-pädagogischen Diskussion des 19. und 20. Jahrhunderts* (1981); Walter Scherf's *Lexikon der Zaubermärchen* (1982) and *Das Märchen Lexikon* (1995); Klaus Doderer's anthology *Über Märchen für Kinder von heute* (1983), with essays by various authors; Paul-Wolfgang Wührl's *Das deutsche Kunstmärchen* (1984); Volker Klotz's *Das europäische Kunstmärchen* (1985); Hermann Bausinger's *Märchen, Phantasie und Wirklichkeit* (1987); and Winfried Freund's *Deutsche Märchen* (1996).

A close examination of these creative works and criticism would reveal to what extent the literary fairy tale as an institution has undergone major transformations. Some short examples of how German writers have maintained a critical dialogue with the Grimms are appropriate here:

"German Fairy Tale"—Yaak Karsunke[29]

This
land has cut its finger
more than once
the blackwhitered children
are told
the old fairy tales
like the one about the young boy
who set out to learn about fear
the grandchildren blink their eyes
at their grandmother:
they do not have to set out
(that's only a fairy tale)
they learn about fear at home
white out of fear
red out of rage
black as the gloom I see in Germany

"Hans My Hedgehog"—Janosch[30]

Once upon a time there was a farmer, and he and his wife had no children. The other farmers poked fun at him in the church and tavern. So one day he said to his wife: "Oh, if you could only have a child, even if it were a hedgehog!"

And then, when his wife had a child, it looked like a hedgehog. Yet, when it was to be baptized, the minister said: "Hedgehogs are not allowed to be baptized."

So they called it: Hans My Hedgehog.

"It could tear my sheets in the bed," the farmer's wife said.

So they placed it in a food box near the oven. Years passed. One day when the farmer was about to go to town and asked everyone what he should bring back for them, the farmer's wife said: "Bring me a good cream for my feet and a television lamp for nineteen dollars."

Then the maid said: "Bring me a pair of stockings, size nine."

But Hans My Hedgehog wanted a harmonica in the key of B flat.

The farmer brought what each one had wanted, and Hans My Hedgehog learned to play the harmonica so perfectly that he could accompany the radio, and the farmhand danced to his music with the maid.

And when the farmer drove into the town again, Hans My Hedgehog asked for a pair of sunglasses. Another time he requested a motorcycle.

"250 cc and four gears," he said. "Then I'll zoom out of here and never, never return."

Since the farmer was glad that he would be rid of him, he bought him a machine that was almost brand new with all the bits and pieces. Hans My Hedgehog took his harmonica, put on his sun glasses, climbed onto the saddle, shifted easily into first gear, and zoomed away as fast as he could. The farmer had given him some money to live on, and it was just enough for a pair of rearview mirrors. Hans My Hedgehog drove into the big city.

Soon he found some friends, and he often played his harmonica on the street with his chrome-plated 250 cc machine glittering beside him. One day a young film director heard him playing. And Hans My Hedgehog was hired for 25 dollars to play the background music for a short film.

Suddenly everyone on the street began whistling the song that Hans My Hedgehog had played. It was broadcast ten times a day on the radio, and records were made of it. When Hans My Hedgehog was to play in his third film, he demanded, "Ten times the royalty! And my bike's got to be in the film."

So Hans My Hedgehog was given fourth lead in the film. He roared across the screen on his bike and zoomed over the prairie while the sun was ablaze. In the evening he played lonely prairie songs on his harmonica that sounded so beautiful that the girls in the movie theaters cried.

Hans My Hedgehog was a superstar. Hans My Hedgehog was no longer called Hans My Hedgehog.

His name was Jack Eagle. He played in one film after another, zoomed across the country, silent like the wind, and he stuck his foot out on the curves.

Suddenly everyone wanted to look like Jack Eagle. Everyone wore jeans like Jack Eagle with a slit up the sides. All the girls, each one wanted to meet a boy like Jack Eagle.

And Jack Eagle married the most beautiful of them all.

And when he went to reveal himself to his father, his father was very happy. The other farmers praised his father in the church and tavern, and many of them had their hair cut just like Hans My Hedgehog from their village.

"Sleeping Beauty and Prince Hasse"—Margaret Kassajep[31]

Once upon a time there was a girl named Elfi. The fairies had given her beauty and virtue at birth, but unfortunately they were not so generous with brains. Consequently, her parents became quite concerned about her. Elfi had to repeat most of her classes and read the Harlequin love romances underneath her desk. When her father finally put serious pressure on her to choose a career, she fell into a deep sleep, and nothing was able to wake her from it.

"A clear case of a psychological defense mechanism!" the family doctor declared after he had given her a thorough checkup.

The beautiful young woman slept and slept and was very pretty to look at. In desperation her parents called upon all kinds of specialists for help. In addition, a faith healer, an herb doctor, and a psychotherapist, who gave advice about minimizing anxiety and whose techniques were quite fashionable. The therapist bent over her sympathetically, and right then she whispered to him in a voice that was barely audible: "Let a prince kiss me awake!"

"If that's all there is to it!" exclaimed the father, who had been listening. "We've got something like that in the firm."

And he contacted Prince Hasse von Hirschbein, district agent for manure fertilizer, who, thank God, was not making his rounds through the villages, and he rushed to the spot. To be sure, he was already 57 years old, thoroughly dull, and cross-eyed, as far as his stuff was concerned, but that did not matter. The beautiful child perked up as soon as he kissed her. Her father arranged a splendid wedding and did not forget to give them a little cabin. Just nine months later they arranged to be divorced in a proper and legal way.

Some time thereafter the beautiful Elfi came across a doctor, who looked just like the doctor in the latest series of Harlequin romances, and there was nothing that could hold her back.

Since her dream partner also played the cello, they lived happily and in harmony until the end of their blessed days.

"Little Red Cap, or: Once a Wolf Always a Wolf"— Burckhard and Gisela Garbe[32]

Once there lived a wolf in the deep, dark woods. He was so large and black and had such shaggy fur that whoever met him would immediately scamper away. Yet, he never intended to harm anyone, by no means, no. Who says that wolves must always be bad? Our wolf was just always alone and lonely and liked to talk a bit with people. But they were afraid of him and ran from him right away.

The only one who was not afraid of the wolf was grandmother who still lived beyond the large dark woods.

"Why must you necessarily be bad?" grandmother asked. "Only because your great-great grandfather, the old bad wolf, was so nasty to people? That's no longer any reason today. No, I don't understand the people," grandmother said, shook her head, and poured another cup of coffee for the wolf. For she had invited him to coffee and cake as she normally did on every Sunday afternoon.

Now grandmother had a granddaughter who was a charming, sweet girl with blue eyes, golden hair and her most favorite little red cap on top. The grandmother had given her the cap one time as a present. Whoever saw Little Red Cap, for that was her name, became fond of her immediately. Yet the girl was mean and terrible and never wanted to do good for anyone, by no means, no. Who says that a cute little girl must always be good and nice? At any rate our Little Red Cap always wanted to sock it to people, and she did it in such a clever way that nobody ever suspected her, and the blame was placed elsewhere.

Little Red Cap certainly did not like the fact that her grandmother was so friendly with the wolf. "He's just taking away that delicious cake from me," she said cursing him, although she knew that this was not true. "And anyway," said Little Red Cap, "It's still true: once a wolf always a wolf. And wolves are bad. I know that." And from then on she thought about how she could do some harm to the two of them.

One Sunday the wolf went through the woods in a cheerful and happy mood. He was looking forward to the Sunday afternoon cake and a friendly talk with grandmother. All of a sudden he met Little Red Cap. The wolf knew her well, but he did not know what a bad girl she was and thus was not afraid of her.

"Good day, wolf," she said.

"Why, thank you, Little Red Cap."

"Where are you going in such a cheerful mood, wolf?"

"To grandmother's. She wanted to bake a fresh butter cake today with a sugar coating."

Little Red Cap thought to herself: "You won't taste it." And they walked a bit together. Then she said, "Wolf, look at the beautiful flowers all around us. I believe you don't even hear how lovely the birds are singing. You're marching straight ahead as though you were going out to poach, and it's so nice to be in the woods."

Now the wolf did not like to hear things about poaching, but he thought to himself: "What does such a young, innocent thing know about these things? Most likely her parents in the town have taught her such things." That's why he did not get angry with her. Then the wolf looked around him, and when he saw the rays of the sun dance between the trees and the beautiful flowers everywhere, he thought: "It would make grandmother so happy if I were to bring her a fresh bouquet of flowers!" So he stopped for a little while and looked for flowers. And when he picked one, he thought that there might be more beautiful ones further on, and he went deeper into the woods. But Little Red Cap went straight to grandmother's house and knocked on the door.

"Who's out there?"

"Little Red Cap, who's come to visit you again since I haven't seen you in such a long time. Open up."

"Just lift the latch," the grandmother called, "I'm too weak and can't get up."

Little Red Cap lifted the latch. The door popped open, and without saying a word, she went to her grandmother's bed, strangled her, and threw her down the deep, deep well outside. Then she put on her grandmother's clothes and bonnet, got into her bed, and pulled the curtains. In the meantime the wolf had run after the flowers and when he had gathered more than he could carry, he remembered the grandmother and set upon his way to her. He was puzzled that the door was open, and when he entered the room, it seemed so strange that he thought: "Oho, my God, how scared I feel today, and I usually feel so good when I'm at grandmother's place!'" He called out "Good day" but did not receive an answer. Thereupon he went to the bed and pulled back the curtains. There lay grandmother, and she had the bonnet down over her face and looked quite strange.

"My, grandmother, what rosy ears you have!"

"The better to hear you with."

"My, grandmother, what sparkling eyes you have!"

"The better to see you with.'

"My, grandmother, what a huge knife you have in your hands!"

"The better to stab you with!"

No sooner had Little Red Cap said that then she jumped out of bed and stabbed the poor wolf right in the middle of his heart.

After she had done that, Little Red Cap took off grandmother's clothes, stuffed them into the jaws of the dead wolf as best she could and laid him in grandmother's bed. Then she ran as fast as she could to the hunter and told him that the wolf had eaten her grandmother. They both rushed quickly to grandmother's house, and when they looked through the window, the wolf lay in grandmother's bed, and scraps of her dress hung out of his jaw. The hunter was filled with rage, took aim through the window, and shot the wolf right in the middle of his heart. Together the hunter and Little Red Cap dragged the wolf from the bed, out of the house, and then threw him into the deep, deep well.

Now the hunter and all the people praised the brave Little Red Cap because she had not been afraid of the wolf. And afterwards her relatives and friends all over the land said: "Just take a look: our innocent Little Red Cap was much smarter than old grandmother. How did she ever get it into her head to invite a wolf for coffee? We've seen it time and again: once a wolf always a wolf!"

"Two Tales about The Wolf and His Stones"— by Chris Schrauff[33]

Once upon a time there was a dwarf who got into the fairy tale by mistake. For there were already seven other dwarfs who did their work. He himself was only the eighth, and nothing was actually prepared for him. So the eighth dwarf trotted about the

> pages in a bad mood and did not know what to do with himself. He came to that spot where the giant was killed, and he found it completely senseless as he always had each time he had come across it. He peevishly sauntered further on until he came to the spot where the handsome prince, who was usually on his knees before the princess, was missing. The dwarf felt so embarrassed that his hair stood on its end, and he rushed away from there. When he did not encounter any of the other dwarfs along the way, he finally ran to the end of the fairy tale. There, however, the dwarf saw that they lived happily ever after. So now he really became furious and trampled on the terrible words with his feet.
>
> ❖ ❖ ❖
>
> Once upon a time there was a wolf who had become gray in his venerable old age. And as he felt his end to be nearing, he said to himself: "Throughout my life I've eaten Little Red Riding Hoods, stones, and kid goats. And what have I gotten from all that? Nothing but dull teeth and a puffed-up belly that I drag through the woods with a great deal of trouble. Now that the time has come, however, I want to grant myself a little pleasure and do something reasonable!" And the old wolf set out on his long way and trotted into the city. There he drank some red wine, as much as he could hold, and spit out the stones, the kid goats, and all the Little Red Riding Hoods right before the feet of the people. Then, to top it all off, the gray old wolf stormed the libraries and ate up all the fairy-tale books.

These radical interrogations of the Grimms' tales and the function of fairy tales themselves occur within a specific German institutionalizing of the literary fairy tale, one that thrives on a self-reflective dialogue about transformations. This does not mean that the institutional framework of the literary fairy tale has remained stable in Germany. In fact, it has substantially and qualitatively expanded, and several significant tendencies have emerged in these transformations.

Ever since the 1920s, avant-garde and political writers have made the fairy tale visible as an institution by attacking the institution of art. German writers have moved in the direction of making the fairy tale more usable in the socialization process.[34] Certainly such explicit use occurred during the period of National Socialism, when the Nazis methodically exploited the fairy-tale genre in an ideological manner to uphold the racist and nationalist supremacy of the German people. Thus the schools, film industry, and publishers were induced to produce fairy tales that subscribed in text and image to *völkisch* ideology.[35] And after 1945, the fairy tale continued to be employed directly by schools, literary organizations, theaters, psychologists, publishers—and, of course, by writers—to influence social attitudes.[36] Albeit, this was not done in a fascist sense, although one cannot talk about a complete rupture with National Socialist thinking and methods in West Germany. The fairy tale retained something *völkisch* about it for many a German, and some Germans continued to identify with the Grimms' tales in a conservative nationalist manner after World War II. Generally speaking, however, fairy tales (primarily the Grimms' tales) were used widely in the schools in a spiritual, religious, and aesthetic manner that downplayed the historical and social significance of the tales and stressed their "marvelous" therapeutic and mystical qualities. Up through the late 1960s the social function of the fairy tales in the schools, endorsed by other outside organizations and societies, was to further the idealist notion of an inner realm of reality that is not connected to material conditions outside the self and that can be shaped organically and morally by the fairy tale. Most striking here was the anthroposophical approach developed by followers of Rudolf Steiner[37] in the Waldorf Schools, which had and still has a wide following outside those schools. Underlying the work of the Waldorf Schools and similar pedagogical approaches was the belief that the fairy tales reflect inner experiences related to natural conditions of primeval times, and that the symbols and images of the fairy tales enable a child to imbibe and grasp the secret laws of nature. Such a spiritual approach to fairy tales, along with *völkisch* and psychological ones, was also common (at first) in one of the largest literary societies in West Germany, the Europäische Märchengesellschaft, which holds large annual meetings and sponsors a series of critical studies about fairy tales. This society, like many others, has become more realistic and historical in its approach to fairy tales since the late 1960s, when there was a major shift in the fairy tale as an institution; unlike any other western country, the German fairy tale at that time underwent a politicization that is connected to the German obsession with the fairy tale.

By 1970, due to the student movement with its antiauthoritarian impulses, there was a crucial shift in the approach to fairy tales and their production. The more progressive writers began formulating their socially symbolic discourse against the grain of the Grimms, while at the same time using the brothers' conventions. The conservative bourgeois value system in the Grimms' tales that also incorporated feudal patriarchal notions was viewed as anachronistic, banal, and escapist. Nevertheless, the fairy tale as an institution was not in and of itself considered escapist as long as one renovated, revised, and re-utilized the Grimms' tales and others in the German cultural heritage. In addition to the critical approach taken by writers and publishing houses, young teachers in the elementary and high schools introduced sociohistorical methods aimed at clarifying the relationship of the Grimms' tales and other fairy tales to social realities and to problems confronting contemporary Germans. With the development of a new sensibility, writers such as Janosch, Waechter, Kassajep, Struck, Ende, Fetscher, Rühmkorf, Grass, and numerous others designed their tales for a new German audience and with the hope that what they were criticizing and developing in the institution of the fairy tale would have some social impact. Whether this has been or even can be achieved by these authors (along with their critics, educators, and publishers) is an open question; some critics in the 1980s saw the fairy tale functioning again to suit a German disposition toward regressive thinking and *Innerlichkeit*.[38] But the very fact that the fairy tale is so openly and prevalently used to discuss social and political relations and is regarded as having a certain communicative potential reveals a great deal about the institution in Germany today. Or, to put it another way, there is something very German in this attitude and hope.

CHAPTER SIX

HENRI POURRAT AND THE TRADITION OF PERRAULT AND THE BROTHERS GRIMM

In their endeavors to assess the significance of Henri Pourrat's remarkable collection of tales, *Le Trésor des Contes* (*The Treasury of Tales*), published in thirteen volumes between 1948–1962, numerous critics have placed Pourrat in the tradition of Charles Perrault and the Brothers Grimm. For instance, Maurice Bémol has remarked:

> Like that of the Brothers Grimm, Henri Pourrat's effort was in effect concentrated on the tale [*conte*]. Like them he incorporated all sorts of proverbs, sentences, expressions, refrains, and small poems, but it was the tale that served to frame those other products of folk culture and that was the principal preoccupation of the author. . . . Within the total corpus of their work, the Brothers Grimm and Pourrat brought together an aesthetic preoccupation with a documentary and scientific one. . . . Henri Pourrat was also just as much attached as his German predecessors to what they called fidelity to the folk tradition in spirit as well as in word.[1]

In contrast to Bémol's high estimation of Pourrat's tales in the tradition of Perrault and the Brothers Grimm, Mark Temmer has asserted:

> In evaluating Pourrat's fairy tales, one should first note that he does not introduce new plots, but relies on well-known motifs without, however, quoting sources, be they oral or literary (Fabliaux, Noël du Fail, Basile's *Pentamerone*, Perrault, the Brothers Grimm, or nineteenth-century French folklore collections). Despite his adherence to traditional themes, Pourrat weakens his versions by being too explicit and thus impairs the spellbinding powers of the *Märchen*. Too many details disenchant. Yet, this passion for accuracy is also a source of strength.[2]

There are numerous other references by literary critics and folklorists comparing or contrasting Pourrat to Perrault and the Brothers Grimm, as in Michel Chrestien's preface to Pourrat's *Contes du vieux-vieux temps* (*Tales of Old-Old Times*).[3] And then there is Pourrat himself, who situates himself against the grain of Perrault's "academic" tradition and more within the current of the Grimms' popular tradition. In a 1946 note to *The Treasury of Tales*, he stated:

> But each folk gives a turn to those tales that are prevalent among them. France has its tales. . . . Perrault edited only a dozen of them, and the peasant culture possessed hundreds. . . . It is precisely the case of Perrault that sheds some light on this kind of disdain. Did he not get mixed up in the Quarrel of the Ancients and the Moderns? Wasn't he among those who tried to combat a literature that was so attached to the Greeks and Romans that it could only view people via antiquity? When all is taken into account, the basis of the Greco-Roman imagination is the same in its mythology as that of the fables and popular tales. But put into operation by the classicists, it could only support classicism. That which was the free play of imagination, imagery, wisdom, and profound formation has become part of academicism.[4]

Like the Brothers Grimm, Pourrat regarded himself as a writer who sought to conserve the values and customs of the common people: "I have written many books, but *L'Homme à la Beche*, *La Bienheureuse Passion*, *Le Sage et son Démon*, *L'Exorciste* form a part of the same project as *Le Trésor:* the endeavor to comprehend what is disappearing from our country's soil, to grasp what should not disappear. All these books are books of allegiance."[5] Though it is clear that Pourrat saw himself closely aligned with a folklore tradition associated more with the Brothers Grimm than with Perrault, the distinction that he makes between the academic and the popular is not as great as he believed. In actuality, Pourrat and the Brothers Grimm worked within the same literary tradition as Perrault, even if their intentions and intended audiences were different. Just what is this tradition? What are the connections between Perrault, the Brothers Grimm, and Pourrat? Will these connections enable us to assess Pourrat's tales in a new light? Before concerning ourselves with these questions, we must first ask: Who is Henri Pourrat, and how did he find his way into the fairy-tale tradition of Perrault and the Brothers Grimm?

Pourrat was born on May 7, 1887, in the small city of Ambert near Clermont-Ferrand.[6] His father was a grocer, and their living conditions were modest. As a young boy, he was sent to a Dominican school, where he learned the basics of reading and writing. By the time he was ready for the *lycée,* he was sent to Paris and received his baccalaureate in 1904. Pourrat intended to continue his studies at the Institut National Agronomique in Paris, but it was discovered that he had tuberculosis. So he returned to his hometown and spent his time trying to recuperate by taking long walks in the forests and mountains of Auvergne. It was also during this time that he took a strong interest in literature and began writing himself. The major influences in this period of his life were Friedrich Nietzsche, Maurice Barrès, and Henri Bergson, and there were distinct elitist if not racist tendencies in his early stories and poems.[7] However, the more he became concerned with regional material and folklore, the more his work took on a populist tone, for Pourrat attributed his recovery from tuberculosis to the pure atmosphere of country life, and he was soon to become a champion of local color and folklore literature. He contributed stories, fables, and fairy tales to regional journals and newspapers, and around 1914 to 1915 he began visiting peasants in the countryside, listening to their tales, taking notes, and recording the tales later at his house. These tales were then revised carefully according to his notions of what pure folklore should be. Pourrat sought to celebrate the true and simple qualities of the Auvergnats; in a text entitled *Nous qui sommes Auvergnats* (*We Who Are Auvergnats*), he asserted: "Race only exists truly by becoming a moral conscience, collective, made of memories and the same hopes."[8] And for Pourrat, his major task as writer was to demonstrate how the rustic soul and lifestyle of the people in the region of Auvergne set moral standards that he implicitly believed were superior to those set by other people and should be adopted by the rest of the nation.

From 1915 until his death in 1959, Pourrat, who led the life of a recluse in Ambert until the late 1920s, published all types of folklore books at a prolific pace. His major breakthrough as a writer came in 1922, when he completed the two-volume novel, *Gaspard des Montagnes* (*Gaspard of the Mountains*), which earned him Le Prix du Figaro in 1922 and Le Grand Prix du roman de L'Académie Française in 1931. Set during the years following the French Revolution in Ambert, this sentimental, if not maudlin, romance concerns the trials and tribulations of young Anne-Marie, who chops off the hand of a marauder when she is left at home by her parents. From this point on, the virtuous country lass is hounded by the villain, who even succeeds in marrying her by disguising himself. Both before and after her unfortunate marriage, Anne-Marie relies on her cousin, the strapping mountaineer Gaspard, who constantly comes to her aid, and though they are intensely in love with each other, they never consummate their love. They remain chaste lovers throughout 28 *veillées,* or approximately 1,000 pages of melodramatic adventures, in which Pourrat seeks to demonstrate the noble and heroic character of these two rustic souls. Gaspard is the epitome of the truthful, faithful, intrepid, wise folk hero, while Anne-Marie is sturdy, devoutly religious, self-sacrificing, silently suffering, and pure in heart. If it were not for the remarkable historical description of customs and traditions and the folk tales and anecdotes that are contained in the novel, it would be tedious reading. As it is, the novel is reminiscent of a sensational American western in which stock characters and situations abound, and its popularity to this very day resides in Pourrat's simplistic style and devotion to the simple people who are the salt of the earth and never abandon their roots.

There is almost an equation drawn in *Gaspard des Montagnes:* Devotion to the pure mountains of the homeland purifies and ennobles his characters, who are exemplary figures, if not members of an elite race of people.

After the success of *Gaspard des Montagnes*, Pourrat continued to publish books in this vein. Some were historical romances, others dealt with the customs, legends, farmers, animals, superstitions, and saints in Auvergne, which he never left. In all, there were 60 titles. During the Pétain regime in France, he was singled out as being one of France's leading writers and won the Prix Goncourt in 1941 for the long essay *Vent de Mars.* Interestingly, it was during the 1930s that Pourrat began concentrating on publishing the enormous number of tales that he had collected and was still collecting. In other words, it was during the rise of patriotism and fascism in France that, in such books as *Les Contes de la Bucheronne*, he sought to bring out tales that championed the pure folk spirit of France. And then, soon after World War II, he capped his career by publishing the 13 volumes of *Le Trésor des contes* from 1948 to 1962.[9] To a certain degree, this enterprise could be considered a sociopolitical gesture, through which Pourrat endeavored to resurrect the "indomitable" French spirit by pointing to the glorious folk tradition of France. Whatever the case may be, the volumes were successful but not bestsellers, by any means. In fact, since Pourrat's death in 1959, he has more or less fallen into oblivion, even though his tales have been republished by Gallimard in seven expensive volumes with superb woodcuts. [10] Perhaps the reason that these volumes have not had a success is because they are something that the "folk" would find difficult to purchase. Of course, there is a smaller and cheaper selection also available in one volume,[11] and in English there is a tiny selection, which was published in 1953 under the title *A Treasury of French Tales*,[12] and a somewhat larger selection with the title *French Folktales* (1989), with an introduction by Royall Tyler.[13] Still, for all intents and purposes, Pourrat, despite the availability of his texts and the centennial celebration of his birth in 1987,[14] is hardly known in France and virtually unknown beyond France's borders.

An undeserved fate? Undoubtedly, for his tales are highly stylized narratives that combine a vast historical knowledge of the customs, lore, and expressions of Auvergne with a fine poetic sensibility for the generic features of the literary fairy-tale tradition. Like Perrault and the Brothers Grimm before him, Pourrat was anxious to construct a national literary monument to his people, though the "folk" that peopled his tales were not necessarily those who had existed in reality. Pourrat romanticized the folk and the folk tradition according to his ideological aspirations. Here he was no different from Perrault and the Brothers Grimm.

Perrault, the Brothers Grimm, and Pourrat were all conscious of the fact that they appropriated anecdotes, fables, jokes, *Zaubermärchen*, journeyman tales, soldier's tales, legends, and cautionary tales from oral *and* literary sources. They were not entirely satisfied with the form and content of those tales, for they shaped and reshaped them according to models they themselves conceived as to what the "genuine" fairy tale or tale type should *read* like. They entered into a dialogue with existing oral and literary versions with the intention of providing aesthetic standards and norms of civility and morality. If we consider the literary tale as a type of speech genre as defined by Mikhail Bakhtin in his essay, "The Problem of Speech Genres,"[15] we may be able to gain a greater sense of the literary tradition in which Perrault, the Brothers Grimm, and Pourrat play such an important role.

Bakhtin understands language as speech realized by individual concrete utterances (oral and written) and enunciated by participants in various areas of human activity:

> For speech can exist in reality only in the form of concrete utterances of individual speaking people, speech subjects. Speech is always cast in the form of an utterance belonging to a particular speaking subject, and outside this form it cannot exist. Regardless of how varied utterances may be in terms of their length, their content, and their compositional structure, they have common structural features as units of speech communication and, above all, quite clear-cut boundaries. (71)

The boundaries are demarcated by the speaker/author of a speech or work, as soon as there is a shift in the narrative voice and position. This means that a sentence, a word, a phrase, and an entire work can be considered an utterance, and the speaker, in choosing a type of linguistic means and referentially semantic sphere, uses a particular speech genre in response to others who have chosen to express themselves with similar compositional and stylistic features. For Bakhtin,

> the work, like the rejoinder in dialogue, is oriented toward the response of the other (others), toward his active responsive understanding, which can assume various forms: educational influence on the readers, persuasion of them, critical responses, influence on followers and successors, and so on. It can determine others' responsive positions under the complex conditions of speech communication in a particular cultural sphere. The work is a link in the chain of speech communion. Like the rejoinder in a dialogue, it is related to other work-utterances: both those to which it responds and those that respond to it. At the same time, like the rejoinder in a dialogue, it is separated from them by the absolute boundaries created by a change of speaking languages. (75–76)

Using Bakhtin's definition of a speech genre, the literary fairy tale can be considered an utterance that relies on known existing themes and compositional techniques in oral and literary communication, and the individual form a tale takes is a response to those preexisting tales and perhaps even to anticipated tales. Most important, the literary tale must be viewed as part of a historically, socially, and linguistically formed dialogue through which various authors choose to make their views on various subjects known. Bakhtin states that "any utterance is a link in the chain of speech communion. It is the active position of the speaker in one referentially semantic sphere or another. Therefore, each utterance is characterized by a particular referentially semantic content"(84). Moreover, there is a subjective emotional evaluation toward the subject matter that enters into the dialogue.

The historical rise of the literary fairy tale in Europe can certainly be comprehended as the rise of a dialogue with the oral tradition, whereby the literary fairy tale distinguishes itself from the oral tale by endeavoring to institutionalize its form and contents in authorial and authoritative ways. The literary fairy tale not only assimilates the experience and appropriates the styles of the oral tradition, but also seeks to establish models of definitive communication in response to other literary fairy tales and sociopolitical conditions. The literary fairy tale is not only a speech genre, it is also a sociocultural institution. That is, as the literary fairy tale became accepted and used for various purposes within the public sphere of Western societies by educated members of these societies, certain stylistic and thematic conventions became established. Moreover, the family, schools, libraries, and publishers instituted specific means of production, communication, and circulation that affected the fairy-tale dialogue itself. To comprehend the signification of the fairy tale as a sociocultural institution means to investigate the unique composition of a text in relation to the preexisting similar texts of the same speech genre, general audience demands and taste, policies of publishers, market conditions, usage of the text by different social groups, censorship, and literary standards established by the dominant authorities of culture in a particular society. In addition, it is important to bear in mind that the literary fairy tale—and this factor distinguishes it from other genres—is particularly susceptible to changes introduced by different publishers and to a re-appropriation by the oral tradition, which, in turn, reshapes and transmits the text as oral tale under different conditions. The dialogic communion between the literary fairy tale and the oral folk tale is vital and never-ending. Each time an author produces a literary tale, it is in response to both an oral and a literary tradition within the historical process of civilization, as I have pointed out in my book *Fairy Tales and the Art of Subversion*. The author's tale does not remain static as a symbolical act, but its signification can be altered by the manner in which it is reinterpreted and republished over the years and by the manner in which people as readers/listeners reabsorb and retell it in an oral tradition.

If we now look more closely at how Perrault, the Brothers Grimm, and Pourrat appropriated the material from the oral and literary tradition for their fairy tales and shaped them to comment on various aspects of the civilizing process,[16] it will become clear to what extent they were in a dialogue with others and each other, a dialogue that marks the shifting historical and aesthetic boundaries of the literary fairy tale as genre.

Under what conditions did Perrault begin writing his fairy tales? With whom was he carrying on a dialogue? The scholarship of Jacques Barchilon,[17] Marc Soriano,[18] Raymonde Robert,[19] Lewis Seifert,[20] and Catherine Velay-Vallantin[21] has demonstrated clearly how Perrault consciously entered into a dialogue with the oral tradition, not only to give it a new shape stylistically, so that it would appeal to an upper-class literate audience, but also to demonstrate the quality of its "modernity" in his quarrel with Nicholas Boileau. Moreover, he was probably aware of Straparola's and Basile's tales and other literary fairy tales written during the seventeenth century.[22] Here, too, his purpose was to respond to these tales in a manner that would exalt what was considered to be common and oral, if not vulgar. In doing so, Perrault sought to make an important contribution to French culture by revealing how popular oral tales and children's tales could be "refined" and contribute to the discussion of manners, comportment, sexuality, and civility. In a certain sense, though he was not acting in the name of the common people (as later the Brothers Grimm and Pourrat did), there is a certain nationalist quality to Perrault's work, for it is part of a dialogue about the possibility of the French language and customs assuming a classical status equal to that of the Greeks. His defense of modernity in the famous debate with Boileau, called "The Quarrel of the Ancients and the Moderns," was in actuality a defense of indigenous French culture. All this occurred at a time when King Louis XIV was trying to maintain the glory of France through wars that actually threatened to undermine the supremacy of French culture.

Perrault's symbolic act, his entry into the fairy-tale discourse, was an endeavor to recuperate and preserve the French oral tradition in a manner that would celebrate and preserve the national prestige of France. But, as Catherine Velay-Vallantin has noted, Perrault violated French orality in aspiring to champion it, and in turn, the oral tradition reconsumed his texts and reworked them in many different and interesting ways:

> In reality, "oral art" is structured. In endeavoring to reconstitute the existing folk tales in the oral tradition, Perrault was necessarily obliged to violate this primordial orality by coagulating a certain version of a certain tale with precise forms in light of the artificial conditions of his collection. The academician himself constituted an "oral folk literature." Thus his *Tales* form part of a totality, that are contradictory and artificial in their own terms,

> a totality that emanated from numerous graftings of elements that, in turn, emanated from very different cultural domains. If Perrault resorted to the "resources" of the literary and intellectual culture, it was in order to fabricate a satisfying orality that could lead one to believe that this orality was genuine—more genuine than nature. . . . If Perrault's *Tales* [when passed on orally] have attained a distinct success as "classics" of folklore and orality, it is because they upset the texts of the author in order to produce those games that have been infinitely developed with the molds that this type of narrative offers.[23]

The "games" between oral folk and literary fairy tales are those symbolical dialogues that formed the communal context and network of the genre that became firmly established in Europe during the eighteenth century. In fact, by the time the Brothers Grimm began collecting oral and literary tales at the beginning of the nineteenth century, the fairy-tale genre had been institutionalized as an accepted mode of communication for adults and children. As I have demonstrated in previous chapters, the Grimms compiled their tales with the help largely of educated, middle-class women, some of whom were influenced by the French Huguenot tradition, and with reference to literary sources. Their goal was to select, study, write and revise them in order to preserve the truths and essence of natural language, associated with the common people and agrarian customs. Like Perrault, they recorded their tales during a period of war and during the formation of a national bourgeoisie that sought to institutionalize its own forms of expression. Unlike Perrault, they were more dedicated to the customs, expressions, mores, and beliefs of the peasantry. They collected and stylized their tales in response to the artificial courtly literature and the *Kunstmärchen* that had become fashionable in Germany at the end of the eighteenth century. There is little irony in their narrative compositions. They did not make fun of superstitions and the miraculous in the original versions as did Perrault. They went to great effort to retain the naiveté, frankness, and simple language of the oral tradition.

Nevertheless, like Perrault, the Grimms did impose their own value system on the oral tradition, and most of their tales were carefully stylized to recreate a "natural" rustic tone in the seven different editions from 1812 to 1857. The Protestant ethic and patriarchalism set the standards of civilization, and the constant revision of the tales reveals that the Grimms sought to superimpose their concept of folklore and folk onto them. In doing so, they, like Perrault, "violated" the oral tradition by seeking to idealize and conserve it. On the other hand, once their printed texts were circulated in Germany and elsewhere, they received the same treatment that Perrault's texts did: They were reabsorbed by the oral tradition, and have served as the basis for new oral versions that in turn have influenced new literary texts.

Though the initial impulse of the Brothers Grimm was to preserve the oral folk tradition, it is important to bear in mind that they, like Perrault, "betrayed" it. In fact, they were writing for a new middle-class audience and responded to the criticisms they received by radically changing their texts and making them more didactic, sentimental, and moralistic. They also made heavy use of literary sources; as they wrote down their tales, they were conscious of maintaining a dialogue on many levels with Basile, Perrault, the German romantics, and various folklorists with whom they were in contact. More than Perrault, they were extremely conscious of being within a broad, institutionalized fairy-tale discourse that had great implications for the future development of German culture. What they did not realize, however, is that their selection of tales and their great artistic reshaping of the oral/literary tradition would have a world-wide impact in socializing children and establishing a fixed canon that in some circles of society is treated as sacred scripture.

There was, indeed, something religious in the zeal and dedication of the Brothers Grimm to uphold the alleged "purity" of folk tales against artificial courtly art. And there was also something definitely religious in the manner in which, 100 years later, Pourrat became dedicated to the people of Auvergne and their folk customs and sought to make them indelible.

> This *Trésor*, what does it intend to be? A general collection of that which was the memory of a people who were still rustic, its formation, its pleasures, its tasks. Perhaps the tales were nothing at all but incantations. Perhaps they emanated out of the need to imagine the things that one wishes might happen—and who knows if that did not help them to happen? . . . Indeed, the tales

> have always tried to become magic if they were sufficiently inspired. They have taken a turn toward the elliptic, the enigmatic, the song, and incantation.[24]

As Sylvia Mittler has demonstrated in her insightful essay, "Le jeune Henri Pourrat: de Barrès et Bergson à l'âme rustique,"[25] Pourrat began to ground his defense of regional folklore very early in his readings of Nietzsche, Barrès, Bergson, Pascal, Carlyle, and Joseph-Arthur de Gobineau.

> Gradually he conceived a philosophy of truth, drafted at first under the form of a quest for an Auvergnian aesthetic, then under the etiquette of race that masked the true meaning. It was in the "powerful" doctrines of Nietzsche and Barrès that he had easily found that which nourished (rather, intensively fed) a spirit desirous of "embarking." Soon the call for racial and personal pride became toned down and became more like sympathy; the cult of individualism became rustic good sense. In dedicating himself to folklore research, Pourrat finally became conscious of the essentiality of the customs, life, and human soul.[26]

In other words, even before he began collecting and rewriting folk tales in 1914, Pourrat had developed a concept of the folk and a critical view of the pretentiousness and decadence of so-called high art and literature emanating from Paris. His commitment to re-creating folk tales so that they retained the essence and purity of the folk became a lifetime project like that of the Brothers Grimm.

Again, like the Brothers Grimm, Pourrat's major problem was to find a form that would transcend the rough and coarse patois of Auvergne and yet retain the unique rustic tone and succinct rhythmic patterns of the regional dialect. Moreover, he had to transform many of the narrow, local references and themes and make them more universal. The result was a style "like a sophisticated osmosis between folk language and literary language," as Dany Hadjady has remarked in agreement with Paul Vemois and Monique Parent.[27] Indeed, Hadjady has done a thorough analysis of how Pourrat undertook a restoration of the oral folk tale by eliminating outmoded dialect phrases, coarse terms, ungrammatical sentence structure, and regional syntax; and by providing greater coherence, more elaborate description, and greater characterization, clarifications, and explanations of a character's motivations and actions. By comparing Pourrat's final literary versions with his oral material, Hadjady shows that Pourrat as a poet creates a marvelous illusion for readers as though they were reading a true folk tale.

Read carefully, however, these "marvelous illusions" are actually illuminations: Pourrat's literary fairy tales illuminate the long historical and stimulating dialogue between orality and literacy, which is filled with controversy and debate about customs, beliefs, values, aesthetics, and politics of the common people and the educated elites. They illuminate the differing opinions of such individual authors as Perrault and the Brothers Grimm and the changing value systems of their respective societies. They illuminate the quest for communion through a speech genre such as the literary fairy tale—the author's quest for shared beliefs and community, as well as the quest of the oral carriers of the tales who represent and express the experiences of common people. Finally, they illuminate the hope of Pourrat that literate and nonliterate people can be brought together as one people or folk through participation in the fairy-tale dialogue. This hope for communion is also an endeavor to set ideological and aesthetic standards to which "good" and "clever" people are expected to conform through their reading. Neither Pourrat, Perrault, nor the Brothers Grimm are impartial collectors and writers of fairy tales.

The distinctive aesthetic features and ideological preferences of Pourrat can best be seen in comparison with those of Perrault and the Brothers Grimm, especially since they participated in the fairy-tale dialogue by revising oral and literary tales and worked on much of the same materials. In Pourrat's *Contes de la Bucheronne* and *Le Trésor des Contes* there are five tales related to Perrault's *Histoires ou Contes du temps passé:* "Blue Beard," "Cinderella," "Ricky with the Tuft," "Little Red Riding Hood," and "Sleeping Beauty." With regard to the Brothers Grimm, there are many more related tales, such as "La trop fière princesse" ("The Princess with too much Pride"), "La branches qui chants" ("The Singing Branch"), "La granulata" ("The Little Frog), "Le dibble et le passion" ("The Devil and the Peasant"), "Les sept frères dans le puits" ("The Seven Brothers in the Well"), and "Misère et Pauvreté" ("Misery and Poverty"). Since it would demand an exhaustive analysis to compare all the similar types of tales written by Perrault, the Brothers Grimm, and Pourrat, I want to concentrate here on four tales: "Sleeping Beauty," "Cinderella," "Little Red Riding Hood," and "Blue Beard."

Pourrat's storytelling is the most poetic and literary of the three. In contrast to the tales by Perrault and the Brothers Grimm, Pourrat's tales display greater description, more realistic motivation, more complex characterization, and smoother transitions. With regard to description and transition, compare, for example, how the three authors depict the scene before the princess discovers the spindle in "Sleeping Beauty":

> At the end of fifteen or sixteen years, the king and queen journeyed to one of their country residences, and one day the princess happened to be running about the castle and climbing from one chamber up to another when she arrived at the top of a tower and entered a little garret, where a good old woman was sitting alone and spinning with her spindle and distaff. (Perrault)[28]

❋ ❋ ❋

> Now, on the day she turned fifteen it happened that the king and queen were not at home, and she was left completely alone in the palace. So she wandered all over the place and explored as many rooms and chambers as she pleased. She eventually came to an old tower, climbed its narrow winding staircase, and came to a small door. A rusty key was stuck in the lock, and when she turned it, the door sprang open, and she saw an old woman in a little room sitting with a spindle and busily spinning flax. (The Brothers Grimm)[29]

❋ ❋ ❋

> One summer, due to the heat that was very strong that year, the king, the queen, and the entire court went to a castle that they had in the heart of the forest. It was in a remote part of the country, and the princess had never been there. She was about fifteen years old at that time. Thus, still a child, delighted by a journey, curious to see a new country, the plants that move along the sides of the road, the water which falls on the sides of the rock, the large bunches of violets springing from the moss, the old red-headed woodpecker flying from branch to branch. At the castle it was the same thing: many stairs, detours, gal-

> leries, stone corridors. And from a narrow window four stories high everything could be seen shooting out from the shadow, stretching into the blue country and losing itself.
>
> The old castle—it was a world—secret like the heart of the forest. It was impossible for the princess to discover all the things that were in it. So many hidden staircases and remote chambers! It seemed to her that a miracle was waiting for her at the end. She constantly ran and searched about. One beautiful night she went about and arrived at a little door completely buried by a shadow at the top of a tower. She opened it. And she entered: it was a small garret, a garret of gray stone. There was an old woman there, so old that it seemed that she had been forgotten in this retreat since the days of King Herod. And this old woman was spinning. She was spinning with a spindle. (Pourrat)[30]

In his elaborate description, Pourrat not only provides greater motivation and better transition for the princess' discovery of the spindle, but he also creates an idyllic rustic setting that is later set in contrast to the palace of the ogress. The composition of Pourrat's text demonstrates how carefully he worked to amplify the action with realistic detail and psychological motivation.

The beginning of his "Blue Beard"—again in contrast to Perrault's tales and the Grimms' "Fichter's Bird" and "Blue Beard"—creates psychological suspense through the introduction of a young woman who is warned by her brothers about Bluebeard, and who nevertheless asserts that she will win in the end. "But she, she did not fear this beard. Lively like a fish, sharp like a bee, and ready to take risks at any time."[31] Indeed, the rest of the tale involves a battle of wits that is won by the courageous young woman without the aid of her brothers.

Pourrat eliminated melodramatic and sentimental aspects of the plot, aspects one can find in the tales of Perrault and the Grimms. There are no sisters, no begging, no new marriage at the end. This is also true in his version of "Little Red Riding Hood," which has fewer moralistic trimmings than do the versions by Perrault and the Brothers Grimm. Pourrat describes realistically and succinctly the dilemma of an eight-year-old peasant girl who does not heed the warning of her grandmother. His depiction does not belabor her "guilt" or naiveté but rather retains an ironic, comic tone that is in keeping with her rescue at the end of the tale.

The succinct, dry tone and staccato rhythm of Pourrat's narrative style enabled him to re-create the same tales told by Perrault and the Grimms in a less didactic and sentimental manner. The beginning of "Cinderella" ("Marie-Cendron") is a good example:

> Once upon a time there was a man, a nobleman, and he and his wife had a little girl named Marie: a Marie extremely good, extremely fine, extremely pretty. They were so very happy on this poor earth that there could be no doubt that their happiness would not last. The mother died, all well and good. . . . The little girl was approaching seven perhaps. Her father believed that everything was going well. So he remarried.[32]

In addition to the lighter and drier tone, the characterization of Marie-Cendron, who goes to church to meet the prince instead of going to a ball, and who is more confrontational than the Cinderellas of Perrault and the Grimms, is psychologically more complex and interesting.

In sum, if we view Pourrat in a dialogue with Perrault and the Brothers Grimm—certainly not an exclusive dialogue—we can see how Pourrat was striving to become more artistic and more realistic in regard to the folklore tradition than Perrault and the Brothers Grimm. He paid much more attention to details of agrarian life; described nature more carefully; drew fuller characters, especially the females; avoided sentimentality and melodrama; and often favored a light comic style. To be sure, in the artful "folkloristic" manner he used to recreate folk tales, Pourrat was closer to the Grimms than he was to Perrault. But he was also more radical than they were in the changes he made to create the illusion of fidelity to folklore. Nevertheless, they all shared a common project: conserving oral tales for posterity according to their respective ideological and aesthetic viewpoints.

As we have seen, Pourrat's vision did not emanate as purely from the folk as he would have us believe. Rather, he created a model of the folk and folk tales through his tales, by which he hoped to illuminate ways toward communion and communication with paradise and happiness. Each of his tales is thus to be read as a narrative strategy in response to questions he posed to himself and posed for future generations within the fairy-tale genre. Ultimately, as in the case of Perrault and the Brothers Grimm, there is something conservative about Pourrat's vision: he wants to conserve a pure world that he imposes on the folk and his readers through literature, and only by the fact that he poses himself as a writer in a dialogue with the oral tradition does he rescue this conservatism from becoming static. His nostalgia for a pure world that harks back to days when wishing still counted was in actuality a utopian wish for change. It is this tension in his own thinking that led him to stay within the tradition of Perrault and the Brothers Grimm, while also endeavoring to break out and seek his own path.

> Aren't the tales the opposite of a pure literature? However, it is artificial to view the discourse even of teaching, of explaining, as opening all possibilities for the imagination. Poetry has become demiurge. But the great mystery, that which counts above all is that which is not expressed.
>
> It is an illusion to think that on a given night on a certain mountain in a remote place, if one were simple enough and subtle enough, one could unravel the tales much better. How is it possible not to view the presence of magic? How is it possible not to find again the ancient idea from which everything undoubtedly emanates: that of happiness promised to man? . . .
>
> Perhaps the tales will be not so much explications or teachings but rather incantations?[33]

CHAPTER SEVEN

RECENT PSYCHOLOGICAL APPROACHES WITH SOME QUESTIONS ABOUT THE ABUSE OF CHILDREN

The bicentennial celebrations of the birthdays of the Brothers Grimm have long since come to an end, and it is time to take stock. Did we really learn something new about the Grimms and their tales during those two years of celebrations and commemorations held fifteen years ago? Or did we honor the Grimms merely by praising them in a conventional and uncritical manner, and did we thereby do them a disservice? Who did the praising and why? This last question is most significant, for numerous associations, institutions, and nations organized ceremonial conferences and symposiums to honor the Grimms, or published books and articles about their significance. Such widespread tribute to the Grimms and their work certainly indicated to what extent the Grimms, and their tales in particular, have transcended German culture to become vital components in the cultural heritages of different nations. In fact, one could probably argue that the Grimms' tales, either in their literally translated editions or in multifarious adaptations, and especially in their mass-mediated forms by Disney and other cinematic corporations, play a crucial role in the socialization of children throughout much of the modern world. The Grimms' tales occupy a central position in the international canon of children's literature and children's mass media. All the more reason why we must ask who has done the canonizing and why all the praise.

Since the bicentennial celebrations assumed many different formats in many different places,[1] I shall limit myself in this chapter to a discussion of the reception of the Grimms and their tales in the Federal Republic of Germany up to 1990 (once upon a time there was an East and West Germany). It was in West Germany, a country "obsessed" by fairy tales, that the Grimms received the most attention, and an analysis of their reception there might enable us to estimate whether any progress has been made toward understanding the impact that their fairy tales have had in different civilizing processes. My focus will be on the historical and philological studies that have generated new discoveries and insights into the Grimms' tales in relation to the psychological approaches that promise so much—and offer so little.

First, a word about the conferences and publications that honored the Grimms. To begin with, there was the monumental exhibition of the Grimms' works, along with paintings and drawings by their brother, Ludwig Grimm, which opened at the Museum Fridericanum in Kassel on June 1, 1985 and later was moved to Berlin and Hanau. This exhibition produced three important publications: *Die Brüder Grimm: Dokumente ihres Lebens und Wirkens*, edited by Dieter Hennig and Bernhard Lauer;[2] *Ludwig Emil Grimm 1790–1863: Maler, Zeichner, Radierer*, edited by Ingrid Koszinowski and Vera Leuschner;[3] and *Die Brüder Grimm in ihrer amtlichen und politischen Tätigkeit* edited by Hans Bernd Harder and Ekkehard Kaufmann.[4] Conferences were organized by the University of Göttingen, the University of Marburg, the Europäische Märchengesellschaft, and the Roter Elefant, a society devoted to the study of children's literature. Two books resulted from two of the conferences: *Jacob und Wilhelm Grimm*,[5] volume 26 of the Göttinger Universitätsreden, with articles by

Karl Stackmann on the Grimms' dictionary, Heinz Rölleke on the tales, Karl Otmar Freiherr von Aretin on the politics of the Grimms, and Werner Ogris on Jacob Grimm and the history of law; and *Das selbstverständliche Wunder: Beiträge germanistischer Märchenforschung*,[6] the proceedings of the Marburg conference, edited by Wilhelm Solms, with contributions exemplifying different approaches to the Grimms' tales by Lutz Röhrich, Annegret Hofius, Bernhard Paukstadt, Rudolf Freudenberg, Hans Henning Smolka, Charlotte Oberfeld, Walter Scherf, and Solms himself.

Two significant biographies, Irma Hildebrandt's *Es waren ihrer Fünf: Die Brüder Grimm und ihre Familie*[7] and Gabriele Seitz's *Die Brüder Grimm: Leben-Werk-Zeit*,[8] provided a fuller sociohistorical picture of the Grimms' family life and their involvement in the political struggles of their times. The journal *Diskussion Deutsch*[9] devoted a special number to the Grimms' tales with diverse approaches by Heinz Rölleke, Dieter Arendt, Walter Scherf, Gertrud Jungblut, Wilhelm Solms, Annegret Hofius, and Michael Sahr, stressing the philological, psychological, feminist, and pedagogical aspects of the tales. The two volumes of the Brüder Grimm-Gesellschaft, *Brüder Grimm Gedenken 6 und 7*[10] (edited by Ludwig Denecke in 1986 and 1987), contain numerous biographical pieces and articles on the fairy-tale illustrations and the reception of the tales in Poland.

Heinz Rölleke, the foremost scholar of the Grimms' tales, has vied with the workaholic Grimms themselves in his productivity. His collected essays, mainly of a philological nature, were published in *"Wo das Wünschen noch geholfen hat": Gesammelte Aufsätze zu den "Kinder- und Hausmärchen" der Brüder Grimm*,[11] and his book *Die Märchen der Brüder Grimm*[12] is the finest short introduction to the Grimms' tales in German. In addition, Rölleke did invaluable work as editor of the Grimms' *Kleine Ausgabe*[13] of 1858 and the facsimile reproduction of the first edition of 1812 and 1815, with the handwritten corrections and comments of the Brothers Grimm.[14] Finally, he contributed the preface to Albert Schindehütte's edition of *Krauses Grimm'sche Märchen*,[15] Krause being one of the more important and interesting informants of the Brothers Grimm.

In the domain of psychology, Verena Kast had already made her debut in 1982 with her optimistic Jungian interpretations in

Wege aus Angst und Symbiose: Märchen psychologisch gedeutet (translated as *Through Emotions to Maturity: Psychological Readings of Fairy Tales*),[16] in which she mapped out ways to overcome anxiety with the use of fairy tales, and has continued to do so throughout the 1990s. About the same time, Eugen Drewermann began a series of psychological and religious interpretations in such books as *Das Mädchen ohne Hände* (The Maiden without Hands, 1981),[17] *Schneeweißchen und Rosenrot* (Snow White and Rose Red, 1983),[18] and *Die kluge Else, Rapunzel* (Clever Else, Rapunzel, 1986),[19] in which he preached harmony through a symbolical understanding of the spiritual meanings in the tales. He, too, has remained prolific in the 1990s. Similar to his series but more Jungian in approach, the Kreuz Verlag of Stuttgart flooded the market with pop-psychology books such as *Aschenputtel: Energie der Liebe* (Cinderella: The Energy of Love, 1984) by Hildegunde Wöller,[20] *Das tapfere Schneiderlein: List als Lebenskunst* (The Brave Little Tailor: Cunning as the Art of Life, 1985) by Lutz Müller,[21] *Der Froschkönig: Geschichte einer Beziehung* (The Frog King: The Story of a Relationship, 1985) by Hans Jellouschek,[22] and *Hänsel und Gretel: Der Sohn im mütterlichen Dunkel* (Hansel and Gretel: The Son in Motherly Darkness, 1986) by Ursula Eschenbach.[23] In addition, Carl Mallet added to his pseudo-Freudian analyses a study of power and violence with his book *Kopf Ab! Gewalt im Märchen* (Head Off! Violence in the Fairy Tale, 1985).[24] Related to the psychological approach but more pedagogically oriented was Elisabeth Müller's feminist analysis, *Das Bild der Frau im Märchen* (The Image of the Woman in Fairy Tales, 1986).[25] In addition, the image of women and various feminist approaches were addressed in *Die Frau im Märchen* (The Woman in Fairy Tales, 1985) edited by Sigrid Früh and Rainer Wehse.[26]

Aside from all the scholarly and analytical treatments that the Grimms' tales received from 1985 through 1987, mention should be made of the numerous republications[27] of the tales themselves, such as *Alte Märchen der Brüder Grimm*, illustrated and selected by Helga Gebert,[28] and the parodies, such as Uta Claus and Rolf Kutschera's *Total Tote Hose: 12 Bockstarke Märchen*,[29] Heinz Langer's *Grimmige Märchen*,[30] and Chris Schrauff's *Der Wolf und seine Steine*.[31]

More can be said about the reception of the Grimms' tales in 1985 and 1986—like the invention of a *Märchenstraße* by the chamber of commerce of Hessia, a "fairy-tale road" that connects landmarks, towns, and cities supposedly associated with the Brothers Grimm, but more intended to attract tourists to an array of fairy-tale kitsch and memorabilia. But enough has been said to indicate that the Grimms were honored sufficiently, and perhaps more than sufficiently, during 1985 and 1986. Now what about new findings and discoveries? Were the celebrations self-serving, or did they serve to reevaluate the Grimms in the context of reassessing the German cultural heritage?

The 1985–1986 celebrations and publications about the Grimms and their tales are the results of approximately two decades of work, largely by professors of German literature, who in the late 1960s began questioning the manner in which fairy tales transmitted conservative bourgeois values to children. This critical questioning, initiated mainly by Marxist-oriented critics,[32] also included theses about the emancipatory nature of fairy tales, à la Ernst Bloch. By the mid-1970s most literary critics, folklorists, historians, educators, and psychologists were following examples set by different Marxist analyses and by Bruno Bettelheim's *The Uses of Enchantment* (translated into German as *Kinder brauchen Märchen*, or "children need fairy tales") to conceive innovative approaches to the Grimms' tales.

By the mid-1980s, new historical aspects of the Grimms' lives and work were being uncovered: details about their everyday life; the immense breadth and quality of their achievements as folklorists, lexicographers, linguists, historians, and literary critics; and their political activities. The historical reexamination of their lives by Irma Hildebrandt, Gabriele Seitz, and Werner Ogris[33] was intended to counter the common and popular picture of the Grimms as retiring scholars who were peacefully ensconced in Kassel and spent their time collecting wonderful tales from peasants and writing voluminous books, including the famous *Deutsches Wörterbuch* (*German Dictionary*). Hildebrandt revealed how traumatic the fall of the Grimm family was for all concerned after the early death of the father in 1796, and how the two older brothers, Jacob and Wilhelm, had to struggle to maintain the good name of the family and hold it together under difficult financial circumstances. Seitz and Ogris also supported this view, but went further to study the political nature of the Grimms' work and their involvement in some of the key political issues of the day, such as the peace negotiations with the French in 1813 and 1814; their opposition to the Kurfürst in Kassel from 1815 to 1829; their role in the refusal of the Göttingen Seven to take an oath of allegiance to Ernst August, the new King of Hannover, in 1837, because he had illegally dissolved the constitution; and their participation in the Revolution of 1848. Instead of appearing as romantic idealists whose emphasis on the love of fatherland and nationalism led them to support reactionary causes and ultimately to contribute to the "blood and soil" politics of Bismarck and the eventual rise of fascism, the Grimms now appear more clearly in these studies: first, as struggling young men seeking to make a career choice that would enable them to pursue their true love—namely the study of old German literature, myths, and customs; second, as worldly young scholars who were politically aware of the disastrous effects the French invasion had for the development of a unified German state; third, as literary historians who devoted their research on German folklore and language in part to restoring a sense of culture and nation to the German people in general; and fourth, as established but versatile scholars with admirable moral integrity who were confident about the value of their various literary and philological projects toward developing a genuine German heritage that would celebrate the democratic will and rights of the German people, and who were not afraid to take a stand for the liberal political cause in Germany—even though they were not outspokenly antimonarchical until their later years.

The historical reinterpretation of the Grimms' lives and the realistic reexamination of their hardships and accomplishments as scholars with a political cause have been matched by the critical exploration of the means by which they collected and shaped their tales. The historical-philological research has indeed produced an abundance of discoveries that have great ramifications not only for the literary, psychological, and historical study of the Grimms' tales, but also for the genre of the fairy tale in general. In his article "Die 'Kinder- und Hausmärchen' der Brüder Grimm in neuer Sicht,"[34] Rölleke sums up some of the significant new findings about the Grimms' methods of work and the formation of the tales:

1. The Grimms rarely if ever collected their tales by traveling into the fields and having peasants narrate stories to them.
2. Most of their informants were females from the well-to-do middle class, and a large portion of the tales was provided by people from aristocratic circles at the Haxthausen estate in Northrhine-Westphalia.
3. Many tales were taken from books, especially after the publication of the 1819 edition.
4. The tales themselves were not purely "Germanic" but were Indo-European in origin, which does not, however, discount the fact that they were stamped by changes made by the German storytellers and informants.
5. From the very beginning the Grimms changed, adapted, and edited the tales to fit their notions of the ideal folk tale and considered their collection to be an *Erziehungsbuch*, an educational manual, which was edited more and more by Wilhelm Grimm over the course of approximately 40 years to address children with good bourgeois upbringing. Therefore, the Grimms pruned the tales of anything sexual, vulgar, and offensive to a middle-class sensibility.
6. Among the changes made by the Grimms—and here it must be noted again that it was mainly Wilhelm, who was in charge of editing the texts after 1815—were the stylistic refinement of the language and structure, which included embroidering the phrases and providing for smoother transitions, adding and inventing proverbs to give the tales a *volkstümlich* tone;[35] emphasizing patriarchal authority and the Protestant ethic by implying the need to domesticate women and to achieve success through industry and cunning; and synthesizing variants of the same tale into their own distinct version.

In short, Rölleke and others demonstrated that the Grimms' tales are definitely not folk tales in the strict sense of the word, but that they are appropriated or mediated tales, which they gathered through educated informants, selected according to their own taste, and shaped and reshaped in a form that corresponded to their conception of an ideal folk tale. All this means that the tales of the Brothers Grimm must be studied individually with regard to the changes they underwent, and they must be considered as artistic products of a discursive process shaped by both the oral and literary traditions in which peasants, middle-class informants, and the Grimms as artists/scholars played an immense role in defining a new genre of the literary fairy tale.

Given these developments in Grimm scholarship, numerous critics of different persuasions whose works were part of the recent celebrations made headway in sifting through and sorting out the layers of narrative input and signification in the Grimms' tales. I want to discuss three of the more stimulating approaches here.

In his essay "Der Froschkönig,"[36] Lutz Röhrich, one of the most astute and esteemed folklorists in Germany, has demonstrated how the Grimms "created a piece of artistic prose out of an artistic narrative"[37] by constantly editing and reshaping it over the course of 42 years. In doing so they introduced or emphasized some interesting motifs, such as the paternal authority of the king and the resistance of the princess who is nevertheless rewarded with a prince for smashing the frog against the wall. Whether this is actually a reward is a question that can be debated,[38] but Röhrich's careful analysis of other similar folk-tale types, the Grimms' compositional techniques, and the literary and advertisement adaptations from the nineteenth century to the present enable us to grasp the changing signification of "The Frog King" in a sociohistorical context and in different cultural processes.

Dieter Arendt's stimulating article "Dümmlinge, Däumlinge und Diebe im Märchen—oder drei Söhne, davon hieß der jüngste der Dümmling (KHM 64)"[39] seeks to understand the connection between simpletons, Tom Thumbs, and thieves in the Grimms' tales, and at the same time to question the traditional folklorist categorization of tale types. He convincingly argues that there are close ties between the simpletons, Tom Thumbs, and thieves, especially when one considers that dumbness is simplicity and as such concealed or even feigned cleverness. Indeed, Wilhelm Grimm correctly pointed out that this dumb fool (*tumbe tor*) is called the "dumb clear one," and suggested that smallness and dumbness are *attributes* that are not to be underestimated. In revealing how dumb is connected to thumb, and that the thieves in many Grimms' tales (and in older tales as well) are often tiny, Arendt argues that the small hero is a figure of the future, pushing forward and seeking subversively to upset the established structures to bring about change. Implied in Arendt's conclusion is that the Grimms had a strong preference for such protagonists and that there is something pedagogically and psychologically significant here that can be elaborated in a beneficial way for readers and students.

Whereas Arendt focuses historically and philologically on the possible utopian aspects of the Grimms' tales about simpletons, Tom Thumbs, and thieves, Gertrud Jungblut is more critical of the paternalistic attitudes in the tales in her essay "Märchen der Brüder Grimm—feministisch gelesen."[40] Much of what she has to say is based on Heide Göttner-Abendroth's provocative book *Die Göttin und ihr Heros*,[41] which focuses on the patriarchalization of myths and tales thousands of years before the onset of the Judeo-Christian era—an era, Göttner-Abendroth argues, that established a basic male framework in which tales were transmitted. Jungblut summarizes the sociohistorical process in which the patriarchalization of tales was brought about and argues that the task of feminists is to uncover the motifs and relics of the feminist tradition within the Grimms' tales, such as "Frau Holle," and to reveal how they can be recuperated from patriarchal thinking connected to power, property, achievement, and domination of nature.

Whereas the above three essays sought to benefit from new research about the Grimms in an historical manner and also endeavored to go beyond the new findings of philologists, psychoanalytical and psychological writers in Germany tended to ignore recent sociohistorical research; instead, they preached about the spiritual benefits of engaging the narratives and explained the messages of the tales as though they could bring about salvation for one and all. The Grimms' tales as therapeutically messianic, as prescriptions for the good housekeeping of childhood development—unfortunately, these general views of the Grimms' tales continue to reign supreme in Germany today. I say "unfortunately" because I do not dismiss the value of a critical psychological approach, one that is critical of traditional psychology and psychoanalysis, while at the same time bringing the issue of history and the historical nature of the Grimms' texts into the arena of contemporary psychoanalytical developments and debates. Indicative of the pop psychology that putters with the Grimms' tales in a seemingly well-intentioned manner is Carl Mallet's work, which to date consists of five books: *Kennen Sie Kinder?* (Do You Know Children? 1980), *Das Einhorn bin ich* (I Am the Unicorn, 1982), *Kopf ab! Gewalt im Märchen* (Head Off! Violence in Fairy Tales, 1985), *Am Anfang War Nicht Nur Adam: Das Bild der Frau in Mythen, Märchen und Sagen* (It Was Not Only Adam at the Beginning: The Image of Woman in Myths, Fairy Tales, and Legends, 1990), and*—und rissen der schönen Jungfrau die Kleider vom Leib: Männlichkeitsmodelle im Märchen* (—And They Ripped the Clothes Off the Beautiful Maiden: Models of Manliness in Fairy Tales, 1995).[42] Mallet's starting point is that fairy tales contain hidden messages that are related to our unconscious drives and needs and should be interpreted as Freud interpreted dreams for us to grasp their psychological significance. All well and good; but Mallet also dismisses the fact that the Grimms' tales—and he works primarily with these tales—are historical and social creations. He considers them primeval narratives reflecting the great folk spirit and universal psyche, and thus containing truths about ourselves that need to come out. Bruno Bettelheim, of course, supports Mallet's work, and in the 1985 paperback edition of Mallet's *Kennen Sie Kinder*,[43] he praises Mallet because Mallet allegedly complements his own work by addressing parents who would do well to learn about children and how to deal with them through a psychoanalytical interpretation of the tales. For instance,[44] to paraphrase Mallet, if Little Red Riding Hood's mother had given her the proper, direct, and clear sexual education she needed before she left her house (as all good mothers should do), then Little Red Riding Hood would not have succumbed to the temptation of the wolf. Mallet makes clear that the mother, who herself was never given the proper sexual education by her own mother, secretly wants sex and is curious about sex because she was never really enlightened. So she unconsciously continues her mis-education by dressing her daughter as a coquette who will attract the wolf; she subliminally encourages her daughter to explore her curiosity about sex. Grandma, too, who invites the wolf into her house when she could have kept him out, is also anxious to fulfill her curiosity about sex. Thus, we have three women who bring about their own sexual molestation or violation, who "ask for it," and who need to be edified—and Mallet is the "edifier" for them and for us.

At this point I would like to suggest that a *male fantasy* about how women bring their own rape on themselves might be at work here, and might be the basis of the narrative itself.[45] Mallet's simplistic and unhistorical psychoanalytic observations are still at work in his book, *Kopf ab!* in which he again proclaims that fairy tales do not have an author and that the tales are not only about idyllic worlds, but filled with scenes of violence and power. By studying these scenes one can learn much about the abuse and use of violence and power. Mallet comes to the conclusion at the end of 258 pages of banal, superficial observations that power and violence are part of human existence and humankind must learn to live with these conditions. Again, the Grimms' collection of tales becomes a manual for learning how to live.

Mallet's therapeutic work is matched if not even "surpassed" by the series called "Weisheit im Märchen" ("Wisdom in Fairy Tales"), published by the Kreuz Verlag in Stuttgart. Since this wisdom is spread in 12 books written by 12 different authors, it would be difficult to summarize their wise words in one short essay. Yet the books tend to incorporate the same pop-psychological tendency, so that a brief discussion of one of the books, such as *Das tapfere Schneiderlein: List als Lebenskunst*, will suffice to demonstrate their pretentious bids at profundity. Each book begins with a short, glowing introduction by the general editor of the series, Theodor Seifert, followed by a reprinting of the tale itself (not based on a definitive edition). The author of each volume—in this case Lutz Müller—then proceeds to take sections of the tale in chronological order and comment on them according to his or her philosophy, invariably based on a superficial understanding of psychology. Müller addresses adults as his primary audience, and he sums up his central idea in his first chapter: "To a certain degree we always remain children of life. We do not know where we come from, who we are and finally where we are going. Faced with our mysterious life and fate we are small, weak children. Life is always greater and stronger than we are. Therefore we can ask ourselves whether the brave little tailor can tell us something about the art of contending with the forces and powers of adult life."[46]

Such platitudes and mystification of reality run rampant in Müller's book as he examines key passages chronologically to demonstrate that the little tailor uses the art of simple means to develop his moral autonomy, and thus serves as a model to emulate in our own lives.

Books, then, about the Grimms fairy tales as self-help manuals on the art of life, the energy of love, and how to resolve problems in heterosexual relations. The Grimms certainly did not intend their "educational manual" as they called it, to be used as material for pop psychology and self-help books. Fortunately, there are more serious and sophisticated psychological approaches to the Grimms' tales. Yet unfortunately, these, too, have not provided any new insights into the tales. Nor have they developed approaches much different from those in the 1969 collection *Märchenforschung und Tiefenpsychologie*, edited by Wilhelm Laiblin. For instance, in his article "Das Märchenpublikum: Die Erwartung der Zuhörer und Leser und die Antwort des Erzählers,"[47] Walter Scherf argues that the audience of the Grimms' tales consists of all those who are willing to participate in the narrative, to identify with and play along, using the configuration of the tale to work through his or her own inner conflicts. Whatever process of maturation and resolution of conflicts the protagonist of a tale goes through enables the reader/listener to contemplate and experience analogous possible changes. Scherf wants to explain what constitutes the attraction of a fairy tale, what makes for its *Wunder* or wondrous quality, and he concludes that the fairy-tale dramaturgy contains a special concept for playing and working through unconscious drives, needs, and conflicts. Now this is a sound thesis, but it is also very self-evident and can be applied to all forms of literature, so that it does not go very far in helping us explain the attraction or significance of the Grimms' tales.

The psychological and psychoanalytical approaches that have emerged during the Grimm commemorative years leave us with disturbing questions. Are the simplistic analyses in Germany an indication that psychological and psychoanalytical theory is incapable of producing new critical insights into the Grimms' tales? Are the tales to be used mainly as therapeutic devices by analysts and patients to relate to psychological problems and maturation in a positivist manner? Why hasn't there been a major attempt to break away from the theories of Freud and Jung to consider what Jacques Lacan, Donald Winnicott, or Alice Miller, to name three interesting theoreticians, might contribute to a psychoanalytical understanding of fairy tales? Indeed, Miller has recently touched on this subject herself but has not investigated it thoroughly enough.[48]

Here I should like to demonstrate briefly how a critic or psychologist might use Miller's works productively to relate what I would call the deeper psycho-historical content of fairy tales to modern psycho-social phenomena and problems. As is well known, Miller, who worked for close to 40 years as a psychoanalyst in Zurich before writing about her experiences and explicating her ideas, has written three significant books concerning the abuse of children by parents and analysts: *Das Drama des begabten Kindes* (*The Drama of the Gifted Child*, 1979), *Am Anfang war Erziehung* (*For Your Own Good: Human Cruelty in Child-Rearing and the Roots of Violence*, 1980), and *Du sollst nicht merken* (*Thou Shalt Not Be Aware: Society's Betrayal of the Child*, 1981).[49] Her basic thesis in all these works is that parents tend to use powerless children for their own needs and take advantage of them whenever they feel the urge or need. Since children are denied their own voice and fulfillment of their needs, they suffer and repress their feelings out of fear, anxiety, and guilt caused by the adults who, both intentionally and unintentionally, manipulate the children's feelings of love for them. As children grow older, they repress the abuse they have experienced because they are unable to accept the adults they love as cruel or manipulative. Given this repression, it is difficult to locate the cause of emotional and physical disorders that children develop as they are "brought up" to become adults. Yet, Miller argues, the perversions, addictions, and self-destructive behavior that people as adolescents and adults exhibit result from the abuse they have experienced as children but want to forget as they mature. Only by realizing and recognizing that there was actual emotional, sexual, or physical abuse in their childhood can they begin to grasp emotional blocks and disturbances that affect them as adults. Miller has charged that analysts, following Freud, have tended to dismiss dreams and stories of abuse to conceal from themselves the way that they themselves were maltreated as children, and that in the analyst-patient situation the analysts often use power in the same manner that power was once used against them. Miller claims that

> the more insight one gains into the unintentional and unconscious manipulation of children by their parents, the fewer illusions one has about the possibility of changing the world or of prophylaxis against neurosis. It seems to me that if we can do anything at all, it is to work through our narcissistic problems and reintegrate our split-off aspects to such an extent that we no longer have any need to manipulate our patients according to our theories but can allow them to become what they really are. Only after painfully experiencing and accepting our own truth can we be relatively free from the hope that we might still find an understanding, emphatic mother—perhaps in a patient—who then would be at our disposal.[50]

Whether it has been due to major shifts in psychoanalytic and therapeutic practice and theory or to major social changes brought about by the women's movement and other progressive groups, the subject of child abuse has become a major issue in Western societies during the past 25 years, and it is now evident that there has been more sexual and psychological harm done to children beneath the surface of our enlightened Western societies than we want to believe. But it is still not easy to get children and adults to discuss the abuse that they have suffered at the hands of people whom they love. Here the fairy tale can play an important role, for, as Miller believes,

> it is the past of every individual, namely his or her early childhood, when knowledge of the world, as it really is, is acquired. Children learn about evil in its undisguised form in their early childhood and store this knowledge in their unconscious. These experiences of early childhood form the source of the adult's productive imagination that is, however, subjected to a censorship. The experiences take the form of fairy tales, legends, and myths, in which the whole truth about human cruelty finds its expression in the way that only a child can experience it. . . . Since the word "fairy tale" by definition connotes unreality, censorship can be weaker here, especially at the end when good triumphs over evil, justice reigns, the evil person is punished and the good person is rewarded; that is, when denial prevents insight into the truth. For the world is not just. Good is seldom rewarded. And the most cruel things are seldom punished. Nevertheless, we tell all this to our children, who, of course, would

> like to believe, as we would, that the world is just like we are presenting it to them [i.e., in fairy tales].[51]

We tend to forget or repress the cruel episodes children experience in the Grimms' fairy tales due to the many happy endings that follow them. Moreover, there has been a sanitization process in the twentieth century throughout the world. Writers, illustrators, and publishers have cleansed the tales of many violent acts in their reprints and adaptations to protect the innocence and sensitive souls of children. For instance, most versions of the Grimms' "classical" tales for children will not depict the wolf swallowing Granny and Little Red Riding Hood, Cinderella's sisters' eyes being pecked out by doves, Gretel shoving the witch into an oven, and so on. Yet there is more, much more. In the corpus of the Grimms' tales there are approximately 25 tales in which the main focus is on children who experience some form of abuse. This is not to mention the numerous tales that begin with children being kidnapped, used as objects in a barter with the devil, or abandoned. Abandonment and continual persecution are central issues in "Brother and Sister" and "Hansel and Gretel." Who else is the stepmother/witch but the real mother of the children? (The Grimms consciously changed mother figures in the tales that they collected into stepmothers.) In "Mother Trudy," a disobedient girl has her curiosity repaid by a witch who turns her into a log of wood that will be burned. In "The Juniper Tree," a boy is murdered by his stepmother because she wants her own daughter to inherit everything from her husband. In "The Stubborn Child," a mother must go to a dead boy's grave and smack his arm so he will die properly. In "The Little Lamb and the Little Fish," a stepmother changes a brother and sister into a lamb and fish and seeks to kill them. In "Going Traveling," a poor son is constantly beaten during his travels because he says the wrong thing. In "The Stolen Pennies," a dead child who has a guilty conscience keeps returning to his home and upsetting his parents because he has stolen some pennies and wants to have his sin absolved. God demonstrates to Eve in "Eve's Unequal Children" that he has created a world in which children will not be treated equally, and God rationalizes his position by claiming that inequality must exist to have people fill the different jobs that must be performed on earth. In "The

Young Boy in the Grave," an orphan boy is beaten by his master and finally driven to suicide. In "The True Bride," an orphan girl is exploited by her stepmother. In two of the omitted tales, the Grimms depict how a child is killed by some other children ("How Children Played at Slaughtering") and how some die of starvation ("The Children of Famine").

These tales indicate that there was widespread child abuse in the eighteenth and nineteenth centuries, and they are clearly symbolic representations by their narrators and writers of disturbed relations in the different types of families that existed at that time. They were not uncommon. The most famous children's book in the world, *Struwwelpeter* (*Slovenly Peter*), was produced by Heinrich Hoffmann in 1845. Under the motto of "spare the rod, spoil the child," he took obvious delight in admonishing children in his funny verses about the horrible punishments that awaited them if they did not learn how to behave properly. He struck such a common chord in parents that his book sold in the millions, continues to sell well, and has been translated into more than 100 languages since its publication.[52] Here it is interesting to note that the Grimms, as collectors and revisers of the tales that featured many of the same warnings, were of like mind. They may have toned down or omitted some of the more cruel episodes of the original tales, such as the one in which children play at butchering, but they kept enough abuse within the frame of the happy-ending narratives to allow insight into real conditions. The history of the family in the eighteenth and nineteenth centuries is filled with reports about long periods of swaddling,[53] child killing, abandonment of children, corporal punishment, sexual abuse, rape, intense sibling rivalry, and maltreatment of children by stepmothers and stepfathers. While these subjects are amply portrayed in the Grimms' tales, they have not been sufficiently explored by literary critics, folklorists, and therapists. One of the reasons why the Grimms' tales have received only superficial psychoanalytical treatment—despite efforts by Freud, Jung, Roheim, Franz, and Bettelheim to take them seriously—is due to the lack of interdisciplinary work and communication. Alan Dundes points to this problem in his significant essay, "The Psychoanalytic Study of the Grimms' Tales with Special Reference to 'The Maiden without Hands' (AT 706)":

> Folklorists and psychoanalysts have for nearly a century analyzed the Grimm tales in almost total ignorance of one another. Folklorists blindly committed to anti-symbolic, anti-psychological readings of folk tales make little or no effort to discover what, if anything, psychoanalysts have to say about the tales they are studying. Psychoanalysts, limited to their twentieth-century patients' free associations to the nineteenth-century Grimm versions of folk tales, are blithely unaware of the existence of hundreds of versions of the same tale types so assiduously assembled by folklorists in archives or presented in painstaking detail in historic-geographic monographs.[54]

To prove the value of the folklorist/psychoanalytic approach in regard to the Grimms' collection, Dundes studies the Grimms' version of "The Maiden Without Hands" in regard to its tale type and the motif of the lecherous father. He argues convincingly that the maiden cuts her hands off not because she wants to help her father against the devil, but because she actually wants to flee her father in fear of incest.

The tale concerns a poor miller who meets an old man in the forest. This man is the devil, who promises him wealth if the miller will give him the first thing he finds behind his mill. The miller agrees because he thinks that there is only an apple tree, but it turns out that his daughter is standing there. When the devil comes to claim her, however, she thwarts him by washing herself clean and drawing a circle around her. Angrily, the devil demands that the miller cut off the maiden's hands, or he will take him away instead of the girl. The father explains his plight to his daughter, and she allows him to cut off her hands. Still, the devil is thwarted from taking her because her tears purify her stumps, and thus his claim is invalidated. Afterwards the miller approaches his daughter and says, "I've become so wealthy because of you that I shall see to it you'll live in splendor for the rest of your life." But she answers, "No, I cannot stay here. I'm going away and shall depend on the kindness of people to provide me with whatever I need."[55] After she departs, she makes her way to a royal garden where an angel helps her obtain fruit. She is discovered by the king, who becomes enchanted by her beauty and goodness, and thus he marries her. He has silver hands made for her, and everything goes well until the devil interferes by intercepting letters between the king, who goes off to a war, and his queen, who is now pregnant and remains at home. The devil changes their letters to make the king believe that his wife has given birth to a monster during his absence. The last letter forged by the devil has the king ordering the queen and child to be put to death. But the king's mother, who knows the truth, saves her and sends her away. So the queen flees with the child and is protected by an angel in a remote forest. When the king realizes his mistake, he goes in search for her and wanders for seven years. Finally, the angel brings about a reconciliation, and the king is reunited with his wife, whose hands have grown back through the grace of God, and with his seven-year-old son.

Can this really be a tale about incest?

By drawing parallels with other similar tale types (collected in the nineteenth century or before) in which the father apparently maltreats or wants to marry his daughter, and by discussing cultural attitudes toward incest, Dundes maintains that the principle of projective inversion is at work in "The Maiden Without Hands." The girl, who believes her father wants to sleep with her, is suffering from an Electra complex. It is she who wants to replace her mother—here a parallel can be drawn to "All Fur"—and because of this, she imagines that her father wants to maltreat her or seduce her. Unconsciously the girl must punish herself for having these thoughts. Thus she wants her hands to be cut off and remains in an "infantile state" (without hands) symbolically until she can transfer her feelings in a mature way to another man. Dundes comments

> that fleeing from her father's advances, the heroine, handless, nevertheless manages to marry royalty (a father substitute) after all, and bear a child. . . . The false accusation that the heroine has given birth to a monster is consonant with the interpretation advanced here. The "monstrous" crime of incest was thought in medieval times to lead to the birth of literal monsters. Marriage leads to the restoration of the heroine's hand. In metaphorical terms, someone appropriate has asked for and received the heroine's hand in marriage. The message, so to speak, is that in society a girl must resist the temptation or impulse to marry her father but must leave home to marry someone else.[56]

Dundes is certainly correct in arguing that "The Maiden Without Hands" is a tale about incest, and that such monstrous crimes and the abuse of children were symbolically related and concealed in folk tales and in the tales collected by the Grimms. However, Dundes has not gone far enough in his analysis because he remains too attached to traditional Freudianism in his exploration of symbols and narrative strategy. First of all, if we approach the tale from a folklorist/psychoanalytic viewpoint, it might be worthwhile to consider the changes made by Wilhelm that reflect the unconscious fears or anxiety of the author in "handling" a delicate subject. For instance, in the first edition of 1812, the version of "The Maiden Without Hands" is much shorter, more succinct, and less Christian than the final 1857 version cited by Dundes. (See the appendix at the end of this chapter for the two complete texts.) In other words, Wilhelm made major changes in the tale from 1819 to 1857. In the 1819 version there is no angel; the miller's daughter must look after chickens for the king; she is married to the king; when the devil exchanges the letters, the devil does not have the king ordering her death but her banishment; the maiden responds, "I did not come here to become queen. I don't have any luck and don't demand any. Bind my child and my hands to my back. Then I shall go out into the world."[57] Her husband, the king, returns, realizes his mistake, and, with the help of a servant, finds her in the forest after a long journey.

The later 1857 version makes the maiden more helpless, more stoic, and dependent on the angel. In addition, the tale becomes much more didactic and moralistic. It is as if one merely had to place trust in God and do the right things, and everything would turn out well. From a psychoanalytical viewpoint, the changes that appear in the 1857 version reveal a great deal about Wilhelm. To begin with, the "betrayal of the father" can be equated with Wilhelm's father's early death. The mistreatment of the girl and her helpless condition can be connected to the mistreatment Wilhelm endured in Kassel, his asthma, and heart troubles. The creation of the strong angelic figure who helps the girl can be related to Jacob, who constantly stood by Wilhelm and came to his aid. The misunderstandings in the marriage that are patched up by the angel may indicate some difficulties in Wilhelm's marriage with Dortchen Wild that were resolved by Jacob. Finally, the general theme of the story can be summed up by the Grimms' family motto: *Tute si recte vixeris*—he cannot go wrong whose life is in the right.

The parallels to Wilhelm's life in the altered version of 1857 are the most obvious, and they need greater investigation—especially if one intends to examine the tales from a psychoanalytical viewpoint. For instance, one must ask why Wilhelm made the second tale both more cruel and more religious? Why did he use pear trees in the royal garden in the 1857 version and not an apple tree? Why did he add the angel, the king's mother, and all the religious references? Why did he change the tale into a religious melodrama? The historical basis of the narration provides the key for grasping psychological expression as a public representation. Once we understand something about the conditions that brought about the cultural formation of a tale, we can begin to explore its greater ramifications. What then becomes important, I believe, are the motifs of child abuse and incest that Wilhelm apparently tried to conceal. One could perhaps argue that he unconsciously rationalized and apologized for them. But here, too, we must go beyond Dundes to consider another possible psychoanalytical interpretation in light of Miller's work.

If we agree that the tale is about child abuse and incest, among other things, then couldn't it be possible that the tale represents the abused child's repressed fears based on actual mistreatment? Did Wilhelm relate to the tale because he, too, had been abused as a child? Have narrators felt drawn to the tale because it contains hidden motifs about the abuse they suffered in their childhood? Instead of interpreting the tale as one of projected inversion, as Freud always did in cases of hysterical women (and most analysts following him), we might want to try to locate the truth of the tale's trauma in actual experience. As we know, Freud's seduction theory itself has come under attack because he changed the evidence about seduction and physical violation that he had collected.[58] Though one cannot dismiss Freud's seduction theory in its entirety, it can be argued to a certain degree that he did not really hear or listen to his female patients and consequently manipulated them. Let us try to avoid this.

In this tale about child abuse and incest, the protagonist is at first without power. She is overwhelmed by her father while her mother remains passive. The father is not terribly concerned about the future of his daughter. He is worried about his impoverishment, and he does not hesitate to chop off her hands. He is a frustrated man, concerned about his inability to succeed—perhaps his virility—and he finds a way to vent his frustration by attacking his child and then rationalizing it. He simply expects her to forgive him because he cannot help himself, because he is afraid of the devil. His violation of her is not treated as a crime but rather as an emergency; she is made to feel guilty if she does not relent. The physical and psychological harm that he causes his daughter will be made up to her, he believes, when he offers her a life of splendor. However, the girl is more willing to place her life in the hands of strangers than to have her father come near her again. Without being too literal and reducing the meaning of "The Maiden Without Hands" to a simple causal situation, then, the signs in this initial incident indicate that the narrator is expressing the difficulties a child feels in confronting an abusive father or mother. It is not by coincidence that the girl marries a man who also threatens to abuse her (with death or banishment). Aided by her mother-in-law (wish-fulfillment), she flees again. Only when the male (the father, the parent, the analyst) recognizes that he is the abuser and does penance for his misuse of power (seven years wandering), can there be a reconciliation. Only then will the maiden have her own hands, her own power, and be able to determine how she will live.

For the last 30 years many therapists have recognized how valuable the Grimms' tales and fairy tales by other authors can be in treating abused children and working with families. In Gainesville, Florida, a therapist who has been working with sexually and physically abused children has employed such tales as "Hansel and Gretel" and "Goldilocks and the Three Bears" to enable the child to speak about his or her feelings of abandonment, manipulation, and abuse. She generally has the children choose their favorite tale, or she reads some tales to the children and then asks them to choose their favorite tale. And on the basis of their choice and emotional response to a tale, she will explore the child's psychological blocks and disturbances. What is significant here is that children in contemporary society respond intuitively to symbolic tales of past experiences that are historical representations of familial problems and problems of power that have continued to hinder the development of compassionate social relations. And, of course, we as adults continue to be attracted to these tales, repressing those that are perhaps too explicit in exposing adult cruelty and choosing those that apparently resolve problems of child abuse. Such resolution eases our conscience and makes it seemingly easy to live with ourselves as we attain power and unintentionally manipulate weaker people, especially children, and often our own children. However, if we return to the tales (all of them) and attempt to examine them in light of Miller's notions (and not only Miller's) and in light of the historical conditions under which they arose, there is a great deal that we can still discover about our childhood and about listening to children's needs today.

These last remarks should serve as an indication that I do not believe psychoanalysis and psychology have reached a dead end in the land of the Grimms' fairy tales or in the United States. But I do want to suggest that the psychoanalytical approach needs some historical grounding and must seek new avenues if it is to keep pace with the progress made by literary historians and critics. If it is true that the Grimms' tales are not authentic folk tales and that the Grimms shaped these tales in a peculiar manner, then it would seem necessary to study the Grimms themselves (their personalities, their psychological problems), as well as family conditions in Central Europe during the eighteenth and nineteenth centuries, to gain an understanding of the nature of the tales and the significance of their formation in relation to familial relations and child rearing. In addition, a sociopsychological approach might enable us to understand why and how the Grimms' tales play such an immense role in the socialization of children and adults alike. Does the character formation of the various figures in the tales correspond to the gender-specific roles that have been developed in bourgeois society? If so, then is it possible that what appears to be a healthy resolution of psychological problems is merely a rationalization of the arbitrary manner in which parents wield power, or a sexist resolution of power relations that keep certain groups, namely women and other minorities, in a place where white males want them to be? Are we constantly attracted to the Grimms' tales because they help us repress the abuse that we have experienced and at the same time allow us to contend with these problems on a subconscious level?

These questions lead me to a brief conclusion about the purpose of all the celebrations of the Grimms and their tales during 1985 and 1986. Obviously, most publishers in the so-called culture industry could not have cared less what serious critics thought about the tales, and to make a profit they produced as many so-called new editions as the market could tolerate. On the other hand, literary critics and historians (without the profit motif dangling before their eyes) tried sincerely to reassess the Grimms and their tales, and are still in the midst of evaluating the central role the Grimms have played in the development of the fairy-tale genre. At times, their positions have focused too much on the utopian and positive values of the tales and thus have failed to explicate the ideological function of the tales within a male-dominated discourse of fairy tales in the nineteenth century. For the most part, however, their analyses have opened up new insights into the work methods, reception, and cultural function of the tales. The psychoanalytical studies of the Grimms produced in West Germany during the 1983–1986 period have done, and continue to do, both psychoanalysis and the Grimms a disservice. Yet they are important to study because they sell in the thousands in Germany, where Germans appear to be enchanted and obsessed by them and the tales. It is through an understanding of this "German" obsession (and perhaps a global obsession with fairy tales and fantasy), as well as through an understanding of the general psychological repression by psychoanalytically-oriented critics, that we might better grasp the distinctive cultural meanings of the Grimms' tales. Their use in our cultural heritage may have more to do with child abuse than we have believed, and their appeal for children may suggest that the tales may be filling an emotional gap and offering more hope for their future than the social institutions and caretakers of their future will ever be able to provide.

APPENDIX

"The Maiden Without Hands" (1812)[59]

A miller, who was so poor that he had nothing more than his mill and a large apple tree behind it, went into the forest to fetch wood. There he met an old man who said, "There's no reason why you have to torture yourself so much. I'll make you rich. In return, just sign over to me what's behind your mill. I'll come and fetch it in three years."

The miller thought to himself, that's my apple tree, said yes, and signed it over to the man. When he returned home, his wife said to him, "Miller, where did we get all this great wealth that's suddenly filled the chests and boxes in our house."

"It's from an old man in the forest. Whatever's behind the mill I signed over to him."

"Oh, husband!" his wife exclaimed in dread. "We'd better be prepared for the worst. That was the devil, and he meant our daughter, who was behind the mill sweeping out the yard."

Now the miller's daughter was beautiful and pious, and after three years the devil came quite early and wanted to fetch her, but she had drawn a circle around herself with chalk and had washed herself clean. So the devil could not approach her, and he spoke angrily to the miller, "Take all the cleansing water away from her so that she can't wash herself anymore. Then I can have power over her."

Since the miller was afraid of the devil, he did as he was told. The next morning the devil came again, but the maiden wept on her hands and made them completely clean. Once more he could not get near her, and he became very mad and ordered the miller, "Chop off her hands, so I can get hold of her!"

But the miller was horrified and replied, "How can I chop off the hands of my own child!"

"You know what I'll do if you don't. I'll come and get you yourself if you don't do it!"

The miller became tremendously afraid, and in his fear he promised the devil to do what he had commanded. So he went to his daughter and said, "My child, if I don't chop off both your hands, the devil will take me away, and since I promised that I'd do it, I want to beg you for forgiveness."

"Father," she said, "do what you want with me."

She extended both her hands and let him chop them off. The devil came a third time, but she had wept so long and so much on her stumps that they were completely clean. So the devil lost all claim to her.

Since the miller had become so wealthy because of her, he promised her that she would live in splendor for the rest of her life. However, she did not want to remain there any longer.

"I want to go away from here, and I shall depend on the kindness of people to provide me with whatever I need to live."

She had both her maimed hands bound to her back, and at dawn she set out on her way and walked and walked the entire day until it was evening. Then she reached the king's garden. There was an opening in the hedge of the garden, and she went through it and found a fruit tree that she shook with her body. And when the apples fell to the ground, she bent over, picked them up with her teeth, and ate them. For two days she lived like that, but on the third day the guards of the garden came and saw her. So they captured her and threw her into the prison house. The next morning she was brought before the king and was to be banished from the land.

"Wait," said the king's son. "It would be better to have her look after the chickens in the yard."

She stayed there a long time and looked after the chickens. And the king's son took a great liking to her. Meanwhile the time came for him to marry. Messengers were sent throughout the wide world in order to find a beautiful bride for him.

"You don't have to send the messengers far," he said. "I know of a bride who lives nearby."

The old king racked his brain, but he was not familiar with any such maiden in the land who was beautiful and rich.

"You don't want to marry that one who looks after the chickens in the yard, do you?"

But the son declared that he would marry no one but her. So the king finally had to yield, and soon thereafter he died. The king's son succeeded him to the throne and lived happily with his wife.

However, at one time the king had to go to war, and during his absence she gave birth to a beautiful child and sent a messenger to him with a letter in which she announced the joyful news. On the way the messenger stopped to rest near a brook and fell asleep. Then the devil, who was still trying to harm the queen, came and exchanged the letter for another one that said that the queen had given birth to a changeling. When the king read the letter, he became quite distressed, but he wrote in reply that his wife and child were to be given good care until his return. The messenger went back with the letter, and when he rested and fell asleep on the exact same spot, the evil devil approached and shoved another letter under him in which the king ordered that the queen and child were to be banished from the land. Despite the fact that everyone at the court was sad and wept, the command had to be carried out.

"I did not come here to become queen. I don't have any luck and don't demand any. Bind my child and my hands to my back. Then I shall go out into the world."

That evening she reached a well in a dense forest where a good old man was sitting.

"Please be so merciful," she said, "and hold my child on my breast until I have given him enough to drink."

The man did that, and thereupon he said to her, "A large tree is standing over there. Go to it and wrap your maimed arms around it three times!"

And after she had done that, her hands grew back again. Afterwards he showed her a house.

"You're to live in there and not to go out. Don't open the door for any person who does not ask for God's sake three times."

In the meantime the king returned home and realized that he had been deceived. He set out in the company of only a single servant, and after a long journey, he wandered about lost for a long time in the same forest in which the queen was living. Indeed, he did not know that she was so near.

"Over there," the servant said, "I see a little light glimmering in a house. Thank God, we can get some rest."

"Not at all," said the king. "I don't want to rest very long. I want to keep searching for my beloved wife. Until then I shall have no rest."

But the servant pleaded so much and complained about being tired that the king agreed out of pity. When they came to the house, the moon was shining, and they saw the queen standing by the window.

"Oh, that must be our queen. She looks just like her," the servant said. "But I see that it can't be her, for she's got hands."

Then the servant asked for lodgings, but she refused because he had not asked for God's sake. He wanted to move on and look for another place to spend the night when the king himself approached.

"Let me in for God's sake!"

"I'm not allowed to let you in until you ask me three times for God's sake."

And when the king asked another two times, she opened the door, and his little son sprang through the door. He led the king to his mother, and the king recognized her right away as his beloved wife. The next morning they all prepared to travel back to their land together, and when they were out of the house, it disappeared behind them.

"The Maiden without Hands" (1857)[60]

A miller had been falling little by little into poverty, and soon he had nothing left but his mill and a large apple tree behind it. One day, as he was on his way to chop wood in the forest, he met an old man whom he had never seen before.

"There's no reason why you have to torture yourself by cutting wood," the old man said. "I'll make you rich if you promise to give me what's behind your mill."

What else can that be but my apple tree, thought the miller, and he gave the stranger his promise in writing.

"In three years I'll come and fetch what's mine," the stranger said with a snide laugh, and he went away.

When the miller returned home, his wife went out to meet him and said, "Tell me, miller, how did all this wealth suddenly get into our house? All at once I've discovered our chests and boxes are full. Nobody's brought anything, and I don't know how it's all happened."

"It's from a stranger I met in the forest," he said. "He promised me great wealth if I agreed in writing to give him what's behind our mill. We can certainly spare the large apple tree."

"Oh, husband!" his wife exclaimed in dread. "That was the devil! He didn't mean the apple tree but our daughter, who was behind the mill sweeping out the yard."

The miller's daughter was a beautiful and pious maiden who went through the next three years in fear of God and without sin. When the time was up and the day came for the devil to fetch her, she washed herself clean and drew a circle around her with chalk. The devil appeared quite early, but he could not get near her, and he said angrily to the miller, "I want you to take all the water away from her so she can't wash herself anymore. Otherwise, I have no power over her."

Since the miller was afraid of the devil, he did as he was told. The next morning the devil came again, but she had wept on her hands and made them completely clean. Once more he could not get near her and said furiously to the miller, "Chop off her hands. Otherwise, I can't touch her."

The miller was horrified and replied, "How can I chop off the hands of my own child!"

But the devil threatened him and said, "If you don't do it, you're mine, and I'll come and get you yourself!"

The father was so scared of him that he promised to obey. He went to his daughter and said, "My child, if I don't chop off both your hands, the devil will take me away, and in my fear I promised I'd do it. Please help me out of my dilemma and forgive me for the injury I'm causing you."

"Dear Father," she answered, "do what you want with me. I'm your child."

Then she extended both her hands and let him chop them off. The devil came a third time, but she had wept so long and so much on the stumps that they too were all clean. Then he had to abandon his game and lost all claim to her.

Now the miller said to his daughter, "I've become so wealthy because of you that I shall see to it you'll live in splendor for the rest of your life." But she answered, "No, I cannot stay here. I'm going away and shall depend on the kindness of people to provide me with whatever I need."

Then she had her maimed arms bound to her back, and at dawn she set out on her way and walked the entire day until it became dark. She was right outside a royal garden, and by the glimmer of the moon she could see trees full of beautiful fruit. She could not enter the garden though because it was surrounded by water. Since she had traveled the entire day without eating, she was very hungry. Oh, if only I could get in! she thought. I must eat some of the fruit or else I'll perish! Then she fell to her knees, called out to the Lord, and prayed. Suddenly an angel appeared who closed one of the locks in the stream so that the moat became dry and she could walk through it. Now she went into the garden accompanied by the angel. She caught sight of a beautiful tree full of pears, but the pears had been counted. Nonetheless, she approached the tree and ate one of the pears with her mouth to satisfy her hunger, but only this one. The gardener was watching her, but since the angel was standing there, he was afraid, especially since he thought the maiden was a spirit. He kept still and did not dare to cry out or speak to her. After she had eaten the pear, and her hunger was stilled, she went and hid in the bushes.

The next morning the king who owned the garden came and counted the pears. When he saw one was missing, he asked the gardener what had happened to it, for the pear was not lying under the tree and had somehow vanished.

"Last night a spirit appeared," answered the gardener. "It had no hands and ate one of the pears with its mouth."

"How did the spirit get over the water?" asked the king. "And where did it go after it ate the pear?"

"Someone wearing a garment as white as snow came down from heaven, closed the lock, and dammed up the water so the spirit could walk through the moat. And, since it must have been an angel, I was afraid to ask any questions or to cry out. After the spirit had eaten the pear, it just went away."

"If it's as you say," said the king, "I shall spend the night with you and keep watch."

When it became dark, the king went into the garden and brought a priest with him to talk to the spirit. All three sat down beneath the tree and kept watch. At midnight the maiden came out of the bushes, walked over to the tree, and once again ate one of the pears with her mouth, while the angel in white stood next to her. The priest stepped forward and said to the maiden, "Have you come from heaven or from earth? Are you a spirit or a human being?"

"I'm not a spirit, but a poor creature forsaken by everyone except God."

"You may be forsaken by the whole world, but I shall not forsake you," said the king.

He took her with him to his royal palace, and since she was so beautiful and good, he loved her with all his heart, had silver hands made for her, and took her for his wife.

After a year had passed, the king had to go to war, and he placed the young queen under the care of his mother and said, "If she has a child, I want you to protect her and take good care of her, and write me right away."

Soon after, the young queen gave birth to a fine-looking boy. The king's mother wrote to him immediately to announce the joyful news. However, on the way the messenger stopped to rest near a brook, and since he was exhausted from the long journey, he fell asleep. Then the devil appeared. He was still trying to harm the pious queen, and so he exchanged the letter for another one that said that the queen had given birth to a changeling. When the king read the letter, he was horrified and quite distressed, but he wrote his mother that she should protect the queen and take care of her until his return. The messenger started back with the letter, but he stopped to rest at the same spot and fell asleep. Once again the devil came and put a different letter in his pocket that said that they should kill the queen and her child. The old mother was tremendously disturbed when she received the letter and could not believe it. She wrote the king again but received the same answer because the devil kept replacing the messenger's letters with false letters each time. The last letter ordered the king's mother to keep the tongue and eyes of the queen as proof that she had done his bidding.

But the old woman wept at the thought of shedding such innocent blood. During the night she had a doe fetched and cut out its tongue and eyes and put them away. Then she said to the queen, "I can't let you stay here any longer. Go out into the wide world with your child, and don't ever come back."

She tied the child to the queen's back, and the poor woman went off with tears in her eyes. When she came to a great wild forest, she fell down on her knees and prayed to God. The Lord's angel appeared before her and led her to a small cottage with a little sign saying "Free Lodging for Everyone." A maiden wearing a snow white garment came out of the cottage and said, "Welcome, Your Highness," and took her inside. She untied the little boy from her back and offered him her breast so he could have something to drink. Then she laid him down in a beautifully made bed.

"How did you know that I'm a queen?" asked the poor woman. "I'm an angel sent by God to take care of you and your child," replied the maiden in white.

So the queen stayed in the cottage for seven years and was well cared for. By the grace of God and through her own piety her hands that had been chopped off grew back again.

When the king finally returned from the wars, the first thing he wanted to do was to see his wife and child. However, his old mother began to weep and said, "You wicked man, why did you write and order me to kill two innocent souls?" She showed him the two letters that the devil had forged and resumed talking. "I did as you ordered," and she displayed the tongue and eyes.

At the sight of them the king burst into tears and wept bitterly over his wife and little son. His old mother was aroused and took pity on him.

"Console yourself," she said. "She's still alive. I secretly had a doe killed and kept its tongue and eyes as proof. Then I took the child and tied him to your wife's back and ordered her to go out into the wide world, and she had to promise me never to return here because you were so angry with her."

"I shall go as far as the sky is blue, without eating or drinking, until I find my dear wife and child," the king said. "That is, unless they have been killed or have died of hunger in the meantime."

The king wandered for about seven years and searched every rocky cliff and cave he came across. When he did not find her, he thought she had perished. During this time he neither ate nor drank, but God kept him alive. Eventually, he came to a great forest, where he discovered the little cottage with the sign "Free Lodging for Everyone." Then the maiden in white came out, took him by the hand, and led him inside.

"Welcome, Your Majesty," she said, and asked him where he came from.

"I've been wandering about for almost seven years looking for my wife and child, but I can't find them."

The angel offered him food and drink, but he refused and said he only wanted to rest awhile. So he lay down to sleep and covered his face with a handkerchief. Then the angel went into the room where the queen was sitting with her son, whom she was accustomed to calling Sorrowful, and said, "Go into the next room with your child. Your husband has come."

So the queen went to the room where he was lying, and the handkerchief fell from his face.

"Sorrowful," she said, "pick up your father's handkerchief and put it over his face again."

The child picked the handkerchief up and put it over his face. The king heard all this in his sleep and took pleasure in making the handkerchief drop on the floor again. The boy became impatient and said, "Dear Mother, how can I cover my father's face when I have no father on earth. I've learned to pray to 'our father that art in heaven,' and you told me that my father was in heaven and that he was our good Lord. How am I supposed to recognize this wild man? He's not my father."

When the king heard this, he sat up and asked her who she was.

"I'm your wife," she replied, "and this is your son, Sorrowful."

When the king saw that she had real hands, he said, "My wife had silver hands."

"Our merciful Lord let my natural hands grow again," she answered.

The angel went back into the sitting room, fetched the silver hands, and showed them to him. Now he knew for certain that it was his dear wife and dear son, and he kissed them and was happy.

"A heavy load has been taken off my mind," he said.

After the Lord's angel ate one more meal with them, they went home to be with the king's old mother. There was rejoicing everywhere, and the king and queen had a second wedding and lived happily ever after.

CHAPTER EIGHT

SEMANTIC SHIFTS OF POWER IN FOLK AND FAIRY TALES

Cinderella and the Consequences

The study of the relationship between orality and literacy has always had great significance for folklorists in their investigations of folk tales and their derivations. However, they have generally felt called upon to defend the "purity" of the oral genre and its resilient character against the "creeping disease" of literary adaptation, and the production of the tales in distorted but attractive forms as commodities to make money. In contrast, literary critics have largely ignored the importance of oral sources and orality in their studies of the literary fairy tale, although there are some exceptions. At most, they make passing reference to oral and popular versions while honoring the consolidated literary form of a finished work. In recent years there have been attempts made by various literary critics, folklorists, anthropologists, and historians—such as Jack Goody,[1] Walter Ong,[2] Heide Göttner-Abendroth,[3] Dieter Richter,[4] August Nitschke,[5] Raymonde

Robert,[6] Rudolf Schenda,[7] and others—to rectify this situation. They have sought to explore the reciprocal effects in the development of both the oral and literary tales and to establish reasons for the canonization of certain tales and authors. In consideration of their work I want to point out some of the productive results that their efforts may have for literary theory by focusing on the *ambivalent* nature of the tensions between the oral folk tale and the literary fairy tale.

In approaching the problematic relationship between the oral folk tale and the literary fairy tale, there are some interesting remarks by Ong that may be helpful in focusing our attention on the cultural dynamics underlying the formation of the literary fairy tales. In his book *Orality and Literacy*, he stresses that: "Writing from the beginning did not reduce orality but enhanced it, making it possible to organize the 'principles' or constituents of oratory into a scientific 'art,' a sequentially ordered body of explanation that showed how and why oratory achieved and could be made to achieve its various specific effects."[8] However, Ong adds later on that this kind of "enhancement" has its ambivalent side, since writing "is a particularly preemptive and imperialist activity that tends to assimilate other things to itself even without the aid of etymologies."[9] In other words, writing imposed and imposes specific grammatical rules, new meanings, and mental and social requirements on oral communication, and often disregarded and disregards customary usage and semantics in oral cultures. Indeed, socialization in Western societies made literature an important agent in the education of children, whereby oral tales gave way to a classical set of literary tales whose rules and themes were challenged only after those who retold the tales knew the rules and themes well.

A case in point is the rise of the literary fairy tale in Europe, which I described in *Breaking the Magic Spell* as the "bourgeoisification" of the oral folk tale. By bourgeoisification of the oral folk tale I meant the manner in which educated people appropriated tales belonging to and disseminated by peasants (largely nonliterate) and the manner in which these educated people, largely of the bourgeoisie, adapted the styles, motifs, topoi, and meanings of the tales to serve the interests and needs of the new and expanding reading audiences—particularly at the end of the eighteenth and the beginning of the nineteenth century. In other words, this appropriation was a kind of "preemptive and imperialist activity," which thrived on an oral tradition and also enriched it. In many instances, the recording of the oral folk tales, such as by the Brothers Grimm, even when it involved major changes, enhanced the orality because it helped define and explain the rhetoric and contents of the tales and allowed residual folk elements to be preserved that otherwise would have disappeared. Memory is selective and historical, and the oral tales can only retain basic elements of tales from other generations before the tales fade. Literature can thus complement the oral tradition. Nevertheless, the stylistic and semantic shifts of power embedded in written language itself indicated that a different social consciousness was organizing and regulating cultural products and stamping its imprint on them.

To be more succinct, one could argue that, with the advent of the literary fairy tale, the "folk" or nonliterate people in Europe were deprived of their tales because the literary fairy tale gradually became the exemplary genre in literate societies for recording what nonliterate people had received differently in earlier historical epochs. By no means do I want to argue that the literary genre has eliminated or replaced the oral tradition, or that the literary texts have been totally predominant in the lives of most people. But there is no doubt that, as literacy and schooling evolved in the nineteenth and twentieth centuries, the governing factors in the reception of the classical fairy tales in the West have been determined by the literary genre as an institution. Such a development has had enormous consequences for the socialization of both children and adults through literature because a specific canon of tales, continually reproduced and used for the last two centuries, emphasizes male adventure and power and female domesticity and passivity.

The sexist and middle-class bias of the classical fairy tales has been analyzed and scrutinized by various critics during the past 20 years.[10] However, as I have tried to demonstrate in *The Trials and Tribulations of Little Red Riding Hood*, there is a danger in looking upon the "classical" literary fairy tale as too monolithic and its impact as too one-dimensional. Certainly, the literary appropriation of the oral tale about a peasant girl meeting a werewolf in the forest transformed a narrative about the initiation of a shrewd girl within a sewing community into a text concerned with the responsibility of a "bourgeois" girl for causing her "rape." Yet the tale is also a warning that makes children aware of the dangers lurking in unfamiliar places. Furthermore, it is a tale about repressed sexual desire that finds its perverted expression in violation.

The study of the literary appropriation of the oral folk tale must take into account the ways and means the literary fairy tale is received by different audiences and how it is reused in oral interaction, social situations, and the media to influence the "dialogic" development of the entrenched literary genre. Let us take the case of the Cinderella cycle to explore the ambivalent relationship between orality and literacy.

In *Soziale Ordnungen im Spiegel der Märchen* by August Nitschke[11] and Heide Göttner-Abendroth's *Die Göttin und ihr Heros,* the oral tale of Cinderella is traced back to matrilineal societies in which the *schenkende Mutter* (the gift-bearing mother), who is dead, provides her daughter with three gifts that enable her to complete tasks in the underworld, sea, and sky so that she can liberate a man, who is in a beastly state (i.e., she "civilizes" him). The man as hero plays a secondary exogenous but important role: As outsider, he demonstrates his integrity after he has been humanized or civilized by the young woman when he integrates himself into another tribe governed by the matrilineal rites of the goddess. As various folklorists and anthropologists have discovered—many of their studies have been gathered in Alan Dundes's useful *Cinderella: A Casebook*[12]—there are thousands of Cinderella versions which have been collected in Egypt, China, Scandinavia, and Africa as well as in Europe and the Americas, and it is not always clear that the *Urmärchen* (the primeval tale), if there is one, has come from a matrilineal society. Nevertheless, I think that both Nitschke and Göttner-Abendroth provide sufficient evidence from ancient relics and our knowledge of moon worship and matriarchal rites to substantiate their claim that a strand of the Cinderella cycle emanated from the matrilineal oral tradition. For instance, there is strong evidence from African,[13] Afghan, and Iranian tales that the Cinderella type 510A may have originated in female rituals. In fact, in her study of a Cinderella variant in the context of a Muslim women's ritual, Margaret Mills demonstrates that the Iranian tale "Mah Pishani" ("Moon-Brow")[14] functions to reinforce female solidarity among Muslim women today when they conduct a food offering and ritual meal in honor of the daughter of Mohammed and the wife of Ali. Here is her account of the tale based on the field notes of the ritual meal with a girl listening to the recital of the tale by an elderly woman.

> A merchant enrolled his daughter in the *madraseh* (religious school). The teacher, a female *axund* or teaching *mulla*, was a widow, and she asked the girl about her family's financial position, which the girl reported was good. She asked the girl what they had in their house, and the girl replied, vinegar. The teacher convinced the girl that she, the teacher, was good and her mother was bad, and she told the girl to tell her mother that she wanted some vinegar, and when she went to get it, to push her in and cover the storage jar. She told her not to tell her father, just to say that she fell in.
>
> The mother was dead when the father found her. (Here the informant mentioned spooning ash and the girl answering "Yes.") Later on, the father found a yellow cow in his stable in the place of the murdered mother. The teacher and the father become engaged; then he had both a wife and the cow, and he sent the daughter out to pasture the cow. The new wife gave birth to a daughter, and she began to mistreat the first daughter, giving her one rotten piece of bread to eat when she took the cow out for the day, and sending her with raw cotton to clean and spin while the cow fed, but no tools to work the cotton. Out in the fields, the girl began to cry because she could not spin, and all she could do was hook the cotton fibers on a thorn and back away from them, twisting them with her fingers.
>
> The cow spoke and asked her why she was crying. She complained about the task, and said, "If I don't do it, my stepmother won't let me back in the house." The cow asked to see her bread. (The informant added that the listening girl continues to say "Yes" at intervals.) The girl gave the bread to the cow, and then the cotton to eat, and the cow shat cotton thread until evening. The girl collected all the thread and took it back to her stepmother.
>
> For three days in a row, the stepmother gave the girl bad bread to eat and more cotton to spin. (Listener: "Yes.") On the third day, when the girl gave the cow the cotton, the wind blew a piece away, and it dropped down a well. The girl was about to go down the well after it, and the cow told her, "When you go into

the well, you'll see an old woman *barzangi*. When you see her, say 'Salam!' and ask for the cotton. The old woman will say, 'Delouse my hair.' You should say, 'Your hair is perfectly all right—it's cleaner than mine.'"

The girl follows directions. When the old woman asks her to delouse her hair, she begins to do it, and the old woman asks, "What does my hair have?" The girl answers, "Nothing, your hair is cleaner than my mother's. Your hair is like a rose, my mother's is full of dirt." The old woman tells her to take her cotton from a certain room. The daughter goes in and sees that the room is full of jewels, but she takes only her cotton, sweeps the room, and leaves, saving goodbye to the *barzangi*. She starts to climb the ladder out of the well, but when she is halfway up, the *barzangi* shakes the ladder to see if she has stolen anything and hidden it in her clothes. When no jewels fall from her clothes, the old woman prays for her to have a moon in the center of her brow. When she reaches the top of the ladder, the *barzangi* shakes it again and blesses her again, "May you have a star on your chin!"

The girl returns to the cow, who tells her to cover her forehead and chin so that her stepmother won't see them. She returns home with the cow. That night, while she sleeps, her veil slips and the stepmother sees the moon and the star. The next day, she sends her own daughter with the cow instead, giving her raw cotton to work and sweet nut bread to eat. The girl can't spin, but she guesses that the cow did the spinning for her sister, so she gives the sweet bread to the cow, and the cotton, but the cow produces only a little thread.

On the third day, her cotton, too, is blown into the well, and she follows it and sees the old woman. She asks for the cotton without saying, "Salam," and the old woman asks her to delouse her hair. When the old woman asks her about her hair, the girl replies, "Your hair is filthy, my mother's is clean." The old woman tells her to go into the room, sweep it and take her cotton. She takes some jewels, which fall from her clothes when the old woman shakes the ladder. The old woman says, "May a donkey's penis appear from your forehead!" At the top of the ladder the old woman shakes it again, and more jewels fall, and she adds a curse, "And a snake from your chin!"

The girl goes back to the cow, who sees the penis and the snake, but says nothing. She takes the cow home, and her mother cuts off the penis and snake with a knife and covers the wounds with salt, but both objects reappear overnight. The stepmother realizes the cow is behind this and feigns sickness, bribing the doctors to tell her husband that she must eat the meat of the yellow cow and have its skin thrown over her, in order to recover. Meanwhile, the first daughter has realized that the yellow cow is her mother, and she feeds her candied chickpeas and bread. One day the cow cries and tells her: "They'll kill me today, and if they kill me, your life will become very hard. When they kill me, don't eat the meat. Collect all the bones in a bag, bury them, and hide them." The daughter cries and goes to plead with her father, saying that all their wealth means nothing to her compared with the yellow cow. The father says the cow must be killed, because it is the only medicine for her stepmother.

The girl follows the cow's instructions, gathering up the bones after she is killed. The stepmother "gets well," and a few days later the family is invited to a wedding in another city. The stepmother and her daughter decide to go, so the mother cuts off the penis and snake and applies salt to the wounds, then mixes millet and *togu* (another tiny seed), places her stepdaughter in front of the empty pool in the garden, and tells her to separate the seeds and to fill the pool with her tears. The two then leave for the wedding. The girl is sitting and crying when she sees a hen with a lot of chickens come into the garden. The hen speaks, telling the girl to put salt and water into the pool, take the horse and good clothes she will find in the stable, and go to the wedding, while the chicks separate the seeds. The hen adds, "When you come back, one of your shoes will fall into the water; don't stop to get it—go quickly so that your stepmother won't know you."

The girl finds a magically provided horse, fine clothes, and gold shoes in the stable, and she rides off to the wedding, with her forehead and chin covered. They place her at the head of the guests in the women's party when the dancing starts. She dances, and the stepsister recognizes her and says to her mother, "This is our Mahpishani (Moon-Brow)."The stepmother says, "Impossible!" but they leave to go and see whether she is at home, to see whether the guest was really she. Mahpishani rushes ahead on the horse to get home before them, but she drops a shoe into some water. When she gets home, she realizes that the hen had changed into the horse. She puts on her old clothes and sits down to separate the few remaining seeds and the pool is full of "tears," and the stepmother says, "I told you so!"

> Two days later, a prince is riding by the waterside, and his horse refuses to drink. He looks down, finds the shoe, and takes it to his father, saying that he wants to wed the owner of the shoe. The king and his viziers try the shoe on everyone, and all wish that it would fit, but it does not. Finally they come to Mahpishani's father's house. The stepmother cleans and cuts her daughter's head, but the shoe does not fit. The vizier is about to leave. The first daughter is locked in the bread oven. A cock flies on top of the oven, and begins to crow:
>
> | | |
> |---|---|
> | A moon in the oven! | *Mahi dar tannur!* |
> | A head is in there, ku-kul! | *Sar ar unjeh, qu, qu!* |
> | Where is the foot, like glass? | *Pa ku ci bolur?* |
> | A head is in there, ku-ku! | *Sar ar unjeh, qzi, qu!* |
>
> The stepmother and her daughter try to catch the cock, who escapes them and crows twice more. The vizier gets annoyed and insists on looking in the oven, where he finds the girl. The shoe fits, and she marries the prince.(185–188)

The motifs of the tale reveal a strong affinity to matrilineal moon worship. Mahpishani completes various tasks successfully, and she is rewarded with the sign of the moon and stars. Moreover, she is guided by her gift-bearing dead mother, and it is she who plays an active role in determining her destiny. Men are incidental to the tale. As Mills remarks,

> Mahpishani ignores male characters as such: the father and the prince are almost completely passive prizes of the women's struggle, male brides. In a performance context from which males are excluded, the humiliation of an evil female is accomplished by the invocation of male symbols. This quintessential female narration of the Cinderella tale reveals that these women see marking (being made conspicuous) as both disastrous and masculine. (191)

But the "markings" in the dominant version of the Cinderella tale in the modern world remain male and obfuscate the matrilineal tradition because of the patriarchalization that has taken place—especially in the literary tradition, but not only there.

In general, the patriarchalization of matrilineal tales, which began in the oral tradition itself as matriarchal societies were conquered or underwent changes by themselves, led to the replacement of female protagonists and rituals celebrating the moon goddess by heroes and rites emphasizing male superiority and sun worship. According to Göttner-Abendroth, the major features of patriarchalization consist of the demonization of the goddess (endowing the virtuous princess with demonic features); the transformation of the major heroine into a hero; the reinforcement of patrilineal marriage; the degradation of female ritualistic symbols; and the deformation of the mythic structure that relied heavily on moon worship. Thus, the Cinderella type heroine was changed during the course of four millennia—approximately 7000 B.C. to 3000 B.C.—from a young active woman who is expected to pursue her own destiny under the guidance of a wise, gift-bearing dead mother; into a helpless, inactive pubescent girl, whose major accomplishments are domestic, and who must obediently wait to be rescued by a male. Such patriarchalization in the oral tradition prepared the ground for the bourgeoisification of the tale in the literary tradition.

The importance of the first three major literary Cinderellas in Europe—by Giambattista Basile, Charles Perrault, and the Brothers Grimm—consists in the manner in which they continue to transmit residues and traces of the matrilineal tradition (perhaps enhancing this tradition by writing them down in script), while also reformulating how oral symbolical motifs and topoi could be used to represent social experience (in, respectively, the sixteenth, seventeenth, and eighteenth centuries). In Basile's "The Cat Cinderella" (1634–1636), Zezolla, the daughter of a prince, is an active young woman who kills her evil stepmother in order to replace her with her apparently sweet and understanding governess. Yet, this kind governess reveals herself to be a conniving shrew who has six daughters of her own! Zezolla is banished to the fireplace in the kitchen and is called the Cat Cinderella. But, thanks to the pigeon of the fairies (a symbolic representation of her dead mother) she receives a date palm, which she cultivates, and which enables her to attend the ball three times. The last time, she loses a slipper, and the king, who is enamored of her, finds her and makes her his queen. Although Basile retained some of the matrilineal features by allowing Zezolla to play an active role in determining her destiny, and though he also used an oral style (he wrote his tales in a mannered dialect of Naples), there are distinct signs of patriarchalization: the demonization of the governess, the domestication of Zezolla before she can marry, and the rescue of Zezolla by a king.

Perrault's tale, printed in 1697, borrowed heavily from Basile and heightened the patriarchalization by emphasizing the helplessness of Cinderella, her industrious and modest nature as housekeeper, and the fashions of King Louis XIV's court. In no way does Perrault suggest ties with an ancient matrilineal tradition; he simply invents a godmother, who is obviously a fairy, just as he invented the glass slipper, which should but does not break. (The slipper appears to have been invented as a joke.) Perrault actually mocked the conventions of nonliterate people while seeking to establish a code of bourgeois-aristocratic *civilité*.[15] This code was in the process of being formed at that time, and it elaborated the proper manner of behavior expected from members of different social classes and the two sexes. In contrast to Perrault, the Brothers Grimm paid more homage in 1812 to the matrilineal tradition in their version of Cinderella by reinstating the connections between the dead mother, dove, and tree—but they, too, domesticated the young woman to make her worthy of a king, and they stressed the virtues of self-denial, obedience, and industriousness, all major qualities of the middle-class Protestant ethic.

By the end of the nineteenth century, the two dominant versions of Cinderella in western Europe and America were those of Perrault and the Brothers Grimm, and often they were mixed together in popular, glossy editions for children. An oral tale (without illustrative frills) that once celebrated the ritualistic initiation of a girl entering womanhood in a matrilineal society had been transformed within a literate code that prescribed the domestic requirements in bourgeois Christian society necessary for a young woman to make herself acceptable for marriage: self-sacrifice, diligence, hard work, silence, humility, patience. Of course, the tale could be read on another, non–gender-specific level as being about an individual who goes from riches to rags and then from rags to riches. It is also a tale about child abuse, the rewards of stoicism, and the difficulties of sibling rivalry. In any case, one must still speak about the literary *preemption of an oral tale* and the celebration of an ascetic way of life (most concretely articulated in the

Grimms' version); the Protestant ethic; and self-denial as a goal in and of itself—something nonliterate people might have had difficulty understanding. The *scripted* Cinderella is in effect the prescribed way of success for young people of both sexes in a society that stresses self-renunciation, thrift, industry, opportunism, and material well-being in the form of heterosexual marriage, in which the male dominates as a wealthy provider. After all, he is the finder and keeper of the slipper!

Despite the fact that the literary script of Perrault and the Grimms has been institutionalized throughout the West, it has not been totally accepted and received on a conscious level in the manner in which I have presented it. Beginning in the nineteenth century, numerous writers composed parodies of Cinderella or revised the Grimm and Perrault versions in a serious vein to suggest alternatives to the ideological import of the classical models, which had established themselves in the minds of educated people, young and old. In addition, numerous oral versions were recorded by folklorists and ethnologists in their fieldwork, and their tales showed the influence of the literary tales even though revised. Often these oral tales came back to influence other literary versions. Finally, the mass media—radio, film, television, and the internet—have presented variations of the Cinderella tale that either reinforce the patriarchal texts or place them in question.

If one were to endeavor to trace the manifold ways in which the Cinderella tale has been put to use since its literary registration in the seventeenth century, one would have to deal with the question of literary appropriation and oral reappropriation on different levels—aesthetic, ideological, psychological, and so on. Important here would be the social and historical context at each point in the investigation. For instance, the various literary parodies and serious adaptations that began appearing in the nineteenth century were certainly influenced by the manner in which the classical tales of Perrault and Grimm were retold orally, memorized, and transmitted in face-to-face encounters at home, in the school, and in the theater. To a certain extent, the literary texts that appear in a given epoch may be considered semiotic constellations or semantic consolidations of shifts in oral interaction, social norms, accepted behavior, and dominant ideologies that point to the ambivalent side of writing.

By semiotic constellations or semantic consolidations, I mean the way in which oral narratives are arranged as literary signs in a particular order and endowed with social content that makes them representative of preferred behavior and thinking, either from the author's viewpoint or from the viewpoint of the dominant class. Insofar as these semiotic constellations become congealed so to speak as literature, or are seen as exemplary in a particular epoch, they are often used to set role models for children. Yet, their meanings eventually change as social and sexual values shift. Standards endorsed by the semiotic constellations of a particular literary tale often become ambivalent or are subverted in oral communication and give rise to new literary rearrangements within an institutionalized discourse. Thus, a fairy tale's cycle must be examined in a sociohistorical context, and such an examination must take into consideration the interaction between orality and literacy.

Using "Cinderella" as an example again, I want to suggest that there have been tendencies in the literary adaptations in America, England, and Germany during the last 20 years that question the aesthetic and thematic features of the classical Cinderella (the versions of Perrault and the Brothers Grimm) and introduce new elements that have their roots in oral invention and literary experimentation. Writers such as Anne Sexton,[16] Iring Fetscher,[17] Richard Gardner,[18] Tanith Lee,[19] Janosch,[20] John Gardner,[21] Olga Broumas,[22] Jay Williams,[23] Margaret Kassajep,[24] Judith Viorst,[25] Roald Dahl,[26] and Jane Yolen[27] have composed Cinderella tales and poems that bear the mark either of feminism or wry skepticism about classical storytelling. Typical of the implicit attitude in many of the Cinderella versions is the beginning of Dahl's witty poem:

I guess you think you know this story.
You don't. The real one's much more gory.
The phoney one, the one you know,
Was cooked up years and years ago,
And made to sound all soft and sappy
Just to keep the children happy.[28]

Like Dahl, most of the writers of the new "Cinderellas" have embarked on a revision of their childhood experiences of reading and hearing fairy tales. They have entered into a dialogue with the entire institution of the genre, and most of them have redesigned the plot of Cinderella (often without using her name) to make readers aware of the conditions underlying the heroine's passivity. For the most part, she is rerepresented either as a young woman who learns to take destiny into her own hands or as a fool for not taking a more active role in determining the course of her life. Here I should like to cite some recent examples of "new Cinderellas" by Ann Jungman, Gail Carson Levine, Philip Pullman, Priscilla Galloway, Francesca Lia Block, Emma Donoghue, and Gregory Maguire, to indicate how semantic shifts reveal changing cultural attitudes toward gender roles, abuse, and the role of the stepmother.

Written and illustrated for young readers, Jungman's *Cinderella and the Hot Air Balloon* (1992)[29] is one of the most hilarious feminist versions of the traditional tale that appeared in the 1990s. Ella, daughter of a rich merchant, prefers to ride horseback and mix with the common people than to dress up and move in high society. When the king invites her and her sisters to a ball at the castle, she sends the servants and her fairy godmother in her place, while she stays at home to bake potatoes and make some pumpkin soup. When her fairy godmother and friends return, they continue to dance at a midnight party that Ella organizes, and soon all the neighbors appear, as does the prince named Bill, who is fleeing his oppressive father. Since Ella takes a liking to him, she helps him escape and flies off with him in a hot air balloon.

While Jungman is concerned with depicting a young woman who knows her own mind and desires, Levine, Pullman, and Galloway all shift the focus from a girl to a boy in novel ways. In *Cinderellis and the Glass Hill* (2000),[30] Levine, who has written a series of princess tales for readers between age 7 and 12, introduces a young farmhand named Ellis, who lives with his two brothers Ralph and Burt in the imaginary kingdom of Biddle. Evidently they are orphans, and Ellis is called Cinderellis because one of his inventions with flying powder backfired, and he became covered with soot and ashes from a chimney. Ellis is always trying to win the attention and respect of his two plodding brothers, but they neglect him, and he suffers from loneliness—as does Princess Marigold, who has no mother, and whose father is always away on quests. Eventually, the father realizes his daughter is ready for marriage, and he prepares a contest to determine what knight might marry her. The king has a glass mountain built, and whoever can climb it on a horse can have Marigold for a bride. With the help of three magical horses and powder, Cinderellis accomplishes the task.

Levine's narrative is comical but too predictable. The problem faced by Ellis and Marigold, two humble and innocent characters who ooze sweetness, is loneliness and neglect, and once they encounter each other, it is clear they will no longer need their brothers or father to live happily ever after. This is certainly not the case with Roger in Pullman's *I Was a Rat!* (1999),[31] which has more tragic-comic overtones than Levine's trivial story. In this novel, a grubby young boy dressed in a tattered page's uniform appears out of nowhere on the doorstep of a cobbler's shop at ten in the evening. An old couple named Bob and Joan provide him with shelter and care. When he tells them he does not have a name, they are puzzled and explain to him what it means to have a name. Bob and Joan do not realize that Roger, as they call him, was once Cinderella's page and had indeed been a rat, but somehow the fairy godmother had not retransformed him into a rat. In his human condition, Roger must learn what it means to be civilized, but at the same time, he is bent on proving to Bob and Joan that he truly was a rat, and this causes quite a stir in the city. Ironically, he soon finds himself persecuted for wanting to be himself. Only Princess Aurelia, who was once Cinderella, can help prove that he is not a subhuman fiend or a venom-dripping beast from the nethermost pit of hell but just a normal little fellow. In the end, Roger gives up his quest to be a rat again because he might be exterminated by people driven to hysteria by the mass media.

Another male figure in a Cinderella tale, "The Prince" (1995),[32] by Priscilla Galloway, also feels misunderstood; he recounts his story in a first-person narrative that reveals just how obnoxious he is. From the very first paragraph it is clear that we are dealing with a highly neurotic and narcissistic character: "Guilt. Guilt. Guilt. My analyst keeps telling me I need to work out my feelings of guilt. Such nonsense. My mother died when I was born. I killed her. My father kept provoking wars so that he'd have to go away and fight them because he couldn't stand the sight of me, and no wonder, always reminding him."[33] In the course of his self-indulgent story we learn that he has had a homosexual affair with Stephen, his tutor, who was put to death by the prince's father because of his disapproval of the relationship. In fact, the father orders a ball and commands the prince to choose a wife, or he will choose one for him. The prince vows he will not marry, but he dances with a princess with glass slippers, and her toes remind him of his former lover Stephen and the foot fetish he had. When the young lady rushes away from him, he is left with a glass slipper and becomes obsessed with finding her.

Galloway's provocative narrative is concerned with obsession and self-absorption. We learn nothing about Cinderella, but all about a pathetic prince. The implications are clear: If this prince is what Cinderella can expect, she will have nothing but trouble for the rest of her life. Galloway's intriguing first-person narrative reveals the ambivalence of the happy ending of most recent Cinderella narratives. We know nothing about the prince except for his foot fetish.

In Emma Donoghue's "The Tale of the Shoe" (1997),[34] we have another first-person narrative, but this time it is Cinderella's voice that we hear, and it is the voice of an awakening and a new beginning. In grief about her mother's death, the unnamed young woman endeavors to deal with her sorrow through work: "Nobody made me do the things I did, nobody scolded me, nobody punished me but me. The shrill voices were all inside. Do this, do that, you lazy heap of dirt. They knew every question and answer, the voices in my head. Some days they asked why I was still alive. I listened out for my mother, but I couldn't hear her among their clamor."[35] Fortunately, one day a stranger appears, a friend of her mother, who describes herself as her mother's tree, and indeed, she provides the support and comfort that the young woman needs. She enables her to attend three balls, but the young girl realizes she is in love with the older woman, and she throws away into the woods the shoe that she did not lose at the ball to leave for home with the strange woman. Donoghue's story is a coming-of-age fairy tale that celebrates the self-awareness of a young woman and the love that she feels for another woman. This story is repeated with a slightly different emphasis in Francesca Lia Block's "Glass" (2000).[36] Told in a third-person narrative, it is the story of a young woman who is somewhat inhibited and likes to stay at home, clean, and tell stories to her sister. She meets a strange woman with red and white hair, young and old, who begins to speak to her in whispers. Unfortunately, Block's story is trite: it waxes sentimental about a young woman who incurs the jealousy of her sisters because she dares to come out of herself and win the attraction of a prince. When she realizes that her sisters despise her because of the attention that the prince shows her, she runs away, loses her shoe, and deprecates herself. However, the prince pursues because he recognizes her for what she is, and his love for her draws her out for good. So Block's coming-of-age tale is a more traditional heterosexual version of love than Donoghue's more unusual lesbian version. What is important in each case is that two women authors focus not so much on child abuse as on the need for love. The focus is on the self-affirmation of a young woman who has been suffering from grief about a dead mother. The intervention of an older, powerful, wise woman in the form of a fairy godmother is the necessary impetus for self-discovery.

Such intervention does not occur in Gregory Maguire's compelling novel, *Confessions of an Ugly Stepsister* (1999),[37] one of the more graphic and provocative Cinderella novels about wicked stepmothers and child abuse to have appeared in recent years. Maguire sets his story in the small city of Haarlem in seventeenth-century Holland, and he has a great eye for capturing the customs and living conditions of the time. His narrative concerns the return of the widow Margarethe Fisher from England with her two daughters: Ruth, an awkward but gentle mute, and Irene, a plain but gifted and compassionate girl. Fierce in her determination to protect her daughters and to provide them with a livelihood, Margarethe finds a job as a servant for a master painter and then as head of the van den Meer household, where Irene is giving English lessons to a beautiful and anxious girl named Clara, who had been abducted and saved from her kidnappers when she was a child. Eventually, Margarethe takes over the household and marries Cornelius van den Meer after the death of his wife. From this point on she rules the domestic affairs of the house with an iron fist, and though Clara and her stepsisters are close and mutually supportive, Margarethe treats Clara with disdain and becomes obsessed with guaranteeing the business success of her new husband and the rise of her own daughters in society.

In fact, Maguire's novel is concerned with the immortality of this stepmother, who is the driving force behind the action of the novel. He is not dismissive of the stepmother figure, nor is he judgmental. The entire narrative, in fact, is composed to represent Ruth's viewpoint, and while her tone is terse and her perspective frank, she has empathy for her mother, as though the conditions of life were such that her mother had little choice but to act the way she did—this was the way mothers had to maneuver to enable daughters to survive if not prosper. Margarethe's motives are no different from those of the others in "good" society. So, Ruth's "confession" is a true story mainly about her mother and her ambitious striving to make sure that her own genetic daughters would have a better life. She acts out of desperation and tries to overcome poverty by any means she can, just as the Dutch merchants ruthlessly deal with one another in the town of Haarlem. Maguire depicts a dog-eat-dog world, and it is no surprise that the crude and domineering Margarethe is not punished in the end, but lives on to represent the indomitable will not just of stepmothers, but of mothers obsessed with protecting their daughters.

There have been a surprising number of published literary adaptations of "Cinderella" in the past ten years, especially in the United States and United Kingdom, indicating a significant cultural disposition to this tale type. In addition to the fictional accounts, there have been critical studies such as Andrea Dworkin's *Woman Hating*, Maria Kolbenschlag's *Kiss Sleeping Beauty Good-Bye*, Marcia Lieberman's "'Some Day My Prince Will Come': Female Acculturation Through the Fairy Tale,"[38] Jane Yolen's "America's Cinderella,"[39] Colette Dowling's *The Cinderella Complex*,[40] Jennifer Waelti-Walters' *Fairy Tales and the Female Imagination*,[41] and Marina Warner's *From the Beast to the Blonde*,[42] in which contemporary women are equated in some fashion with Cinderella and charged with being too passive, comatose, and self-defeating because they have subscribed to the message of the tale. Other critics have blamed the tale for playing a role in the socialization of women along sexist lines. Consequently, the fairy godmother and prince must be forgotten if women are to come into their own.

Such a rejection of the Cinderella role appears to have had some remarkable effects in our social behavior, which may indeed be due to the feminist movement, social reforms, and the oral and literary recasting of the role that women in particular are expected to play in reality. For instance, there was an interesting development in New Mexico some years ago that J. Godwin, C. G. Cawthorne, and R. T. Roda reported in the pages of the *American Journal of Psychiatry* as the "Cinderella Syndrome."[43] Three girls between the ages of nine and ten were living in three different foster homes. They were each apparently neglected and maltreated by their foster parents, in particular their foster mothers. The girls were each dressed in tattered clothes and disheveled when the authorities found them and took them away. At the time, each of the girls claimed that she had been given her clothes by her foster parents. Upon investigation, however, the authorities found that the girls had all "lied" and had dressed themselves in "rags" on purpose to attract attention to the fact that they were in danger of being mistreated and abused by their foster mothers, who themselves had case histories similar to those of their daughters, and each of whom had been sexually and physically abused.

What is interesting here is that the girls rejected the Cinderella role by assuming the Cinderella guise and acting *against* passivity. Moreover, they intuitively went to the psychological core of the fairy tale that the happy end tends to repress—the abuse. As we have seen in Alice Miller's remarks about the fairy tale in the previous chapter, the fairy-tale frame, with its happy-end closure, tends paradoxically to belie the reality and the ugly truths that it also seeks to expose. If we know subconsciously that the happy end of "Cinderella" is based on delusion, then it becomes more apparent why we keep returning to the tale: The abuse of girls and boys continues, the sibling rivalries remain intense, and parents do not listen to the needs of their children. In fact, they are more often than not the oppressors when children are abused. Recasting Cinderella in our daily actions and literary imaginations remains part of a crucial dialogue within the civilizing process.[44]

The dialogue can be retraced historically in the series of semantic shifts of power in the Cinderella cycle from oral tales celebrating the initiation of a young woman into womanhood; oral tales reflecting the patriarchalization of society and the changing image of women and men; literary tales representing the proper domestication of the female and requirements for marriage set by men; literary tales consciously depicting a Horatio Alger myth of rags to riches; and literary tales portraying a Cinderella, who aims to overcome her prescribed role. These shifts indicate a constant utopian need, especially on the part of the disadvantaged in society, to reshape the prescribed plots of their lives. The shifts also enable us to see clearly that there has been a certain subversion and democratization of the writing process, or human forces at work that seek to undermine writing as "preemptive and imperialist." By focusing on the shifts in orality and literacy, we shall see that the fairy tale plays an unusually significant role in modern society as myth and antimyth, which have ideological repercussions in programs involved in the social reform of schooling and literacy. To tell or write a fairy tale is, after all is said and done, a means to seize knowledge and power and to take charge of one's destiny.

EPILOGUE

This chapter is the revised version of a paper that I delivered at the annual meeting of the Modern Language Association (December 1984) in Washington, D.C. The session was on orality and literacy. After I concluded my talk, a woman approached me and told me that she was a teacher in an elementary school where fairy tales were constantly being retold, largely by the girls. She then asked me whether I wanted to hear a Cinderella version that was told by some girls in the fifth and sixth grades at her school. Of course, I said. Well, she said, the plot is basically the same except that Cinderella is told by her fairy godmother that her vagina will turn into a pumpkin if she does not return to her house on time. When the prince dances with her, she is not particularly impressed by him. In fact, she is more concerned about having fun with other people and returning home on time. However, the prince is so dazzled by her beauty that he asks her to marry him. She refuses. He persists. Finally she asks him his name. Peter Peter Pumpkin-Eater, he says. Well, then, Cinderella replies, that's a different story.

And, indeed, it is and will be a different story.

CHAPTER NINE

FAIRY TALE AS MYTH/ MYTH AS FAIRY TALE

The Immortality of Sleeping Beauty and Storytelling

1

(She speaks . . .)
I wish the Prince had left me where he found me,
Wrapped in a rosy trance so charmed and deep
I might have lain a hundred years asleep.
I hate this new and noisy world around me!
The palace hums with sightseers from town,
There's not a quiet spot that I can find.
And worst of all, he's chopped the brambles down –
The lovely briars I've felt so safe behind.

But if he thinks that with a kiss or two
He'll buy my dearest privacy, or shake me
Out of the cloistered world I've loved so long,

tern of my dream, he's wrong.
umsy trespasser can do
uch my heart, or really wake.

2

(He speaks . . .)
I used to think that slumbrous look she wore,
The dreaming air, the drowsy-lidded eyes,
Were artless affectation, nothing more.
But now, and far too late, I realize
How sound she sleeps, behind a thorny wall
Of rooted selfishness, whose stubborn strands
I broke through once, to kiss her lips and hands,
And wake her heart, that never woke at all.

I wish I'd gone away that self-same hour,
Before I learned how, like her twining roses,
She bends to her own soft, implacable uses
The pretty tactics that such vines employ,
To hide the poisoned barb beneath the flower,
To cling about, to strangle, to destroy.

—*Sandra Henderson Hay, "The Sleeper"*[1]

When we think of the fairy tale today, we primarily think of the classical fairy tale. We think of those fairy tales that are the most popular in the Western world: "Cinderella," "Snow White," "Little Red Riding Hood," "Sleeping Beauty," "Rapunzel," "Beauty and the Beast," "Rumpelstiltskin," "The Ugly Duckling," "The Princess and the Pea," "Puss in Boots," "The Frog King," "Jack and the Beanstalk," "Tom Thumb," "The Little Mermaid," and so on. It is *natural* to think mainly of these fairy tales, as if they had always been with us, as if they were part of our nature. Newly written fairy tales, especially those that are innovative and radical, are unusual, exceptional, strange, and artificial because they do not conform to the patterns set by the classical fairy tale. And, if they do conform and become familiar, we tend to forget them after a while, because the classical fairy tale suffices. We are safe with the familiar. We shun the new, the real innovations. The classical fairy tale makes it appear that we are all part of a universal community with shared values and norms; that we are all striving for the same happiness; that there are certain dreams and wishes which are irrefutable; that a particular type of behavior will produce guaranteed results, like living happily ever after with lots of gold in a marvelous castle, *our* castle and fortress, which will forever protect us from inimical and unpredictable forces of the outside world. We need only have faith and believe in the classical fairy tale, just as we are expected to have faith and believe in the American flag as we swear the pledge of allegiance.

The fairy tale is myth. That is, the classical fairy tale has undergone a process of mythicization. Any fairy tale in our society, if it seeks to become natural and eternal, must become myth. Only innovative fairy tales are anti-mythical, resist the tide of mythicization, and comment on the fairy tale as myth. Even the classical myths are no longer valid as Myths with a capital "M" but with a small "m." That is, the classical myths have also become ideologically mythicized, dehistoricized, and depoliticized to represent and maintain the hegemonic interests of the bourgeoisie. Classical myths and fairy tales are contemporary myths that pervade our daily lives in the manner described by Roland Barthes in *Mythologies*[2] and in *Image—Music—Text.*[3] For Barthes, myth is a collective representation that is socially determined and then inverted so as not to appear as a cultural artifact.

> Myth consists in overturning culture into nature or, at least, the social, the cultural, the ideological, the historical into the "natural." What is nothing but a product of class division and its moral, cultural and aesthetic consequences is presented (stated) as being a "matter of course"; under the effect of mythical inversion, the quite contingent foundations of the utterance become Common Sense, Right Reason, the Norm, General Opinion, in short the *doxa* (which is the secular figure of the Origin).[4]

As a message and type of verbal or visual speech, contemporary myth is derived from a semiological system that has undergone and continues to undergo a historical-political development. Paradoxically, the myth acts to deny its historical and systematic development. It takes material that already has a signification and reworks it parasitically to make it suitable for communication in an ideological mode that appears nonideological. Barthes argues

Figure 9.1. Household Stories from the Collection of the Brothers Grimm, *Trans. Lucy Crane, London: Macmillan, 1882.* Illustration: *Walter Crane.*

that "myth is a double system; there occurs in it a sort of ubiquity: its point of departure is constituted by the arrival of a meaning."[5] Essentially, it is the concept behind the formation of the myth that endows it with a value or signification so that the form of the myth is totally at the service of the concept. Myth is manipulated speech. Or, as Barthes defines it, "myth is a type of speech defined by its intention . . . much more than by its literal sense . . . and in spite of this, its intention is somehow frozen, purified, eternalized, *made absent* by this literal sense."[6] As frozen speech, myth

> suspends itself, turns away and assumes the look of a generality: it stiffens, it makes itself look neutral and innocent. . . . On the surface of language something has stopped moving: the use of the signification is here, hiding behind the fact, and conferring on it a notifying look; but at the same time, the fact paralyses the intention, gives it something like a malaise producing immobility: in order to make it innocent, it freezes it. This is because myth is speech *stolen and restored.* Only, speech which is restored is no longer quite that which was stolen: when it was brought back, it was not put exactly in its place. It is this brief act of larceny, this moment taken for a surreptitious faking, which gives mythical speech its benumbed look.[7]

The fairy tale, which has become the mythicized classical fairy tale, is indeed petrified in its restored constellation: It is a stolen and frozen cultural good, or *Kulturgut,* as the Germans might say. What belonged to archaic societies, what belonged to pagan tribes and communities, was passed down by word of mouth as a good—only to be hardened into script, Christian and patriarchal. It has undergone and undergoes a motivated process of revision, reordering, and refinement. All the tools of modern industrial society (the printing press, the radio, the camera, the film, the record, the videocassette) have made their mark on the fairy tale to make it classical, ultimately in the name of the bourgeoisie, which refuses to be named and denies involvement, for the fairy tale must appear harmless, natural, eternal, ahistorical, and therapeutic. We are to live and breathe the classical fairy tale as fresh, free air. We are led to believe that this air has not been contaminated and polluted by a social class that will not name itself, wants us to continue believing that all air is fresh and free, and all fairy tales spring from thin air.

Take Sleeping Beauty. Her story is frozen. It appears to have always been there, and with each rising sun, she, too, will always be there, flat on her back, with a prince hovering over her, kissing her or about to kiss her. In Charles Perrault's version we read:

> He approached, trembling and admiring, and knelt down beside her. At that moment, the enchantment having ended, the princess awoke and bestowed upon him a look more tender than a first glance seemed to warrant.
>
> "Is it you, my prince?" she said. "You have been long awaited."[8]

In the *Children's and Household Tales* of the Brothers Grimm, we read: "Finally, he came to the tower and opened the door to the small room in which Brier Rose was asleep. There she lay, and her beauty was so marvelous that he could not take his eyes off her. Then he leaned over and gave her a kiss, and when his lips touched hers, Brier Rose opened her eyes, woke up, and looked at him fondly."[9]

Just the presence of a man in the Perrault version of 1697 is enough to break the enchantment and revive the princess. The Grimms added the kiss in 1812 to bring her back to life. What noble men the princes of Perrault and the Grimms are! They make us forget their literary ancestors in the fourteenth-century romance *Perceforest* and in Giambattista Basile's *Pentamerone*, two works that prefigured the revised tales by Perrault and the Grimms. We are not to remember that the anonymous author of *Perceforest* mocked the chivalrous code of courtly love and portrayed a more realistic picture of a knight taking advantage of a sleeping lady.[10] We are not to recall the scene in Basile's tale, "Sun, Moon, and Talia," which reads as follows:

> The king ordered one of his attendants to knock at the door, thinking that someone was living there. But after he had knocked for a long time, the king sent a servant to find a ladder that was used in the vineyards so that he could climb up himself and see whether there was someone inside. And after he climbed up and entered the palace and walked all over, he was perplexed that he had encountered not a single soul in the place. Finally, he reached the room in which Talia was sitting, as if under a

Figure 9.2. Les Contes de Perrault, *Paris: J. Hetzel, 1867*. Illustrator: *Gustav Doré*.

> magic spell, and as soon as the king saw her, he thought she was asleep. So he called to her, but she did not awake, no matter how much he touched her or cried out to her. Her beauty, however, set him afire, and he carried her in his arms to a bed, where he gathered the fruits of life and then left her asleep in the bed. Afterward he returned to his kingdom, where, for a long time, he forgot about all that had happened.[11]

This material and similar motifs from *Perceforest*, in which the sleeping woman is violated, became the stuff of myth.[12] Crucial here is the notion of salvation: How is the princess to be saved? The act of resolution is a moral act, and it is apparent that the salvation of a sleeping princess in the Baroque period was secondary to the fulfillment of male sexual passion and power. That is, the description of the raw power of princes and knights who exploited sleeping women corresponded to social reality. In such situations it was predictable and permissible for a man to take advantage of a defenseless woman. Later, in Perrault's times, this behavior continued, but it was not openly condoned, and thus Perrault pointed to a different moral resolution when he rewrote Basile's tale. But Perrault's version still incorporated some vulgar aspects in the depiction of the ogress, and contained a strange second part with the prince's mother, an ogress, involved in cannibalistic acts. So, eventually, it was the Grimms' shorter, more prudent version that became frozen into a bourgeois myth about the proper way that males save and are to save comatose women. In our day its consummate representation is the Disney film adaptation, which made many myths out of the already "bourgeoisified" fairy tale of the Grimms. Here Sleeping Beauty as a housewife-in-training sings "some day my prince will come," and the prince as "the great white hope," not unlike Rocky, does battle with the black forces of evil. Disney was a mythomaniac in the broadest sense of the word, and in his hands, "Sleeping Beauty" conveyed numerous seemingly innocent and neutral messages as maxims:

1. Women are all naturally curious, and, as we know, curiosity kills cats and even sweet, innocent princesses.
2. Men are daring, persistent, and able to bestow life on passive or dead women whose lives cannot be fulfilled until rescued by a prince.
3. Women are indeed helpless without men, and without men they are generally catatonic or comatose, eternally waiting for the right man, always in a prone, death-like position, dreaming of a glorious marriage.
4. Male energy and will power can restore anything to life, even an entire castle filled with people in a coma, perhaps even all the people in an immense kingdom. We just need the right man for the job.

These are still the mythic messages of "Sleeping Beauty" today. The ancient, communal signification and the literary antecedents are buried and lost—although there are signs here and there that the oral tale with the sleeping beauty motif may have come from a tradition of resurrection, from a reawakening. In general, the tale's history (and her-story) are made speechless by the restored, symbolic constellation that was told in different forms hundreds of years ago and first molded in script back in the fourteenth century. Whatever the tale enunciated hundreds of years ago is less important than the myth it has become and its mythic components, which are singled out and issued as enjoyable and enchanting commodities. We find replications of the classical version everywhere, in illustrated books, in advertisements, on the internet, in daily enactments on the streets, and in our homes.

Yet, just as the classical fairy tale could not totally rob the older folk versions and the literary predecessors of their signification, the myth cannot rob the classical fairy tale of the utopian impulse of the earlier versions. There is something historically indelible about the utopian wish for a better life in a first-told tale, even though we may never know when it was first told or written down. The myth, which is artificial, can only live and seem natural because the essence of the ancient folk tale refuses to die. *The contemporary myth is not only an ideological message but also a fairy tale that cannot totally abandon its ancient utopian origins.*

"Sleeping Beauty" is not only about female and male stereotypes and male hegemony, it is also about death, our fear of death, and our wish for immortality. Sleeping Beauty is resurrected. She triumphs over death. As the eternal brier rose, she rises from the dead to love and to fulfill her desires. The rising from the dead is an uprising, an attack on the borders of mortality. After her uprising, Sleeping Beauty will know how to avoid danger and death, as indeed she does in the aftermath of the first sequence in the Perrault version. Once awakened, Sleeping Beauty is the knowing one, and we know, too.

The first-told fairy tale imparts knowledge about the world and illuminates ways to better it in anticipation of a better world to be created by humankind. It is wise and sincere in tendency, and no matter how hardened and ideologically classical it becomes, it retains a good deal of its original wisdom and sincerity. Each innovative retelling and rewriting of a well-known tale in the cultural heritage is an independent human act seeking to align itself with the original utopian impulse of the first-told tale. On the other hand, the myth is pretentious and deceitful. It seeks to distort the utopian essence and tendency of fairy tales by making "ideographs" out of them. Myth lulls to sleep, to complacency. However, the creative wish to change, to narrate one's own destiny, to bring the utopian dream to fruition, remains alive and awake beneath the intended perversion. It knows what it wants.

But the classical fairy tale's knowing and knowledgeable core, awake and alive as it is, will not be realized as long as myth fetishizes it as a commodity. The myth can only be seen again as fairy tale when the myth is estranged. This means that the frozen constellation must become unfamiliar again; it must be thawed by innovative tales that disassemble the used components of knowing and knowledge and reassemble them into anti-mythic stories.

The revival or resurrection of Sleeping Beauty, our symbolic figure of hope against the forces of death, cannot occur for us in the classical version today, for its sexist closure, its pristine heterosexual and patriarchal resolution, is a coffin of another kind. The resurrection must take place, take its place outside the mythic framework in such re-creations as Anne Sexton's *Transformations*, Olga Broumas's *Beginning with O*, Jane Yolen's *Sleeping Ugly*, and Martin Waddell's *The Tough Princess*. Both Sexton and Broumas, in particular, seek to break the prisonhouse of male discourse. Sexton writes:

> I must not sleep
> for while asleep I'm ninety
> and think I'm dying.[13]

She questions whether the awakening is an awakening, and thus opens our eyes to the desperate situation of women, whose "resurrected" lives may be just as bad as their deaths.

> God help—
> this life after death?[14]

Whereas Sexton is overly pessimistic in her "transformations," Broumas is stridently optimistic in her version of "Sleeping Beauty" and flaunts society's taboos.

> we cross the street, kissing
> against the light, singing, *This*
> *is the woman I woke from sleep, the woman that woke*
> *me sleeping.*[15]

Though not as radical as Sexton's and Broumas' poetical versions, which were intended for adults, Yolen's *Sleeping Ugly*,[16] with humorous pictures by Diane Stanley, is a compelling parody of "Sleeping Beauty" for children that makes one question the mythic ramifications of the classical tale. It concerns the beautiful Princess Miserella, who is nasty and mean. She gets lost in the woods, kicks a little old fairy, and demands that she help her find her way out of the woods. Instead of helping her, however, the fairy takes her to Plain Jane's cottage, where they are hospitably received. Impressed by Plain Jane's manners and good heart, the fairy grants her three wishes. However, out of kindness, Plain Jane is compelled to use two of them to save Princess Miserella from the magic spells of the fairy, who punishes the princess for her temper tantrums. Then, when she wants to punish the princess a third time, the fairy accidentally puts the two young women and herself to sleep for 100 years. At the end of the 100 years, a poor but noble prince named Jojo, the youngest son of a youngest son, finds them, and being a reader of fairy tales, he knows that he can wake the princess with a kiss. Since he is out of practice, however, he warms up by kissing the fairy and Plain Jane, who then uses her third wish to hope he will fall in love with her. Indeed, Jojo turns to kiss the princess but stops because she reminds him of his two cousins who are pretty on the outside but ugly within. So he proposes to Plain Jane. They marry, have three children, and use the sleeping princess either as a conversation piece or a clothes tree in their hallway. Moral of the story: "Let sleeping princesses lie or lying princesses sleep, whichever seems wisest."[17]

Though provocative, Yolen's tale ends on a traditional, homespun note that subverts her questioning of the classical tale. Much more interesting and daring is Waddell's *The Tough Princess*, with illustrations by Patrick Benson.[18] This unusual tale concerns a king and queen who are not very good at what they do. They keep losing wars and kingdoms, and end up living in a caravan in some deep dark wood. When the queen becomes pregnant, they hope their child will be a boy who will grow up to be a hero, marry a princess, and restore their fortunes. Instead, they have a daughter, who grows up to be very tall and tough-minded. Her parents try to find a bad fairy who will get the princess into trouble so a prince will come and rescue her. But the Princess Rosamund knocks out a fairy and goes off on the king's bike to find her own prince. She has numerous adventures, yet she cannot find a prince worthy of her. Then she hears of an enchanted prince in an enchanted castle. She bashes up several goblins, ghouls, and fairies until she finds a sleeping prince, whom she kisses. He jumps out of bed and puts up his fists, and she puts her fists up, too, ready to fight. However, their eyes meet, and they fall in love. So they bike off together and live happily ever after. This radical parody, with unusual illustrations depicting a tattered feudal world mixed with modern inventions and notions, undermines the mythic constellation of the classical "Sleeping Beauty." Intended for young audiences, the book is a delight for all ages, demanding a rereading and rethinking of what we hold to be true and beautiful.

The innovative adaptations by Sexton, Broumas, Waddell, and Benson—and there are many others[19]—make the fairy-tale genre more fluid. They start again as tales that revitalize the tradition of first-told tales, rather than freezing it. Innovative tales explore the dormant potential of the classical tales to bestow knowledge on us, and unlike myth, they free ancient knowledge in the *name* of an author who is not afraid to declare her or his allegiance. Innovative fairy tales take sides, are partial, and name their class allegiance. They question the illusion of happiness and universality in the classical tales and make us realize how far we have yet to go to bring the anticipatory illuminations of concrete utopia to fulfillment. They do not deceive with their symbols and metaphors, but illuminate. "Once upon a time" in the classical fairy tale refers to the point in the past that was a *genuine* beginning. There was no myth then, and even though myth is the dominant form of the fairy tale today, it cannot freeze the genuine beginning forever. "Once upon a time" keeps shining, and its rays seep through the mythic constellation to tell the tale again on its own terms, on our own new terms, which embody that which has yet to come. The myth—despite itself—urges us to innovate in the form of a fairy tale that has not completely forgotten its utopian origins.

But to recall the utopian impulse of fairy-tale narrative, to keep the utopian impulse of the sociocultural act alive, it is not only necessary to demythicize the classical fairy tales but also to expose the mythic connotations of fairy-tale illustrations. Therefore, in analyzing "Sleeping Beauty," it is not only the printed text that must be considered but the pictures and images. Yet even before we begin an analysis of different contemporary illustrated versions of "Sleeping Beauty," we must go back in history to gain a perspective on the present signification of fairy-tale illustration.

If we date the rise of the printed fairy tale with the development of the literary fairy-tale vogue in France at the end of the seventeenth century,[20] it is apparent that fairy tales were hardly, if ever, illustrated. (Even in the early nineteenth century the tales were rarely illustrated. The first edition of the Grimms' tales had none.) This is due to the fact that fairy tales were originally written down for adults, who were to use their imaginations to conceive the contours of fairy realms. In addition, it was technically difficult and costly to print illustrations. If they were produced, then they were individual engravings or woodcuts to highlight a pivotal scene of the narrative. Many such illustrations could be found in the early chapbooks. The situation remained essentially the same in Europe and America until the end of the eighteenth century. Then, as fairy tales became more acceptable for children and as technical inventions made it less expensive to print illustrations, more and more fairy-tale pictures began to appear.

Thus it was during the nineteenth century that precedents were set for fairy-tale illustrations which have exerted a great influence up to the present:

1. There was the single illustration of a tale in an anthology of fairy tales or treasury of stories for children or in a chapbook for a general audience. The single illustration tended to capture the essence of the tale in a specific scene and reinforce a particular message either explicitly or implicitly.
2. The broadsheet, also known as the broadside, the *Bilderbogen,* the *image populaire,* was a single sheet of cheap paper with anywhere from 9 to 24 small pictures in a sequence with captions that related the basic incidents of the tale. The broadsheets, inexpensively printed in black and white and color and developed for a mass audience, were the forerunners of the comic book.
3. Collections by a single author such as Charles Perrault, the Grimms, Hans Christian Andersen, Ludwig Bechstein, and Wilhelm Hauff were often illustrated with one

or more pictures per tale, depending on the size of the edition.

4. Single tales were often fully illustrated by the end of the nineteenth century in the form of toybooks. Previous to the toybooks, there were cheap penny books with black and white woodcuts.
5. Fairy-tale illustrations were used for the advertisements of commodities such as shoes, soap, cereals, medicine, and so on.
6. Fairy-tale postcards were produced illustrating a single scene, or sometimes six or more cards were manufactured to illustrate a series of key scenes from a tale.

During the nineteenth century, the illustrator was generally presented with a text and instructed as to how many scenes were to be depicted and how to design them according to the taste of the intended audience. Depending on what method was being used—woodcutting, engraving, lithography, and so on—the illustrator would work with a craftsman who would engrave a drawing. If the illustrations were to be in color, the illustrator would also work with the printer to make sure that the colors suited his design and taste.

Publishers did not choose to print fairy tales with illustrations because they were connoisseurs and believed that the illustrations would enhance the artistic merit of the texts. They chose to print fairy-tale illustrations because the market for fairy tales had changed: The tales gradually became acceptable wares for children of the middle class during the nineteenth century, and the illustrations made the books more attractive. In addition, fairy tales were cheap to print and illustrate as old texts were used or adapted, and new authors did not have to be paid. Often the texts were quickly written and translated and poorly produced. This type of sloppy work was also true of most of the fairy-tale illustration in the nineteenth century: It was considered hack work to be done by hack illustrators or craftsmen. Nevertheless, there were gifted artists who came to dedicate their skills to the development of fairy-tale illustration, such as George Cruikshank, Ludwig Grimm, Gustav Doré, Richard Doyle, Arthur Hughes, Alfred Crowquill, Ludwig Richter, Walter Crane, and Warwick Goble.

Figure 9.3. *Sir Arthur Quiller-Couch.* The Sleeping Beauty and Other Fairy Tales, *London: Hodder and Stoughton, 1910.* Illustrator: *Edmund Dulac.*

In other words, the production of fairy-tale illustrations was at first in the hands of men, who were commissioned by publishers (generally men) to design illustrations for a particular book. Fairy-tale illustration and production were established and designed in accordance with male fantasies. The imaginative fairy-tale projections served the underlying desires and ideas of a patriarchal culture. The source of production of a fairy-tale illustration was constituted by: the artist, the author/editor, the technician, the book designer, and last but not least, the publisher.

Depending on the publisher's policy and the type of publication, the illustration could have such different functions as: (1) decoration; (2) analogue of the text; (3) commentary on the text. As an analogue to the text, the illustration had a denotative function to reinforce the lines of the text to which it referred without deviating from the apparent, literal meaning of those lines. As a commentary on the text, the illustration had a connotative function to refer to a concept (or signified) beyond the apparent meaning of the text. Naturally, the illustration could be and often is analogue and commentary at the same time. Yet, for the most part, fairy-tale illustration was developed along ideological lines as an intended commentary on the text. In his essay "Rhetoric of the Image," Barthes makes the following point about drawings, which are applicable to illustrations:

> The coded nature of the drawing can be seen at three levels. Firstly, to reproduce an object or a scene in a drawing requires a set of *rule-governed* transpositions; there is no essential nature of the pictorial copy and the codes of transposition are historical (notably those concerning perspective). Secondly, the operation of the drawing (the coding) immediately necessitates a certain division between the significant and the insignificant: the drawing does not reproduce *everything* (often it reproduces very little), without its ceasing, however, to be a strong message; whereas the photograph, although it can choose its subject, its point of view and its angle, cannot intervene *within* the object (except by trick effects).... Finally, like all codes, the drawing demands an apprenticeship.... It is certain that the coding of the literal prepares and facilitates connotation since it at once establishes a certain discontinuity in the image: the "execution" of a drawing itself constitutes a connotation.[21]

The connotative aspect of the "Sleeping Beauty" illustrations is its most intriguing one since it demonstrates how little the story's ideological mythic message has changed since the nineteenth century to the present. If we study three recent "Sleeping Beauty" books by a group of unusually gifted writers and illustrators, we shall see how astonishingly little has been altered since the early nineteenth century with regard to the sociopolitical gesture of text and image. The three books I propose to analyze are *The Sleeping Beauty* retold and illustrated by Trina Schart Hyman,[22] *The Sleeping Beauty* retold and illustrated by Mercer Mayer,[23] and *The Sleeping Beauty* retold by Jane Yolen and illustrated by Ruth Sanderson.[24]

A few general preliminary remarks before I comment on the works separately. Each edition is large, approximately 8 x 11", and sumptuously illustrated in lavish colors. In hardback, they cost $12.95, $13.95, and $14.95, respectively—expensive when they were first published, so that it is apparent that the books were *not* intended for the eyes of *most* children. When such books are bought, then they will be purchased most likely by the affluent in our society, and one must pose the question whether the text and illustrations confirm the myths by which affluent people govern their lives, and indirectly intend to set models for anyone who comes into contact with them. On the other hand, we must not forget that the mass public is treated to cheaper versions, such as Walt Disney's *Sleeping Beauty* in book and film versions, so that the myth of Sleeping Beauty is widespread and is intended to confirm *not* the make-believe but what we believe to be true and natural. As myths, fairy-tale illustrations are presented as statements of fact, of naturalness, of maxims.

Hyman's *Sleeping Beauty* is the only book with a cover that depicts the prince sitting on the ledge of a wide arched window with vines and flowers on its borders and peering into the distance, which has a road leading to sun-lit mountains. The rugged-looking prince definitely has a goal in mind. We can tell this by his determined look, and his look will impel him and us to take a journey to a faraway realm, which is sequentially depicted in autumn, winter, and spring as we turn to the title pages. And, if we flip the book to the back, we can see immediately what his goal is: He stands and holds his prize, a young, beautiful and smiling princess,

Figure 9.4. *From* The Sleeping Beauty, *retold and illustrated by Trina Schart Hyman. Copyright © 1977 by Trina Schart Hyman. By permission of Little, Brown and Company.*

in his powerful arms. It is as if she were swept off her feet. This scene takes place seemingly before the same stone-edged arched window trimmed by the same vines and flowers that we encountered at the onset of his adventure. But this time, there is a castle in the background with a path leading to it. Given the front and

Figure 9.4. *From* The Sleeping Beauty, *retold and illustrated by Trina Schart Hyman. Copyright © 1977 by Trina Schart Hyman. By permission of Little, Brown and Company.*

back cover, it is really not necessary to look at the rest of the pictures or the text: There are no contents. There is no substance. The meaning of the narrative has been framed and formalized from the moment we look at the prince looking into the distance, and it is defined explicitly on the back cover. The goal of every prince (every man) is fulfilled by a beautiful, long-haired young woman with a fair complexion, and she is connected to a castle or money and power. The sleeping beauty's meaning in life was introduced to us on the cover. It is through the prince's kiss that she is resurrected.

Hyman does nothing original in her retold version or in her illustrations. In fact, the text is incidental to the pictures. She has 21 double-page illustrations, all more or less shaped in the form of an arch or an arched window to emphasize the motif of gazing, peeking, peering. This appears to be associated with a utopian motif in her artwork: It is in the distance, beyond us, that we can find the answer to the mystery of life. Yet this apparent openness is deceptive, for everything is preordained in Hyman's illustrations by her adherence to the text and to the myth of patriarchal order. The ordering of the pictures and the opulent forms do not reveal the slightest questioning of the mythic connotations of the Grimm text, which she has barely altered. Her artwork is cute and decorative, intended to make the misfortune of a young woman appear to be adventurous and fortunate.

In contrast to Hyman, Mercer Mayer endeavors to question the mythic narrative of "Sleeping Beauty" by altering the classical Grimm text in an original manner. In this version the king, who marries a stable girl and makes her his queen, causes the Blue Faerie to cast two curses on them because of his negligence and jealousy. One of them leads their daughter to fall into a deep sleep, and she can only be wakened if one who loves her more than life finds her. One hundred years later the son of the Blue Faerie, a prince, who knew the story of Sleeping Beauty and felt destined to save her, sets out to find her. His mother had disappeared, and his father the king cannot dissuade him. First, however, he must prove that he is willing to forfeit his life for her if he is to be successful. After surviving difficult temptations and overcoming obstacles, the prince finds and kisses the princess, who had followed his adventures in her dreams. At their marriage, the Blue Faerie appears in an attempt to destroy them, but her own evil causes her downfall. Sleeping Beauty and her prince have children and eventually die, "but beyond time they live in eternity as we shall all do."[25]

Mayer's version adds interesting dimensions to the characters and plot of the narrative. Sleeping Beauty's mother is a remarkable woman, whereas her father shows certain weaknesses. The evil faerie is much more complex, and so is the prince, her son, who seeks to undo the bad that she has done. Once wakened, Sleeping Beauty takes an active role in determining her future. These textual alterations were apparently made to counter the sexist bias and mythic connotations of the classical text. However, without a more radical revision and questioning of the Sleeping Beauty myth, the illustrations convey many of the same messages of those renditions that merely repeat the classical tale. Mayer provides 16 pastel drawings to illustrate his story set apart from the text, thus emphasizing the need to look at both text and illustration, since not all the scenes may be familiar. However, the key scenes are all there: the birth, the curse, the spindle, the awakening, and the marriage. And though they are charming due to the simple, elegant lines and soft colors, Mayer's illustrations remain traditional and re-posit the myth of male adventure and prowess in slightly different hue and form. The key scene on the cover, repeated toward the end of the book, represents a tender male hovering over a beautiful, long-haired princess dressed in jewels and a gold-trimmed green gown. His clothes are torn, for he has made his way through the thorn bushes, and the jeweled handle of his sword protrudes from his scabbard. We cannot fail to get the message.

Nor can we fail to get the message from the cover of Ruth Sanderson's *The Sleeping Beauty*. Even though her technique is flawless, the results are disappointing. Sanderson states:

> Because I wanted the people in the book to look as if they actually lived and breathed, I sought out models who embodied as closely as possible my ideal conceptions of the characters. (Often, though, I had to greatly exaggerate a model's features to get the effect I wanted.) After having all the costumes made for all the characters, I took photographs, and, consulting these photographs and other reference materials (books on castles, etc.), I drew sketches for the entire book. Then I painted the illustrations in oils on stretched canvas. All the paintings are about three times the size of the printed illustrations. I work on this larger scale because I enjoy adding many details to the pictures, and because they look even sharper when reduced.[26]

Figure 9.5. *From* The Sleeping Beauty *by Jane Yolen, illustrated by Ruth Sanderson. Copyright © 1986 by The Tempest Co. Used by permission of Alfred A. Knopf, a division of Random House, Inc.*

But what does all this work yield? Another stone-edged arched window trimmed with vines and flowers. In contrast to Hyman's cover, we are asked this time to look inside at a handsome young prince dressed in a medieval costume hovering over a sleeping, long-haired, fair princess. This portrayal is no doubt an accurate representation of Yolen's text. Or is it Yolen's text? She did not change the Grimms' version in any remarkable fashion except to make it flow better. Are the illustrations really Sanderson's? She has used the Pre-Raphaelites as models and designed a book with renaissance flavor and taste, but her technique and her compositions are imitative and only serve to repeat what we have always known to be true about sleeping princesses: They will never wake up to face reality unless wakened by a valorous, handsome prince.

The illustrations by Hyman, Mayer, and Sanderson, despite their artistic qualities, reveal nothing new about Sleeping Beauty and nothing new about the myth that surrounds her sleep. The compositions are not critical commentaries on the text but extensions bound by prescriptions that tie the artists' hands to draw not what they see and know but what the text and society mean to uphold. We pride ourselves in the days of postmodernism, poststructuralism, postindustrialism, and post–women's liberation that we have left the sexist connotations of children's books and illustrations behind us. Perhaps my discussion of Sleeping Beauty, the fairy tale as myth, will reveal that it is not so much Sleeping Beauty who needs to be wakened from a trance, but we as readers and creators of fairy tales—that is, if we want our imaginations really to be challenged and our eyes to behold new horizons qualitatively different from the scenes of our present illustrated fairy-tale books.

CHAPTER TEN

THE STRUGGLE FOR THE GRIMMS' THRONE

The Legacy of the Grimms' Tales in East and West Germany since 1945

No sooner did World War II come to a close than explanations were urgently sought to explain why the Germans had committed such atrocious acts as those discovered in the concentration camps. Given the importance that fairy tales played in the German socialization process, particularly the Grimms' tales, it was not by chance that the occupation forces, led by the British, briefly banned the publication of fairy tales in 1945.[1] According to the military authorities, the brutality in the fairy tales was partially responsible for generating attitudes that led to the acceptance of the Nazis and their monstrous crimes. Moreover, the tales allegedly gave children a false impression of the world that made them susceptible to lies and irrationalism.

The decision by the occupation forces led the Germans themselves to debate the value of fairy tales,[2] and it should be noted that the Grimms' tales were practically synonymous with the general use of the term *Märchen*. That is, the Grimms' collection, especially during the Nazi regime, had become identical with a German national tradition and character, as if all the Grimms' tales were "pure" German and belonged to the German cultural tradition. Therefore, unless a distinction was made in the discussions about fairy tales and folk tales after 1945, it was always understood that one meant the Grimms' tales. They ruled the realm of this genre, and thus they were also held partially responsible for what had happened during the German Reich.

Although the ban against publishing fairy tales was lifted by 1946, the discussion about their brutality and connection to Nazism continued into the early 1950s. There were two general arguments in this debate: (1) the Grimms' tales had conditioned German children to accept brutal acts and prepared them for a savage regime; and (2) the tales had nothing to do with the barbarism of the Nazis, but rather, the cruelty of the Nazis had to be understood in light of traditional German authoritarianism and socioeconomic factors. The controversy over the Grimms' tales was never resolved, largely because the viewpoints expressed could not be documented and because very little research had been done about the effects of fairy tales on children and adults. However, the debate about the Grimms' tales set the tone for their reception in both Germanies, where there were, once upon a time, two distinctive Grimm traditions, in the Federal Republic of Germany (FRG) and the German Democratic Republic (GDR), respectively.

In fact, the overall reception of the Grimms' tales in the postwar period is a complex one, and there are numerous factors that must be taken into consideration, such as: (1) the customary attitude of the German people toward the Grimms' tales as part of their cultural legacy; (2) the policies of publishers and the government; (3) the use of the Grimms' tales at home and in schools, libraries, and the mass media; (4) the influence of scholarly and critical works on the Grimms by academics, psychologists, and folklorists; (5) the differences in the reception of the Grimms' tales by children and adults as well as gender differences; and (6) the references to the Grimms' tales in advertisements, commercials, and cartoons. Since it would be impossible to deal with all these factors in a short chapter, my focus will be limited to the manner in which creative writers in East and West Germany responded to the Grimms' tales in short prose narratives and sought to dethrone the Grimms in one way or another as the ideological rulers of fairy tales. That is, I am concerned most with the *critical and productive* attitudes that German writers bring to their revisions of the Grimms' tales and how their attitudes are articulated in the reformulations of the Grimms' tales. Interestingly, the experiments with the Grimms' tales are not simply to be considered innovative attempts by contemporary writers to come to terms with the legacy of the Brothers Grimm, but they must also be regarded as endeavors that explored, challenged, and defined the cultural determinants and parameters of West and East Germany. In this regard, though there are clear differences between the Grimms' revised tales for children and those for adults, I shall not deal with them at length since these differences are often blurred, and since I am more concerned with the general manner in which the production of new "Grimm-like" tales goes against or with the grain of the Grimms' tradition. In addition, a new phase of "challenges" to the Grimms' throne began after the fall of the Berlin Wall in 1989, and has yet to define itself. What is interesting, however, is that this new phase of German unification may be less nationalistic than the one that occurred in 1876, which in itself was not what the Grimms had envisioned. Ironically, the more recent unification, with Germany representing itself as a "model European" state, might have been much more to the Grimms' liking.

WEST GERMANY

Once the Federal Republic was established in 1949, there was an apparent need to make compromises with the Nazi past and create propitious conditions to reclaim the German classics in the name of democratic humanism. Historians and other academics have often referred to the period of the 1950s as one of nonideology, when Germans were afraid of ideological extremes and preferred a middle if not neutral path in politics. In keeping with the general tendency of so-called nonideology in the 1950s, the Grimms'

Kinder- und Hausmärchen was published and circulated again in the thousands, and many of the tales were published individually in single volumes. Nonideology is a deceptive term. In fact, the prevalent ideological position at this point was anticommunist and procapitalist, with many Germans fearful of conflict and another war. Nonideological, therefore, meant a rejection of Nazism, an avoidance of radical politics of any kind, an acceptance of a capitalist welfare state, and partiality for the conservative middle stream that promised economic security above everything else. Given the conservative, if not patriarchal, nature of the Grimms' tales, they were clearly suited to this period. Moreover, the model of the cleaner, rational bourgeois hero, the Tom Thumb type, would be appealing in this context.

Despite the short ban on fairy tales and the debate about their effect, the reception of the Grimms' tales never really experienced a rupture within the German socialization process. If there was a major change during the 1950s in West Germany, it was the elimination of the explicit racist interpretations and the more violent episodes of the tales in editions intended for children. Otherwise, the Grimms' tales quickly made their way back into the school curricula, libraries, theaters, radio, and even television. A major fairy-tale society called Die Gesellschaft zur Pflege des Märchengutes (The Society for the Preservation of the Fairy-Tale Treasure)[3] was founded in 1955 to perpetuate the fairy-tale tradition, and this group had strong folk, if not "völkisch," tendencies. Indeed, the climate for the reception of the Grimms' tales in the 1950s had not changed radically from that of the 1930s and 1940s: The Grimms' tales were considered "purely" German and healthy for the soul, young and old. The only thing missing was the explicit Nazi ideological framework that had previously set the conditions for the reception of the Grimms' tales.

If one were to talk about schools of thought that influenced the reception from 1949 to approximately the mid-1960s, there were basically four that were all in agreement about the positive nature of the tales: the psychological, the anthroposophical, the structural, and the moralistic. Though their approaches to the tales were and still are different, each one of these currents stressed the healing and educational nature of fairy tales. In the case of the psychological movement, the Jungian school, which had successfully triumphed over Freudian psychology during the 1930s and 1940s, remained dominant. The Jungians traced universal archetypes in all the Grimms' tales and preached the harmony of the anima and animus (that is, the feminine and the masculine) in their interpretations. Readers, so it was and is claimed even today, can learn to become whole, if not wholesome, through the absorption of fairy tales. Closely related to Jungian ideology, the anthroposophical mode of thinking, influenced by Rudolf Steiner and developed in practice at the Waldorf schools, stressed that fairy tales can help us regain touch with the innocence of childhood and oneness with nature. The structural approaches to fairy tales were elaborated in different ways, but they were all geared toward the appreciation of the aesthetic composition of the tales as marvelous artifacts. Content and history were disregarded in favor of the morphological study of the tales, which were purported to be universal statements about the ontological nature of humankind. Here the moralistic approach complemented the structural, insofar as it placed more emphasis on contents. The tales were often treated as transmissions of morals and ethics that contributed to the building of character. Through the emulation of a particular protagonist, one could learn to develop Christian charity, the proper work habits, patience, and so on.

From 1946 to 1966 there were hardly any major revisions of the Grimms' tales. It was as if they were sacrosanct and part of the healing process necessary for the rebuilding of a humanist German culture. There were new collections of folk and fairy tales by other authors, but they were neither explicit nor implicit commentaries on the Grimms' tales, though they may have been somewhat influenced by the Grimms' tales. More important was the prevailing desire of wanting to cure and reconstruct the German nation. Indicative of this attitude was the short preface that Ernst Wiechert wrote for the publication of his two volumes of *Märchen* (*Fairy Tales*) in 1946:

> This book was begun during the last winter of the war when hate and fire scorched the earth and our hearts. It was written for all of the poor children of all of the poor people and for my own heart so that I would not lose my faith in truth and justice. For the world as it is depicted in the fairy tale is not the world of

> miracles and magicians but that of the great and final justice about which the children and people of all times have dreamed.[4]

The more notable collections along the lines of Wiechert's compassionate and stimulating fairy tales published from the immediate postwar period up to 1965 were: Otto Flake, *Kinderland* (*The Land of Children;* 1946), Ina Seidel, *Das wunderbare Geißleinbuch (The Wonderful Book about the Kid Goats,* 1949); Hans Watzlik, *Girliz und Mixel* (1949); Hanns Arens, ed., *Märchen deutscher Dichter der Gegenwart* (*Fairy Tales by Contemporary German Writers,* 1951); and Paul Alverdes, *Vom Schlaraffenland* (*About the Topsy-Turvy World,* 1965). Most of these works were not directly related to the Grimms' tales, but the general conciliatory attitude toward the fairy tale determined the overall reception of the Grimms' tales during this period. Most German writers regarded the tales as a means to cure the evils of the past and to regain a lost innocence. The fairy tales were intended to help bring about a redemption both for children and adults. In those instances where the Grimms' tales were used as the basis for "new" tales, the references to World War II and postwar conditions were also redemptive. Two good examples are Seidel's *Das wunderbare Geißleinbuch* and Arens' *Märchen deutscher Dichter der Gegenwart.*

Though published first in 1925, Seidel's *Geißleinbuch* was reissued in 1949 and reprinted until 1962, and its popular reception reveals how strong the nostalgia for the Grimms' tales and the atavistic mythic tradition remained among Germans. The plot and setting of the book recall a longing for an idyllic, teutonic lifestyle. Young Peter lives with his mother and father on the edge of a forest because his father is a forester. Each night his mother tells him a story, and one evening she tells him the tale about "The Wolf and the Seven Kids." During the narration, Peter asks many questions, and when it is over, his mother has him say his prayers and wishes him sweet dreams about the seven kids. From this point on, Peter has several dreams about visiting the mother goat and her seven kids, and each dream is an adventure that includes characters from the Grimms' tales: Red Riding Hood, her grandmother, the hunter, the Bremen Town Musicians, Hansel and Gretel, and the seven dwarfs. Toward the end of the book, he attends a wedding of a prince and princess and experiences a storm, in which the father goat scares him because the goat, related to the Germanic goat who pulls Thor's coach during storms, jumps all over the place. Peter is comforted by the mother goat, who in the end turns into his own mother holding him on her lap and whispering that it was only a dream.

Seidel's narrative can be considered a maternal discourse: The tone and style are predicated on nurturing the imagination of the protagonist/young reader and especially on comforting the hero. All the gruesome elements in the Grimms' tales are modified and defused so that the fairy-tale characters appear to be part of one happy family. In fact, the restoration of the family and German tradition through the fairy tale is the major theme of the book, and its atavistic quality made it useful for the healing of the wounds of the postwar period—but it did not point to utopian alternatives for a better future.

Jens Tismar has argued that most of the fairy tales printed or written in the immediate postwar period were mainly concerned with reestablishing continuity with German tradition in an unhistorical and uncritical way.[5] In particular, he criticizes Arens' collection, *Märchen deutscher Dichter der Gegenwart*, for its retrogressive tendencies, and claims that the title is misleading since most of the 41 tales were written before 1945, and many of the authors had contributed to the *völkisch* cause during the Nazi period, including Arens himself.

Evidently Arens' keywords, "contemporary German writers," were to include that period from the end of the nineteenth century to the postwar years as a continuity not to be questioned. In other words, since the Nazi period could not be undone, this fairy-tale book obfuscated the question of politics and art during the fascist period. Instead, it tried to provide the consolation that there were writers who stood above their times and made something beautiful that would last over the years and beyond catastrophes, for none of the contributions to the volume sheds clear light on the postwar historical situation.[6]

As Tismar points out, there are only two tales in this collection that had immediate relevance for the postwar conditions in Germany, and interestingly, they are tales with a direct reference to the Grimms' "The Sweet Porridge" ("Der süße Brei"): Otto Flake's "Das Milchbrünnchen" ("The Little Spring of Milk") and

Luise Rinser's "Das Märchen vom Mäusetöpfchen" ("The Fairy Tale about the Little Mouse Pot"). Flake's tale originally appeared in 1931 and drew an apparent analogy with the great depression of that time. A water spring wishes to provide milk for all those who visit it, and the Christ child grants the spring its wish. However, the people abuse the abundant supply of milk, and the owner of the land makes a business out of it. The Christ child returns to the spring and empowers the spring to provide milk only for helpless animals and those children who tell it a fairy tale in return for the milk. Rinser's tale, written after World War II, involved a poor cleaning woman and her daughter Hanni, who finds a dirty pot among some rubbish. The pot is magical and steals food and supplies from a grocer to help the poor family. The grocer tries to catch and get rid of the pot, but he is put to shame when he learns how poverty-stricken Hanni and her mother are. From that point on, the pot is no longer necessary, for the grocer decides to provide food and provisions for Hanni and her mother at no cost.

The emphasis in both these tales is on Christian charity, compassion for the downtrodden, and survival. Throughout the 1950s these themes reappeared in the analysis of the Grimms' tales, which were regarded as cultural treasures, and in new literary fairy tales, whether or not they relied on motifs and topoi from the Grimms' tales. By the late 1960s, however, the cultural climate and economic conditions in West Germany had changed, and there was little talk about reverence for German tradition, philanthropy, and healing the wounds of the past. If anything, the key slogans of this period had more to do with anti-authoritarianism, rebellion, revamping German tradition, and alternative cultural choices for the future.

In fact, there was a radical break in the reception of the Grimms' fairy tales, and several factors must be considered if one is to grasp the plethora of anti-Grimm fairy tales that have been produced since the 1970s.[7]

- The student movement revolted against all the traditional institutions of culture and education and sought radical models from the Weimar period on which to base their own collective experiments to bring about greater democracy in West Germany, if not socialism. In particular, the work of such progressive educators and psychologists as Siegfried Bernfeld, Otto Kranitz, Otto Rühle, Alfred Adler, and Wilhelm Reich were rediscovered, their ideas were implemented in schools and collective daycare centers, and students began demanding and writing children's books that corresponded to the anti-authoritarian ideology that prevailed from 1968 to 1972.

- Radical fairy-tale proponents and writers from the Weimar period such as Edwin Hoernle, Hermynia zur Mühlen, and Walter Benjamin were rediscovered, and their ideas stimulated contemporary writers to experiment with the traditional fairy tales. Pirate editions of Zur Mühlen's tales and Benjamin's theories were published by radical collectives and had a strong influence on writers and publishers, who began producing anti-authoritarian and feminist fairy tales.
- In keeping with the student movement, left-wing publishing houses were established to promote a progressive children's literature: Basis Verlag, Oberbaum, and Das rote Kinderbuch in Berlin, and Weissmann Verlag in Munich. Major publishers such as Rowohlt, Insel, Campe, and Beltz developed new series of experimental children's books. Radical journals of education were founded such as *betrifft:erziehung* and *päd. extra,* and children's literature became a topic that was discussed in leading journals throughout West Germany. In general, the entire publishing industry underwent a shift in its attitude toward publishing books for children and young adults. While the traditional editions of the Grimms' tales kept appearing, major attempts were made to address pressing social issues that ranged from war, racism, sexism, and economic exploitation to domestic problems, in experimental fairy tales and in a more "realistic" literature that did not address young people in a condescending manner.
- During the 1970s a whole new generation of young teachers entered the school system and initiated reforms that led to a greater demand for new kinds of literature for children that were antisexist, nonracist, and antimilitaristic. These teachers supported cultural experimentation in all the media, including children's theater, films, television, and so on.

- The desire to produce new radical fairy tales came from students and adults, who apparently felt on some deep level that the Grimms' tales, which were so much a part of their early socialization, needed to be reformed. That is, the initiative to topple the Grimms from their throne came from adults and still comes from adults, who imaginatively project alternatives for personal and social action to the deceptive, happy-end closures depicted in the Grimms' tales. In fact, the new fairy-tale realms are often utopian and dystopian options that provoke readers to reconsider the ideological message of the Grimms' tales as well as the prevailing ideology in their immediate surroundings.

Before discussing the different types of fairy tales produced from 1968 to the present by experimental writers, who have explicitly sought to generate fairy tales that have a different sociopolitical tendency than the Grimms' tales, I would like to discuss the significance of a few transitional works to indicate that there were already writers during the 1960s who were dissatisfied with the reception of the Grimms' tales and who desired to embark on a new more adventurous path with the Grimms' tales in mind.

Strikingly, two of the first endeavors to break with the Grimms' tradition were revisions of "Hansel and Gretel"[8]: Hans Traxler's *Die Wahrheit über Hansel und Gretel* (*The Truth about Hansel and Gretel,* 1963) and Paul Maar's "Die Geschichte vom bösen Hänsel, der bösen Gretel und der Hexe" ("The Story about Evil Hansel, Evil Gretel and the Witch," 1968). If any tale from the Grimms' collection had represented the perfect ideological picture of familial reconciliation for Germans after 1945, then it was certainly this tale, which was often performed on stage during Christmas in Engelbert Humperdinck's operatic version. Nothing could be more holy than "Hansel and Gretel" for Germans, and this is exactly why Traxler and Maar created their anti-authoritarian tales. Traxler's book is a sober, tongue-in-cheek scholarly study that purports to demonstrate through photos and sketches of ruins, relics, manuscripts, and other documents that Hansel and Gretel were actually bakers who stole the recipe for the Nürnberger Lebkuchen (Nuremberg gingerbread) from an old woman who lived alone in a forest. Indeed, claims Traxler, who bases his evidence on the work of the researcher Georg Ossegg, Hansel and Gretel killed the old woman to obtain her recipe and became rich and famous because of the old woman's Lebkuchen.

Traxler's book, which has a format similar to a scholarly study, is a parody of the work of folklorists and traditional academics, while at the same time it debunks the idyllic *biedermeier* reception of the tale by transforming it into a tale of murder. Traxler indicates that there is something dark, dangerous, and evil beneath the superficial happy end that the Grimm tale wants to conceal.[9] Like Traxler, Maar reveals in his collection of tales, *Der tätowierte Hund* (*The Tattooed Dog*), intended for young readers, that the poor witch was indeed murdered by Hansel and Gretel, despite the fact that she was kind and wanted to help them. His short tale provokes readers to reconsider the truth about the tale and witches, for he asserts that the witch had lost her powers and had retired to the forest to build the most beautiful "Hexenhaus" in the world. Hansel and Gretel have no respect for her work or her age. Their only concern is to fill their stomachs and steal her jewels—obviously a reference to the pursuit of material well-being of Germans in the 1950s.

Both Traxler and Maar do not want simply to question the "truth" of the Grimms' "Hänsel und Gretel." They want to compel readers to consider possible alternatives to the Grimms' tales and to change the manner in which they receive fairy tales. The truth of the tale is not so much in the contents of the tale itself but in the authoritative and authoritarian rules that govern the way tales are disseminated, interpreted, and accepted.

The key factor at the beginning of the movement to revise the manner in which Germans, young and old, received the Grimms' tales was insubordination. The innovative writers of fairy tales did not want to follow the Grimms' tradition blithely and to subordinate themselves to ideas, rules, laws, and customs that had become suspect. Most typical of the new breed of writer/publisher was Hans-Joachim Gelberg, who played a major role in bringing about a new more emancipatory children's literature in West Germany. Soon after joining the Beltz Verlag, he edited a series of "Jahrbücher der Kinderliteratur" ("Yearbooks of Children's Literature") and promoted the publication of highly experimental fairy tales that departed greatly in style and tone from the Grimms' tale. In section two of his first yearbook, *Geh und Spiel mit dem Riesen* (*Go and Play with the Giant*, 1971), he published 20 different fairy tales in prose, verse, and cartoon, four of which (by Richard Bletschacher, Janosch, Lisa Loviscach, and Iring Fetscher) are direct parodies of Grimms' tales. Gelberg argued in his "Afterword for Adults" that

> the child's need for entertainment is not limited to traditional forms. There are many possibilities to create tension, and a good deal in children's literature begins new and entirely differently every year. Poems, plays, reports, letters, pictures, photos—even the slick advertisements that resound in our ears every day can be fused to new contents if we learn to regard the entertainment of children, their encounter with language and form, not just in a one-dimensional traditional way. And it is in this way that even the good old fairy tale will take on a new aspect.[10]

As an example of what direction he thought the "new" fairy tale should take, he quoted the East German writer Franz Fühmann's poem "Lob des Ungehorsams" ("Praise of Disobedience," 1966), which is important to record in full here:

> They were seven young kids
> and were allowed to look into everything
> with the exception of the clock case,
> for that could ruin the clock,
> so their mother had said.
>
> They were seven good young kids,
> who wanted to look into everything
> with the exception of the clock case,
> for that could ruin the clock,
> so their mother had said.
>
> There was a disobedient kid
> who wanted to look into everything
> even into the clock case,
> and so it ruined the clock,
> just as his mother had said.
>
> Then came the big bad wolf.
>
> There were six good young kids,

> who hid themselves when the wolf came,
> under the table, under the bed, under the chair,
> none in the clock case.
> They were all eaten by the wolf.
>
> There was one naughty young kid,
> who jumped into the clock case,
> for it knew that it was empty.
> The wolf did not find it there,
> and so it remained alive.
>
> Indeed the mother goat was quite glad.[11]

In keeping with the spirit of disobedience, Gelberg published Janosch's "Der Däumling" ("Thumbling"), which is a terse narrative about a son who leaves home forever because he can never please his father, no matter what he accomplishes. Rebellion against fathers and patriarchy was a major theme in German literature of the 1970s. To a certain extent, all the major "revisionist" writers of the Grimms' fairy tales since 1970 break with their fathers via the Brothers Grimm. That is, their rupture with the Grimms or challenge to the Grimms can be viewed as a critique of the older generation in Germany and a desire to project the possibilities for other modes of living and thinking. Chief among the rebellious fairy tale writers is Janosch, whose remarkable book *Janosch erzählt Grimm's Märchen* (1972) signaled that the time for toppling the Grimms from their throne had come. As Gelberg, his publisher in this common affair, remarked in his afterword to this edition:

> The fairy tales of the Brothers Grimm originated in a time long since past and have been passed on by word of mouth. They present social structures that we have since then surpassed or rejected. Their tales indicate that the poor must be humble and obedient—only this way can the poor man from the common people be rewarded, or the miller's daughter marry the rich prince. . . . In many variations and ideas that are often shrewd and continually new, Janosch blurs the schemes of the Grimms' fairy tales and parodies them without forcing anything. There are not many writers who could come to terms with these rigid fairy tales—Janosch senses with a reliable instinct where and

> how the tone of the folk can become captured in language. And yet his [fifty] fairy tales retain something of the timeless "truth" of fairy tales.[12]

Nothing and nobody are sacred for Janosch. His tales debunk the good, clean bourgeois values of the Grimms and reveal how inappropriate they are in the contemporary *Leistungsgesellschaft* (achievement society),[13] in which achievement and money are the standards by which we measure ourselves. In his version of "Hans mein Igel" ("Hans My Hedgehog"), for example, Hans is gladly sent packing by his father because of his strange looks and habits. However, as soon as Hans becomes a famous rock and roll star, he is welcomed back by his father and the entire village. In "Doktor Allwissend" ("Doctor Know-It-All"), a farmer transforms himself into a rich doctor with the help of his wife, who has learned that charlatanism is at the basis of the medical knowledge that most doctors dispense. In "Vom tapferen Schneider" ("About the Brave Tailor"), a tailor is constantly rewarded for killing a king's enemies from afar with weapons that the king places at his disposal. Finally, when the tailor has weapons enough to destroy entire lands, he uses all his courage to connect them, after which he pushes a button, and blows up the entire world. In "König Drosselbart" ("King Thrushbeard"), the daughter of a rich man defies her father, who wants her to marry a wealthy man with a chin like a thrushbeard. She runs away, joins up with a young hippie, and tramps about Europe until life becomes too hard for her. Then she returns home, only to discover that the young hippie is the son of the man with the thrushbeard, and she consents to marry him since he has returned to the fold as well.

Janosch's tales, which he revised and expanded in 1991,[14] deal with generational conflicts, hypocrisy, war, greed, the false dreams of the petty bourgeoisie, and sexism. His drawings and language are terse, sober, and unpretentious. It is as if he were the child from Andersen's "The Emperor's Clothes," seeking to denude the Grimms' tales and the artificiality of contemporary German society.

Indeed, one could summarize the general attitude of the best fairy-tale writers since 1970 as one that seeks to denude the Grimms while exposing all that is false in West German society. But perhaps the expression used by Erich Kaiser is more apropos in describing the attitude of most of the writers who have revised the Grimms' tales. He uses the term *ent-Grimm-te Märchen* (de-Grimmed fairy tales)[15] to describe those tales created by authors who have reacted to an overdose of Grimms' tales and want to get rid of a bad habit by cleansing the tales of negative and useless elements. For him, "the common denominator of the de-Grimmed fairy tales, which are incidentally very different from one another, is therefore the rejuvenation of the basic components that can be utilized by the respective authors for pedagogical, sociopolitical, critical, parodistic, or free poetical purposes."[16]

While "de-Grimmed" can be a useful term for many of the revised Grimms' tales, it suggests depletion or cleansing, and this process does not actually take place. I prefer the political term *Umfunktionierung*, or reutilization, because it suggests that German authors have taken the Grimms' tales and turned their function around so that the motifs and themes of the tales work against the old anachronistic ones through new, more rigorous forms and formulations. A "reutilized" Grimms' tale breaks down the closure of the original to open up new perspectives not only on the original version but on contemporary social conditions and aesthetics. Since there are so many techniques that West German authors have used to reutilize the Grimms' tales, it is not easy to pigeonhole them into categories. However, certain categories can be helpful in describing the various types of experimentation that have been conducted with the Grimms' tales since 1970. In all, I would suggest that there are five basic types: (1) social satire; (2) utopian; (3) pedagogical; (4) feminist; (5) comic parody; and (6) spiritual. Incidentally, such experimentation can be found throughout the world in the twenty-first century. In considering some examples of these types, I would like to emphasize again that I am using them primarily for descriptive purposes because they enable us to understand the critical and productive attitudes of the authors. Of course, the attitudes are often complex, and many of the tales can be considered under two or three headings. For example, a feminist tale may not only be a tale written against sexism and on behalf of women, but it may also be utopian and satirical. In essence, a tale may contain different voices (often depending on the reader) and carry on several dialogues all at the same time. Yet, at bottom, *all* the reutilized Grimms' tales form a dialogue with the famous Brothers and their legacy.

Social Satire

The satirical fairy tales generally have a twofold purpose of debunking the style and ideology of the Grimms' tales and of mocking the prevailing ideology of what was formerly West Germany. Unlike the utopian revisions of the Grimms' tales, no alternatives to the existing social conditions are indicated. As we have seen in the works of Traxler, Maar, and Janosch, most authors of satirical tales demonstrate the destructive, hypocritical, and pathetic aspects of the Grimms' tales and West German society without leaving the reader with much hope for a better future. The general aim of the social satires is provocative and subversive: The reader is to reflect critically about the status quo of the Grimms' tales as classics and their relationship to contemporary social conditions and is challenged *not* to accept the accepted.

Some examples:

Max von der Grün's "Rotkäppchen" ("Little Red Cap," 1972) published in Jochen Jung's anthology *Bilderbogengeschichten* (*Stories from Broadsheets*),[17] transforms the Grimms' tale into a biting satire about conformism in West Germany. Whereas the underlying message of the Grimms' tale is to warn youngsters and set a lesson of obedience, Von der Grün speaks out against conformity by showing how it can lead to fascistic behavior. His little girl, who receives a red cap with a silver star on it as a present, is driven into an outcast state and ultimately attacked by a band of school children because she is different. Such stigmatization recalls Nazi behavior, for only after the girl and her family are beaten into submission, so to say, are they reintegrated into the German community.

Iring Fetscher's *Wer hat Dornröschen wachgeküßt?* (*Who Kissed Sleeping Beauty Awake?* 1972) contains 13 sardonic versions of Grimms' tales, which also mock different critical approaches to the tales such as the philological, psychoanalytical, and historical materialist methods. In his version of Cinderella, entitled "Cinderella's Awakening," Fetscher depicts how the poor exploited maiden does not wait for a fairy godmother to help her. Instead, she organizes all the maids in her town to demand better wages and working conditions. After she founds a union and has success, the prince hears about her, and upon meeting her, he proposes. However, she does not want to betray her working-class movement and tells the prince that if he really loves her, he will convince his father the king to do away with the feudal conditions in his land and to recognize the union. The king reacts violently and has Cinderella arrested. After she serves a prison term, she emigrates to America where there are no princes and kings, and the prince is said to have committed suicide.

In Peter Paul Zahl's "Die Rückkehr der Meisterdiebe" ("The Return of the Master Thieves"), published in the anthology *Deutsche Märchen* (*German Fairy Tales*), edited by Günter Kämpf and Vilma Link,[18] two brothers return home one after the other, after many years of separation, to their poor parents, who live in the Kreuzberg section of Berlin. Since the first one is a common thief, his parents turn him in to the police, and he is imprisoned. The second one is a rich real estate speculator, and he takes care of his parents by sending them to an old age home. Then he buys their decrepit building and has it torn down to make way for a profitable parking lot. Zahl ends his story by commenting, "if he hasn't died yet, he's still, since we live in times in which mere wishing does not help, living today in a splendid villa in the south side of the city."[19]

The acrimonious tone of Zahl's and also Janosch's tales and the sarcastic critique of the false values resulting from the so-called economic miracle in West Germany can also be found in Margaret Kassajep's amusing book, *"Deutsche Hausmärchen" frisch getrimmt* (*"German Household Tales" Freshly Trimmed*, 1980). Her 28 radical tales were originally published in the newspaper *Die Süddeutsche* with a focus on the savage and brutal quality of life in West Germany. For instance, in "Rotkäppchen mit Sturzhelm" ("Little Red Cap with Crash Helmet"), the granddaughter and her friend Wolfi kill grandmother in an old age home because they want her money. Then the two lovers take off for Copenhagen on Wolfi's Suzuki, feeling no remorse about their crime. In "König Drosselbarts Ende" ("The End of King Thrushbeard"), a ruthless entrepreneur drives another businessman into bankruptcy because the businessman's daughter had mocked him during a tennis match and had called him King Thrushbeard. Now poor, the businessman's daughter is driven to study and work hard at menial jobs until she is finally employed by Thrushbeard. Then she puts to use everything she has learned to drive Thrushbeard into bankruptcy and opens her own large bank account in Switzerland.

Utopian Fairy Tales

Whereas the satirical fairy tale often has a skeptical or cynical viewpoint about social change, the plot of the utopian fairy tale most often maps out the possibility for alternative lifestyles. Implicit is a major critique of those Grimms' tales primarily concerned with individual happiness and power: Utopian fairy tales depict change through collective action and equal participation in the benefits of such work. The humor in these tales tends to be more of a burlesque nature than satirical, and the central theme is the overcoming of oppression.

The early children's books of Basis Verlag published at the beginning of the 1970s all tend to have a utopian message. For example, *Zwei Korken für Schlienz* (*Two Corks for Schlienz*) is a highly innovative revision of the Grimms' "How Six Made their Way in the World." Using photographs of real people acting out fictitious roles in contemporary Berlin as illustrations, the story focuses on housing problems and exploitation by landlords. Four young people (all in their twenties) decide to live together: Schlienz, who can smell extraordinarily well; Minzl, who can hear long distances; Gorch, who can run faster than cars; and Atta, who is tremendously strong. They rent an apartment, and the landlord tries to cheat them. However, they are too smart for him, ultimately organizing the tenants in the entire building to fight an arbitrary hike in the rent. Despite the fact that they use their extraordinary talents to the collective's advantage, they have difficulties because the tenants come from different classes (they are a teacher, a bank clerk, a metal worker, an insurance inspector, and a railroad worker) and have different interests. So the landlord is able to play upon the divisiveness in the coalition and, with the help of the police, defeat the tenants' strike. Schlienz, Minzl, Gorch, and Atta are arrested. Nevertheless, while in prison, they reconsider their strategy and make plans so that they can be successful the next time they try to organize the tenants. Although the four heroes (two men and two women) do not succeed, the plot indicates that they are not dejected and hope to learn from their mistakes. Here the emphasis is not so much on gaining a victory but on creating a sense of need for collective action.

However, in Friedrich Karl Waechter's *Tischlein deck dich and Knüppel aus dem Sack* (*Table Be Covered and Stick Out of the Sack*, 1972), there is a victory of the collective, and it is sweet. Waechter's tale takes place in a small town named Breitenrode a long time ago. (From the illustrations by Waechter himself, the time can be estimated to be the early twentieth century.) Fat Jacob Bock, who owns a large lumber mill and most of the town, exploits his workers as much as he can. When a young carpenter named Philip invents a magic table that provides all the food one can eat upon command and a powerful stick that jumps out of a sack to hit people, Bock appropriates these inventions, because they were done on company time. However, Philip, aided by his fellow workers and an elf named Xram (an anagram for Marx spelled backwards), band together and expose Bock's duplicitous ways. Eventually, they drive him out of town and share the fruits of their labor with one another. The reading process of this tale (along with the visuals) becomes a learning process about socialization and work in capitalist society. The workers experience how the products of collective labor are expropriated by Bock, and with the help of Xram (the insights of Marx) they learn to take control of the products of their own labor and share them equally among themselves.

The utopian fairy tales are generally based on wish-fulfillments, yearnings for a better life. In Irmela Brender's "Das Rumpelstilzchen hat mir immer leid getan" ("I Always Felt Sorry for Rumpelstiltskin," 1976), the author suggests that Rumpelstiltskin must have been a gifted but very lonely man, and that if the miller's daughter had proposed to him to join her, the king, and their child, he probably would have accepted, and they *all* would have lived happily ever after. "But the way it is now in the fairy tale, there's no justice."[20]

Pedagogical Fairy Tales

Though they have a similar positive outlook on the possibility for social change as the utopian narratives, the pedagogical fairy tales are more concerned with eliminating violence, sexism, racism, and other elements that the authors consider harmful for children. Therefore, these major revisions of the Grimms' tales pertain to deletions of elements detrimental to the authors' conception of what a good socialization should be. The focus is on depicting the possibilities for harmony and a "healthy" development. There is very little humor in these tales, and whatever innovation there is, is often compromised by a didactic message and contrived closures.

Among the more prominent writers of the pedagogical movement in the early 1970s was Otto F. Gmelin. His critical study, *Böses kommt aus Kinderbüchern* (*Evil Comes from Children's Books*, 1972), argued that "books for children must be oriented functionally in regard to the total social strategy. They must be dialectical insofar as they must first cancel out the perpetual nonsynchronicities and contradictions according to the programmatic sense of an antipatriarchal action put into practice."[21] To present examples of his theories, Gmelin published with Doris Lerche *Märchen für tapfere Mädchen* (*Fairy Tales for Brave Girls*, 1978), in which he changed "Little Red Cap" so it ended with the wolf transformed into a young boy with black eyebrows and blond hair, who remains with Little Red Cap and her grandmother. In addition, he changed the brave little tailor into a brave little seamstress, who does not marry a prince in the end but celebrates her triumph with servants in the forest. His Hansel and Gretel go into the woods voluntarily to help their poor parents. After they get lost, they encounter an old woman who had been banished to the forest by the villagers because she was no longer productive. She does not want to kill and eat the children. However, she does want to exploit them and make them work for her. After a while they manage to escape, not by killing her but by using some magical instruments, and they return to both their parents, who are glad to see them. As we can see, Gmelin diminishes the anxiety children might feel in reading this tale by making the children much more active in determining their fate. Gone is the nasty stepmother, the expulsion of the children, the cannibalistic witch, the helpless Gretel, the killing of the witch, the return home with jewels just to the father.

Like Gmelin, Burckhard and Gisela Garbe have retold the Grimms' tales from a more progressive viewpoint. Their book, *Der ungestiefelte Kater* (*Puss without Boots*, 1985) contains 32 revised Grimms' tales, and according to Burckhard Garbe, he sought to retain such values as

> honesty, friendliness, helpfulness, gratitude, industriousness, and courage from the original Grimms' tales. To be sure I eliminated such authoritarian "virtues" that serve the state as humility, obsequiousness, fatalism, inaction on the part of the individual as a result of submission to God, fate, or men, the acceptance of social injustice on the basis of axiomatic faith in God's justice, the non-questioning of the "necessity" of war, one-dimensional fixing of roles for women and men to the disadvantage of women."[22]

Garbe's version of "Hansel and Gretel" reveals a different pedagogical viewpoint than Gmelin's. The mother beats the children and makes them work hard. However, when she proposes to the father that they get rid of Hansel and Gretel in the woods, he refuses and joins forces with the children. Together they desert the mother in the woods, and she makes her way to a wise woman, who punishes her by making her work as hard as she made her children toil. Meanwhile. Hansel and Gretel live peacefully and happily with their father even though they never become rich. In general, Garbe favors simple role reversals in his tales, so that "King Thrushbeard" becomes "Princess Thrushbeard," in which the theme of the taming of the shrew is changed into the taming of the male chauvinist.

Feminist Fairy Tales

Obviously, the feminist revisions of the Grimms' tales are related to the pedagogical fairy tales because, basically, they want to teach non-sexist behavior or to impart notions that contradict the stereotypical images of male-female relations found in the Grimms' tales. However, the focus is not so much on the pedagogical aspect. Feminist fairy tales[23] tend to be confrontational and provocative, and often there is no strict ideological line that they follow.

Typical of those tales that expose the Grimms' patriarchal attitudes and confront male exploitation today is Rosemarie Kunzler's "Rumpelstilzchen" (1976),[24] in which the miller's daughter refuses to give Rumpelstiltskin her child or to marry the king. Of course Rumpelstiltksin becomes enraged and stamps his foot so deep into the ground that the door of the chamber flies open, and the miller's daughter flees into the wide world. The rejection of manipulation by men is also apparent in Annette Laun's "Rapunzel" (1985),[25] in which the prince seduces Rapunzel with sweet promises and then abandons her. Later Rapunzel cuts off her hair and goes to live in a city, where she gives birth to twins. One day she passes the castle of the prince, who meanwhile had become the king, and she enters a tower where she hears sad tones from the queen. She calls her and tells her to cut off her black hair and make a ladder out of it. The queen joins Rapunzel, and together they live on. This notion of female solidarity is perhaps best exemplified in Christa Reinig's tale, "Kluge Else, Katy und Gänsemagd als Bremerstadtmusikanten" ("Clever Else, Katy, and the Goose Girl as the Bremen Town Musicians," 1976),[26] based on three Grimms' tales. Clever Else becomes tired of being mocked by her father and fiancé. So she leaves home and recruits Katy, whose husband has locked her out of her house, and the goose girl, who has left her husband, to go with her to Bremen and start a rock band. On their way through the forest they scare a group of soldiers, who think the women are the Russians. The men abandon the house they were using as headquarters, and the women set up a home together.

While most feminists, like Reinig, have radically altered the Grimms' tales, there are some like Svende Merian, who, in her book *Der Mann aus Zucker* (*The Man Made of Sugar*, 1985), has added slight variations to alter the passive roles and sexist ideology of the Grimms' tales. There are more scholarly studies like *Schneewittchen hat viele Schwestern* (*Snow White Has Many Sisters*) by Ines Köhler-Zülch and Christine Shojaei Kawan, which demonstrate that there is a large variety of tales with women as the major protagonists. Finally, unusual feminist fairy tales with motifs from the Grimms' tales can be found in various anthologies and journals, such as the special issue of *Schreiben* entitled "Blut im Schuh: Märchen" ("Blood in the Shoe: Fairy Tales").[27]

Comic Parody

Though related to the socially satirical tales, the fairy tale as comic parody tends to mock the conventions of the Grimms' fairy tales without necessarily providing a socially relevant message. Nothing is sacred in the parody, and often both the Grimms' tradition and contemporary mores are mocked at the same time. Typical of the types of Grimm parodies that have been produced are three works: Uta Claus and Rolf Kutschera's *Total Tote Hose* (*Total Dead Pants*, 1984); Heinz Langer's *Grimmige Märchen* (*Grim Fairy Tales*, 1984); and Chris Schrauff's, *Der Wolf und seine Steine* (*The Wolf and his Stones*, 1986). All three books have highly amusing illustrations that reinforce the comic nature of the revisions of a Grimms' tale. Claus has taken 12 well-known tales and rewritten them in the slang and hip language of contemporary German youth. Thus, for example, her version of "Snow White" starts like this: "The whole story all started because Whitey's filthy rich dad couldn't keep going without some broad. So he brought a horny old lady back to their place. She was an unbelievable mess, and the only thing buzzing in her bean was makeup and clothes. And whenever she saw another woman that looked more tremendous than she did, she became mad as a hatter. Well, Whitey looked amazingly sharp, and that's why the old bag wanted to bump her off."[28] Claus follows the basic plot line of the Grimms' tale, but her witty slang undermines the romantic aspect of the classical version, and all the characters and virtues of "Snow White" are totally debunked.

Langer's technique is completely different from Klaus's use of slang. He parodies 38 Grimms' tales with full-page illustrations facing brief passages from the classical versions. The illustrations are generally totally different from the texts, and the disparity between text and image creates the parody. For instance, in one illustration of "Snow White and the Seven Dwarfs"[29] he depicts two dwarfs standing by the side of the road and trying to hitch a ride. Next to them is the glass coffin with Snow White, who has the core of an apple jutting from her mouth. Down the road one can see a hearse heading toward the dwarfs. In another illustration, of "Cinderella,"[30] he shows the prince, who has tripped over roller skates, flying through the air in the entrance of a disco. Throughout the book the anachronistic language and ideas of the Grimms' text are contrasted by cartoons that mix modern settings and characters with traditional fairy-tale motifs.

Finally, Schrauff, whose terse narratives are illustrated by Karl Volkmann, mocks various aspects of the Grimms' tales by jolting the reader with unexpected combinations of motifs. For instance, one of his versions reads: "Once upon a time there was a prince, who found a sleeping Snow White. And since she lay there so beautiful and peaceful, he slit her throat, took her apple, and ate it himself."[31] There is a touch of cynicism in all his tales since there is never a happy ending. One prince who looks for Snow White finds her coffin empty and is himself turned into one of the common dwarfs. A frog, tired of being thrown against walls by princesses who want to see if he is a prince, decides to throw a princess against a wall, but she dies from the collision. Like Claus and Langer, Schraff focuses on implied meanings of the old tales for contemporary audiences. Most of all, it is by causing their readers to laugh at irreconcilable contradictions between the Grimms' mode of writing and thinking and contemporary conditions that these authors' parodies achieve their effects.

Spiritual Tales

The so-called spiritual tales are either religious or moralistic in nature and tend to employ the Grimms' tales in a therapeutic and didactic way so that the reader may be uplifted. Generally speaking, the Grimms' version is not so much revised as it is reinterpreted to reveal its benefits for the individual reader's edification. Leading the way in promoting the spiritual effect of the fairy tales is the Kreuz Verlag with its series "Weisheit im Märchen" ("Wisdom in the Fairy Tale") edited by Theodor Seifert.[32] All the editions have basically the same format: The classical version of the particular Grimms' tale is reprinted, and then there are several explicatory chapters about the essential nature of the tale and how it leads to wholesome living.[33] In Seifert's own edition of "Snow White," interpreted as a demonstration of how one can win back a happy life that seems to have been lost, he begins by advising: "Let the fairy tale calmly have an effect on you. Try to capture the feelings that it stimulates. Let yourself be enchanted by its own power and vision. Let yourself be surprised by your own reactions. . . . Fairy tales are counselors and anticipatory images of the most different situations and difficulties of life. That is why we can use them with trust to orient ourselves because there is no personal intention of a particular author behind them."[34] Seifert then examines passages from "Snow White," giving advice to his readers on how they too might deepen their spiritual lives and see alternatives to a life that appears deadened.

While Seifert's tips for better living tend to be obvious and his tone somewhat simplistic if not condescending, Johann Friedrich Konrad's revisions of nine Grimms' tales in *Hexen-Memoiren* (*Witch Memoirs*, 1981) are modern and amusing. For instance, "The Frog King" is entitled "Der Lustfrosch" ("The Lecherous Frog") and is told in the first person from the frog's perspective. All he can think of is seducing the princess, but when he realizes how much revulsion he causes and how much he makes the princess suffer, he decides not to pursue her anymore. To his surprise, his decision makes him feel humane, and the princess is then free herself to treat him with compassion. In Konrad's notes for the use of his tales at home and in the school, he comments: "The revision has been conceived with a view toward adolescents and is intended to help in connection with other media and texts to free sex and eros from egotism, exploitation, and boasting, and also from inhibition, besmirching and smut and to enable them to form a partnership that lives from consideration and fulfillment."[35] In another note, about "Bearskin," he states: "This revision of 'Bearskin' is basically a fairy-tale sermon about Jesus' words: 'One cannot serve God and Mammon,' and 'A camel will sooner go through the eye of a needle before a rich man is allowed to enter God's kingdom.'"[36]

EAST GERMANY

The postwar debate about the harmful effects of the Grimms' tales was always tied in the German Democratic Republic to questions about the cultural heritage. That is, once the communists solidified their power in 1949, all literature considered bourgeois was to be evaluated and appropriated in a dialectical sense to further the nation's progress toward genuine socialism and eventually communism.[37] The Grimms' tales were rather easy to appropriate since they were considered part of the oral folk tradition and thus depicted how people from the lower classes overcame oppression and fought to improve their lot. Two early scholarly works of the 1950s by Gerhard Kahlo and Waltraut Woeller elaborated this position to show the folk tale's connection to the historical reality of the life experiences of the peasantry. In other words, it was argued that the Grimms' tales and other German folk tales contained positive elements of the class struggle and were part of a grand European tradition that corresponded to the internationalist aspect of communism. Moreover, the tales were considered helpful in developing the moral character of young people. As Anneliese Kocialek stated in her work, *Die Bedeutung des Volksmärchens für Unterricht und Erziehung in der Unterstufe der deutschen demokratischen Schule* (*The Meaning of the Folk Tale for Instruction and Education in the Primary Grades of the German Democratic School*, 1951):

> The moral and aesthetic education of pupils through folk tales in the primary levels of the schools in the German Democratic Republic are inseparably fused with one another. The special attributes of the artistic fairy-tale forms make the children more receptive to the moral content and simultaneously provide aesthetic pleasure. The tales of our own people are superbly suited to maintain in our children a love for their homeland, and the tales of other peoples waken in them a respect for their cultural achievements.[38]

Since specific criteria for the moral and political development of the people in the GDR were stringently set by the state and party leadership, the Grimms' tales came under close scrutiny, and beginning in 1952, the early editions of the Grimms' tales all underwent revision so that they conformed to the value system of the state: Racist and religious elements were eliminated, violence and brutality were diminished, and moral statements were added. It was not until 1955 that the first unabridged, complete edition of the Grimms' tales was published, but even after that event, the censorship and/or revision of the Grimms' tales continued. The result was a dehistorization of the Grimms' tales due to an endeavor to transform them into genuine folk tales that could be used for the moral and political elevation of the people. From 1952 to 1975, there were 48 different editions of the Grimms' tales published in the GDR,[39] with very little criticism of the possible regressive elements in the tales and with changes based on a one-dimensional view of what a folk tale is or should be. The Grimms' tales were considered sacrosanct: perfect for the moral upbringing of children, and perfect for making adults aware of the class struggle. It was, in fact, during this period that the most exceptional contributions to the Grimm legacy began.

One of the best kept secrets of the Cold War was East Germany's production of marvelous fairy-tale films for children.[40] Fortunately, with the fall of the Berlin Wall, there are very few secrets left, and we now have access to these cinematic treasures created by DEFA, the state film company of the former East Germany. More than 25 fairy-tale films were produced from 1950 to 1989, and they emphasize the profound humanitarian aspect of the fairy tales written by the Brothers Grimm and by other writers, such as Gisela von Arnim and Wilhelm Hauff, who enriched the European folklore tradition with original works. In addition, DEFA adapted Mongolian, Ugurian, and Arabian fairy tales for the screen in an effort to go beyond the European tradition and introduce children to other cultures that have marvelous stories about the valorous deeds of common people.

In contrast to the animation work that is popular in America, the DEFA films, which are now shown throughout Germany and have been distributed through videos and DVDs in America, use live characters in realistic settings that recall the historical background of the fairy tales. But this realism quickly becomes fantastic and magical, and the films, which vary in style because different directors made them, blend imaginative plots with messages that stimulate young viewers to think about social issues that involve greed, vanity, envy, tyranny, racism, exploitation, and hypocrisy.

Originally, the DEFA films were looked upon with a certain skepticism by the East German cultural authorities, who did not believe fairy tales were the proper means to convey and promote socialist ideas and morals. However, the filmmakers soon proved the government wrong by transforming and, in many cases, changing the tales into dramatic allegorical depictions of moral dilemmas. Films like *Six Go Round the World*, *Snow White*, *The Singing Ringing Tree*, *Little Redcap*, *Iron Jack*, and *The Tinderbox* stress the need for cooperation and mutual respect to defeat evil tyrants and predators. The focus in most of the fairy tales is on the little hero or the oppressed heroine, so that young viewers can better identify with the protagonists. Thus, the diminutive young man in *The Brave Little Tailor* shows how a small person can use his wits to succeed in life. Here success turns out not to be defined by a royal marriage and the acquisition of money. In fact, the tailor chooses a servant as his bride after the king and his haughty daughter leave the kingdom. In *How to Marry a King*, based on the Grimms' "The Clever Peasant's Daughter," the young protagonist, Marie, also demonstrates her cunning in original ways so that she not only marries a king but also teaches him a lesson in justice. In *Who's Afraid of the Devil*, a peasant boy named Jacob luckily avoids a death sentence by the king and then uses his brains to disguise himself, outsmart the devil, and then win the king's daughter for his bride. Finally, in *The Story of Little Muck*, an old hunchback man tells the local children the story of his life in order to make them aware of their ruthless behavior, which smacks of anti-Semitism. Gradually, the children learn that Muck, who was an orphan, had used magic gifts to help his friends, and in the end the children learn to respect the man they have mistreated.

All the fairy-tale films are filled with learning processes that stimulate critical thinking in young viewers. Two of the films, *Bearskin* and *The Blue Light*, depict how young men are mistreated by kings after they have served their countries in war. The discharged soldiers seek their revenge by making pacts with demonic characters, but they learn that friendship, kindness, and generosity are more important than revenge and money. Other characters also learn that the greed for money can turn them into callous people. Thus, in *The Cold Heart*, Peter Munk, the charcoal burner, almost loses his heart in his striving to become the richest and most powerful man in his village. Only his humility and love for his poor wife save him in the end. In *The Dwarf Magician*, the king, who only thinks about straw spun into gold by the miller's daughter, realizes that his newborn son is more important to him than all the money in the world.

The lessons to be learned in the DEFA fairy-tale films are not overly didactic or preachy. They arise almost magically and often comically from the stories themselves, which the screenwriters and directors have retold and altered in innovative ways. There is practically no graphic violence in any of these films, and there is an implicit message that any human being is capable of changing for the better.

Given the high status of the Grimms' tales, the DEFA film adaptations, and fairy-tale plays, GDR writers were not encouraged to tamper with them, unless they could bring out a socialist-humanitarian message. They were certainly not to mock them, for the tales were considered part of a folk heritage. The only major East German writer who rewrote them in a critical manner before 1970 was Franz Fühmann, who published compelling verse renditions of the Grimms' tales in *Die Richtung der Märchen* (*The Direction of the Fairy Tales*, 1962) that generally addressed the theme of the Nazi past and problems of authoritarianism. For instance his poem "In Frau Trudes Haus" ("In Mother Trudy's House") begins this way:

> When the child entered Mother Trudy's house,
> it saw a black man standing on the stairs,
> his head was a dead skull,
> claws were on his fingers.
>
> My child, said Mother Trudy, all that you see
> is what you've been imagining,
> it was only the good charcoal burner,
> who's brought me wood to burn.[41]

In contrast to the Grimms' "Mother Trudy," in which a child is approvingly burned as a log because of its disobedience, Fühmann's poem recalls images of Nazi Germany, and the child is murdered because the young person sees everything only too clearly.

Fühmann's 1962 poems were indeed an exception in East Germany,[42] and it was only after there was a change in the government leadership from Walther Ulbricht to Erich Honecker in 1971 that writers were encouraged to write more imaginative, if not fantastic literature.[43] This does not mean that there were no fairy tales whatsoever produced before 1971. In fact, there was a fair amount produced that departed from the Grimms' tales in interesting ways. For instance, Friedrich Wolf published some interesting tales for children following World War II, as did such writers as Lilo Hardel, Fred Rodrian, Werner Heiduczek, Benno Pludra, and Stefan Heym.[44] Yet, like the fairy tales published in West Germany during this period, these tales tended to create a sense of harmony and to stress the importance of moral behavior commensurate with the expectations of the state. However, they reflected little about the hard realities of life in the GDR during the 1950s and 1960s. Ironically, it was only with the thaw of socialist realism that writers dared to address social contradictions and produce highly innovative fairy tales that broke with the Grimms' tradition in a critical way. The important factors that led to the endeavors to rewrite the Grimms' tales[45] were: (1) the influence of West German writers, whose work was known in the GDR; (2) a more positive reception of German romanticism; (3) the great overall familiarity of the writers and their public with the Grimms' tales, which thus could be used more effectively as shared symbolical vehicles to criticize the state; (4) and greater cultural freedom, which allowed writers to address social problems in a more obvious manner.

Since the production of reutilized Grimms' tales was much more limited in the GDR than in the FRG and only achieved significance during the 1970s and 1980s, I want to focus my discussion largely on tales taken from three important anthologies, *Die Rettung des Saragossameeres* (*The Rescue of the Saragossa Sea*, 1976), *Die Verbesserung des Menschen* (*The Improvement of the Human Being*, 1982), and *Es wird einmal* (*Once Upon a Time in the Future*, 1988), to consider tales representative of some of the best work accomplished in East Germany. Most of these tales were first published in individual volumes by their authors, and they, too, can be loosely categorized according to their satirical, parodistic, feminist, and pedagogical aspects like those in West Germany, although there are no religious or spiritual narratives. The common thread running throughout most of them is political, and although there was no anti-authoritarian movement at the end of the 1960s in the German Democratic Republic, insubordination also plays a role in the Grimms' tales that have been *umfunktioniert*.

In his essay "Metamorphose des Märchens," Joachim Walther, one of the editors of *Die Rettung des Saragossameeres*, associated the endeavor to write new literary fairy tales in the GDR with the radical antibourgeois and utopian tales of early German romanticism, not with the Grimms' "folk" tales. In fact, he argued that "the form of the folk tale that has been handed down to us cannot become the model for the new contents."[46] Walther maintained that the changed conditions of production and the social needs of the people in the GDR had to serve as the basis for new fairy tales, which should possess a utopian tendency if the literary fairy tale was to overcome a transitional phase in which it mixed elements from different genres and was to assume an important social function. In his anthology, there are several examples in which authors attempt to use the Grimms' tales as models that can be revised with new contents to address social problems in the GDR, yet they are anything but utopian. Klaus Rahn's "Frau Holle" ("Mother Holle") recalls an episode in which a young Polish woman named Irina was raped by a German farmer during World War II. Irina burns down the farm and herself, muttering "Mother Holle" before she dies. Her story lives on in contemporary East Germany, and the narrator stimulates East German readers to recall, through surrealistic imagery, the landscape and country where it happened, and to associate the racist act of the German farmer with contemporary attitudes toward the Poles. Waltraud Jähnichen's "Dornröschen" ("Brier Rose") is less serious than Rahn's tale and pokes fun at the state ceremonies in the GDR. A top chef is missing on the day of an important celebration, and nobody knows the recipe for the pastry. The kitchen boy is sent to the state library to try to discover it but cannot get the book he needs. So, he finally looks into a thick fairy-tale book and wakes the chef (in the Grimms' tale) who was about to give the kitchen-boy a slap in the face. Now the chef gets mad again and is about to slap the kitchen boy from Berlin, but the minister president's young wife pricks her finger accidentally with a thorn. Everyone falls asleep, and the next day the top chef returns and is puzzled to find everyone in a coma with the fairy-tale book turned to the tale of "Brier Rose." More complex and more sardonic than Jähnichen's parody is Martin Stade's "Der Traum vom Hühnchen und Vom Hähnchen (nach Grimm)" ("The Dream of the Little

Hen and the Little Rooster [according to Grimm]"), in which Stade interweaves passages from the Grimms' tale with a first-person recollection of a futuristic dream. The reader is compelled to reconcile the fatalistic old Grimm tale about "The Death of the Hen" with the narrator's recollection of a sterile automated future.

Interestingly, the three tales by Rahn, Jähnichen, and Stade are all satirical and open-ended. The revised Grimms' tales reflect more about the difficulties of resolving contradictions in GDR society than indicating utopian alternatives and tendencies. This is also true of Günter Kunert's fairy tales in *Die geheime Bibliothek* (*The Secret Library*, 1973), which preceded the publication of *Die Rettung des Saragossameeres* by three years. In particular, his "Dornröschen" ("Brier Rose") is a brief recapitulation of the tale, in which he seeks to undermine the idyllic happy ending and belief in a rosy future by showing the reality as it must have been for the prince, who supposedly makes his way through the thorny hedges after 100 years have passed: "He enters the castle, runs up the stairs, enters the chamber where the sleeping woman is resting, her toothless mouth half-opened, slobbering, sunken lids, her hairless skull rippled on the temples by blue wormlike veins, spotted, dirty, a snoring hag. Oh blessed are all, who, dreaming of Brier Rose, died in the hedge and in the belief that behind the hedge a time would prevail in which time would finally stop once and for all and be definite."[47] Obviously Kunert, a dissident, was casting doubt on the future of the GDR, as did other writers of fairy tales in the early 1970s—many who had been prevented from developing fairy tales and other genres of fantasy literature. The questioning spirit of all the revised Grimms' tales during the 1970s is skeptical because the writers were still dubious about whether the thaw would bring about a new flood of suppression of cultural freedoms.

A good example of the skeptical nature of the satirical fairy tales based on a Grimms' tale is Arnim Stolper's "Der Wolf, nicht totzukriegen" ("The Wolf That Can't Be Killed," 1979). The focus is on a German professor who tries to dissuade Little Red Riding Hood from believing in fantastic stories such as fairy tales. He is a man of reason, who represents the cultural authorities of the GDR. When he sees Little Red Riding Hood returning from her grandmother's house, he refuses to believe what happened to her. And even when he is eaten by a wolf, he tries to repress the reality of fantasy. However, after several years in the wolf's stomach, he discovers his own subjectivity, is transformed into a young man in his best years, and goes home with Little Red Riding Hood and her fairy-tale book.

Another parody of a Grimms' tale with an implicit critique of higher authorities in the GDR is Karl Hermann Roehricht's "Von einem, der auszog, die Höflichkeit zu lernen" ("About a Young Man, Who Went Out to Learn about Politeness," 1980). Here, a young simpleton leaves his hometown with the advice from an old woman to say only one sentence to the people he meets: "From the bottom of my heart I am sorry." However, this sentence and two others that he thinks up cause him to have difficulties with kings, who incarcerate him. Finally, fed up with kings, he returns to his hometown with the sentence "I have complete understanding for everything." Eventually, even though he remains simple-minded, people turn to him for advice in his old age, and he becomes a professor who teachers the art of politeness.

Like Roehricht's parody, Lothar Kusche's "Froschkönig" ("The Frog King," 1979) mocks audience expectations concerning fairy tales while presenting a critique of contemporary society. A young woman loses an earring in a fountain, and the frog visits her in her apartment, where she flings him against a wall because he becomes too irksome. When he is transformed into the Prince Alwin von und zu Schaumburg-lippe auf Knödelstein von Hessen-Nassau with an upper-class nasal manner of speaking, she compels him to leave because she does not want to have anything to do with princes. Kusche concludes that the tale explains the repulsion that most people have toward frogs, for they fear that a frog could be transformed unexpectedly into an old German prince.

Aside from the socially critical fairy tales that debunk authoritarianism and any form of class hegemony, there have been various parodies basically intended to mock the old versions of the Grimms and to provide amusement for readers. For instance Stefan Heym's "Wie es mit Rotkäppchen weiterging" ("The Further Adventures of Little Red Cap," 1979) pokes fun at Little Red Riding Hood's desire for more fame after she has told her neighbors and villagers about her encounter with the wolf.[48] She becomes bored at home and neglects Felix the boy next door. Therefore, she hopes that she will meet another wolf and become famous again on another visit to Granny. However, neither her grandmother nor the son of the big bad wolf agree to repeat the previous adventure, and she returns home, where Felix invites her to play the game of Little Red Riding Hood and the Wolf, in which she will be gobbled up out of love. The ironical sexual innuendo of the narrative is the explicit meaning of all the short illustrated parodies of Thomas Schleusing's *Es war einmal . . .* (*Once Upon a Time . . .*, 1979). Similar to the technique employed by the West German caricaturist Heinz Langer, Schleusing takes a short passage from the traditional Grimm tale and then juxtaposes it with an erotic illustration that brings out some of the underlying sexual meanings of the tale. In his "Der Froschkönig" ("The Frog King") he quotes the part where the frog says he is tired and wants to sleep with her and then shows the princess in a revealing nightie with a frog between her legs. As she looks down at him, she remarks, "Oh, don't be a frog."[49] Even more explicit in its sexual (if not sexist) connotation is his version of "Rapunzel," based on the part where the prince calls her to let her hair down. There she is pictured smiling from a window in her tower as a group of princes have formed a line to take their turn having their pleasure with her.

Although most of the reutilized fairy tales in the GDR are comic in tone, there are some that are deadly serious and do away with magic and fantasy. For instance, Horst Matthies' collection of tales *Der goldene Fisch* (*The Golden Fish*) has the subtitle "Not a Fairy-Tale Book" ("Kein Märchenbuch"), and indeed his revisions of such tales as "The Wolf and the Seven Young Kids," "Brier Rose," "Lucky Hans," and "The Devil With the Three Golden Hairs" have more to do with stark realism than with symbolic literature. Moreover, Matthies focuses specifically on the problems that women encountered since the foundation of the GDR in 1949, and he exposes the romantic myths underlying the Grimms' fairy tales. In "The Wolf and the Seven Kids," Matthies focuses on a young woman, who in a span of 18 years has 7 girls with different fathers. Most of the time she is treated shabbily by men, and she also has shabby jobs since she has never been able to educate herself or qualify for high-skilled jobs. She constantly tells her daughters to beware of men taking advantage of them, and when she goes on her vacation one summer, she returns to find that a repairman is sleeping in her apartment because of major repairs he must make on the gasline in the building. After an initial distrust on the mother's part, she soon learns to accept him and gets married. On the steps of the city hall, she then says to her daughters: "What's rumbling and pumbling around in my stomach . . . ?"[50] This delightful ending can be contrasted to Matthies' version of "Brier Rose," in which a young woman loses her mother in an air attack a day or so before World War II ends. An orphan, she takes a job as an archivist in a small town and spends the rest of her life afraid to make contact with men yet waiting for a man to save her. However, life passes her by, and she remains a lonely anxious person whose deep desires will never be fulfilled.

⁂

What is one to conclude from all the experiments with the Grimms' fairy tales in East and West Germany? Have the Grimms been toppled from their throne? Will it ever be possible to surpass the Grimms' fairy tales, which are second only to the Bible as a bestseller in Germany? If we begin with a comparison of the "productive reception" of the Grimms' tales in the FRG and GDR, we can note that there have been distinctly different historical phases—and yet, writers in both countries arrived at the same point by 1989.

In West Germany up to 1968, the Grimms' tales were more or less treated as gems of the German cultural tradition that were therapeutic and could help heal the wounds of World War II. The anti-authoritarian movement and student revolts brought about a radical change in the attitude toward the Grimms' tales, so that those major writers who reutilized them exposed their regressive ideological aspects and deceptive idyllic messages. The experimentation with the Grimms' fairy tales was based on *insubordination* or a healthy skeptical attitude toward blind acceptance of the so-called humanistic German cultural tradition. In this respect, the Grimms' tales were touchstones in a literary discourse within the public sphere. They served as symbolic reference points for critical writers who reutilized them to have a dialogue about sex, politics, social conditions, religion, and so on. From 1949 to 1971 in the GDR, there was a similar "religious" attitude toward the

Grimms' tales that were being produced in the FRG, with one *major* difference. Whereas the overriding ideological reception in West Germany was connected to traditional religious and bourgeois values and served a social function of healing and reinforcing a mood of existentialism, mystery, and miracle, the reception in the GDR was linked to a rationalization and legitimization of the so-called socialist policies of the state. The ethics and morals of the tales were shaped to promote class struggle, and the social function of the tales was to promote an understanding of how one must strive to overcome exploitation. Since the Grimms' tales were considered part of the GDR's cultural heritage, it was taboo to criticize them up to 1971. After that year, East German writers purposely used the Grimms' tales in much the same way that West German writers did, with one important exception. There were no endeavors to continue or to reconstruct an anthroposophical, Jungian, or Christian discourse through the Grimms' tales. The reutilization of the Grimms' tales was part of a vigorous dialogue pertaining to state policies and social conditions in the GDR. It is in this sense that writers in East and West Germany came together, for in both cases their tales were socially symbolic gestures that sought to open up questions about the German past and point to ways to change the institutions of their respective public spheres.

For the most part the reutilized Grimms' tales in East and West Germany are *not* utopian, whereas it is easy to point to the utopian aspects of the original Grimms' tales—tales written during a revolutionary period, when the bourgeoisie was on the rise and establishing the norms of its civilizing process. To the extent that this civilizing process has expanded and remains intact (even though it was qualitatively different in both the GDR and FRG), it will be difficult to topple the Grimms from their fairy-tale throne. Their tales continue to represent basic values and norms of German and other Western societies that have been heavily influenced by the Protestant ethos, patriarchy, and corporate capitalism. Nevertheless, it can be clearly seen that the "realm" of fairy-tale production changed immensely in both Germanies since 1970,[51] and experimentation in literary fairy tales and fantasy transcended the ideology of the Grimms' tales. In this regard, one must extend the study of the reception of the Grimms' tales to see how they have been fully transformed or surpassed in other contemporary fairy tales.

Moreover, ever since the two Germanies became united in the fall of 1990, there have been fairy tales of different kinds addressing the problems of nationalism and reunification, and there has also been a marked influence of American and British tales that have become popular in Germany through the mass media. The unification of Germany has been more unsettling than harmonious. For the past 12 years, the differences between the attitudes of Germans who were raised in East and West Germany from 1945 to 1990 have been exacerbated by the apparent economic and social advantages that people in the West have, as well as their prejudices against the former East German "police state" and its huge spy system. If anything, there has not really been unification after 1990, but instead discord and compromise. The East Germans have had to yield to the West German way of life, and there is strong resentment in the eastern sectors to the manner in which unification has been established. The "rebuilding" of East Germany and its integration into a Western-style capitalist system has been fraught with struggles, aggravated by the revelations of corruption in the Christian Democratic government, the rise of right-wing groups, racism, economic recession, and the collapse of the fragile coalition between the Social Democratic Party and the Greens. The cultural production in the unified Germany during the last 12 years has reflected the crises of faith in the government and questioning of national identity. The issue of national identity is closely tied to shifts in the culture industry oriented more and more toward European interests. The role of the fairy tale in the cultural life of Germans today has become less clear. While the traditional tales of the Grimms continue to be reproduced and are well known, and while there are many fairy-tale films, videos, advertisements, and children's books imported from other Western countries, there has not been an exceptionally new challenge to the Grimms' legacy that might reflect a different social and cultural attitude. While nationalism helped to foster the Grimms' collecting and writing of tales that, they hoped, would bring about German unification, nationalism has become an "ugly" term today, and writers and artists are reluctant to use the fairy tale or the Grimms' tales to display a new kind of nationalism.

Perhaps the greatest "sensation" and most important publication in the realm of the Brothers Grimm adaptations since 1990 has been the publication of 100 tales selected by the highly talented illustrator Nikolaus Heidelbach for his book *Die Märchen der Brüder Grimm* (*The Fairy Tales of the Brothers Grimm*, 1995).[52] The texts, based mainly on the second and third editions of *Children's and Household Tales*, have not been altered, but the color and ink illustrations by Heidelbach do alter our vision. By themselves the illustrations tell their own stories, which bring out the somber and macabre aspects of the tales; they are startling in comparison to the majority of sweet, cute, and artificial illustrations, some of which were discussed in the previous chapter. For instance, in Heidelbach's illustrations for "Sleeping Beauty," he has the queen swimming in an ordinary pond with her head above water speaking to a frog that informs her she will give birth to a daughter. The second image shows the prince on his dappled horse looking at a castle on top of a gray mountain and facing what appears to be an insurmountable task. Nothing is settled in the images. There is a sense of mystery, and the figures are earthy types. In fact, throughout the book, there are very few "beautiful" people. Most of the characters, even the kings and queens, are stocky, broad, and unappealing—and in some cases, hideous. Often we do not even see their faces, as is the case in "Snow White"; the mirror shows no reflection, and later we only catch a glimpse of Snow White's black hair in a glass coffin while one of the dwarfs covers his face in sorrow. In "Hansel and Gretel," we are shown the grim stepmother pulling her husband by one arm while he has a menacing ax in the other. On the next page, the large witch dressed in a brown skirt and dark blue apron is more menacing: she stoops over and leads two diminutive children into a gingerbread house, which resembles a prison cell more than it does an appetizing house. We do not see her, only her enormous backside. Throughout the book it is the grotesque, the rustic, the macabre, the extraordinary, and the ruddy and hard side of the peasant world that is featured and evokes characters from the worlds of Bruegel, Bosch, and Dürrer. There is no hint of a "new" Germany here, no sense of optimism or hope.

Are Heidelbach's illustrations signs of the time? It is difficult to say. There are other more delightful versions of the Grimms' tales, such as Rotraut Susanne Berner's comic illustrations in her book *Rotraut Susanne Berners Märchen-Stunde* (*Rotraut Susanne Berner's Fairy-Tale Hour,* 1998),[53] and thousands of traditional kitsch editions are distributed every year by many different publishers. These are the commercialized Grimms' tales that even appear in Americanized forms throughout Europe. As Germany enters a new historical phase, there are bound to be even more "new German" fairy tales about the legacy of the Grimms, the direction that the united Germany will take, and the hopes and wishes of the German people, who have longed to overcome the dark past of Nazism. But that is another story with an ending that has yet to be written . . .

NOTES

2002 PREFACE

1. Haydn Middleton, *Grimm's Last Fairy Tale* (London: Abacus, 1999), 248.
2. In another novel about the Grimms, *Darkest Desire: The Wolf's Own Tale* (New Jersey: The Ecco Press, 1998), Anthony Schmitz suggests that the Grimms abandoned their concern for truth in pursuit of sensational stories. See the review of Schmitz's book by Louise Speed in *Marvels & Tales* 14 (2000): 323–325.
3. He followed this work with the republication of the 1812/15 and 1819 editions of the Grimms' tales with new annotations. More recently, he has published a highly significant collection of his philological studies in *Märchen der Brüder Grimm* (Trier: Wissenschaftlicher Verlag Trier, 2000) and edited the correspondence between the brothers in *Briefwechsel zwischen Jacob und Wilhelm Grimm* (Stuttgart: Hirzel, 2001).
4. Mention should also be made of the valuable work of Ines Köhler-Zülch, Ulrich Marzolph, Christine Shojaei Kawan, and Hans-Jörg Üther.
5. There is very little consideration given to the publications outside this field, with the exception of Marie-Louise von Franz's Jungian opus or Bruno Bettelheim's neo-Freudian work, which has become more and more questionable in the last decade. There is indeed a great deal of provincialism in the psychological and pedagogical works produced in Germany, but I think this may be characteristic of most of the psychological studies of the Grimms' tales, which are trivialized by therapists who want to save our souls through fairy tales, and it is not only characteristic of German psychology. Some of the psychological works of Kast, Drewermann, and Mallet have been translated into English, and there are also followers or disciples in the United States and United Kingdom who want to do good for humanity but don't do the Grimms any good.
6. Actually, they have not looked at philosophical, political, and sociological advances made in their own country. They remain bound to an old fashioned notion of *Geistesgeschichte* or intellectual history and are immersed in German idealism. Such predilection makes much of their work reductive. I could cite other books that are not "wrong" in their interpretation of the Grimms' fairy tales or fairy tales in general, such as Wilhelm Solms' book,

Die Moral von Grimms Märchen (Darmstadt: Wissenschaftliche Buchgesellschaft, 1999), which is simplistic in its notion of moralism and has no references to crucial philosophical debates on moralism inside and outside Germany.

7. I could also cite examples to show that there is very little contact between German scholars and critics who write on the Grimms in France and Italy, two countries with which I am familiar. Of course, the case with France is unusual because the French tend to be consumed by Perrault and the French fairy-tale tradition. This was apparent at a recent conference held at the Bibliothèque Nationale de France in the spring of 2001 and the book published to commemorate an exhibit and the conference, edited by Olivier Piffaut, *Il était une fois . . . Les contes de fées* (Paris: Seuil, 2001). The national receptions of the Grimms throughout the world and "national" approaches to folklore and fairy tales are often very distinct and need to be studied more carefully. I am basically concerned in this introduction with differences among German, American, and British scholars.
8. Among the more productive books that followed the works of Tatar and Bottigheimer were: Donald Haase's edited collection, *The Reception of the Grimms' Fairy Tales* (1993); James McGlathery's *Grimms' Fairy Tales: A History of Criticism on a Popular Classic* (1993); Marina Warner's *From the Beast to the Blonde: On Fairy Tales and their Tellers* (1995); Steven Swann Jones' *The Fairy Tale: The Magic Mirror of Imagination* (1995); Cristina Bacchilega's *Postmodern Fairy Tales: Gender and Narrative Studies* (1997); Graham Anderson's, *Fairy Tale in the Ancient World* (2000); and more recently, Elizabeth Wanning Harries' *Twice Upon a Time: Women Writers and the History of the Fairy Tale* (2001) and Shawn Jarvis and Jeannine Blackwell's anthology with notes, *The Queen's Mirror: Fairy Tales by German Women, 1780–1900* (2001).

1988 PREFACE

1. Dan Sperber, *Explaining Culture: A Naturalistic Approach* (London: Blackwell, 1996), 61. See also Sperber's early essay, "Anthropology and Psychology: Towards an Epidemiology of Representations." *Man* 20 (1984): 73–89.

CHAPTER 1

1. In particular, see the work of Heinz Rölleke, *"Wo das Wünschen noch geholfen hat": Gesammelte Aufsätze zu den "Kinder- und Hausmärchen der Brüder Grimm* (Bonn: Bouvier, 1985) and *Die Märchen der Brüder Grimm* (Munich Artemis, 1985). Rölleke summarizes most of the important research in Germany. See also chapter 7 of the present volume, "Recent Psychological Approaches with Some Questions about the Abuse of Children," which provides a summary of contemporary scholarship.
2. See John Ellis, *One Fairy Story too Many: The Brothers Grimm and Their Tales* (Chicago: University of Chicago Press, 1983). Cf. My review, "Mountains out of Mole Hills, a Fairy Tale," *Children's Literature* 13 (1985): 215–219.

3. There are numerous works on these topics. Among the most provocative are: Andrea Dworkin, *Woman Hating* (New York: Dutton, 1974); Robert Moore, "From Rags to Witches: Stereotypes, Distortions and Anti-humanism in Fairy Tales," *Interracial Books for Children* 6 (1975): 1–3; Lilyane Mourey, *Introduction aux contes de Grimm et de Perrault* (Paris: Minard, 1978); Jennifer Waelti-Walters, "On Princesses: Fairy Tales, Sex Roles and Loss of Self," *International Journal of Women's Studies* 2 (March/April 1979): 180–188.
4. Cf. Bruno Bettelheim, *The Uses of Enchantment: The Meaning and Importance of Fairy Tales* (New York: Knopf, 1976).
5. Cf. Ruth Bottigheimer, *Grimms' Bad Girls and Bold Boys: The Moral and Social Vision of the Tales* (New Haven: Yale University Press, 1987); Maria Tatar, *The Hard Facts of the Grimms' Fairy Tales* (Princeton: Princeton University Press, 1987); and Marina Warner, *From the Beast to the Blonde: On Fairy Tales and Their Tellers* (London: Chatto & Windus, 1995).
6. The major exceptions in English are Christa Kamenetsky, *The Brothers Grimm and Their Critics: Folktales and the Quest for Meaning* (Athens: Ohio University Press, 1992) and James M. McGlathery, *Grimms Fairy Tales: A History of Criticism on a Popular Classic* (Columbia, SC: Camden House, 1993). In Germany, the work of Heinz Rölleke, Lothar Bluhm, and contributors to the publications of the Brüder Grimm-Gesellschaft tend to base their philological studies on careful historical research related to the lives of the Grimms.
7. Ruth Michaelis-Jena, *The Brothers Grimm* (New York: Praeger, 1970), 10.
8. Jacob Grimm, "Selbstbiographie" in *Auswahl aus den Kleinen Schriften* (Hamburg: Gutenberg, 1904), 19–20.
9. In Irma Hildebrandt, *Es waren ihrer Fünf: Die Brüder Grimm und ihre Familie* (Cologne: Diederichs, 1984), 34–35.
10. See Wilhelm Schoof, "Aus der Jugendzeit der Brüder Grimm," *Hanausches Magazin* 13 (1934): 81–96, and 14 (1935): 1–15.
11. Schoof, "Aus der Jugendzeit," 83. Letter of October 6, 1798.
12. "Selbstbiographie," 24.
13. Wilhelm Grimm, *Kleinere Schriften*, Vol. 1 (Berlin: 1881–87), 12.
14. Heinz Rölleke, ed., *Briefwechsel zwischen Jacob und Wilhelm Grimm* (Stuttgart: Hirzel, 2001), 30.
15. See Hermann Grimm, Gustav Hinrichs, and Wilhelm Schoof, eds., *Briefwechsel zwischen Jacob und Wilhelm Grimm aus der Jugendzeit*, 2d rev. ed. (Weimar: Hermann Böhlaus, 1963) and Rölleke, ed., *Briefwechsel zwischen Jacob und Wilhelm Grimm* (2001).
16. In Gabriele Seitz, *Die Brüder Grimm: Leben—Werk—Zeit* (Munich: Winkler, 1984), 48.
17. In Gunhild Ginschel, *Der junge Jacob Grimm* (Berlin: Akademie-Verlag, 1967), 40.
18. G. Ronald Murphy, *The Owl, the Raven, the Dove: The Religious Meaning of the Grimms' Magic Fairy Tales* (New York: Oxford University Press, 2000), 3–4. See also Wilhelm Solms, *Die Moral von Grimms Märchen* (Darmstadt: Wissenschaftliche Buchgesellschaft, 1999).

19. Jürgen Habermas, *Strukturwandel der Öffentlichkeit* (Berlin: Luchterhand, 1962).
20. Manfred Kluge, ed., *Die Brüder Grimm in ihren Selbstbiographien* (Munich: Heyne, 1985), 64.
21. Rölleke, *Briefwechsel zwischen Jacob und Wilhelm Grimm*, 137–138.
22. Michaelis-Jena, *The Brothers Grimm*, 86–87.
23. Cf. Hans Bernd Harder and Ekkehard Kaufmann, eds., *Die Brüder Grimm in ihrer amtlichen und politischen Tätigkeit* (Kassel: Weber & Wiedemeyer, 1985), 70–71.
24. Cf. Ludwig Denecke, "Die Göttinger Jahre der Brüder Jacob und Wilhlem Grimm," *Göttinger Jahrbuch* 25 (1977): 139–155.
25. See Jacob's defense of his position in his essay, "Über meine Entlassung" (1838), published in Jacob Grimm, *Reden und Aufsätze*, ed. Wilhelm Schoof (Munich: Winkler, 1966), 34–63.
26. See Hartwig Schulz, ed. *Der Briefwechsel Bettina von Arnim mit den Brüdern Grimm 1838–1841* (Frankfurt am Main: Insel, 1985).
27. Michaelis-Jena, *The Brothers Grimm*, 130.
28. See Holger Ehrhardt, *Briefwechsel der Brüder Grimm mit Hermann Grimm* (Kassel: Verlag der Brüder Grimm-Gesellschaft, 1998).
29. Cf. Roland Feldmann, *Jacob Grimm und die Politik* (Kassel: Bärenreiter, 1970); and Wilhelm Bleek, "Die Brüder Grimm und die deutsche Politik," *Politik und Zeitgeschichte*, Beilage zur Wochenzeitung *Das Parlament*, 1 (January 4, 1986): 3–15.
30. Seitz, *Die Brüder Grimm*, 154.

CHAPTER 2

1. Reprinted in Heinz Rölleke, *Die Märchen der Brüder Grimm* (Munich: Artemis, 1987), 63–69.
2. Jacob Grimm, *Circular wegen Aufsammlung der Volkspoesie*, ed. Ludwig Denecke, afterword Kurt Ranke (Kassel: Brüder Grimm-Museum, 1968), 3–4.
3. For excellent accounts of the sources of the Grimms' collection and the background of the informants, see Wilhelm Schoof, *Zur Entstehungsgeschichte der Grimmschen Märchen* (Hamburg: Hauswedell, 1959), 59–130; Heinz Rölleke's three essays, "Die 'stockhessischen Märchen' der 'Alten Marie'" (1975), "Von Menschen denen wir Grimms' Märchen verdanken" (1987), and "Neue Ergebnisse zu den *Kinder- und Hausmärchen* der Brüder Grimm" in *Die Märchen der Brüder Grimm: Quellen und Studien* (Trier: Wissenschaftlicher Verlag Trier, 2000), 9–22, 23–36, 37–44; and Christa Kamenetsky, *The Brothers Grimm and Their Critics: Folktales and the Quest for Meaning* (Athens: Ohio University Press, 1993), 113–177.
4. See Albert Schindehütte, ed., *Krauses Grimm'sche Märchen* (Kassel: Stauda, 1985). This book contains all of Kraus's tales, along with biographical and historical information and documents edited by Heinz Rölleke and Heinz Vonjahr.
5. Heinz Rölleke, *Die älteste Märchensammlung der Brüder Grimm* (Cologny-Geneva: Martin Bodmer Fondation, 1975).

6. Gunhild Ginschel, "Der Märchenstil Jacob Grimms," in *Jacob Grimm: Zur Wiederkehr seines Todestages*, ed. Wilhelm Fraenger and Wolfgang Steinitz (Berlin: Akademie-Verlag, 1963), 131–168.
7. Heinz Rölleke, "Clemens Brentano und die Brüder Grimm im Spiegel ihrer Märchen," in *Die Märchen der Brüder Grimm*, 61. See also *Nebeninschriften. Brüder Grimm—Arnim und Brentano—Droste-Hülshoff. Literarhistorische Studien* (Trier: Wissenschaftlicher Verlag Trier, 1980).
8. For a full discussion of contamination and the Brothers Grimm, see my essay "The Contamination of the Fairy Tale," in *Sticks and Stones: The Troublesome Success of Children's Literature from Slovenly Peter to Harry Potter* (New York: Routledge, 2000), 99–125.
9. See Ines Köhler-Zülch, "Der Diskurs über den Ton: Zur Präsentation von Märchen und Sagen in Sammlungen des 19. Jahrhunderts," in *Homo narrans: Studien zur populären Erzählkultur*, ed. Christoph Schmitt (Münster: Waxmann, 1999), 25–50.
10. Rölleke, *Die älteste Märchensammlung der Brüder Grimm*, 246–248.
11. Walter Killy, ed., *Kinder-und Hausmärchen der Brüder Grimm* (Frankfurt am Main: Fischer, 1962), 150–151.
12. *Ibid.*, 39.
13. Jacob and Wilhelm Grimm, *The Complete Fairy Tales of the Brothers Grimm*, ed. and trans. Jack Zipes (New York: Bantam, 1987), 8–9.
14. Killy, *Kinder-und Hausmärchen der Brüder Grimm*, 41.
15. Grimm, *The Complete Fairy Tales*, 55.
16. Jacob und Wilhelm Grimm, *Kinder- und Hausmärchen der Brüder Grimm: Vollständige Ausgabe in der Urfassung*, ed. Friedrich Panzer (Wiesbaden: Emil Ollmer, n.d.), 70–71.
17. Jacob and Wilhelm Grimm, *The Complete Fairy Tales*, 12–20.
18. For a thorough discussion about the sources for this tale, see Heinz Rölleke, "Märchen von einem, der auszog, das Fürchten zu lernen: Zur Überlieferung und Bedeutung des KJM 4," in *Die Märchen der Brüder Grimm: Quellen und Studien* (Trier: Wissenschaftlicher Verlag Trier, 2000), 136–148.
19. See Annemarie Verweyen, "'Wenig Bücher sind mit solcher Lust entstanden . . . '," in *Börsenblatt* 77 (September 27, 1985): 2465–2473.
20. See the important work by Hannjost Lixfeld, *Folklore and Fascism: The Reich Institute for German Volkskunde*, ed. and trans. James R. Dow (Bloomington: Indiana University Press, 1994).
21. Cf. the chapter, "The Fight Over Fairy-Tale Discourse: Family, Friction, and Socialization in the Weimar Republic and Nazi Germany," in Jack Zipes, *Fairy Tales and the Art of Subversion* (New York: Methuen, 1983), 134–169, and James R. Dow and Hannjost Lixfeld, eds., *The Nazification of an Academic Discipline: Folklore in the Third Reich* (Bloomington: Indiana University Press, 1994).
22. Cf. Jack Zipes, *The Trials and Tribulations of Little Red Riding Hood* (1983; rev. and exp. second ed. New York: Routledge, 1993).
23. In particular, see Bruno Bettelheim, *The Uses of Enchantment: The Meaning and Importance of Fairy Tales* (New York: Knopf, 1976).

24. For an excellent summary of the psychoanalytic scholarship, see Alan Dundes, "The Psychoanalytic Study of Folklore," *Annals of Scholarship* 3 (1985): 1–42.
25. See the reprint of Charlotte Bühler's *Das Märchen und die Phantasie des Kindes* with an additional essay by Josephine Belz, 4th ed. (Berlin: Springer, 1977).
26. Géza Roheim, "Psychoanalysis and the Folk-Tale," *International Journal of Psychoanalysis* 3 (1922): 180–186.
27. C. J. Jung, "The Phenomenology of the Spirit in Fairy Tales," in *Psyche and Symbol*, ed. Violet S. de Laszlo (New York: Anchor, 1958), 61–112.
28. Aniela Jaffé, *Bilder und Symbole aus E. T. A. Hoffmanns Märchen "Der goldene Topf,"* (second rev. ed., Zurich: Gerstenberg, 1978).
29. Joseph Campbell, *The Hero with a Thousand Faces* (Cleveland: Meridian, 1956) and *The Flight of the Wild Gander: Explorations in the Mythological Dimension* (New York: HarperCollins, 1990).
30. Marie von Franz, *Problems of the Feminine in Fairytales* (New York: Spring, 1972).
31. Verena Kast, *Mann und Frau im Märchen: Eine psychologische Deutung* (Olten, Switzerland: Walter, 1983) and *Familienkonflikte im Märchen: Eine psychologische Deutung* (Olten, Switzerland: Walter, 1984). See also Mario Jacoby, Verena Kast, and Ingrid Riedel, *Witches, Ogres, and the Devil's Daughter: Encounters with Evil in Fairy Tales*, trans. Michael H. Kohn (Boston: Shambhala, 1992).
32. Erich Fromm, *The Forgotten Language* (New York: Grove, 1957).
33. Julius Heuscher, *A Psychiatric Study of Fairy Tales* (Springfield, Il: Thomas, 1963).
34. Bettelheim, *The Uses of Enchantment.*
35. André Favat, *Child and Tale: The Origins of Interest* (Urbana, Il.: National Council of Teachers of English, 1977).
36. Vladimir Propp, *Morphology of the Folktale*, ed. Louis Wagner and Alan Dundes, second rev. ed. (Austin: University of Texas Press, 1968).
37. Max Lüthi, *Das europäische Volksmärchen*, second rev. ed. (Bern: Francke, 1960); and *Once Upon a Time: On the Nature of Fairy Tales* (New York: Ungar, 1970).
38. Ludwig Denecke, *Jacob Grimm und sein Bruder Wilhelm* (Stuttgart: Metzler, 1971).
39. Rölleke, *Die Märchen der Brüder Grimm.*
40. Lothar Bluhm, *Grimm-Philologie: Beiträge zur Märchenforschung und Wissenschaftsgeschichte* (Hildesheim: Olms-Weidmann, 1995).
41. Dieter Richter and Johannes Merkel, *Märchen, Phantasie und soziales Lernen* (Berlin: Basis, 1974).
42. Christa Bürger, "Die soziale Funktion volkstümlicher Erzählformen—Sage und Märchen," in *Projekt Deutschunterricht 6*, ed. Heinz Ide (Stuttgart: Metzler, 1971): 26–56.
43. Bernd Wollenweber, "Märchen und Sprichwort," in *Projekt Deutschunterricht 6*, ed. Heinz Ide (Stuttgart: Metzler, 1974): 12–92.

44. Cf. Ernst Bloch, *The Utopian Function of Art and Literature*, trans. Jack Zipes and Frank Mecklenburg (Cambridge: MIT Press, 1987). This volume contains two essays that specifically deal with fairy tales, as well as essays that incorporate Bloch's notion of anticipatory illumination.
45. See the chapter, "The Culture Industry: Enlightenment as Mass Deception," in Max Horkheimer and Theodor Adorno, *Dialectic of Enlightenment*, trans. John Cumming (New York: Seabury Press, 1972), 120–167.
46. Pierre Bourdieu, *The Field of Cultural Production* (New York: Columbia University Press, 1993), 42.
47. Jürgen Kocka, ed., *Bürger und Bürgerlichkeit im 19. Jahrhundert* (Göttingen: Vandenhoeck & Ruprecht, 1987).
48. *Ibid.*, 43.
49. See Paul Münch, ed., *Ordnung, Fleiß und Sparsamkeit* (Munich: dtv, 1984), 9–38.
50. Cf. Dietz-Rüdger Moser, "Exempel—Paraphrase—Märchen: Zum Gattungswandel christlicher Volkserzählungen im 17. und 18. Jahrhundert am Beispiel einiger 'Kinder- und Hausmärchen' der Brüder Grimm," in *Sozialer und kultureller Wandel in der ländlichen Welt des 18. Jahrhunderts*, ed. Ernst Hinrichs and Günther Wegelmann (Wolfenbüttel: Herzog August Bibliothek, 1982), 117–148.
51. Cf. my introduction and essay, "Cross-Cultural Connections and the Contamination of the Classical Fairy Tale," in *The Great Fairy Tale Tradition*, ed. Jack Zipes (New York: Norton, 2001), xi-xiv and 845–869.
52. Cf. Jacques Barchilon, *Le Conte Merveilleux Français de 1690 à 1790* (Paris: Champion, 1975); Lewis C. Seifert, *Fairy Tales, Sexuality and Gender in France, 1690–1715: Nostalgic Utopias* (Cambridge: Cambridge University Press, 1996); Patricia Hannon, *Fabulous Identities: Women's Fairy Tales in Seventeenth-Century France* (Amsterdam: Rodopi, 1998); Shawn Jarvis and Jeannine Blackwell, eds., *The Queen's Mirror: Fairy Tales by German Women, 1780–1900* (Lincoln: University of Nebraska Press, 2001); and Elizabeth Wanning Harries, *Twice Upon a Time: Women Writers and the History of the Fairy Tale* (Princeton: Princeton University Press, 2001).
53. Cf. Jack Zipes, ed., *Don't Bet on the Prince: Contemporary Feminist Fairy Tales in North America and England* (New York: Methuen, 1986); Marina Warner, *From the Beast to the Blonde: On Fairy Tales and their Tellers* (London: Chatto & Windus, 1995).
54. Simon Bronner, "The Americanization of the Brothers Grimm," in *Following Tradition: Folklore in the Discourse of American Culture* (Logan, Utah: Utah State University Press, 1998), 187.
55. Many other critics are even more severe than I am. For example, see Henry A. Giroux, *The Mouse That Roared: Disney and the End of Innocence* (Lanham, Md: Rowman and Littlefield, 1999). For the most balanced study of Disney, his life, and the development of the Disney corporation, see Steven Watts, *The Magic Kingdom: Walt Disney and the American Way of Life* (Boston: Houghton Mifflin, 1997). Recently Janet Wasko has published an excellent critical and analytical study, *Understanding Disney: The Manufacture of Fantasy* (Cambridge: Polity, 2001).

CHAPTER 3

1. Jacob and Wilhelm Grimm, *The Complete Fairy Tales of the Brothers Grimm*, trans. Jack Zipes (New York: Bantam, 1987), 92. All further page references cited in the text.
2. See such other tales as "The Girl without Hands," "The Robber Bridegroom," "Fitcher's Bird," "The Six Swans," "The Knapsack, the Hat, and the Horn," "The Golden Goose," "The Miller's Drudge and the Cat," "The Two Traveling Companions," "The Donkey Lettuce," "Simelei Mountain," "The Three Green Branches," and "The Hazel Branch."
3. Hermann Grimm, Gustav Hinrichs, and Wilhelm Schoof, eds., *Briefwechsel zwischen Jacob und Wilhelm Grimm aus der Jugendzeit*, second rev. ed. (Weimar: Böhlaus, 1963), 49.
4. Gabriele Seitz, *Die Brüder Grimm: Leben—Werk—Zeit* (Munich: Winkler, 1984).
5. See Jack Zipes "The Fight Over Fairy-Tale Discourse: Family, Friction, and Socialization," in *Fairy Tales and the Art of Subversion* (New York: Methuen, 1983), 134–169; Lucia Borghese, "Antonio Gramsci und die Grimmschen Märchen," in *Brüder Grimm Gedenken*, ed. Ludwig Denecke, vol. 3 (Marburg: Elwert, 1981), 374–390.
6. Cf. Simon Bronner, "The Americanization of the Brothers Grimm," in *Following Tradition: Folklore in the Discourse of American Culture* (Logan, Utah: Utah State University Press, 1998), 184–236.
7. Eugen Weber, "Fairies and Hard Facts: The Reality of Folktales," *Journal of the History of Ideas* 42 (1981): 93–113.
8. Robert Darnton, *The Great Cat Massacre and Other Episodes in French Cultural History* (New York: Basic Books, 1984). In particular, see the chapter "Peasants Tell Tales: The Meaning of Mother Goose," 9–72.
9. Cf. Elfriede Moser-Rath, *Predigtmärlein der Barockzeit: Exempel, Sage, Schwank und Fabel in geistlichen Quellen des oberdeutschen Raums* (Berlin: de Gruyter, 1964); Rudolf Schenda, "Orale und literarische Kommunikationsformen im Bereich von Analphabeten und Gebildeten im 17. Jahrhundert," in *Literatur und Volk im 17. Jahrhundert: Probleme populärer Kultur in Deutschland*, ed. Wolfgang Brückner, Peter Blickle, and Dieter Breuer (Wiesbaden: Harrasowitz, 1985), 447–464; Rudolf Schenda, "Vorlesen: Zwischen Analphabetentum und Bücherwissen," *Bertelsmann Briefe* 119 (1986): 5–14.
10. Peter Taylor and Hermann Rebel, "Hessian Peasant Women, Their Families, and the Draft: A Social-Historical Interpretation of Four Tales from the Grimm Collection," *Journal of Family History* 6 (Winter, 1981): 347–378. Hereafter page references cited in the text.
11. For information about the sources, see Heinz Rölleke, ed., *Kinder- und Hausmärchen*, vol. 3 (Stuttgart: Reclam, 1980), 441–543.
12. Lothar Bluhm, *Grimm-Philologie: Beiträge zur Märchenforschung und Wissenschaftsgeschichte.* (Hildesheim: Olms-Weidmann, 1995), 23–24. For an English translation of the complete essay by Deborah Lokai Bischof, see "A New Debate about 'Old Marie'? Critical Observations on the Attempt to

Remythologize Grimms' Fairy Tales from a Sociohistorical Perspective," *Marvels & Tales* 14 (2000): 287–311. My translation is slightly different.

13. For the historical derivation of the tales, see the entries in Walter Scherf's excellent study, *Das Märchen Lexikon*, 2 vols. (Munich: Beck, 1995).
14. Hermann Rebel, Why not 'Old Marie' . . . or someone very much like her? A reassessment of the question about the Grimms' contributors from a social historical perspective," *Social History* 13 (January 1988): 9.
15. Again, see the excellent essay by Lothar Bluhm that defends Rölleke's position in great detail while developing important socio-historical theses for social history: "Neuer Streit um die 'Alte Marie'? Kritische Bemerkungen zum Versuch einer sozialgeschichtlichen Remythisierung der *Kinder- und Hausmärchen*" in *Grimm-Philologie*, 1–24.
16. Dietz-Rüdiger Moser, "Theorie- und Methodenprobleme der Märchenforschung," *Ethnologia Bavaria* 10 (1981): 61.
17. *Ibid.*, 61.
18. See Alice Eisler, "Recht im Märchen," *Neophilologus* 66 (1982): 422–430.
19. The number in parentheses indicates the total number of tales in which the social type plays the major role in the narrative.
20. Cf. Antti Aarne, *The Types of the Folktale: A Classification and Bibliography*, trans. and enlarged by Stith Thompson, second rev. ed., FF Communications Nr. 3 (Helsinki: Suomalainen Tiedekatemia, 1961).
21. Cf. Stith Thompson, *Motif-Index of Folk-Literature*, 6 vols. (Bloomington: University of Indiana Press, 1955).
22. Cf. Wolfgang Mieder, "Wilhelm Grimm's Proverbial Additions in the Fairy Tales," and "Sprichwörtliche Schwundstufen des Märchens. Zum 200. Geburtstag der Brüder Grimm," *Proverbium* 3 (1986): 59–83; 257–271; see also his book *"Findet; so werdet ihr suchen!" Die Brüder Grimm und das Sprichwort* (Bern: Peter Lang, 1986).
23. If one were to include "Herr Fix und Fertig," which was part of the 1812 edition (source: Johann Friedrich Krause) and eliminated in 1819, there would be 11 soldier tales. I have translated this tale as "Herr Fix-It-Up" in *The Complete Fairy Tales of the Brothers Grimm*, 647–650.
24. The titles in German are: "Die drei Schlangenblätter," "Sechse kommen durch die ganze Welt," "Bruder Lustig," "Bärenhäuter," "Des Teufels rußiger Bruder," "Das blaue Licht," "Der Teufel und seine Großmutter," "Die zertanzten Schuhe," "Der Stiefel von Büffelleder," and "Der Grabhügel."
25. The following remarks about soldiers are based to a large extent on the findings of Jürgen Kuczynski, *Geschichte des Alltags des deutschen Volkes, 1650–1810*, vol. 2 (Cologne: Pahl-Rugenstein, 1981).
26. Heinz Rölleke, ed., *Briefwechsel zwischen Jacob und Wilhelm Grimm* (Stuttgart: Hirzel, 2001), 300.
27. The titles in German are: "Das tapfere Schneiderlein," "Der Schneider im Himmel," "Tischlein deck dich, Goldesel und Knüppel aus dem Sack," "Däumlings Wanderschaft," "Die beiden Wanderer," "Vom klugen Schneiderlein," "Die klare Sonne bringt's an den Tag," "Der gläserne

Sarg," "Lieb und Leib teilen," "Geschenke des kleinen Volkes," and "Der Riese und der Schneider."

28. For clarification of the distinction between master tailors and journeymen and the conflicts between them, see James F. Farr, *Artisans in Europe 1300–1914* (Cambridge: Cambridge University Press, 2000), 191–221, and Hans-Ulrich Thamer, "On the Use and Abuse of Handicraft: Journeymen Culture and Enlightened Public Opinion in 18th and 19th Century Germany" in *Understanding Popular Culture*, ed. Steven L. Kaplan (Berlin: 1984).
29. Cf. Frieder Stöckle, ed., *Handwerkermärchen* (Frankfurt am Main: Fischer, 1986), 7–39. For a general picture of the living and working conditions of the artisans in Germany, see Reinhard Sieder, *Sozialgeschichte der Familie* (Frankfurt am Main: Suhrkamp, 1987): 103–124. This chapter deals with "Die Familien der Handwerker."
30. Cf. Geoffrey Crossick and Heinz-Gerhard Haupt, eds., *Shopkeepers and Master Artisans in Nineteenth-Century Europe* (London: Methuen, 1984), and Wolfgang Renzsch, *Handwerker und Lohnarbeiter in der frühen Arbeiterbewegung* (Göttingen: Vandenhoeck & Ruprecht, 1980).
31. Renzsch, *Handwerker und Lohnarbeiter*, 71–72.
32. Cf. Jacob's 1848 speech in the Church of St. Paul in Frankfurt am Main, "Über Adel und Orden" in *Reden und Aufsätze*, ed. Wilhelm Schoof (Munich: Winkler, 1966), 63–69.
33. For information about Riehl, see the excellent critical study by Mary Beth Stein, "Wilhelm Heinrich Riehl and the Scientific-Literary Formation of *Volkskunde*," *German Studies Review* 24 (October 2001): 461–486.
34. Wilhelm H. Riehl, *Die Naturgeschichte des deutschen Volkes* (Leipzig: Kröner, 1935), 73.
35. *Ibid.*, 73.

CHAPTER 4

1. Ingeborg Weber-Kellermann, ed., *Kinder- und Hausmärchen*, vol. 1 (Frankfurt am Main: Insel, 1976),14–15.
2. Heinz Rölleke, *Die Märchen der Brüder Grimm* (Munich: Artemis, 1985), 25.
3. Jack Zipes, *Fairy Tales and the Art of Subversion: The Classical Genre for Children and the Process of Civilization* (New York: Methuen, 1983).
4. Cf. Andrea Dworkin, *Woman Hating* (New York: Dutton, 1974); Heide Göttner-Abendroth, *Die Göttin und ihr Heros* (Munich: Frauenoffensive, 1980); and the various essays in Sigrid Früh and Rainer Wehse, eds. *Die Frau im Märchen* (Kassel: Erich Röth, 1985).
5. See Jennifer Waelti-Walters, *Fairy Tales and the Female Imagination* (Montreal: Eden Press, 1982); Jack Zipes, ed., *Don't Bet on the Prince: Contemporary Feminist Fairy Tales in North America and England* (New York: Methuen, 1986); Ruth B. Bottigheimer, *Grimms' Bad Girls and Bold Boys: The Moral and Social Vision of the Tales* (New Haven: Yale University Press, 1987); Marina Warner, *From the Beast to the Blonde: On Fairy Tales and Their Tellers* (London: Chatto & Windus, 1994).

6. For two stimulating studies on this topic, see Katalin Horn, *Der aktive und der passive Märchenheld* (Basel: Schweizerische Gesellschaft für Volkskunde, 1983) and Maria M. Tatar, "Born Yesterday: Heroes in the Grimms' Tales," in *Fairy Tales and Society: Illusion, Allusion, and Paradigm*, ed. Ruth B. Bottigheimer (Philadelphia: University of Pennsylvania Press, 1986), 95–112.
7. In Früh and Wehse, eds., *Die Frau im Märchen*, 72–88.
8. Max Horkheimer and Theodor Adorno, *Dialectic of Enlightenment*, trans. John Cumming (New York: Seabury, 1972), 43–80.
9. *Ibid.*, 57.
10. *Ibid.*, 62.
11. Cf. Ruth B. Bottigheimer, "Silenced Women in the Grimms' Tales: The 'Fit' Between Fairy Tales and Society in Their Historical Context," in *Fairy Tales and Society*, ed. Ruth B. Bottigheimer, 115–131.
12. Cf. Tatar, "Born Yesterday: Heroes in the Grimms' Fairy Tales," 98–105.
13. Gustav Hinrichs, ed., *Kleinere Schriften*, vol. 1 (Berlin: Dümmlers, 1881), 356.
14. See my translation in Jacob and Wilhelm Grimm, *The Complete Fairy Tales of the Brothers Grimm* (New York: Bantam: 1987), 708–713.
15. For a comprehensive analysis of the Polyphemus tradition and the place of the Grimms' "The Robber and His Sons" within it, see Lutz Röhrich, "Die mittelalterichen Redaktionen des Polyphem-Märchens und ihr Verhältnis zur außerhomerischen Tradition," in Röhrich, *Sage und Märchen: Erzählforschung heute* (Freiburg: Herder, 1976), 234–251.
16. Gustav Hinrichs, ed. *Kleinere Schriften*, vol. 4 (Gütersloh: Bertelsmann, 1887), 428–462.
17. *Ibid.*, 461.
18. Mikhail M. Bakhtin, "The Problem of Speech Genres," in *Speech Genres and Other Late Essays*, ed. Caryl Emerson and Michael Holquist, trans. Vern W. McGee (Austin University of Texas Press, 1986), 88–89.

CHAPTER 5

1. *The Economist* (August 11, 1984), 37.
2. In Jack Zipes, *The Trials and Tribulations of Little Red Riding Hood* (South Hadley, MA: Bergin & Garvey, 1983), 256.
3. Robert Darnton, *The Great Cat Massacre and Other Episodes in French Cultural History* (New York: Basic Books, 1984), 50.
4. John Ellis, *One Fairy Story Too Many* (Chicago: University of Chicago Press, 1983), 100.
5. See Martine Segalen, *Mari et femme dans la societé paysanne* (Paris: Flammarion, 1980); Reinhard Sieder, *Sozialgeschichte der Familie* (Frankfurt am Main: Suhrkamp, 1987),12–72; and James R. Farr, *Artisans in Europe, 1300–1914* (Cambridge: Cambridge University Press, 2000).
6. Cf. Zipes, *The Trials and Tribulations of Little Red Riding Hood.* In particular, see the introduction to the second rev. edition (New York: Routledge, 1993).
7. Ellis, *One Fairy Story Too Many*, 35.
8. In particular, see Heinz Rölleke, ed., *Die älteste Märchensammlung der Brüder Grimm* (Cologny-Geneva: Fondation Martin Bodmer, 1975).

9. Donald Ward, "New Misconceptions about Old Folktales: The Brothers Grimm," in *The Brothers Grimm and Folktale*, ed. James M. McGlathery (Urbana: University of Illinois Press, 1988), 93.
10. Cf. Ingeborg Weber-Kellermann's introduction to *Kinder- und Hausmärchen gesammelt durch die Brüder Grimm*, vol. 1 (Frankfurt am Main: Insel, 1976), 9–18, and Heinz Rölleke's afterword to Brüder Grimm, *Kinder- und Hausmärchen* (Stuttgart: Reclam, 1980), 590–617.
11. Wilhelm Schoof, *Zur Entstehungsgeschichte der Grimmschen Märchen* (Hamburg: Hauswedell, 1959), 147.
12. In his afterword to the *Kinder- und Hausmärchen*, Rölleke makes the point that the Grimms were very conscious of their audience and sought to mold the tales to suit the needs of their readers.
13. Cf. Ernst Bloch, *Ästhetik des Vor-Scheins*, ed. Gert Ueding, 2 vols. (Frankfurt am Main: Suhrkamp, 1974). Many of the same essays in this book are contained in Ernst Bloch, *The Utopian Function of Art and Literature*, trans. Jack Zipes and Frank Mecklenburg (Cambridge: MIT Press, 1987).
14. See Antti Aarne, *The Types of the Folktale: A Classification and Bibliography*, trans. and enlarged by Stith Thompson, second rev. ed., F. F. Communications Nr. 3 (Helsinki: Suomalainen Tiedekatemia, 1961).
15. Cf. my discussion of the international and national aspects of the tales in "The Contamination of the Fairy Tale," in *Sticks and Stones: The Troublesome Success of Children's Literature from Slovenly Peter to Harry Potter* (New York: Routledge, 2000), 99–125.
16. Peter Bürger, "Institution Kunst als literatursoziologische Kategorie," in *Seminar: Literatur- und Kunstsoziologie*, ed. Peter Bürger (Frankfurt am Main: Suhrkamp, 1978), 261.
17. *Ibid.*, 262.
18. Cf. Mary Elizabeth Storer, *La Mode des contes des fées (1685–170)* (Paris: Champion, 1928); Jacques Barchilon, *Le conte merveilleux français de 1690 à 1790* (Paris: Champion, 1975); and Raymonde Robert, *Le conte des fées littéraire en France de la fin du XVIIe à la fin du XVIIIe siècle* (Nancy: Presses Universitaires de Nancy, 1982). For comments on how women writers used the discourse to express their criticisms of court conventions and social practices, see Lewis Seifert, *Fairy Tales, Sexuality and Gender in France, 1690–1715: Nostalgic Utopias* (Cambridge: Cambridge University Press, 1996); Patricia Hannon, *Fabulous Identities: Women's Fairy Tales in Seventeenth-Century France* (Amsterdam: Rodopi, 1998); and Jean Mainil, *Madame D'Aulnoy et le Rire des Fées: Essai sur la subversion féerique et le merveilleux comique sous l'ancien régime* (Paris: Klimé, 2001).
19. Bürger, "Institution Kunst," 269.
20. *Ibid.*, 264.
21. Most of these tales have been translated into English. See Frank G. Ryder and Robert Browning, eds., *German Literary Fairy Tales* (New York: Continuum, 1983) and Jack Zipes, ed., *Spells of Enchantment: The Wondrous Fairy Tales of Western Culture* (New York: Viking, 1991).

22. For a more thorough critique of how Americans' notions of the Grimms' tales have been influenced by Disney, see my book *Happily Ever After: Fairy Tales, Children, and the Culture Industry* (New York: Routledge, 1997).
23. Cf. Fred E. Schrader, *Die Formierung der bürgerlichen Gesellschaft, 1550–1850* (Frankfurt am Main: Fischer Taschenbuch, 1996).
24. See Shawn Jarvis and Jeannine Blackwell, *The Queen's Mirror: Fairy Tales by German Women, 1780–1900* (Lincoln: University of Nebraska Press, 2001).
25. See Ulrike Bastian, *Die "Kinder- und Hausmärchen" der Brüder Grimm in der literaturpädagogischen Diskussion des 19. und 20. Jahrhunderts* (Giessen: Haag & Herchen, 1981).
26. Walter Benjamin, "The Storyteller," in *Illuminations*, trans. Harry Zohn (New York: Harcourt, Brace & World, 1968), 102.
27. Ernst Bloch, "Bessere Luftschlösser in Jahrmarkt und Zirkus, in Märchen und Kolportage" in *Ästhetik des Vor-Scheins*, ed. Gert Ueding, Vol. 1 (Frankfurt am Main: Suhrkamp, 1974), 73–4. See the translation, "Better Castles in the Sky at the County Fair and Circus, in Fairy Tales and Colportage," in *The Utopian Function of Art and Literature*, 169.
28. Elias Canetti, *Die Provinz des Menschen: Aufzeichnungen 1942–1972* (Munich: Hanser, 1972), 48.
29. Yaak Karsunke, "Deutsches Märchen," in *Mädchen, pfeif auf den Prinzen: Märchengedichte von Günter Grass bis Sarah Kirsch*, ed. Wolfgang Mieder (Cologne: Diederichs, 1983), 35.
30. Janosch, "Hans Mein Igel," in *Janosch erzählt Grimm's Märchen* (Weinheim: Beltz & Gelberg, 1972), 170–175.
31. Margaret Kassajep, "Dornröschen und Prinz Hasse," in *Deutsche Hausmärchen frischgetrimmt* (Dachau: Baedeker & Lang, 1980), 84–86.
32. Burckhard and Gisela Garbe, "Rotkäppchen oder: Wolf bleibt Wolf," in *Der ungestiefelte Kater: Grimms Märchen umerzählt* (Göttingen: sage & schreibe, 1985), 87–90.
33. Chris Schrauff, *Der Wolf und seine Steine* (Hannover: SOAK, 1986), 108–110.
34. For a discussion of the development of the fairy tale in the 1920s and 1930s, see the chapter "The Fight over Fairy-Tale Discourse: Family, Friction, and Socialization in the Weimar Republic and Nazi Germany" in Jack Zipes, *Fairy Tales and the Art of Subversion* (New York: Methuen, 1983), 134–169.
35. See Jack Zipes, "Grimms in Farbe, Bild und Ton: Der deutsche Märchenfilm für Kinder im Zeitalter der Kulturindustrie," in *Aufbruch zum neuen bundesdeutschen Kinderfilm*, ed. Wolfgang Schneider (Hardeck: Eulenhof, 1982): 212–224.
36. See Bastian, *Die "Kinder- und Hausmärchen" der Brüder Grimm*, 226–318. Bastian also discusses the postwar development in East Germany that is important to investigate in order to obtain a complete picture of the fairy tale as institution in German-speaking countries. See 186–225 and also chapter 10 in this volume.
37. For a general overview of his notions, see Rudolf Steiner, *Märchendichtungen im Lichte der Geistesforschung: Märchendeutungen* (Dornach, Switzerland:

Verlag der Rudolf Steiner-Nachlassverwaltung, 1969). These two essays were first held as talks in 1913 and 1908, respectively.

38. Cf. Andreas von Prondczynsky, *Die unendliche Sehnsucht nach sich selbst: Auf den Spuren eines neuen Mythos: Versuch über eine "unendliche Geschichte"* (Frankfurt am Main: dipa, 1983).

CHAPTER 6

1. Maurice Bémol, "Henri Pourrat et 'Le Trésor des Contes,'" *Annales Universitatis Saraviensis* 10 (1961): 180–181.
2. Mark J. Temmer, "Henri Pourrat's 'Trésor des Contes,'" *French Review* 38 (October, 1964): 46.
3. Henri Pourrat, *Contes du vieux-vieux temps*, ed. Michel Chrestien (Paris: Gallimard, 1970). See preface by Chrestien, 7–16.
4. Henri Pourrat, *Les fées*, ed. Claire Pourrat (Paris: Gallimard, 1983), 11.
5. Henri Pourrat, *Le Trésor des Contes*, vol. 5 (Paris: Gallimard, 1954), 277.
6. The best study of Pourrat's life and work is Bernadette Bricout, *Le Savoir et la saveur: Henri Pourrat et Le Trésor des contes* (Paris: Gallimard, 1992). Interestingly, one of the first portrayals of his life and writings was by Arno Ringelmann, a German, who was interested in the racial and folk aspects of Pourrat's early works. See *Henri Pourrat: Ein Beitrag zur Kenntnis der Littérature terrienne"* (Würzburg: Kilian, 1936). Depending on one's viewpoint, one could translate "littérature terrienne" as "blood and soil" or local color literature.
7. Cf. Sylvia Mittler, "Le jeune Henri Pourrat: de Barrès et Bergson à l'âme rustique," *Travaux de Lingustique et de Littérature* 15 (1977): 193–215.
8. Cited in Mittler, "Le jeune Henri Pourrat," 200.
9. Three of the volumes were published posthumously after Pourrat's death in 1962.
10. See the following volumes all edited by Claire Pourrat and published by Gallimard in Paris: *Le Diable et ses diableries* (1977), *Les Brigands* (1978), *Au Village* (1979), *Les Amours* (1981), *Les Fées* (1983), *Les Fous et les sages* (1986), and *Le Bestiaire* (1986).
11. See Henri Pourrat, *Contes* (Paris: Gallimard, 1987).
12. Henri Pourrat, *A Treasury of French Tales*, trans. Mary Mian (London: Allen & Unwin, 1953).
13. Henri Pourrat, *French Folktales*, trans. Royall Tyler (New York: Pantheon, 1989).
14. There was an exhibit of his work in Clermont-Ferrand and a catalogue published about the exhibit. See *Le Monde à l'envers dans le Trésor des Contes d'Henri Pourrat* (Clermont-Gerrand: Bibliothèque municipale et universitaire, 1987) and *Actes du Colloque du Centenaire:* "Henri Pourrat et le *Trésor des contes*," *Cahiers Henri Pourrat*, no. 6 (Bibliothèque municipale et interuniversitaire de Clermont-Ferrand, 1988).
15. Mikhail M. Bakhtin, "The Problem of Speech Genres," in *Speech Genres and Other Late Essays*, trans. Vern W. McGee and ed. Caryl Emerson and

Michael Holquist (Austin: University of Texas, 1986), 60–102. Hereafter page references cited in the text.

16. With regard to the mutual influences and dialogue, there have been two interesting studies concerned with Perrault's influence on the Grimms. See Harry Velten, "The Influence of Charles Perrault's Contes de ma Mère L'Oie on German Folklore," *Germanic Review* 5 (1930): 14–18, and Rolf Hagen, "Perraults Märchen und die Brüder Grimm," *Deutsche Philologie* 74 (1955): 392–410.
17. Jacques Barchilon, *Perrault's Tales of Mother Goose: The Dedication Manuscript of 1695 reproduced in collotype Facsimile with Introduction and Critical Text* (New York: The Pierpont Morgan Library, 1956).
18. Marc Soriano, *Les Contes de Perrault: Culture et traditions populaires* (Paris: Gallimard, 1968).
19. Raymonde Robert, *Le conte des fées littéraire en France de la fin du XVIIe à la fin du XVIIIe siècle* (Nancy: Presses Universitaires de Nancy, 1982).
20. Lewis Seifert, *Fairy Tales, Sexuality, and Gender in France, 1690–1715: Nostalgic Utopias* (Cambridge: University of Cambridge Press, 1996).
21. Catherine Velay-Vallantin, "Le miroir des contes: Perrault dans les Bibilothèques bleues," in *Les usages de l'imprimé*, ed. Roger Chartier (Paris: Fayard, 1987), 129–185.
22. Cf. Jack Zipes, "Les origines italiennes du conte de fées: Basile et Straparola," in *Il était une fois . . . les contes de fées*, ed. Olivier Piffault (Paris: Seuil, 2001), 66–74.
23. Velay-Vallantin, "Le miroir des contes," 179–180, 181–182.
24. Pourrat, *Le Trésor des Contes*, vol. 5, 271, 275.
25. Mittler, "Le jeune Henri Pourrat," 193–215.
26. *Ibid.*, "Le jeune Henri Pourrat," 214.
27. Dany Hadjady, "Du 'releve de folklore' au conte populaire: avec Henri Pourrat, promenade aux fontaines du dire," in *Frontières du conte*, ed. François Marotin (Paris: Editions du Centre National de la Recherche Scientifique, 1982), 55–67.
28. Charles Perrault, *Contes*, ed. Gilbert Rouger (Paris: Garnier, 1967), 98–99. My translation.
29. Heinz Rölleke, ed., *Kinder- und Hausmärchen*, vol. 1 (Stuttgart: Reclam, 1980), 258. My translation.
30. Pourrat, *Le Trésor des Contes*, vol. 5, 40. Unless otherwise indicated, all translations of Pourrat's tales are my own.
31. Pourrat, *Contes de la Bucheronne* (Tours: Maison Mame, 1935), 184.
32. Pourrat, *Les Fées* (Paris: Gallimard, 1983), 49.
33. Pourrat, *Le Trésor des Contes*, vol. 3 (Paris: Gallimard, 1951), 281–222.

CHAPTER 7

1. There were major celebrations in Kassel; Marburg; Berlin; Munich; Belgrade; Tokyo; Santiago; New York; and Urbana, Illinois, to name but a few.

2. Dieter Hennig and Bernhard Lauer, eds., *Die Brüder Grimm: Dokumente ihres Lebens und Wirkens* (Kassel: Weber & Weidemeyer, 1985).
3. Ingrid Koszinowski and Vera Leuschner, eds., *Ludwig Emil Grimm 1790–1863: Maler, Zeichner, Radierer* (Kassel: Weber & Weidemeyer, 1985).
4. Hans Bernd Harder and Ekkehard Kaufmann, eds., *Die Brüder Grimm in ihrer amtlichen und politischen Tätigkeit* (Kassel: Weber & Weidemeyer, 1985).
5. *Jacob und Wilhelm Grimm: Vorträge und Ansprachen in den Veranstaltungen der Akademie der Wissenschaften und der Georg-August-Universität in Göttingen* (Göttingen: Vandenhoeck & Ruprecht, 1986).
6. Wilhelm Solms, ed., *Das selbstverständliche Wunder: Beiträge germanistischer Märchenforschung* (Marburg: Hitzroth, 1986).
7. Irma Hildebrandt, *Es waren ihrer Fünf: Die Brüder Grimm und ihre Familie* (Cologne: Diederichs, 1984).
8. Gabriele Seitz, *Die Brüder Grimm: Leben—Werk—Zeit* (Munich: Winkler, 1984).
9. *Diskussion Deutsch* 17/91 (October/November 1986).
10. Ludwig Denecke, ed., *Brüder Grimm Gedenken 6 und* 7, vol. 6 (Marburg: Elwert, 1986) and vol. 7 (Marburg: Elwert, 1987).
11. Heinz Rölleke, *"Wo das Wünschen noch geholfen hat": Gesammelte Aufsätze zu den "Kinder- und Hausmärchen" der Brüder Grimm* (Bonn: Bouvier, 1985).
12. Heinz Rölleke, *Die Märchen der Brüder Grimm* (Munich: Artemis, 1985).
13. Heinz Rölleke, ed., *Kleine Ausgabe* (Frankfurt am Main: Insel, 1985).
14. Heinz Rölleke and Ulrike Marquardt, eds., *Kinder- und Hausmärchen Gesammelt durch die Brüder Grimm: Vergrösserter Nachdruck der zweibändigen Erstausgabe von 1812 und 1815 nach dem Handexemplar des Brüder Grimm-Museums Kassel mit sämtlichen handschriftlichen Korrekturen und Nachträgen der Brüder Grimm sowie einem Ergänzungsheft* (Göttingen: Vandenhoeck & Ruprecht, 1986).
15. Albert Schindehütte, ed., *Krauses Grimm'sche Märchen*, preface by Heinz Rölleke (Kassel: Stauda, 1985).
16. Verena Kast, *Wege aus Angst und Symbiose: Märchen psychologisch gedeutet* (Olten, Switzerland: Walter, 1982); *Through Emotions to Maturity: Psychological Readings of Fairy Tales*, trans. Douglas Whitcher (New York: Fromm International, 1993).
17. Eugen Drewermann, *Das Mädchen ohne Hände* (Freiburg: Olten, 1981).
18. Eugen Drewermann, *Schneeweißchen und Rosenrot* (Freiburg: Olten, 1983).
19. Eugen Drewermann, *Die kluge Else, Rapunzel* (Freiburg: Olten, 1986).
20. Hildegunde Wöller, *Aschenputtel: Energie der Liebe* (Stuttgart: Kreuz, 1984).
21. Lutz Müller, *Das tapfere Schneiderlein: List als Lebenskunst* (Stuttgart: Kreuz, 1985).
22. Hans Jellouschek, *Der Froschkönig: Geschichte einer Beziehung* (Stuttgart: Kreuz, 1985).
23. Ursula Eschenbach, *Hänsel und Gretel: Der Sohn im mütterlichen Dunkel* (Stuttgart: Kreuz, 1986).
24. Carl Mallet, *Kopf Ab! Gewalt im Märchen* (Hamburg: Rasch und Röhring, 1985).

25. Elisabeth Müller, *Das Bild der Frau im Märchen: Analysen und erzieherische Betrachtungen* (Munich: Profil, 1986).
26. Sigrid Früh and Rainer Wehse, eds., *Die Frau im Märchen* (Kassel: Röth, 1985).
27. There were well over 60 during the two-year period 1985–87. See Annemarie Verweyen, "Jubiläumsausgaben zu den Märchen der Brüder Grimm: 'Wenig Bücher sind mit solcher Lust entstanden . . . ,'" *Börsenblatt* 77 (August 27, 1985): 2465–2473.
28. Helga Gebert, ed., *Alte Märchen der Brüder Grimm* (Weinheim: Beltz & Gelberg, 1985).
29. Uta Claus and Rolf Kutschera, *Total Tote Hose: 12 Bockstarke Märchen* (Frankfurt am Main: Eichborn, 1984).
30. Heinz Langer, *Grimmige Märchen* (Munich: Hugendubel, 1984).
31. Chris Schrauff, *Der Wolf und seine Steine* (Hannover: SOAK-Verlag, 1986).
32. Cf. Christa Bürger, "Die soziale Funktion volkstümlicher Erzählformen—Sage und Märchen," in *Projekt Deutschunterricht 1*, ed. Heinz Ide (Stuttgart: Metzler, 1971), 26–56; Bernd Wollenweber, "Märchen und Sprichwort," in *Projektunterricht 6*, ed. Heinz Ide (Stuttgart: Metzler, 1974): 12–92; Dieter Richter and Johannes Merkel, *Märchen, Phantasie und soziales Lernen* (Berlin: Basis, 1974).
33. See Werner Ogris, "Jacob Grimm und die Rechtsgeschichte," in *Jacob und Wilhelm Grimm* (Göttingen: Vandenhoeck & Ruprecht, 1986), 67–96.
34. Heinz Rölleke, "Die 'Kinder- und Hausmärchen' der Brüder Grimm in neuer Sicht," *Diskussion Deutsch* 91 (October/November 1986): 458–464.
35. Cf. Rudolf Freudenberg, "Erzähltechnik und 'Märchenton'" in *Das selbstverständliche Wunder: Beiträge germanistischer Märchenforschung*, ed. Wilhelm Solms (Marburg: Hitzeroh, 1986), 121–142; and Wolfgang Mieder, "Sprichwörtliche Schwundformen des Märchens. Zum 200. Geburtstag der Brüder Grimm," *Proverbium* 3 (1986): 257–272.
36. Lutz Röhrich, "Der Froschkönig," in Solms, ed., *Das selbstverständliche Wunder*, 7–41.
37. *Ibid.*, 9.
38. Wolfgang Mieder also deals with parodies and variations of "The Frog King" in an interesting manner. See the essay "Grimm Variations: From Fairy Tales to Modern Anti-Fairy Tales" in his book *Tradition and Innovation in Folk Literature* (Hannover: University Press of New England, 1987), 13–22.
39. Dieter Arendt, "Dümmlinge, Däumlinge und Diebe im Märchen—oder: 'drei Söhne, davon hieß der Jüngste der Dümmling' (KHM 64)," *Diskussion Deutsch* 91 (October 1986): 465–478.
40. Gertrud Jungblut, "Märchen der Brüder Grimm—Feministisch gelesen," *Diskussion Deutsch* 91 (October 1986): 497–510.
41. Heide Göttner-Abendroth, *Die Göttin und ihr Heros* (Munich: Frauenoffensive, 1980).
42. For an English translation of Mallet's early work, *Kennen Sie Kinder?*, see *Fairy Tales and Children: The Psychology of Children Revealed through Four of Grimm's Fairy Tales* (New York: Schocken, 1984).

43. Carl Mallet, *Kennen Sie Kinder?* (Munich: dtv, 1985).
44. Mallet, *Ibid.*, 67–92.
45. Cf. Jack Zipes, *The Trials and Tribulations of Little Red Riding Hood* (South Hadley: Bergin & Garvey, 1983).
46. Müller, *Das tapfere Schneiderlein*, 24.
47. Walter Scherf, "Das Märchenpublikum: Die Erwartung der Zuhörer und Leser und die Antwort des Erzählers," *Diskussion Deutsch* 91 (October 1986): 479–496.
48. See Alice Miller, *Du sollst nicht merken: Variationen über das Paradies-Thema* (Frankfurt am Main: Suhrkamp, 1983), 294–300.
49. All of Miller's books were first published in Germany by the Suhrkamp Verlag in Frankfurt am Main.
50. Alice Miller, *The Drama of the Gifted Child*, trans. Ruth Ward (New York: Basic Books, 1981), 27.
51. Miller, *Du sollst nicht merken*, 295–296. My translation, which is slightly different from the one in *Thou Shalt Not Be Aware*, 232.
52. Cf. Heinrich Hoffmann, *Struwwelpeter: Fearful Stories and Vile Pictures to Instruct Good Little Folks*, illustr. Sarita Vendetta, intro. Jack Zipes (Venice, CA: Feral House, 1999).
53. C. Alan Dundes, *Life Is Like a Chicken Coop Ladder: A Portrait of German Culture Through Folklore* (New York: Columbia University Press, 1984). Dundes tries to explain some aspects of the German national character by understanding the German interest in anal practices and products as expressed in proverbs, slang, and folk customs. "I believe Mayhew was on the right track and that he correctly anticipated psychoanalytic theory which postulates a connection or correlation between infant care and adult personality. The continued use of the German expression 'Der ist falsch gewickelt' (He was swaddled wrongly) suggesting that a misguided individual was damaged as an infant through poor child care hints that the folk themselves may have sensed the connection between infant care and adult personality. One might suppose, for example, that the important twentieth-century German notion of Lebensraum (living space) might reflect something more than political history or the particularities of the personality of Hitler. Lebensraum may conceivably go back to the painful discomfort of severe swaddling techniques. As an infant seeks more 'living space,' so adults in the same culture might find great appeal in a concept that offered the nation (and its citizens) a chance to move around and spread out," 101–102.

    Though overstated, Dundes's thesis is worth pursuing, since there may indeed be a connection between swaddling and the raising of children in Germany and the depiction of abuse and cruel treatment of children in the Grimms' tales and also in children's books like the famous *Struwwelpeter* (1845), or in Hans Christian Andersen's fairy tales that began appearing in 1835.
54. Alan Dundes, "The Psychoanalytic Study of the Grimms' Tales with Special Reference to 'The Maiden Without Hands' (AT 706)," *Germanic Review* 42 (Spring, 1987): 54.

55. Jacob and Wilhelm Grimm, *The Complete Fairy Tales of the Brothers Grimm*, trans. and ed. Jack Zipes (New York: Bantam, 1987), 120.
56. *Ibid.*, 62.
57. Walter Killy, ed., *Kinder- und Hausmärchen in der ersten Gestalt* (Frankfurt am Main: Fischer, 1962), 91.
58. Cf. Jeffrey M. Masson, *Assault on Truth: Freud's Suppression of the Seduction Theory* (New York: Farrar, Straus & Giroux, 1984).
59. My translation based on the 1812 text in *Kinder- und Hausmärchen*, 89–92.
60. Based on my translation in *The Complete Fairy Tales of the Brothers Grimm*,118–123. I have made some minor changes.

CHAPTER 8

1. Jack Goody, *The Domestication of the Savage Mind* (Cambridge: Cambridge University Press, 1977).
2. Walter Ong, *Orality and Literacy* (London: Methuen, 1982).
3. Heide Göttner-Abendroth, *Die Göttin und ihr Heros* (Munich: Frauenoffensive, 1982).
4. Dieter Richter, *Schlaraffenland: Geschichte einer populären Phantasie* (Cologne: Diederichs, 1984).
5. August Nitschke, *Soziale Ordnungen im Spiegel der Märchen*, vols. 1 and 2 (Stuttgart: Frommann-Holzboog, 1976–77).
6. Raymonde Robert, *Le conte des fées littéraire en France de la fin du XVIe à la fin du XVIIe siècle* (Nancy: Presses Universitaires de Nancy, 1982).
7. Rudolf Schenda, "Orale und literarische Kommunikationsformen im Bereich von Analphabeten und Gebildeteten im 17. Jahrhundert," in *Literatur und Volk im 17. Jahrhundert: Probleme populärer Kultur in Deutschland*, ed., Wolfgang Brückner, Peter Blickle, and Dieter Breuer (Wiesbaden: Harrasowitz, 1985), 447–464; and *Folklore e letteratura popolare: Italia—Germania—Francia* (Rome: Istituto della Enciclopedia, 1986).
8. Ong, *Orality and Literacy*, 2.
9. *Ibid.*, 12.
10. Cf. Andrea Dworkin, *Woman Hating* (New York: Dutton, 1974); Maria Kolbenschlag, *Kiss Sleeping Beauty Good-bye* (New York: Doubleday, 1979); Jennifer Waelti-Walters, *Fairy Tales and the Female Imagination* (Montreal: Eden Press, 1982); the essays by Marcia Lieberman, Karen Rowe, Susan Gubar and Sandra Gilbert in *Don't Bet on the Prince*, ed. Jack Zipes (New York: Methuen, 1986); Ruth Bottigheimer, *Grimms' Bad Girls and Bold Boys: The Moral and Social Vision of the Tales* (New Haven: Yale University Press, 1987), and Marina Warner, *From the Beast to the Blonde: On Fairy Tales and their Tellers* (London: Chatto & Windus, 1995).
11. Nitschke also discusses his theses in his essay "Aschenputtel aus der Sicht der historischen Verhaltensforschung," in *Und wenn sie nicht gestorben sind . . . Perspektiven auf das Märchen*, ed. Helmut Brackert (Frankfurt am Main: Suhrkamp, 1980), 71–88.
12. Alan Dundes, ed. *Cinderella: A Casebook* (New York: Garland, 1982).

13. See William Bascom, "Cinderella in Africa," in *Cinderella: A Casebook*, ed. Dundes, 148–168.
14. See Margaret A. Mills, "A Cinderella Variant in the Context of a Muslim Women's Ritual," in *Cinderella: A Casebook*, ed. Dundes, 180–92. Hereafter page references cited in the text.
15. Cf. Jack Zipes, *Fairy Tales and the Art of Subversion* (New York: Methuen, 1983).
16. Anne Sexton, *Transformations* (Boston: Houghton Mifflin, 1971).
17. Iring Fetscher, *Wer hat Dornröschen wachgeküßt? Das Märchen Verwirrbuch* (Hamburg: Classen, 1972).
18. Richard Gardner, *Dr. Gardner's Fairy Tales for Today's Children* (Englewood Cliffs: Prentice-Hall, 1974).
19. Tanith Lee, *Princess Hynchatti and Some Other Surprises* (London: Macmillan, 1972).
20. Janosch, *Janosch erzählt Grimm's Märchen* (Weinheim: Beltz, 1972).
21. John Gardner, *Gudgekin the Thistle Girl and Other Tales* (New York: Knopf, 1976).
22. Olga Broumas, *Beginning with O.* (New Haven: Yale University Press, 1977).
23. Jay Williams, *The Practical Princess and Other Liberating Tales* (New York: Parents' Magazine Press, 1979).
24. Margaret Kassajep, *"Deutsche Hausmärchen" frisch getrimmt* (Dachau: Baedeker & Lang, 1980).
25. Judith Viorst, *If I Were in Charge of the World* (New York: Atheneum, 1982).
26. Roald Dahl, *Revolting Rhymes* (London: Jonathan Cape, 1982).
27. Jane Yolen, *Tales of Wonder* (New York: Schocken, 1983).
28. Dahl, *Revolting Rhymes*, 1.
29. Ann Jungman, *Cinderella and the Hot Air Balloon*, illustr. Russell Ayto (London: Frances Lincoln, 1992).
30. Gail Carson Levine, *Cinderellis and the Glass Hill*, illustr. Mark Elliott (New York: Harper Collins, 2000).
31. Philip Pullman, *I Was a Rat!* (New York: Knopf, 1999).
32. Patricia Galloway, "The Prince," in *Truly Grim Tales* (New York: Bantam Doubleday Dell, 1995).
33. *Ibid.*, 124.
34. Emma Donoghue, "The Tale of the Shoe," in *Kissing the Witch: Old Tales in New Skins* (New York: HarperCollins, 1997).
35. *Ibid.*, 2.
36. Francesca Lia Block, "Glass," in *The Rose and The Beast: Fairy Tales Retold* (New York: HarperCollins, 2000).
37. Gregory Maguire, *Confessions of an Ugly Stepsister*, illustr. Bill Sanderson (New York: Regan Books, 1999).
38. Marcia Lieberman, "'Some Day My Prince Will Come': Female Acculturation Through the Fairy Tale," *College English* 34 (1972): 383–395.
39. Jane Yolen, "America's Cinderella," *Children's Literature in Education* 8 (1977): 21–29.
40. Colette Dowling, *The Cinderella Complex* (New York: Simon and Schuster, 1981).

41. Jennifer Waelti-Walters, *Fairy Tales and the Female Imagination* (Montreal: Eden Press, 1982).
42. Marina Warner, *From the Beast to the Blonde: On Fairy Tales and Their Tellers* (London: Chatto & Windus, 1995).
43. See J. Godwin, C. G. Cawthorne, and R. T. Rada, "Cinderella Syndrome: Children Who Simulate Neglect," *American Journal of Psychiatry* 137 (1980): 1223–1225.
44. For the various ways children and adults respond to "Cinderella" and thus participate in the dialogue, see Mary Jeffrey Collier, "The Psychological Appeal in the Cinderella Theme," *American Imago* 18 (1961): 399–406; Beryl Sandford, "Cinderella," *The Psychoanalytic Forum* 2 (1967): 127–144; and Barbara Herrnstein Smith, "Narrative Versions, Narrative Theories," *Critical Inquiry* 7 (1980): 213–236.

CHAPTER 9

1. Sara Henderson Hay, *Story Hour* (Fayetteville: University of Arkansas Press, 1982): 6–7.
2. London: Granada, 1973.
3. New York: Hill and Wang, 1977.
4. "Change the Object Itself: Mythology Today," in *Image—Music—Text*, trans. Stephen Heath (New York: Hill and Wang, 1977), 165.
5. *Mythologies*, trans. Annette Lavers (London: Granada, 1973), 123.
6. *Ibid.*, 124.
7. *Ibid.*, 125.
8. Charles Perrault, "Sleeping Beauty," in *The Great Fairy Tale Tradition: From Straparola and Basile to the Brothers Grimm*, trans. Jack Zipes (New York: Norton, 2001), 691.
9. Jacob and Wilhelm Grimm, *The Complete Fairy Tales of the Brothers Grimm*, trans. and ed. Jack Zipes (New York: Bantam, 1987), 189.
10. There are four different fifteenth-century manuscripts of *Le Roman de Perceforest:* two in the Bibliothèque Nationale (Paris), one in the Bibliothèque de l'Arsenal (Paris), and one in the British Museum. The romance was composed by an anonymous author, and it is in the grail tradition. In chapter 46 of book 3 there is an episode that deals with the birth of Princess Zellandine. She is given various gifts by three goddesses but is sentenced to eternal sleep when one of them is offended. Zellandine is destined to prick her finger while spinning and then to fall into a deep sleep. As long as a chip of flax remains in her finger, she will continue to sleep. Troylus meets her before she pricks her finger and falls in love with her. The love is mutual, but Troylus must perform some adventures before seeing her again. In the meantime Zellandine pricks her finger, and her father, King Zelland, places her completely nude in a tower that is unaccessible except for one window to protect her. When Troylus returns to King Zelland's court, he discovers what has happened to Zellandine, and with the help of a kind spirit, Zephir, who carries him up through the window, he manages to gain entrance to Zellandine's room. There, urged on by Venus,

he gives way to his desire and has sexual intercourse with Zellandine. Then he exchanges rings with Zellandine and departs. Nine months later she gives birth to a child, and when the child mistakes her finger for her nipple, he sucks the flax chip out of it, and she awakes. After grieving about her lost virginity, Zellandine is comforted by her aunt. Soon after, a bird-like creature comes and steals her child. Again Zellandine grieves, but since it is spring, she recovers quickly to think about Troylus. When she looks at the ring on her finger, she realizes that it was he who had slept with her. Some time later Troylus returns from his adventures to take her away with him to his kingdom.

The best modern edition of *Perceforest* is Gilles Roussineau, ed. *Perceforest*, 6 vols. (Geneva: Droz, 1987–2001). For the most exhaustive account of the romance, see Jeanne Lods, *Le Roman de Perceforest* (Geneva: Droz, 1951).

The episode between Zellandine and Troylus served as the basis for two Catalan versions, *Blandin de Cornoualha* and *Frayre de Joy e Sor de Plaser* in the Middle Ages. (See Esther Zago, "Some Medieval Versions of Sleeping Beauty: Variations on a Theme," *Studi Francesci*, 69 (1979): 417–431.) It is more than likely that Basile read *Perceforest*, and there is clear evidence that Perrault was acquainted with Basile's *Pentamerone*. In other words, the tale of *Sleeping Beauty* is essentially within the literary tradition. However, there are similar motifs in the oral tradition, and there is no doubt but that the literary *Sleeping Beauty* did work its way into the oral tradition to influence many different authors. The Grimm source was a tale by Marie Hassenpflug, whose family was of French Huguenot origins, and Wilhelm Grimm kept shaping the different versions to match that of Perrault.

11. Giambattista Basile, "Sun, Moon, and Talia" in *The Great Fairy Tale Tradition: From Straparola and Basile to the Brothers Grimm*, trans. Jack Zipes (New York: Norton, 2001), 685–686.
12. For the most comprehensive treatment of the historical transformations of the motifs and themes of *Sleeping Beauty*, see Giovanna Franci and Ester Zago, *La bella addormentata. Genesi e metamorfosi di una fiaba* (Bari: Dedalo, 1984). Cf. also, Alfred Romain, "Zur Gestalt des Grimmschen Dornröschenmärchens," *Zeitschrift für Volkskunde* 42 (1933): 84–116; Jan de Vries, "Dornröschen," *Fabula* 2 (1959): 110–121; and Ester Zago, "Some Medieval Versions of Sleeping Beauty: Variations on a Theme," *Studi Francesci* 69 (1979): 417–431.
13. "Briar Rose (Sleeping Beauty)" in *Transformations* (Boston: Houghton Mifflin, 1971), 111.
14. *Ibid.*, 112.
15. *Beginning with O* (New Haven: Yale University Press, 1977), 62.
16. Jane Yolen, *Sleeping Ugly* (New York: Coward, McCann & Geoghegan, 1981).
17. *Ibid.*, 64.
18. *The Tough Princess* (New York: Philomel, 1986).
19. For example, see Wolfgang Mieder's two editions, *Disenchantments: An Anthology of Modern Fairy Tale Poetry* (Hanover: University Press of New Eng-

land, 1985) and *Grimmige Märchen* (Frankfurt am Main: R.G. Fischer, 1986), and Jack Zipes, ed., *Don't Bet on the Prince: Contemporary Feminist Fairy Tales in North America and England* (New York: Methuen, 1986). All three books contain bibliographies or references to other collections.

20. See Jacques Barchilon, *Le Conte Merveilleux Français de 1690 à 1790* (Paris: Champion, 1975).
21. "Rhetoric of the Image," in *Image—Music—Text*, 43.
22. Boston: Little Brown, 1977. I am using the third printing of 1986.
23. New York: Macmillan, 1984.
24. New York: Knopf, 1986.
25. Mayer, *The Sleeping Beauty*, final page of unnumbered pages.
26. Yolen/Sanderson, "Illustrator's Note," *The Sleeping Beauty*, final page of unnumbered text.

CHAPTER 10

1. Ulrike Bastian, *Die "Kinder- und Hausmärchen" der Brüder Grimm in der literaturpädagogischen Diskussion des 19. und 20. Jahrhunderts* (Frankfurt am Main: Haag & Herchen, 1981), 186.
2. Cf. Johannes Langfeldt, "Märchen und Pädagogik," *Pädagogische Rundschau* 2 (1940): 521–25; W. Gong, "Vorschule der Grausamkeit?" *Der Tagesspiegel* (February 7, 1947); Gerhard Boettger, "Das Gute und Böse im Märchen," *Lehrerrundbrief* 3 (1948): 290–291; Werner Lenartz, "Von der erzieherischen Kraft des Märchens," *Pädagogische Rundschau* 2 (1948): 330–336; Wolfgang Petzet, "Verteidigung des Märchens gegen seine Verleumder," *Prisma* 1 (1947): 3, 11.
3. In 1981 the society changed its name to the *Europäische Märchengesellschaft* and indicated that it was becoming more open to sociological, philological, and historical approaches to the folk and fairy-tale tradition.
4. Ernst Wiechert, *Märchen*, vol. 2 (Munich: Kurt Desch, 1946), 7.
5. Jens Tismar, *Das deutsche Kunstmärchen des zwanzigsten Jahrhunderts* (Stuttgart: Metzler, 1981), 133–39.
6. *Ibid.*, 133.
7. For more detailed treatments of this period, see Birgit Dankert, "Die antiautoritäre Kinder- und Jugendliteratur," in *Jugendliteratur in einer veränderten Welt*, ed. Karl Ernst Maier (Bad Heilbrunn: Julius Klinkhardt, 1972), 68–84; Heinz Hengst, "Emanzipatorische Belletristik für Kinder! Probleme politischer Sozialisation in linken Kinderbüchern," in *Die heimlichen Erzieher: Kinderbücher und politisches Lernen*, ed. Dieter Richter and Jochen Vogt (Reinbek: Rowohlt, 1974): 91–100; Jack Zipes, "Down with Heidi, Down with Struwwelpeter, Three Cheers for the Revolution: Towards a New Socialist Children's Literature in West Germany," *Children's Literature* 5 (1976): 162–180.
8. For other revisions of "Hansel and Gretel," see Wolfgang Mieder, ed., *Grimms Märchen—modern* (Stuttgart: Reclam, 1979), 9–34, and Wolfgang Mieder, ed., *Grimmige Märchen* (Frankfurt am Main: R.G. Fischer, 1986), 91–112. Among the German authors who have created their own versions

of the Grimms' tale are: Wolfram Siebeck, Günter Bruno Fuchs, Michael Ende, Karin Struck, Josef Wittmann, Julius Nef, and Josef Reding.

9. One of the most gifted political satirists in West Germany, Traxler often works together with Robert J. Gernhardt, F.W. Bernstein, and Friedich K. Waechter. In fact, some interesting political fairy tales can be found in F.W. Bernstein, Robert Gernhardt, and F.K. Waechter, *Die Drei* (Frankfurt am Main: Zweitausendeins, 1981). It contains some of their best work of the last 20 years.
10. Hans-Joachim Gelberg, *Erstes Jahrbuch der Kinderliteratur 1: Geh und spiel mit dem Riesen.* (Weinheim: Beltz & Gelberg, 1971), 341.
11. Published first in *Die Richtung der Märchen: Fünfzig ausgewählte Märchen für Kinder von heute* (Berlin: Aufbau, 1962).
12. Janosch, *Janosch erzählt Grimm's Märchen* (Weinheim: Beltz & Gelberg, 1972), 250, 252.
13. The term *Leistungsgesellschaft* was coined by the German philosopher Herbert Marcuse and used widely by students and intellectuals in the late 1960s and 1970s to critique the capitalist society in West Germany and America for placing too much emphasis on achievement and not caring about humanity.
14. See Janosch, *Janosch erzählt Grimm's Märchen: Vierundfünfzig ausgewählte Märchen für Kinder von heute*, rev. ed. (Weinheim: Beltz und Gelberg, 1991).
15. Erich Kaiser, "Ent-Grimm-te Märchen?," *Westermanns Pädagogische Beiträge* 8 (1975): 448.
16. Ibid., 449–450.
17. Jung commissioned 28 leading contemporary authors to choose an old broadside from the nineteenth century and to write their own tale based on the images of the broadside. Among those authors who chose a Grimms' tale are: Ilse Aichinger, Jürgen Becker, Nicolas Born, Peter O. Chotejewitz, Jörg Drews, Fabius von Gugel, Peter Härtling, Herbert Heckmann, Katrine von Hutten, Marie Luise Kaschnitz, Karl Krolow, Barbara König, Hermann Lenz, Friederike Märöcker, and Jung himself. Most of the tales fall under the category of social satire.
18. The format of this book is somewhat similar to that of Jochen Jung's anthology. The editors took fairy-tale collages (based on Grimms' tales) by the artist Heinrich Dreidoppel and sent them to 70 German writers asking them to react to the images by writing new fairy tales, "in which actual experiences would be connected to historical ones and German traumas would perhaps be given new expression" (151). The authors who participated in this experiment are: Peter Härtling, Karin Struck, Jochen Link, Robert Jarowoy, Hans-Jügen Linke, Bernd Bohmeier, Vilma Link, Jens Hagen, Rolf Haubl, Bernd Hackländer, Norbert Relenberg, Walter Höllerer, Karl Riha, Hans-Dieter Eberhard, Eckhard Henscheid, Gertrude von Wasmuth, Jochen Gerz, Urs Jaeggi, Fritz Teufel, and Peter Paul Zahl.
19. Peter Paul Zahl, "Die Rückkehr der Diebe," in *Deutsche Märchen*, ed. Günter Kämpf and Vilma Link (Gießen: Anabas-Verlag, 1981), 148.
20. Irmela Brenda, "Das Rumpelstilzchen hat mir immer leid getan," in *Neues vom Rumpelstilzchen und andere Märchen von 43 Autoren*, ed. Hans Joachim Gelberg (Weinheim: Beltz & Gelberg, 1976), 200.

21. Otto F. Gmelin, *Böses kommt aus Kinderbüchern: Die verpaßten Möglichkeiten kindlicher Bewußtseinsbildung* (Munich: Kindler, 1972), 112.
22. Burckhard & Gisela Garbe, *Der ungestiefelte Kater: Grimms Märchen umerzählt* (Götttingen: sage & schreibe, 1985), 225–226.
23. Ursula Eggli has also written some important feminist fairy tales in *Fortschritt in Grimmsland: Ein Märchen für Mädchen und Frauen* (Bern: RIURS, 1983). Many feminist fairy tales can be found in collections that are mixed, such as Gmelin's and Garbe's books, as well as in Gelberg's anthologies.
24. This tale was published in Gelberg's anthology, *Neues vom Rumpelstilzchen.*
25. This tale is in Brigitte Heidebrecht's anthology, *Dornröschen nimmt die Heckenschere: Märchenhaftes von 30 Autorinnen* (Bonn: verlag kleine schritte, 1985), 50–52.
26. Gelberg, ed., *Neues vom Rumpelstilzchen*, 63–69.
27. See also Henriette Beese, ed., *Von Nixen und Brunnenfrauen* (Berlin: Ullstein, 1982); Claudia Schmölders, ed., *Die wilde Frau* (Cologne: Diederichs, 1983); Hanna Moog, ed., *Die Wasserfrau* (Cologne: Diederichs, 1987).
28. Uta Claus and Rolf Kutschera, *Total Tote Hose: 12 bockstarke Märchen* (Frankfurt am Main: Eichborn Verlag, 1984), 39.
29. Heinz Langer, *Grimmige Märchen* (Munich: Heinrich Hugendubel, 1984), 26–7.
30. *Ibid.*, 56–57.
31. Chris Schrauff, *Der Wolf und seine Steine* (Hannover: SOAK Verlag, 1986). No page numbers are indicated in the book.
32. Among the titles published by the Kreuz Verlag in Seifert's series are: Angela Waiblinger, *Rumpelstilzchen: Gold Statt Liebe* (1983); Theodor Seifert, *Schneewittchen: Das fast verlorene Leben* (1983); Hildegunde Wöller, *Aschenputtel: Energie der Liebe* (1984); Lutz Müller, *Das tapfere Schneiderlein: List als Lebenskunst* (1985); Hans Dieckmann, *Der blaue Vogel: Der chamante Held und seine Heldin* (1985); Hans Jellouschek, *Der Froschkönig: Geschichte einer Beziehung* (1985); Helmut Hark, *Gevatter Tod: Auseinandersetzung mit der Sterblichkeit* (1985); Marie-Louise von Franz, *Die Katze: Entwicklung des Weiblichen* (1986); Ursula Eschenbach, *Hänsel und Gretel: Der Sohn im mütterlichen Dunkel* (1986).
33. Cf. my critical discussion of the Kreuz series in chapter seven.
34. Seifert, *Schneewittchen: Das verlorene Leben*, 8–9.
35. Johann Friedrich Konrad, *Hexen-Memoiren: Märchen, entwirrt und neu erzählt* (Frankfurt am Main: Eichborn, 1981), 125.
36. *Ibid.*, 122.
37. See Wolfgang Steinitz, "Das deutsche Volksmärchen: Ein wichtiger Teil nationalen Kulturerbes," *Neues Deutschland* (November 17, 1951): 1951.
38. Anneliese Kocialek, *Die Bedeutung der Volksmärchen für Unterricht und Erziehung in der Unterstufe der deutschen demokratischen Schule.* Dissertation: Humboldt-Universität, Berlin, 1951), 183.
39. Cf. Isa Bennung, *Das deutsche Märchen als Kinderliteratur: Eine Untersuchung von den Anfängen bis zur Entwicklung in der DDR*, doctoral dissertation (Halle: Martin-Luther-Universität, 1975), 292, and Bastian, 225.

40. See Ingelore König, Dieter Wiedemann, and Lothar Wolf, eds. *Märchen: Arbeiten mit DEFA-Kinderfilmen* (Munich: KoPäd, 1998).
41. Franz Fühmann, *Die Richtung der Märchen* (Berlin: Aufbau, 1962).
42. Another exception was Günter de Bryn, who parodied the works of Fühmann, Erwin Strittmatter, and Johannes Bobrowski using Grimms' tales in *Maskeraden* (Berlin: 1966).
43. Cf. Hanne Castein, "Nachwort," *Es wird einmal: Märchen für morgen* (Frankfurt am Main: Suhrkamp, 1988), 198.
44. See Bennung, 296–305.
45. Cf. Hanne Castein, "Arbeiten mit der Romantik heute: Zur Romantikrezeption der DDR, unter besonderer Berücksichtung des Märchens," *Deutsche Romantik und das 20. Jahrhundert*, ed. Hanne Castein and Alexander Stillmark (Stuttgart: Hans-Dieter Heinz Akademischer Verlag, 1986), 5–23.
46. Joachim Walther, "Die Metamorphose des Märchens," in *Die Rettung des Saragossameeres: Märchen*, eds. Joachim Walther and Manfred Wolter (Berlin: Buchverlag der Morgen, 1976), 132.
47. Günter Kunert, "Dornröschen," in *Es wird einmal. Märchen für morgen*, ed. Hanne Castein (Frankfurt am Main: Suhrkamp, 1988), 8.
48. For an entirely different version of *Little Red Cap* that pokes fun at male chauvinism, see Hans Joachim Schädlich's "Kriminalmärchen," in *Versuchte Nähe* (Reinbek: Rowohlt, 1977).
49. Thomas Schleusing, *Es war einmal . . . Märchen für Erwachsene* (Berlin: Eulenspiegel Verlag, 1979), 41.
50. Horst Matthies, *Der goldene Fisch: Kein Märchenbuch* (Halle: Mitteldeutscher Verlag, 1980), 35.
51. See the works by Irmtraud Morgner in the GDR and Michael Ende in the FRG.
52. Nikolaus Heidelbach, illustr., *Die Märchen der Brüder Grimm* (Weinheim: Beltz & Gelberg, 1995).
53. Rotraut Susanne Berner, *Rotraut Susanne Berners Märchen-Stunde* (Weinheim: Beltz & Gelberg, 1998).

BIBLIOGRAPHY

EDITIONS OF THE BROTHERS GRIMM

Altdeutsche Wälder. 3 vols. 1813–1816. Reprint. Darmstadt: Wissenschaftliche Buchgesellschaft, 1966.

Deutsche Sagen. 2 vols. 1816–18. Reprint, Dartmstadt: Wissenschaftliche Buchgesellschaft, 1972.

German Legends. Trans. Donald Ward. 2 vols. Philadelphia: Institute for the Study of Human Issues, 1981.

Kinder- und Hausmärchen. Vollständige Ausgabe in der Urfassung. Ed. Friedrich Panzer. 1st ed. Wiesbaden: Emil Vollmer, n.d.

Kinder- und Hausmärchen. Vergrößerter Nachdruck von 1812 und 1815 nach dem Handexemplar des Brüder Grimm-Museums Kassel mit sämtlichen handschriftlichen Korrekturen und Nachträgen der Brüder Grimm. Eds. Heinz Rölleke and Ulrike Marquardt. 1st ed. 2 vols with an additional notebook. Göttingen: Vandenhoeck & Ruprecht, 1986.

Kinder- und Hausmärchen. Nach der zweiten vermehrten und verbesserten Auflage von 1819. Ed. Heinz Rölleke. 2d ed. 2 vols. Cologne: Diederichs, 1982.

Kinder- und Hausmärchen gesammelt durch die Brüder Grimm. Vollständige Ausgabe auf der Grundlage der dritten Auflage (1837). Ed. Heinz Rölleke. Frankfurt am Main: Deutscher Klassiker Verlag, 1985.

Kinder- und Hausmärchen gesammelt durch die Brüder Grimm. Intr. Ingeborg Weber-Kellermann. 7th ed. 3 vols. Frankfurt am Main: Insel, 1976.

Kinder- und Hausmärchen. Ausgabe Letzter Hand mit den Originalanmerkungen der Brüder Grimm. Ed. Heinz Rölleke. 7th ed. 3 vols. Stuttgart: Philipp Reclam, 1980.

Kinder- und Hausmärchen. Nach der Großen Ausgabe von 1857, textkritisch revidiert, kommentiert und durch Register erschlossen. Ed. Hans-Jörg Uther. 7th ed. Darmstadt: Wissenschaftliche Buchgesellschaft, 1996.

Kinder- und Hausmärchen gesammelt durch die Brüder Grimm. Kleine Ausgabe von 1858. Illustr. Ludwig Peitsch. Afterword Heinz Rölleke. 10th printing. Small Ed. Frankfurt am Main: Insel, 1985.

The Complete Fairy Tales of the Brothers Grimm. Trans. and Ed. Jack Zipes. Rev. and exp. ed. New York: Bantam, 1992.

Rölleke, Heinz. *Die älteste Märchensammlung der Brüder Grimm. Synopse der handschriftlichen Urfassung von 1810 und der Erstdrucke von 1812.* Cologny-Geneva: Fondation Martin Bodmer, 1975.

———, ed. *Märchen aus dem Nachlaß der Brüder Grimm.* 3d rev. ed. Bonn: Bouvier, 1983.

———, ed. *Die wahren Märchen der Brüder Grimm.* Frankfurt am Main: Fischer Taschenbuch, 1989.

———, ed. *Grimms Märchen wie sie nicht im Buch stehen.* Frankurt am Main: Insel, 1993.

Seitz, Gabriele, ed. *Im Himmel steht ein Baum, Dran häng ich meinen Traum. Volkslieder, Kinderlieder, Kinderzeichnungen.* Munich: Winkler, 1985.

JACOB GRIMM

Auswahl aus den Kleinen Schriften. Hamburg: Gutenberg, 1904.

Circular wegen Aufsammlung der Volkspoesie. Vienna: 1815. Facsimile ed. by Ludwig Denecke, preface by Kurt Ranke. Kassel: Brüder-Grimm Museum, 1968.

Deutsche Mythologie. 1835. Reprint, Graz: Akademische Druck- und Verlagsanstalt, 1953.

Deutsche Rechstsalterthümer. 2 vols. 1828. Reprint, Darmstadt: Wissenschaftliche Buchgesellschaft, 1965.

Kleinere Schriften. 8 vols. 1869–1890. Reprint, Hildesheim: Georg Olms, 1965–66.

Reden und Aufsätze. Ed. Wilhelm Schoof. Munich: Winkler, 1966.

WILHELM GRIMM

Altdänische Heldenlieder, Balladen, und Märchen. Heidelberg: Mohr und Zimmer, 1811.

Irische Land- und Seemärchen. Gesammelt von Thomas Crofton Croker. Ed. Werner Moritz and Charlotte Oberfeld. Marburg: Elwert, 1986.

Kleinere Schriften. Ed. Gustav Hinrichs. 4 vols. Berlin: Dümmlers, 1881–1887. Volume 4 published by Bertelsmann in Gütersloh.

CORRESPONDENCE

Ehrhardt, Holger, ed. *Briefwechsel der Brüder Grimm mit Herman Grimm.* Kassel: Brüder-Grimm Gesellschaft, 1998.

Göres, Jörn, and Wilhelm Schoof, eds. *Unbekannte Briefe der Brüder Grimm.* Bonn: Athenäum, 1960.

Grimm, Hermann, Gustav Hinrichs, and Wilhelm Schoof, eds. *Briefwechsel zwischen Jacob und Wilhelm Grimm aus der Jugendzeit.* 2d rev. ed. Weimar: Hermann Böhlhaus, 1963.

Grothe, Ewald, ed. *Briefwechsel der Brüder Grimm mit Ludwig Hassenpflug.* Kassel: Brüder-Grimm Gesellschaft, 2000.

Gürtler, Hans, and Albert Leitzmann, eds. *Briefe der Brüder Grimm.* Jena: Verlag der Fromannschen Buchhandlung, 1923.

Rölleke, Heinz, ed. *Briefwechsel zwischen Jacob und Wilhelm Grimm*. Stuttgart: Hirzel, 2001.

REFERENCE WORKS

Aarne, Antti. *The Types of the Folktales. A Classification and Bibliography*. Rev. and en. by Stith Thompson. 2d rev. ed. FF Communications Nr. 3. Helsinki: Suomalainen Tiedeakatemia, 1961.

Alpers, Paul. "Paul Wigand eine Lebensfreundschaft mit den Brüdern Grimm." *Hessisches Jahrbuch für Landesgeschichte* 14 (1964): 271–327.

Anderson, Graham. *Fairytale in the Ancient World*. London: Routledge, 2000.

Arendt, Dieter. "Dümmlinge, Däumlinge und Diebe im Märchen—oder: "drei Söhne, davon hieß der jüngste der Dümmling' (KHM 64)." *Diskussion Deutsch* 91 (October 1986): 465–478.

Arnold, Klaus, ed. *Kind und Gesellschaft im Mittelalter und Renaissance. Beiträge zur Geschichte der Kindheit*. Padeborn: Schönigh, 1980.

Bacchilega, Cristina. *Postmodern Fairy Tales: Gender and Narrative Strategies*. Philadelphia: University of Pennsylvania Press, 1997.

Bakhtin, Mikhail M. *Speech Genres and Other Late Essays*. Ed. Caryl Emerson and Michael Holquist. Trans. Vern W. McGee. Austin: University of Texas Press, 1986.

Barchilon, Jacques. *Le Conte Merveilleux Français de 1690 à 1790*. Paris: Champion, 1975.

———. "Vers L'inconscient de *La Belle au Bois Dormant*." *Cermeil* 2 (February, 1986): 88–92.

Barthes, Roland. *Mythologies*. Trans. Annette Lavers. London: Granada, 1973.

———. *Image—Music—Text*. Trans. Stephen Heath. New York: Hill and Wang, 1977.

Bastian, Ulrike. *Die "Kinder- und Hausmärchen" der Brüder Grimm in der literaturpädagogischen Diskussion des 19. und 20. Jahrhunderts*. Giessen: Haag & Herchen, 1981.

Bausinger, Hermann. *Märchen, Phantasie und Wirklichkeit*. Frankfurt am Main: dipa-Verlag, 1987.

———. "Bürgerlichkeit und Kultur." In *Bürger und Bürgerlichkeit im 19. Jahrhundert*. Ed. Jürgen Kocka. Göttingen: Vandenhoeck & Ruprecht, 1987. 121–142.

———. "Concerning the Content and Meaning of Fairy Tales." *The Germanic Review* 42 (Spring, 1987): 75–82.

Bélmont, Nicole. *Poétique du conte: Essai sur le conte de tradition orale*. Paris: Gallimard, 1999.

Bémol, Maurice. "Henri Pourrat et 'Le Trésor des Contes.'" *Annales Universitatis Saraviensis* 10 (1961): 179–182.

Benjamin, Walter. *Illuminations*. Trans. Harry Zohn. New York: Harcourt, Brace & World, 1968.

———. *Gesammelte Schriften*. Ed. Rolf Tiedemann and Hermann Schweppenhäuser. 6 vols. Frankfurt am Main: Suhrkamp, 1977.

Berendsohn, Walter A. *Grundformen volkstümlicher Erzählkunst in den Kinder- und Hausmärchen der Brüder Grimm.* 2d rev. ed. Wiesbaden: Sändig, 1973.

Bettelheim, Bruno. *The Uses of Enchantment. The Meaning and Importance of Fairy Tales.* New York: Knopf, 1976.

———. "A Return to the Land of Fairies." *New York Times* section 2, July 12, 1987, 1,33.

Bleek, Wilhelm. "Die Brüder Grimm und die deutsche Politik." *Aus Politik und Zeitgeschichte* 1 (January 4, 1986), 3–15.

Bloch, Ernst. *Das Prinzip Hoffnung.* 3 vols. Frankfurt am Main: Suhrkamp, 1959.

———. *Ästhetik des Vor-Scheins.* Ed. Gert Ueding. 2 vols. Frankfurt am Main: Suhrkamp, 1974.

———. *The Utopian Function of Art and Literature.* Trans. Jack Zipes and Frank Mecklenburg. Cambridge: MIT Press, 1987.

Bluhm, Lothar. *Grimm-Philologie: Beiträge zur Märchenforschung.* Hildesheim: Olms-Weidmann, 1995.

———. "A New Debate about 'Old Marie'? Critical Observations on the Attempt to Remythologize Grimms' Fairy Tales from a Sociohistorical Perspective." *Marvels & Tales* 14 (2000): 287- 311.

Bluhm, Lothar and Achim Hölter, eds. *Romantik und Volksliteratur: Beiträge des Wuppertaler Kolloquiums zu Ehren von Heinz Rölleke.* Heidelberg: C. Winter, 1999.

Bolte, Johannes, and George Polivka. *Anmerkungen zu den "Kinder- und Hausmärchen."* 5 vols. 1913–1932; Hildesheim: Georg Olms, 1963.

Borghese, Lucia. "Antonio Gramsci und die Grimmschen Märchen." In *Brüder Grimm Gedenken.* Ed. Ludwig Dennecke. Vol. 3. Marburg: Elwert, 1981. 374–390.

Bottigheimer, Ruth B., ed. *Fairy Tales and Society: Illusion, Allusion, and Paradigm.* Philadelphia: University of Pennsylvania Press, 1986.

———. *Grimms' Bad Girls and Bold Boys: The Moral and Social Vision of the Tales.* New Haven: Yale University Press, 1987.

Bourdieu, Pierre. *The Field of Cultural Production.* New York: Columbia University Press, 1993.

Brackert, Helmut, ed. *Und wenn sie nicht gestorben sind . . . Perspektiven auf das Märchen.* Frankfurt am Main: Suhrkamp, 1980.

Bricout, Bernadette. "A Propos d'un conte d'Henri Pourrat: Le Cycle de la fausse gageure." In *Mélanges de littérature du moyen age au XXe siècle.* Vol. 2. Paris: L'Ecole Normale Supérieure de Jeunes Filles, 1978. 778–792.

———. *Le Savoir et la saveur: Henri Pourrat et le trésor des contes.* Paris: Gallimard, 1991.

Bronner, Simon. "The Americanization of the Brothers Grimm." In *Following Tradition: Folklore in the Discourse of American Culture.* Logan: Utah State University Press, 1998. 184–236.

Bühler, Charlotte and Josefine Bilz. *Das Märchen und die Phantasie des Kindes.* Berlin: Springer, 1977.

Bülow, Werner von. *Märchendeutungen durch Runen. Die Geheimsprache der deutschen Märchen.* Hellerau bei Dresden: Hackenkreuz-Verlag, 1925.

Bürger, Christa. "Die soziale Funktion volkstümlicher Erzählformen—Sage und Märchen." In *Projekt Deutschunterricht 1.* Ed. Heinz Ide. Stuttgart: Metzler, 1971. 26–56.

———. *Tradition und Subjektivität.* Frankfurt am Main: Suhrkamp, 1980.

Büttner, Christian, and Aurel Ende, eds. *Kinderleben in Geschichte und Gegenwart.* Weinheim: Beltz, 1984.

Campbell, Joseph. *The Hero with a Thousand Faces.* Cleveland: Meridian, 1956.

———. *The Flight of the Wild Gander: Explorations in the Mythological Dimension.* New York: HarperCollins, 1990.

Cashdan, Sheldon. *The Witch Must Die: How Fairy Tales Shape Our Lives.* New York: Basic Books, 1999.

Chartier, Roger, ed. *Les usages de l'imprimé.* Paris: Fayard, 1987.

Clifford, James, and George E. Marcus. *Writing Culture: The Poetics and Politics of Ethnography.* Berkeley: University of California Press, 1986.

Collier, Mary Jeffrey. "The Psychological Appeal in the Cinderella Theme." *American Imago* 18 (1961): 399–406.

Crossick, Geoffrey, and Gerhard Haupt, eds. *Shopkeepers and Master Artisans in Nineteenth-Century Europe.* London: Methuen, 1984.

Culhane, John. "'Snow White' at 50: Undimmed Magic." *New York Times* section 2, July 12, 1987, 19, 31.

Darnton, Robert. *The Great Cat Massacre and Other Episodes in French Cultural History.* New York: Basic Books, 1984.

Dégh, Linda. *Folktales and Society: Storytelling in a Hungarian Peasant Community.* Trans. Emily M. Schlossberg. Bloomington: Indiana University Press, 1969.

———. "Grimm's Household Tales and Its Place in the Household: The Social Relevance of a Controversial Classic." *Western Folklore* 38 (1979): 83–103.

Denecke, Ludwig. *Jacob Grimm und sein Bruder Wilhelm.* Stuttgart: Metzler, 1971.

———. "Die Göttinger Jahre der Brüder Jacob und Wilhelm Grimm." *Göttinger Jahrbuch* 25 (1977): 139–155.

———. "Grimm, Jacob Ludwig Carl." In *Enzyklopädie des Märchens: Handwörterbuch zur historischen und vegleichenden Erzählforschung.* Ed. Kurt Ranke, et al. Vol. 5. Berlin: Walter de Gruyter, 1989), 171–86.

———, ed. *Brüder Grimm Gedenken.* Vol. 1. Marburg: Elwert, 1963.

———, ed. *Brüder Grimm Gedenken.* Vol. 2. Marburg: Elwert, 1975.

———, ed. *Brüder Grimm Gedenken.* Vol. 3. Marburg: Elwert, 1981.

———, ed. *Brüder Grimm Gedenken.* Vol. 4. Marburg: Elwert, 1984.

———, ed. *Brüder Grimm Gedenken.* Vol. 5. Marburg: Elwert, 1985.

———, ed. *Brüder Grimm Gedenken.* Vol. 6. Marburg: Elwert, 1986.

———, ed. *Brüder Grimm Gedenken.* Vol. 7. Marburg: Elwert, 1987.

Diederichs, Ulf. *Who's who im Märchen.* Munich: dtv, 1995.

Dielmann, Karl. "Märchenillustrationen von Ludwig Emil Grimm." *Hanauer Geschichtsblätter* 18 (1962): 281–306.

Doderer, Klaus, ed. *Über Märchen für Kinder von heute.* Weinheim: Beltz, 1983.

Dow, James R., and Hannjost Lixfeld, eds. *The Nazification of an Academic Discipline: Folklore in the Third Reich.* Bloomington: University of Indiana Press, 1994.

Drewermann, Eugen. *Das Mädchen ohne Hände.* Olten, Switzlerand: Walter, 1981.

———. *Schneeweißchen und Rosenrot. Märchen Nr. 161 aus der Grimmschen Sammlung*. Freiburg: Walter, 1983.

———. *Die kluge Else, Rapunzel.* Freiburg: Walter, 1986.

———. *Rapunzel, Rapunzel, laß dein Haar herunter: Grimms Märchen tiefenpsychologisch gedeutet.* Munich: dtv, 1994.

———. *Schneewittchen: Märchen Nr. 53 aus der Grimmschen Sammlung.* Zurich: Walter, 1997.

———. *Der Wolf und die sieben jungen Geißlein; Der Wolf und der Fuchs.* Düsseldorf: Walter, 2000.

Dundes, Alan, ed. *Cinderella: A Casebook.* New York: Garland, 1982.

———. *Life Is Like a Chicken Coop Ladder: A Portrait of German Culture through Folklore.* New York: Columbia University Press, 1984.

———. "The Psychoanalytic Study of Folklore." *Annals of Scholarship* 3 (1985): 1–42.

———. "The Psychoanalytic Study of the Grimms' Tales with Special Reference to 'The Maiden without Hands' (AT 706)." *The Germanic Review* 42 (Spring, 1987): 50–65.

Dworkin, Andrea. *Women Hating.* New York: Dutton, 1974.

Ebel, Else, ed. *Wilhelm Grimms Nibelungenkolleg.* Marburg: Elwert, 1985.

Eisler, Alice. "Recht im Märchen." *Neophilologus* 66 (1982): 422–430.

Elias, Norbert. *Über den Prozeß der Zivilisation.* 2 vols. Frankfurt am Main: Suhrkamp, 1977.

Ellis, John. *One Fairy Story Too Many: The Brothers Grimm and Their Tales.* Chicago: University of Chicago Press, 1983.

Farr, James R. *Artisans in Europe, 1300–1914.* Cambridge: Cambridge University Press, 2000.

Favat, André F. *Child and Tale: The Origins of Interest.* Urbana: National Council of Teachers of English, 1977.

Fehling, Detlev. *Amor und Psyche: Die Schöpfung des Apuleius und ihre Einwirkung auf das Märchen.* Wiesbaden: Steiner, 1977.

Fehr, Hans. "Die Brüder Jacob und Wilhelm Grimm und Friedrich Karl von Savigny." *Zeitschrift für Schweizerisches Recht* 72 (1971): 437–443.

Feldmann, Roland. *Jacob Grimm und die Politik.* Kassel: Bärenreiter, 1970.

Fink, Gonthier-Louis. *Naissance et apogée du conte merveilleux en Allemagne 1740–1800.* Paris: Les Belles Lettres, 1966.

Fraenger, Wilhelm and Wolfgang Steinitz, eds. *Jacob Grimm: Zur 100. Wiederkehr seines Todestages.* Berlin: Akademie-Verlag, 1963.

Franci, Giovanna and Ester Zago. *La bella addormentata. Genesi e metamorfosi di una fiaba.* Bari: Dedalo, 1984.

Franz, Marie-Louise von. *An Introduction to the Interpretation of Fairy Tales.* New York: Spring, 1970.

———. *Problems of the Feminine in Fairytales.* New York: Spring, 1972.

Freudenberg, Rudolf. "Erzähltechnik und 'Märchenton.'" In *Das selbstverständliche Wunder. Beiträge germanistischer Märchenforschung.* Ed. Wilhelm Solms. Marburg: Hitzeroth, 1986. 121–142.

Freudenburg, Rachel. "Illustrating Childhood—'Hansel and Gretel.'" *Marvels & Tales* 12 (1998): 263–318.

Freund, Winfried. *Deutsche Märchen.* Munich: Fink, 1996.

Fromm, Erich. *The Forgotten Language.* New York: Grove, 1957.

Früh, Sigrid, and Rainer Wehse, eds. *Die Frau im Märchen.* Kassel: Erich Röth, 1985.

Gardes, Roger. "Le *Conte des yeux rouges* et *Gaspard des Montagnes* d'Henri Pourrat." In *Frontières du conte.* Ed. François Marotin. Paris: Editions du Centre Nationale de la Recherche Scientifique, 1982. 69–76.

Gelberg, Hans-Joachim, ed. *Werkstattmagazin: "Die Brüder Grimm und ihre Märchen."* Weinheim: Beltz & Gelberg, 1995.

Gerstner, Hermann. "Deutsche Künstler illustrieren Märchenbücher." *Imprimatur* IV (1963/64): 26–59.

———. *Brüder Grimm in Selbstzeugnissen und Bilddokumenten.* Hamburg: Rowohlt, 1973.

Ginschel, Gunhild. "Der Märchenstil Jacob Grimms." In *Jacob Grimm: Zur 100. Wiederkehr seines Todestages.* Eds. Wilhelm Praenger and Wolfgang Steinitz. Berlin: Akademie-Verlag, 1963. 131–168.

———. *Der junge Jacob Grimm.* Berlin: Akademie Verlag, 1967.

———. "Jacob Grimm und die Dichtung des Mittelalters." *Forschungen und Fortschritte* 41 (1967): 174–181.

Girard, Marc. *Les Contes de Grimm: Lecture Psychoanalytique.* Paris: Imago, 1990.

Göttner-Abendroth, Heide. *Die Göttin und ihr Heros.* Munich: Frauenoffensive, 1980.

Godwin, J., C. G. Cawthorne, and R. T. Rada, "Cinderella Syndrome: Children Who Simulate Neglect." *American Journal of Psychiatry* 137 (1980): 1223–1225.

Goody, Jack. *The Domestication of the Savage Mind.* Cambridge: Cambridge University Press, 1977.

Haase, Donald, ed. *The Reception of Grimms' Fairy Tales: Responses, Reactions, Revisions.* Detroit: Wayne State University Press, 1993.

————. "Reviewing the Grimm Corpus: Grimm Scholarship in an Era of Celebrations." *Monatshefte* XCI (1999): 121–131.

Habermas, Jürgen. *Strukturwandel der bürgerlichen Öffentlichkeit.* Neuwied: Luchterhand, 1962.

Hadjadj, Dany. "Du 'releve de folklore' au conte populaire: avec Henri Pourrat, promenade aux fontaines du dire." In *Frontières du conte.* Ed. François Marotin. Paris: Editions du Centre Nationale de la Recherche Scientifique, 1982. 55–67.

Hagen, Rolf. "Perraults Märchen und die Brüder Grimm." *Zeitschrift für deutsche Philologie* 74 (1955): 392–410.

Hain, Mathilde. "Der nie stillstehende Fluß lebendiger Sitte und Sage." *Zeitschrift für Volkskunde* 59 (1963): 177–191.

Hamann, Hermann. *Die literarischen Vorlagen der "Kinder- und Hausmärchen" und ihre Bearbeitung durch die Brüder Grimm.* Berlin: Mayer und Müller, 1906.

Hannon, Patricia. *Fabulous Identities: Women's Fairy Tales in Seventeenth-Century France.* Amsterdam: Rodopi, 1998.

Harder, Hans Bernd, and Ekkehard Kaufmann, eds. *Die Brüder Grimm in ihrer amtlichen und politischen Tätigkeit.* Kassel: Weber & Weidemeyer, 1985.

Harries, Elizabeth Wanning. *Twice Upon a Time: Women Writers and the History of the Fairy Tale.* Princeton: Princeton University Press, 2001.

Heindrichs, Ursula, and Heinz-Albert Heindrichs, eds. *Märchen und Schöpfung*. Regensburg: Erich Röth, 1993.

———, eds. *Zaubermärchen: Forschungsberichte aus der Welt der Märchen*. Munich: Eugen Diederichs, 1998.

Hennig, Dieter and Bernhard Lauer, eds. *Die Brüder Grimm. Dokumente ihres Lebens und Wirkens*. Kassel: Weber & Weidemeyer, 1985.

Hennig, John. "The Brothers Grimm and T. C. Croker." *Modern Language Review* 41 (1946): 44–54.

Hermann, Liselotte. "Jacob Grimm und die sprachtheoretischen Konzeptionen der französischen Aufklärung." *Wissenschaftliche Zeitschrift der Humboldt Universität zu Berlin* 14 (1965): 447–453.

Hetmann, Frederik. "Die mündlichen Quellen der Grimms oder die Rolle der Geschichtenerzähler in den *Kinder- und Hausmärchen*." *The Germanic Review* 42 (Spring, 1987): 83–89.

Hettinga, Donald R. *The Brothers Grimm: Two Lives, One Legacy*. New York: Clarion, 2001.

Heuscher, Julius E. *A Psychiatric Study of Fairy Tales*. Springfield, Illinois: Thomas, 1963.

Heyden, Franz. *Volksmärchen und Volksmärchen-Erzähler. Zur literarischen Gestaltung des deutschen Volksmärchens*. Hamburg: Hanseatische Verlagsanstalt, 1922.

Hildebrandt, Irma. *Es waren ihrer Fünf. Die Brüder Grimm und ihre Familie*. Cologne: Diederichs, 1984.

Hildebrandt, Reiner, and Ulrich Knoop, eds. *Brüder-Grimm-Symposion zur historischen Wortforschung*. Berlin: Walter de Gruyter, 1986.

Hinrichs, Ernst, and Günther Wiegelmann, eds. *Sozialer und kultureller Wandel in der ländlichen Welt des 18. Jahrhunderts*. Wolfenbüttel: Herzog August Bibliothek, 1982.

Höck, Alfred. *Die Brüder Grimm als Studenten in Marburg*. Marburg: Elwert, 1978.

Hoffmann, Gerd and Heinz Rölleke, eds. *Der unbekannte Bruder Grimm. Deutsche Sagen von Ferdinand Philipp Grimm*. Cologne: Diederichs, 1979.

Horkheimer, Max, and Theodor W. Adorno. *Dialectic of Enlightenment* Trans. John Cumming. New York: Seabury Press, 1972.

Horn, Katalin. *Der aktive und der passive Märchenheld*. Basel: Schweizerische Gesellschaft für Volkskunde, 1983.

Jacob und Wilhelm Grimm. Vorträge und Ansprachen in den Veranstaltungen der Akademie der Wissenschaften und der Georg-August-Universität in Göttingen. Talks by Karl Stackmann, Heinz Rölleke, Karl Ottmar Freiherr von Aretin, and Werner Ogris. Gottingen: Vandenhoeck & Ruprecht, 1986.

Jacoby, Mario, Verena Kast, and Ingrid Riedl. *Witches, Ogres, and the Devil's Daughter: Encounters with Evil in Fairy Tales*. Boston: Shambhala, 1992.

Jaffé, Aniela. *Bilder und Symbole aus E.T.A. Hoffmanns "Der goldene Topf."* 2d rev. ed. Zurich: Gerstenberg, 1978.

Jameson, Fredric. *The Political Unconscious: Narrative as a Socially Symbolic Act*. Ithaca: Cornell University Press, 1981.

Jolles, André. *Einfache Formen*. Tübingen: Niemeyer, 1958.

Jones, Steven Swann. *The Fairy Tale: The Magic Mirror of Imagination*. New York: Twayne, 1995.

Jung, C. G. *Psyche and Symbol.* New York: Doubleday, 1958.

Jungblut, Gertrud. "Märchen der Brüder Grimm—feministisch gelesen." *Diskussion Deutsch* 91 (October, 1986): 497–510.

Kahn, Walter, ed. *Die Volksmärchen in unserer Kultur. Berichte über Bedeutung und Weiterleben der Märchen.* Frankfurt am Main: Haag und Herchen, 1993.

Kaiser, Erich. "Ent-Grimm-te Märchen." *Westermanns Pädagogische Beiträge* 8 (1975): 448–459.

Kamenetsky, Christa. "Folklore as a Political Tool in Nazi Germany." *Journal of American Folkore* 85 (1972): 221–235.

———. "Folktale and Ideology in the Third Reich." *Journal of American Folklore* 90 (1977): 168–178.

———. *The Brothers Grimm and Their Critics: Folktales and the Quest for Meaning.* Athens: Ohio University Press, 1993.

Kampers, Fr. "Das Märchen vom Dornröschen." *Mitteilungen der schlesischen Gesellschaft für Volkskunde* 17 (1915): 181–187.

Karlinger, Felix. "Schneeweißchen und Rosenrot in Sardinien. Zur Übernahme eines Buchmärchens in die volkstümliche Erzähltradition." *Brüder Grimm Gedenken.* Ed. Ludwig Dennecke. Vol. 2. Marburg: Elwert, 1963. 585–593.

———. *Grundzüge einer Geschichte des Märchens im deutschen Sprachraum.* Darmstadt: Wissenschaftliche Buchgesellschaft, 1983.

———, ed. *Wege der Märchenforschung.* Darmstadt: Wissenschaftliche Buchgesellschaft, 1973.

Kast, Verena. *Wege aus Angst und Symbiose: Märchen psychologisch gedeutet.* Olten, Switzlerland: Walter, 1982.

———. *Mann und Frau im Märchen. Eine psychologische Deutung.* Olten, Switzerland: Walter, 1983.

———. *Familienkonflikte im Märchen. Eine psychologische Deutung.* Olten, Switzerland: Walter, 1984.

———. *Märchen als Therapie.* Olten, Switzerland: Walter, 1986.

———. *Through Emotions to Maturity: Psychological Readings of Fairy Tales.* Trans. Douglas Whitcher. New York: Fromm International, 1993.

———. *Folktales as Therapy.* Trans. Douglas Whitcher. New York: Fromm International, 1995.

———. *Vom gelingenden Leben: Märcheninterepretationen.* Zurich: Walter, 1998.

———. *The Mermaid in the Pond: An Erotic Fairy Tale for Adults.* Trans. Vanessa Agnew. New York: Continuum, 1999.

Kluge, Manfred, ed. *Die Brüder Grimm in ihren Selbstbiographien.* Munich: Heyne, 1985.

Kocka, Jürgen, ed. *Bürger und Bürgerlichkeit im 19. Jahrhundert.* Göttingen: Vandenhoeck & Ruprecht, 1987.

Köhler-Zülch, Ines, and Christine Shojaei Kawan. *Schneewittchen hat viele Schwestern: Frauengestalten in europäischen Märchen.* Gütersloh: Mohn, 1988.

König, Ingelore, Dieter Wiedermann and Lothar Wolf, eds. *Märchen: Arbeiten mit DEFA-Kinderfilmen.* Munich: KoPäd, 1998.

Kolb, Herbert. "Karl Marx und Jacob Grimm." *Archiv für das Studium der neueren Sprachen und Literaturen* 206 (1969): 96–114.

Kolbenschlag, Maria. *Kiss Sleeping Beauty Good-bye.* New York: Doubleday, 1979.

Kosack, Wolfgang. "Der Gattungsbegriff 'Volkserzählung.'" *Fabula* 12 (1971): 18–47.
Koszinowski, Ingrid, and Vera Leuschner, eds. *Ludwig Emil Grimm 1790–1863. Maler, Zeichner, Radierer.* Kassel: Weber & Weidemeyer, 1985.
Knodt, Hermann. "Zur Familiengeschichte der Brüder Grimm." *Hessische Heimat,* 16 (July 31, 1963), 61–64.
Krauses Grimm'sche Märchen. Kassel: Stauda, 1985.
Kretzenbacher, Leopold. "Wissenschaftliche Jacob Grimm-Konferenz der Serbischen Akademie der Wissenschaften und Künste zu Belgrad." *Zeitschrift für Volkskunde* 11 (1986): 61–65.
Kuczynski, Jürgen. *Geschichte des Alltags des deutschen Volkes, 1650–1810.* Vol. 2. Cologne: Pahl-Rugenstein, 1981.
Kürthy, Tamas. *Dornröschens zweites Erwachen. Die Wirklichkeit in Mythen und Märchen.* Hamburg: Hoffmann und Campe, 1985.
Kugler, Harmut, Bernhard Lauer, Lutz Röhrich, and Ruth Schmidt-Wiegand, eds. *Jahrbuch der Brüder Grimm-Gesellschaft.* Vol. 6. Kassel: Brüder-Grimm Gesellschaft, 1996.
———, eds. *Jahrbuch der Brüder-Grimm Gesellschaft.* Vol. 7. Kassel: Brüder-Grimm Gesellschaft, 1997.
Laiblin, Wilhelm, ed. *Märchenforschung und Tiefenpsychologie.* Darmstadt: Wissenschaftliche Buchgesellschaft, 1969.
Laiblin, Wilhelm and Verena Kast, eds. *Märchenforschung und Tiefenpsychologie.* 5th rev. ed. Darmstadt: Wissenschaftliche Buchgesellschaft, 1995.
Leyen, Friedrich von der. *Das Märchen.* Leipzig: Quelle & Meyer, 1917.
———. *Das deutsche Märchen und die Brüder Grimm.* Düsseldorf: Diederichs, 1964.
Lieberman, Marcia. "Some Day My Prince Will Come: Female Acculturation Through the Fairy Tale." *College English* 34 (1972): 383–395.
Lixfeld, Hannjost. *Folklore and Fascism: The Reich Institute for Volkskunde.* Ed. and trans. James R. Dow. Bloomington: University of Indiana Press, 1994.
Lods, Jeanne. *Le Roman de Perceforest.* Geneva: Droz, 1951.
Los Hermanos Grimm Conferencias. Concepcion: Instituto Chileno-Aleman de Cultura de Concepcion, 1986.
Löther, Burkhard. "Kritische Aneignung des Erbes und bürgerliche Jacob-Grimm Rezeption." In *Erbe, Vermächtnis und Verpflichtung: Zur sprachwissenschaftlichen Forschung in der Geschichte der Akademie der Wissenschaften.* Berlin: Akadmie-Verlag, 1977. 60–82.
Lüthi, Max. *Die Gabe im Märchen und in der Sage.* Bern: Francke, 1943.
———. *Das europäische Volksmärchen.* 2d rev. ed. Bern: Francke, 1960.
———. *Volksmärchen und Volkssage.* 2d rev. ed. Bern: Francke, 1966.
———. *Once Upon a Time. On the Nature of Fairy Tales.* Trans. Lee Chadeayne and Paul Gottwald, New York: Ungar, 1970.
———. "Familie und Natur im Märchen." In *Volksliteratur und Hochliteratur.* Bern: Francke, 1970. 63–78.
———. *Das Volksmärchen als Dichtung.* Cologne: Diederichs, 1975.
———. *The European Folktale: Form and Nature.* Trans. John D. Niles. Philadelphia: Institute for the Study of Human Issues, 1982.
———. *The Fairy Tale as Art Form and Portrait of Man.* Trans. Jon Erickson. Bloomington: University of Indiana Press, 1985.

Lutz, Robert. *Wer war der gemeine Mann? Der dritte Stand in der Krise des Spätmittelalters.* Munich: R. Oldenbourg, 1979.

Mainil, Jean. *Madame D'Aulnoy et le Rire des Fées: Essai sur la Subversion Féerique et le Merveilleux Comique sous l'Ancien Régime.* Paris: Klimé, 2001.

Mallet, Carl-Heinz. *Kennen Sie Kinder?* Hamburg: Hoffmann und Campe, 1980.

———. *Das Einhorn bin ich.* Hamburg: Hoffman und Campe, 1982.

———. *Fairy Tales and Children: The Psychology of Children Revealed through Four of Grimm's Fairy Tales.* New York: Schocken, 1984.

———. *Kopf ab! Gewalt im Märchen.* Hamburg: Rasch und Röhring, 1985.

———. *Am Anfang war nicht nur Adam: Das Bild der Frau in Mythen, Märchen und Sagen.* Munich: Knesebeck & Schuler, 1990.

———. *—und rissen der schönen Jungfrau die Kleider vom Leib: Männlichkeitsmodelle im Märchen.* Düsseldorf: Walter, 1995.

Masson, Jeffrey M. *Assault on Truth: Freud's Suppression of the Seduction Theory.* New York: Farrar, Straus and Giroux, 1984.

Mayer, Mathias, and Jens Tismar. *Kunstmärchen.* 3rd. rev. ed. Stuttgart: Metzler, 1997.

McGlathery, James M. *Grimms' Fairy Tales: A History of Criticism on a Popular Classic.* Columbia, SC: Camden House, 1993.

———, ed. *The Brothers Grimm and Folktale.* Urbana: University of Illinois Press, 1988.

Meyer, Rudolf. *Die Weisheit der deutschen Märchen.* Stuttgart: Verlag der Christengemeinschaft, 1935.

Michaelis-Jena, Ruth. *The Brothers Grimm.* New York: Praeger, 1970.

Mieder, Wolfgang. "Wilhelm Grimm's Proverbial Additions in the Fairy Tales." *Proverbium* 3 (1986): 59–83.

———. *Tradition and Innovation in Folk Literature.* Hanover: University Press of New England, 1987.

———. "Sprichwörtliche Schwundstufen des Märchens. Zum 200. Geburtstag der Brüder Grimm." *Proverbium* 3 (1986): 257–71.

———. *"Findet, so werdet ihr suchen!" Die Brüder Grimm und das Sprichwort.* Bern: Peter Lang, 1986.

———. "Grimm Variations: From Fairy Tales to Modern Anti-Fairy Tales." *The Germanic Review* 42 (Spring, 1987): 90–102.

Miller, Alice. *Das Drama des begabten Kindes.* Frankfurt am Main: Suhrkamp, 1979. Trans. *The Drama of the Gifted Child.* Trans. Ruth Ward. New York: Basic Books, 1981.

———. *Am Anfang war Erziehung.* Frankfurt am Main: Suhrkamp, 1980. Trans. *For Your Own Good: Hidden Cruelty in Child-Rearing and the Roots of Violence.* Trans. Hildegarde and Hunter Hannum. New York, 1983.

———. *Du sollst nicht merken.* Frankfurt am Main: Suhrkamp, 1983. Trans. *Thou Shalt Not Be Aware: Society's Betrayal of the Child.* Trans. Hildegarde and Hunter Hannum. New York: Farrar, Straus & Giroux, 1986.

Miller, Elisabeth. *Das Bild der Frau im Märchen. Analysen und erzieherische Betrachtungen.* Munich: Profil, 1986.

Mills, Margaret A. "A Cinderella Variant in the Context of a Muslim Women's Ritual." In *Cinderella: A Casebook.* Ed. Alan Dundes. New York: Garland, 1982. 180–192.

Mittler, Sylvia. "Le jeune Henri Pourrat: de Barrès et Bergson à l'âme rustique." *Travaux de Linguistique et de Littérature* 15 (1977): 193–215.

Le Monde à l'envers dans Le Trésor des Contes d'Henri Pourrat. Clermont-Ferrand: Bibliothèque municipale et interuniversitaire, 1987.

Moore, Robert. "From Rags to Witches: Stereotypes, Distortions and Anti-humanism in Fairy Tales." *Interracial Books for Children* 6 (1975): 1–3.

Moser, Dietz-Rüdiger. "Theorie- und Methodenprobleme der Märchenforschung." *Ethnologia Bavarica* 10 (1981): 47–64.

———. "Keine unendliche Geschichte. Die Grimm'schen Märchen—eine Treppe in die Vergangenheit." *Journal für Geschichte* 3 (May/June, 1984): 18–23.

Moser, Hugo. "Volks- und Kunstdichtung in der Auffassung der Romantiker." *Rheinisches Jahrbuch für Volkskunde* 4 (1953): 69–89.

Moser-Rath, Elfriede. *Predigtmärlein der Barockzeit. Exempel, Sage, Schwank und Fabel in geistlichen Quellen des ober-deutschen Raums.* Berlin: de Gruyter 1964.

———. *"Lustige Gesellschaft": Schwank und Witz des 17. und 18. Jahrhunderts in kultur- und sozialgeschichtlichen Kontext.* Stuttgart: Metzler, 1984.

Mourey, Lilyane. *Introduction aux contes de Grimm et de Perrault.* Paris: Minard, 1978.

Müller, Elisabeth. *Das Bild der Frau im Märchen. Analysen und erzieherische Betrachtungen.* Munich: Profil, 1986.

Müller, Lutz. *Das tapfere Schneiderlein.* Stuttgart: Kreuz, 1985.

Münch, Paul, ed. *Ordnung, Fleiß und Sparsamkeit: Texte und Dokumente zur Entstehung der "bürgerlichen Tugenden."* Munich: dtv, 1984.

Murphy, Ronald. *The Owl, the Raven, and the Dove: The Religious Meaning of the Grimms' Magic Fairy Tales.* New York: Oxford University Press, 2000.

Nissen, Walter. *Die Brüder Grimm und ihre Märchen.* Göttingen: Vandenhoeck & Ruprecht, 1984.

Nitschke, August. *Soziale Ordnungen im Spiegel der Märchen.* 2 vols. Stuttgart: Frommann-Holzboog, 1976–1977.

———. "Aschenputtel aus der Sicht der historischen Verhaltensforschung." In *Und wenn sie nicht gestorben sind . . . Perspektiven auf das Märchen.* Ed. Helmut Brackert. Frankfurt am Main: Suhrkamp, 1980. 71–88.

———. "Fairy Tales in German Families before the Grimms." In *The Brothers Grimm and Folktale.* Ed. James M. McGlathery. Urbana: University of Illinois Press, 1988. 164–177.

Nøjgaard, Morten, Johan de Mylius, Iørn Piø, and Bengt Holbek, eds. *The Telling of Stories: Approaches to a Traditional Craft.* Odense: Odense University Press, 1990.

Ogris, Werner. "Jacob Grimm und die Rechtsgeschichte." In *Jacob und Wilhelm Grimm.* Göttingen: Vandenhoeck & Ruprecht, 1986. 67–96.

Ong, Walter. *Orality and Literacy.* London: Methuen, 1982.

Otto, Eduard. *Das deutsche Handwerk.* Leipzig: Teubner, 1913.

Paetow, Eva. "Märchen und Wirklichkeit." *Unitarische Blätter* 37 (Nov./Dec., 1986): 245–250.

Paetow, Karl. *Märchen und Sagen um Fraue Holle und Rübezahl—Sagen und Legenden.* Husum: Husum Verlag, 1986.

Parent, Monique. "Langue littéraire et langue populaire dans les 'contes' d'Henri Pourrat." In *La Littérature narrative d'imagination. Des genres littéraire aux techniques d'expression.* Paris: Presses Universitaires de France, 1961. 157–172.

Peppard, Murray B. *Paths Through the Forest: A Biography of the Brothers Grimm.* New York: Holt, Rinehart and Winston, 1971.

Pourrat, Claire. "Inventaires du *Trésor.* Les 1009 contes de Pourrat et le millier d'images qui les accompagnent." In Henri Pourrat. *Le Bestiaire.* Ed. Claire Pourrat. Paris: Gallimard, 1986. 323–338.

Praesent, Wilhelm. "Im engen Kreis. Haus und Kleinstadt im Leben der Brüder Grimm." *Hessenland,* 53 (1942): 30–34.

Prestel, Josef. *Märchen als Lebensdichtung. Das Werk der Brüder Grimm.* Munich: Max Hueber, 1938.

Propp, Vladimir. *Morphology of the Folktale.* Ed. Louis Wagner and Alan Dundes. Trans. Laurence Scott. 2d rev. ed. Austin: University of Texas Press, 1968.

———. *Theory and History of Folklore.* Trans. Adriadna Y. Martin and Richard P. Martin. Ed. Anatoly Liberman. Minneapolis: University of Minnesota Press, 1984.

Psaar, Werner, and Manfred Klein. *Wer hat Angst vor der bösen Geiß? Zur Märchendidaktik und Märchenrezeption.* Braunschweig: Westermann, 1976.

Rabinow, Paul. "Representations are Social Facts: Modernity and Post-Modernity in Anthropology." In *Writing Culture: The Poetics and Politics of Ethnography.* Ed. James Clifford and George E. Marcus. Berkeley: University of California Press, 1986. 234–261.

Ranke, Kurt. "Betrachtungen zum Wesen und Funktion des Märchens." *Studium Generale,* 11 (1958): 647–664.

———. "Der Einfluß der Grimmischen 'Kinder- und Hausmärchen' auf das volkstümliche deutsche Erzählgut." *Papers of the International Congress of Western Ethnology.* Ed. Sigurd Erixon. Stockholm: International Commission on Folk Arts and Folklore, 1951.

Rebel, Hermann. "Why Not 'Old Marie' . . . or Someone Very Much Like Her? A Reassessment of the Question about the Grimm's Contributors from a Social Historical Perspective." *Social History* 13 (1988): 1–24.

Renzsch, Wolfgang. *Handwerker und Lohnarbeiter in der frühen Arbeiterbewegung.* Göttingen: Vandenhoeck & Ruprecht, 1980.

Richter, Dieter. *Schlaraffenland. Geschichte einer populären Phantasie.* Cologne: Eugen Diederichs, 1984.

———. *Das fremde Kind. Zur Entstehung des bürgerlichen Zeitalters.* Frankfurt am Main: Fischer, 1987.

Richter, Dieter, and Johannes Merkel. *Märchen, Phantasie und soziales Lernen.* Berlin: Basis, 1974.

Riehl, Wilhelm H. *Die Naturgeschichte des deutschen Volkes.* Ed. Gunther Ipsen. Leipzig: Kröner, 1935.

Ringelmann, Arno. *Henri Pourrat. Ein Beitrag zur Kenntnis der 'littéraire terrienne.'* Würzburg: P. Kilian, 1936.

Robert, Raymonde. *Le conte des fées littéraire en France de la fin du XVIIe à la fin du XVIIIe siècle.* Nancy: Presses Universitaires de Nancy, 1982.

Röhrich, Lutz. *Gebärden—Metapher—Parodie.* Düsseldorf: Schwann, 1967.

———. *Märchen und Wirklichkeit.* Wiesbaden: Steiner, 1974.

———. *Sagen und Märchen. Erzählforschung heute.* Freiburg: Herder, 1976.

———. "Der Froschkönig." In *Das selbstverständliche Wunder. Beiträge germanistischer Märchenforschung.* Ed. Wilhelm Solms. Marburg: Hitzeroth, 1986. 7–41.

Rölleke, Heinz. *'Nebeninschriften': Brüder Grimm—Arnim und Brentano—Droste-Hülshoff. Literarische Studien.* Bonn: Bouvier, 1980.

———. "Texte, die beinahe 'Grimms Märchen' geworden wären." *Zeitschrift für deutsche Philologie* 102 (1983): 481–500.

———. *Die Märchen der Brüder Grimm.* Munich: Artemis, 1985.

———. *"Wo das Wünschen noch geholfen hat." Gesammelte Aufsätze zu den "Kinder- und Hausmärchen" der Brüder Grimm.* Bonn: Bouvier, 1985.

———. "Die 'Kinder- und Hausmärchen' der Brüder Grimm in neuer Sicht." *Diskussion Deutsch* 91 (October 1986): 458–464.

———. *Die Märchen der Brüder Grimm: Quellen und Studien.* Trier: Wissenschaftlicher Verlag Trier, 2000.

———, ed. *Märchen aus dem Nachlaß der Brüder Grimm.* 3rd rev. ed. Bonn: Bouvier, 1983.

Romain, Alfred. "Zur Gestalt des Grimmschen Dornröschenmärchens." *Zeitschrift für Volkskunde*, 42 (1933): 84–116.

Rowe, Karen E. "To Spin a Yarn: The Female Voice in Folklore and Fairy Tale." In *Fairy Tales and Society: Illusion, Allusion, and Paradigm.* Ed. Ruth B. Bottigheimer. Philadelphia: University of Pennsylvania, 1986.

Rüttgers, Severin. *Die Dichtung in der Volksschule.* Leipzig: R. Voigtländers, 1914.

Sahr, Michael. "'Stell Dir vor, daß Rotkäppchen Blaukäppchen heißt!' Über den unterrichtlichen Umgang mit Märchen herkömmlicher und neuer Art." *Diskussion Deutsch* 91 (October 1986): 535–546.

Sale, Roger. *Fairy Tales and After: From Snow White to E. B. White.* Cambridge: Harvard University Press, 1978.

Sandford, Beryl. "Cinderella." *The Psychoanalytic Forum* 2 (1967): 127–144.

Schenda, Rudolf. *Volk ohne Buch.* Frankfurt am Main: Klostermann, 1970.

———. *Die Lesestoffe der Kleinen Leute.* Munich: Beck, 1976.

———. "Folkloristik und Sozialgeschichte." In *Erzählung und Erzählforschung im 20. Jahrhundert.* Ed. Rolf Kloepfer and Gisela Janetke-Dillner. Stuttgart: Kohlhammer, 1981. 441–448.

———. "Alphabetisierung und Literarisierung in Westeuropa im 18. und 19. Jahrhundert." In *Sozialer und kultureller Wandel der ländlichen Welt des 18. Jahrhunderts.* Eds. Ernst Hinrichs and Günter Wiegelmann. Wolfenbüttel: Herzog August Bibliothek, 1982. 1–20.

———. "Mären von deutschen Sagen. Bemerkungen zur Produktion 'Volkserzählungen' zwischen 1850 und 1870." *Geschichte und Gesellschaft* 9 (1983): 26–48.

———. "Volkserzählung und nationale Identität: Deutsche Sagen im Vormärz." *Fabula* 25 (1984): 296–303.

———. "Volkserzählung und Sozialgeschichte." *Il Confronto Lettario*, 1.2 (1984): 265–279.

———. "Der Bilderhändler und seine Kunden im Mitteleuropa des 19. Jahrhunderts." *Ethnologia Europaea* 14 (1984): 163–175.

———. "Orale und literarische Kommunikationsformen im Bereich von Analphabeten und Gebildeten im 17. Jahrhundert." In *Literatur und Volk im 17. Jahrhundert. Probleme populärer Kultur in Deutschland.* Eds. Wolfgang Brückner, Peter Blickle, and Dieter Breuer. Wiesbaden: Harrasowitz, 1985. 447–464.

———. "Jacob und Wilhelm Grimm: Deutsche Sagen Nr. 103, 298, 337, 340, 350, 357 und 514." *Schweizerisches Archiv für Volkskunde* 81 (1985): 196–206.

———. "Vorlesen: Zwischen Analphabetentum und Bücherwissen." *Bertelsmann Briefe* 119 (1986): 5–14.

———. "Telling Tales—Spreading Tales: Change in the Communicative Forms of a Popular Genre." In *Fairy Tales and Society: Illusion, Allusion, and Paradigm*. Ed. Ruth B. Bottigheimer. Philadelphia: University of Pennsylvania Press, 1986.

———. *Folklore e Letteratura Popolare: Italia—Germania—Francia*. Rome: Istituto della Enciclopedia Italiana, 1986.

Scherf, Walter. *Lexikon der Zaubermärchen*. Stuttgart: Kröner, 1982.

———. "Das Märchenpublikum. Die Erwartung der Zuhörer und Leser und die Antwort des Erzählers." *Diskussion Deutsch* 91 (October 1986): 479–96.

———. *Das Märchen Lexikon*. 2 vols. Munich: Beck, 1995.

Schöll, Friedrich. *Gott-Natur in Mythos und Märchen*. Munich: Verlag Deutsche Unitarier, 1986.

Schoof, Wilhelm. "Aus der Jugendzeit der Brüder Grimm." *Hanausches Magazin* 13 (1934): 81–96; 14 (1935): 1–15.

———. "Beziehungen Wilhelm Grimms zu seiner Vaterstadt Hanau." *Hanausches Magazin* 15 (1936): 1–5.

———. "Brief der Brüder Grimm beim Tod ihrer Schwester Lotte." *Neues Magazin für Hanauische Geschichte* 2 (1954): 88–95.

———. "Der Verwandtenkreis der Brüder Grimm." *Hessische Familienkunde* 4 (October 1957): 193–202.

———. *Zur Entstehungsgeschichte der Grimmschen Märchen*. Hamburg: Hauswedell, 1959.

———. "Jacob Grimms Abkehr von der Rechtswissenschaft." *Zeitschrift für schweizerisches Recht* 104 (1963): 269–282.

Schoof, Wilhelm, and Ingeborg Schnack, eds. *Briefe der Brüder Grimm an Savigny*. Berlin: Erich Schmidt, 1953.

Schott, Georg. *Weissagung und Erfüllung im Deutschen Volksmärchen*. Munich: Wiechmann, 1925.

Schrader, Fred E. *Die Formierung der bürgerlichen Gesellschaft, 1550–1850*. Frankfurt am Main: Fischer Taschenbuch, 1996.

Schultz, Hartwig, ed. *Der Briefwechsel Bettine von Arnims mit den Brüdern Grimm 1838–1841*. Frankfurt am Main: Insel, 1985.

Schumann, Thomas B. "Französische Quellen zu den Grimmschen 'Kinder- und Hausmärchen.'" *Philobiblon* 21 (1977): 136–140.

Schwartz, Emanuel K. "A Psychoanalytic Study of the Fairy Tale." *Journal of American Psychotherapy* 10 (1956): 740–762.

Segalen, Martine. *Mari et femme dans la societé paysanne*. Paris: Flammarion, 1980.

Seifert, Lewis. *Fairy Tales, Sexuality and Gender in France, 1690–1715: Nostalgic Utopias*. Cambridge: Cambridge University Press, 1996.

Seifert, Theodor. *Schneewittchen. Das fast verlorene Leben*. Stuttgart: Kreuz, 1983.

Seitz, Gabriele. *Die Brüder Grimm. Leben—Werk—Zeit*. Munich: Winkler, 1984.

Sellers, Susan. *Myth and Fairy Tale in Contemporary Women's Fiction*. London: Palgrave, 2001.

Semrau, Eberhard. "Die Illustrationen zu Grimms Märchen im 19. Jahrhundert." *Zeitschrift für die Buchillustration* 14 (1977): 15–25.

———. "Die Illustrationen zu Grimms Märchen. Zweite Folge: Zwischen 1900 und 1945." *Zeitschrift für die Buchillustration* 14 (1977): 79–84.

Sieder, Reinhard. *Sozialgeschichte der Familie.* Frankfurt am Main: Suhrkamp, 1987.

Sielaff, Erich. "Zum deutschen Volksmärchen." *Der Bibliothekar* 12 (1952): 816–829.

———. "Bemerkungen zur kritischen Aneignung der deutschen Volksmärchen." *Wissenschaftliche Zeitschrift der Universität Rostock* 2 (1952/53): 241–301.

Smith, Barbara Herrnstein. "Narrative Versions, Narrative Theories." *Critical Inquiry* 7 (1980): 213–236.

Solheim, Svale. "Die Brüder Grimm und Asbjørnsen und Moe." *Wissenschaftliche Zeitschrift der Ernst-Moritz-Arndt-Universität Greifswald* 13 (1964): 15–20.

Solms, Wilhelm. *Die Moral von Grimms Märchen.* Darmstadt: Wissenschaftliche Buchgesellschaft, 1999.

———, ed. *Das selbstverständliche Wunder. Beiträge germanistischer Märchenforschung.* Marburg: Hitzeroth, 1986.

Solms, Wilhelm, and Annegret Hofius. "Der wunderbare Weg zum Glück. Vorschlag für die Behandlung der 'Kinder- und Hausmärchen' der Brüder Grimm im Deutschunterricht." *Diskussion Deutsch* 91 (October, 1986): 511–34.

Soriano, Marc. *Les Contes de Perrault. Culture savante et traditions populaires.* Paris: Gallimard, 1968.

———. *Le Dossier Charles Perrault.* Paris: Hachette, 1972.

———. *Guide de littérature pour la jeunesse.* Paris: Flammarion, 1975.

Sperber, Dan. *Rethinking Symbolism.* Trans. Alice L. Morton. Cambridge: Cambridge University Press, 1975.

———. "Anthropology and Psychology: Towards an Epidemiology of Representations." *Man* 20 (1984): 73–89.

———. *On Anthropological Knowledge.* Cambridge: Cambridge University Press, 1985.

———. *Explaining Culture: A Naturalistic Approach.* London: Blackwell, 1996.

Spiess, Karl von. *Das deutsche Volksmärchen.* Leipzig: Teubner, 1917.

Spiess, Karl von, and Edmund Mundrak. *Deutsche Märchen—Deutsche Welt.* 2d ed. Berlin: Stubenrauch, 1939.

Spörk, Ingrid. *Studien zu ausgewählten Märchen der Brüder Grimm. Frauenproblematik—Struktur—Rollentheorie—Psychoanalyse—Überlieferung—Rezeption.* Königstein/Taunus: Hain, 1985.

Spreu, Arwed, and Wilhelm Bondzio, eds. *Sprache, Mensch und Gesellschaft—Werk und Wirkungen von Wilhelm von Humboldt und Jacob und Wilhelm Grimm.* 3 vols. Berlin: Humboldt-Universität zu Berlin, 1986.

Stein, Mary Beth. "Wilhelm Heinrich Riehl and the Scientific-Literary Formation of *Volkskunde.*" *German Studies Review* 24 (October 2001): 461–86.

Steiner, Rudolf. *Märchendichtungen im Lichte der Geistesforschung. Märchendeutungen.* Dornach, Switzerland: Verlag der Rudolf Steiner-Nachlassverwaltung, 1969.

Stöckle, Frieder. *Fahrende Gesellen. Des alten Handwerkssitten und Gebräuche.* 1980.

Storer, Mary Elizabeth. *La Mode des contes des fées (1685–1700).* Paris: Champion, 1928.

Tatar, Maria M. "Born Yesterday: Heroes in the Grimms' Fairy Tales." In *Fairy Tales and Society: Illusion, Allusion, and Paradigm.* Ed. Ruth B. Bottigheimer. Philadelphia: University of Pennsylvania Press, 1986.

———. *The Hard Facts of the Grimms' Fairy Tales.* Princeton: Princeton University Press, 1987.

Taylor, Peter, and Hermann Rebel. "Hessian Peasant Women, Their Families, and the Draft: A Social-historical Interpretation of Four Tales from the Grimm Collection." *Journal of Family History* 6 (Winter, 1981): 347–378.

Temmer, Mark J. "Henri Pourrat's 'Trésor des Contes.'" *French Review* 38 (October 1964): 42–51.

Tenèze, Marie Louise, ed. *Approches de nos traditions orales.* Paris: Maisonneuve et Larose, 1970.

Thamer, Hans-Ulrich. "On the Use and Abuse of Handicraft: Journeymen Culture and Enlightened Public Opinion in 18th and 19th Century Germany." In *Understanding Popular Culture.* Ed. Steven L. Kaplan. Berlin, Mouton 1984.

Thomas, Hayley. "Undermining a Grimm Tale: A Feminist Reading of 'The Worn-Out Dancing Shoes' (KHM 133)." *Marvels & Tales* 13 (1999): 170–183.

Thompson, Stith. *Motif Index of Folk Literature.* 1932–36. 6 vols. Reprint, Bloomington: University of Indiana Press, 1955.

———. *The Folktale.* New York: Holt Rinehart & Winston, 1946.

Tismar, Jens. *Kunstmärchen.* Stuttgart: Metzler, 1977.

———. *Das deutsche Kunstmärchen des zwanzigsten Jahrhunderts.* Stuttgart: Metzler, 1981.

Töppe, Frank. *Das Geheimnis des Brunnens. Versuch einer Mythologie der Märchen.* Meerbusch bei Düsseldorf: Erb, 1985.

Turley, Richard Marggraf. "Nationalism and the Reception of Jacob Grimm's *Deutsche Grammatik* by English-Speaking Audiences." *German Life and Letters* LIV (July, 2001): 234–252.

Velay-Vallantin, Catherine. "Le miroir des contes. Perrault dans les Bibliothèques bleues." In *Les usages de l'imprimé.* Ed. Roger Chartier. Paris: Fayard, 1987. 129–185.

Velten, Harry. "The Influence of Charles Perrault's Contes de ma Mère L'Oie on German Folklore." *The Germanic Review* 5 (1930): 14–18.

Verweyen, Annemarie. "Jubiläumsausgaben zu den Märchen der Brüder Grimm. 'Wenig Bücher sind mit solcher Lust entstanden . . . '" *Börsenblatt* 77 (August 27, 1985): 2465–2473.

Viergutz, Rudolf F. *Von der Weisheit unserer Märchen.* Berlin: Widukind-Verlag, 1942.

Vries, Jan de. "Dornröschen." *Fabula* (1959): 110–21.

Waelti-Walters. "On Princesses: Fairy Tales, Sex Roles and Loss of Self." *International Journal of Women's Studies* 2 (March/April, 1979): 180–88.

———. *Fairy Tales and the Female Imagination.* Montreal: Eden Press, 1982.

Waiblinger, Angela. *Rumpelstilzchen. Gold statt Liebe.* Stuttgart: Kreuz, 1983.

Waldmann, Elisabeth and Richard. *Wo hinaus so früh, Rotkäppchen?* Zurich: Schweizerisches Jugendbuch-Institut, 1985.

Ward, Donald. "New Misconceptions about Old Folktales: The Brothers Grimm." In *The Brothers Grimm and Folktale*. Ed. James M. McGlathery. Urbana: University of Illinois Press, 1988. 92–100.

Warner, Marina. *From the Beast to the Blonde: On Fairy Tales and Their Tellers*. London: Chatto & Windus, 1995.

Wasko, Janet. *Understanding Disney: The Manufacture of Fantasy*. Cambridge: Polity, 2001.

Watts, Stephen. *The Magic Kingdom: Walt Disney and the American Way of Life*. Boston: Houghton Mifflin, 1997.

Weber, Eugen. "Fairies and Hard Facts: The Reality of Folktales." *Journal of the History of Ideas* 42 (1981): 93–113.

Weber-Kellermann, Ingeborg. *Die deutsche Familie*. Frankfurt am Main: Suhrkamp, 1974.

———. *Die Kindheit*. Frankfurt am Main: Insel, 1979.

Wegehaupt, Heinz, and Renate Riepert, ed. *150 Jahre 'Kinder- und Hausmärchen' der Brüder Grimm*. Berlin: Deutsche Bibliothek, 1964.

Wegehaupt, Heinz. *Die Märchen der Brüder Grimm*. Munich: Internationale Jugendbibilothek, 1984.

Wenk, Walter. *Das Volksmärchen als Bildungsgut*. Langensalza: Beyer, 1929.

Wesselski, Albert. *Märchen des Mittelalters*. Berlin: Stubenrauch, 1925.

Wigand, Paul. "Jacob Grimm." *Novellen-Zeitung* 2 (1864): 200–202, 216–218, 232–234, 247–250.

Williams, Raymond, ed. *Contact: Human Communication and Its History*. London: Thames and Hudson, 1981.

Wittmann, Reinhard, ed. *Buchmarkt und Lektüre im 18. und 19. Jahrhundert. Beiträge zum literarischen Leben 1750–1880*. Tübingen: Niemeyer, 1982.

Wöller, Hildegunde. *Aschenputtel. Energie der Liebe*. Stuttgart: Kreuz, 1984.

Woeller, Waltraut. *Der soziale Gehalt und die soziale Funktion der deutschen Volksmärchen*. Habilitations-Schrift der Humboldt-Universität zu Berlin, 1955.

———. "Die Bedeutung der Brüder Grimm für die Märchen- und Sagenforschung." *Wissenschaftliche Zeitschrift der Humboldt-Universität zu Berlin* 14 (1965): 507–514.

Wollenweber, Bernd. "Märchen und Sprichwort." In *Projektunterricht 1*. Ed. Heinz Ide. Stuttgart: Metzler, 1974. 12–92.

Wührl, Paul-Wolfgang. *Das deutsche Kunstmärchen*. Heidelberg: Quelle & Meyer, 1984.

Wyss, Ulrich. *Die wilde Philologie. Jacob Grimm und der Historismus*. Munich: Beck, 1979.

Yolen, Jane. "America's Cinderella." *Children's Literature in Education* 8 (1977): 21–29.

Zago, Ester. "Some Medieval Versions of Sleeping Beauty: Variations on a Theme." *Studi Francesci* 69 (1979): 417–431.

———. "La Belle au Bois Dormant: Sens et Structure." *Cermeil* 2 (February, 1986): 92–96.

Zipes, Jack. *Breaking the Magic Spell: Radical Theories of Folk and Fairy Tales*. London: Heinemann, 1979.

———. "Grimms in Farbe, Bild, und Ton: Der deutsche Märchenfilm für Kinder im Zeitalter der Kulturindustrie." In *Aufbruch zum neuen bundesdeutschen Kinderfilm.* Ed. Wolfgang Schneider. Hardeck: Eulenhof, 1982. 212–224.

———. *The Trials and Tribulations of Little Red Riding Hood: Versions of the Tale in Socio-Cultural Context.* South Hadley: Bergin & Garvey, 1983.

———. *Fairy Tales and the Art of Subversion: The Classical Genre for Children and the Process of Civilization.* London: Heinemann, 1983.

———. "Mountains out of Mole Hills, a Fairy Tale." *Children's Literature* 13 (1985): 215–219.

———. "The Enchanted Forest of the Brothers Grimm: New Modes of Approaching the Grimms' Fairy Tales." *The Germanic Review* 42 (Spring 1987): 66–74.

———. *Sticks and Stones: The Troublesome Success of Children's Literature from Slovenly Peter to Harry Potter.* New York: Routledge, 2000.

———. "Les origines italiennes du conte de fées: Basile et Straparola." In *Il était une fois . . . les contes de fées.* Ed. Olivier Piffault. Paris: Seuil, 2001. 66–74.

———, ed. *Don't Bet on the Prince. Contemporary Feminist Fairy Tales in North America and England.* New York: Methuen, 1986.

———, ed. *The Oxford Companion to Fairy Tales.* Oxford: Oxford University Press, 2000.

WEBSITES

Ashliman, D. L. "Folklore and Mythology Electronic Texts, http://www.pitt.edu/~dash/folktexts.html

Blais, Joline, Keith Frank, and Jon Ippolito. "Fair e-Tales," http://www.three.org/fairetales/

Brown, David K. "Cinderella Stories," http://ucalgary.ca/~dkbrown/cinderella.html

"SurLaLune Fairy Tale Pages," http//members.aol.com/surlalune/frytales/index.htm

"The Cinderella Project," http://www-dept.usm.edu/~engdept/cinderella/cinderella.html

Vandergrift, Kay. "Kay Vandergrift's Snow White Page," http://www/scils.rutgers.edu/special/Kay/ snow white.html

Windling, Terri. "The EndiCott Studio of Mythic Arts," http://www.endicott-studio.com/

PROSE, FICTION AND POETRY

Hoffmann, Heinrich. *Struwwelpeter: Fearful Stories and Vile Pictures to Instruct Good Little Folks.* Illustr. Sarita Vendetta. Intro. Jack Zipes. Venice, CA: Feral House, 1999.

Loggia, Wendy. *Ever After: A Cinderella Story.* New York: Dell, 1998.

Middleton, Hayden. *Grimm's Last Fairytale.* New York: St. Martin's Press, 2001.

Roussineau, Gilles, ed. *Perceforest.* 6 vols. Geneva: Droz, 1987–2001.

Schmitz, Anthony. *Darkest Desire: The Wolf's Tale.* New Jersey: The Ecco Press, 1998.

FILMS

The Wonderful World of the Brothers Grimm. Metro-Goldwyn-Mayer, 1962. Video Tape: Turner Entertainment, 1989. Director: Henry Levin. Director of fairy tales: George Pal. Screenplay: David Harmon, Charles Beaumont, and William Roberts. Lead actors: Lawrence Harvey, Claire Bloom, Karl Boehm, Walter Slezak, Oscar Homolka, and Barbara Eden.

Once Upon a Brothers Grimm. 1977. Video Tape: Video Communications, 1992. Director: Mitch Leigh. Lead actors: Dean Jones and Paul Sand.

FAIRY TALES AND FAIRY TALE COLLECTIONS

Arens, Hanns, ed. *Märchen deutscher Dichter der Gegenwart.* Esslingen: Bechtle, 1951.

Artmann, H.C. *Das im Walde verlorene Totem. Prosadichtungen 1949–1953.* Salzburg: Residenz, 1970.

Basile, Giambattista. *The Pentamerone.* Trans. Richard Burton. London: Spring, n.d.

Beese, Henriette, ed. *Von Nixen und Brunnenfrauen.* Berlin: Ullstein, 1972.

Berner, Rotraut Susanne. *Rotraut Susanne Berners Märchen-Stunde.* Weinheim: Beltz & Gelberg, 1998.

Bernstein, F. W., Robert Gernhardt, and F. K. Waechter. *Die Drei.* Franktfurt am Main: Zweitausendundeins, 1981.

Biermann, Wolf. *Das Märchen von dem Mädchen mit dem Holzbein.* Cologne: Kiepenheuer und Witsch, 1979.

Block, Francesca Lia. *The Rose and the Beast: Fairy Tales Retold.* New York: HarperCollins, 2000.

Blut im Schuh: Märchen deutscher Dichter. Spec. Issue of *Schreiben.* Bremen: Zeichen + Spuren, 1984.

Brackert, Helmut, ed. *Das große deutsche Märchenbuch.* Königstein/Taunus: Athenäum, 1979.

Brenda, Irmela. "Das Rumpelstilzchen hat mir immer leid getan." In *Neues vom Rumpelstilzchen und andere Haus-Märchen von 43 Autoren.* Ed. Hans Joachim Gelberg. Weinheim: Beltz & Gelberg, 1976, 198–200.

Brezan, Jurij. *Der Mäuseturm.* Berlin: Verlag Neues Leben, 1970.

Broumas, Olga. *Beginning with O.* New Haven: Yale University Press, 1971.

Bruyn, Günter de. *Maskeraden.* Halle: Mitteldeutscher Verlag, 1966.

Castein, Hanne, ed. *Es wird einmal: Märchen für morgen.* Frankfurt am Main: Suhrkamp, 1988.

Chotjewitz, Peter O. *Kinder, Kinder! Ein Märchen aus sieben Märchen.* Hannover: Fackelträger, 1973.

Claus, Uta and Rolf Kutschera. *Total Tote Hose. 12 bockstarke Märchen.* Frankfurt am Main: Eichborn, 1984.

Dahl, Roald. *Revolting Rhymes.* London: Jonathan Cape, 1982.

Donoghue, Emma. *Kissing the Witch: Old Tales in New Skins.* New York: HarperCollins, 1997.

Eggli, Ursula. *Fortschritt in Grimmsland: Ein Märchen für Mädchen und Frauen.* Bern: RIURS, 1983.

Ende, Michael, *Momo*. Stuttgart: Thienemann, 1973.
———. *Unendliche Geschichte*. Stuttgart: Thienemann, 1979.
Fetscher, Iring. *Wer hat Dornröschen wachgeküßt? Das Märchenverwirrbuch*. Hamburg: Claasen, 1972.
———. *Der Nulltarif der Wichtelmänner. Märchen- und andere Verwirrspiele*. Hamburg: Claasen, 1982.
Fuchs, Günter Bruno. *Neue Fibelgeschichten*. Berlin: Literarisches Colloquium, 1971.
Fühmann, Franz. *Die Richtung der Märchen*. Berlin: Aufbau, 1962.
———. *Märchen auf Bestellung*. Rostock: Hinstorff, 1982.
Galloway, Priscilla. *Truly Grimm Tales*. New York: Bantam, 1995.
Garbe, Burckhard and Gisela. *Der ungestiefelte Kater. Grimms Märchen umerzählt*. Göttingen: sage & schreibe, 1985.
Gardner, John. *Gudgekin the Thistle Girl and Other Tales*. New York: Knopf, 1976.
Gardner, Richard. *Dr. Gardner's Fairy Tales for Today's Children*. Englewood Cliffs: Prentice-Hall, 1974.
Gebert, Helga. *Alte Märchen der Brüder Grimm*. Weinheim: Beltz & Gelberg, 1985.
Gelberg, Hans-Joachim, ed. *Erstes Jahrbuch der Kinderliteratur 1: Geh und spiel mit dem Riesen*. Weinheim: Beltz & Gelberg, 1971.
———, ed. *Zweites Jahrbuch der Kinderliteratur 2: Am Montag fängt die Woche an*. Weinheim: Beltz & Gelberg, 1973.
———, ed. *Drittes Jahrbuch der Kinderliteratur 3: Menschengeschichten*. Weinheim: Beltz & Gelberg, 1975.
———, ed. *Neues vom Rumpelstilzchen und andere Hausmärchen von 43 Autoren*. Weinheim: Beltz & Gelberg, 1976.
———, ed. *Viertes Jahrbuch der Kinderliteratur 4: Der fliegende Robert*. Weinheim: Beltz & Gelberg, 1977.
Gernhardt, Robert. *Die Blusen des Böhmen*. Frankfurt am Main: Verlag Zweitausendeins, 1977.
Gmelin, O. F. and Doris Lerche. *Märchen für Tapfere Mädchen*. Gießen: Schlot, 1978.
Goes, Albrecht. "Sterntaler." In *Gedichte*. Frankfurt am Main: Fischer, 1958, 116.
Grimm, Albert Ludwig. *Kindermährchen*. Heidelberg: Mohr und Zimmer, 1808.
———. *Lina's Mährchenbuch. Eine Weynachtsgabe*. Frankfurt am Main: Wilmans, 1816.
———. *Kindermährchen*. 3d rev. ed. Frankfurt am Main: Brönner, 1839.
———. *Mährchen der Tausend und Einen Nacht für Kinder*. 4 vols. Frankfurt am Main: Wilmans, 1821–22.
———. *Mährchen aus dem Morgendland für Kinder*. Hamburg: Heubel, 1844.
———. *Deutsche Sagen und Märchen*. Leipzig: Gebhardt, 1867.
Grünler, Jörg, Hoschby Tießler, and Theo Geißler. *Knacks sagt das Ei, die ganze Luft ist voller Bilder*. Berlin: Klopp, 1977.
Gugel, Fabius von. *Aschen-Brödel oder Der verlorene Schuh*. Munich: Moos, 1981.
Günzel, Manfred. *Deutsche Märchen*. Frankfurt am Main: Metopen-Verlag, 1968.
Hägele, Rainer. *Ich dachte, es wäre der Froschkönig*. Stuttgart: Spectrum, 1984.
Härtling, Peter. *Zum laut und leise Lesen*. Darmstadt: Luchterhand, 1975.

Hammer, Klaus, ed. *Der Holzwurm und der König: Märchenhaftes und Wundersames für Erwachsene.* Halle: Mitteldeutscher Verlag, 1985.

Hannover, Heinrich. *Die Birnendiebe vom Bodensee.* Frankfurt am Main: März, 1975.

Hardel, Lilo. *Otto und der Zauberer Faulebaul.* Berlin: Kinderbuchverlag, 1956.

Hay, Sara Henderson. *Story Hour.* Fayetteville: University of Arkansas Press, 1982.

Heidebrecht, Brigitte, ed. *Dornröschen nimmt die Heckenschere: Märchenhaftes von 30 Autorinnen.* Bonn: Verlag Kleine Shritte, 1985.

Heidelbach, Nikolaus, Illustr. *Märchen der Brüder Grimm.* Weinheim: Beltz & Gelberg, 1995.

Heidtmann, Horst, ed. *Die Verbesserung des Menschen: Märchen von Franz Fühmann, Peter Hacks, Irmtraud Morgner, Anna Seghers und vielen anderen Autoren aus der DDR.* Darmstadt: Luchterhand, 1982.

Heiduczek, Werner. *Jana und der kleine Stern.* Berlin: Kinderbuchverlag, 1968.

Heißenbüttel, Helmut. *Eichendorffs Untergang und andere Märchen.* Stuttgart: Klett-Cotta, 1978.

Heym, Stefan. *Der kleine König, der ein Kind kriegen mußte und andere neue Märchen für kluge Kinder.* Munich: Goldmann, 1979.

———. *Märchen für kluge Kinder.* Munich: Goldmann, 1998.

Hinze, Christa, ed. *Märchen, die die Brüder Grimm nicht kannten.* Cologne: Diederichs, 1975.

Hohler, Franz. *Der Riese und die Erdbeerkonfitüre.* Illustr. Nikolaus Heidelbach. Ravensburg: Otto Maier, 1993.

Holtz-Baumert, Gerhard. *Sieben und dreimal sieben Geschichten.* Berlin: Kinderbuchverlag, 1979.

Hyman, Trina Shart. *The Sleeping Beauty.* Boston: Little Brown, 1977.

Janosch (Horst Eckert). *Janosch erzählt Grimm's Märchen: Fünfzig ausgewählte Märchen für Kinder von heute.* Weinheim: Beltz und Gelberg, 1972.

———. *Not Quite as Grimm.* Trans. Patricia Crampton. London: Abelard-Schuman, 1974.

———. *Janosch erzählt Grimm's Märchen: Vierundfünfzig ausgewählte Märchen für Kinder von heute.* Rev. ed. Weinheim: Beltz und Gelberg, 1991.

Jarvis, Shawn, and Jeannine Blackwell, eds. *The Queen's Mirror: Fairy Tales by German Women, 1780–1900.* Lincoln: University of Nebraska Press, 2001.

Jung, Jochen, ed. *Bilderbogengeschichten—Märchen, Sagen, Abenteuer.* Munich: Moos, 1974.

Jungman, Ann. *Cinderella and the Hot Air Balloon.* Illustr. Russell Ayto. London: Frances Lincoln, 1992.

Kämpf, Günter and Vilma Link. *Deutsche Märchen.* Gießen: Anabas-Verlag, 1981.

Kaschnitz, Marie-Luise. "Bräutigam Froschkönig." In *Überallnie: Ausgewählte Gedichte 1928–1965.* Munich: dtv, 1950.

Kassajep, Margaret. *"Deutsche Hausmärchen" frisch getrimmt.* Dachau: Baedeker & Lang, 1980.

Konrad, Johann Friedrich. *Hexen-Memoiren: Märchen, entwirrt und neu erzählt.* Frankfurt am Main: Eichborn, 1981.

Körner, Heinz., ed. *Die Farben der Wirklichkeit: Ein Märchenbuch.* Fehlbach: Körner, 1983.

Kraus, Barbara. *Gestohlene Märchen.* Munich: Trikont, 1979.
Kriegel, Volker. *Der Rock'n Roll-König.* Frankfurt am Main: Sauerländer, 1982.
Kübler, Roland. *Die Mondstein Märchen.* Munich: Knauer, 1988.
———. *Der Märchenring.* Munich: Knaur, 1995.
Kühn, Dieter. *Es fliegt ein Pferd ins Abendland.* Frankfurt am Main: Fischer Taschenbuch, 1994.
———. *Der fliegende König der Fische.* Frankfurt am Main: Fischer Taschenbuch, 1996.
Kunert, Günter. *Die geheime Bibliothek.* Berlin: Aufbau, 1973.
———. *Jeder Wunsch ein Treffer.* Velber: Middelhauve, 1976.
Kunze, Reiner. *Der Löwe Leopold: Fast Märchen, fast Geschichten.* Frankfurt am Main: Fischer, 1974.
Langer, Heinz. *Grimmige Märchen.* Munich: Hugendubel, 1984.
Lee, Tanith. *Princess Hynchatti and Some Other Surprises.* London: Macmillan, 1972.
Levine, Gail Carson. *Cinderellis and the Glass Hill.* Illustr. Mark Elliott. New York: HarperCollins, 2000.
Maar, Paul. *Der tätowierte Hund.* Hamburg: Oetinger, 1968.
Maguire, Gregory. *Confessions of an Ugly Stepsister.* Illustr. Bill Sanderson. New York: Regan Books, 1999.
Matthies, Horst. *Der goldene Fisch: Kein Märchenbuch.* Halle: Mitteldeutscher Verlag, 1980.
Mayer, Mercer. *The Sleeping Beauty.* New York: Macmillan, 1984.
Merian, Svende. *Der Mann aus Zucker: Mein Märchenbuch.* Darmstadt: Luchterhand, 1985.
Merkel, Johannes. *Zwei Korken für Schlienz.* Berlin: Basis, 1972.
Middelhauve, Gertraud, and Gert Loschütz, eds. *Das Einhorn sagt zum Zweihorn. Schriftsteller schreiben für Kinder.* Cologne: Middelhauve, 1974.
Mieder, Wolfgang, ed. *Grimms Märchen—modern.* Stuttgart: Reclam, 1979.
———, ed. *Disenchantments: An Anthology of Modern Fairy Tale Poetry.* Hanover: University Press of New England, 1985.
———, ed. *Grimmige Märchen.* Frankfurt: R.G. Fischer, 1986.
Nöstlinger, Christine. *Wir pfeifen auf den Gurkenkönig.* Weinheim: Beltz, 1972.
Péhan, Wolfgang. *Grimm 2000. Gedanken zur zeitgemäßen Gestaltung überlieferter Volksmärchen.* Vienna: Intercity, 1977.
Perrault, Charles. *Contes.* Ed. Gilbert Rouger. Paris: Garnier, 1967.
———. *Perrault's Tales of Mother Goose. The Dedication Manuscript of 1695 reproduced in collotype Facsimile with Introduction and Critical Text.* Ed. Jacques Barchilon. New York: The Pierpont Morgan Library, 1956.
———. *The Fairy Tales of Charles Perrault.* Trans. Angela Carter. New York: Avon, 1977.
Pourrat, Henri. *Contes de la Bucheronne.* Tours: Maison Mame, 1935.
———. *Le Trésor des Contes.* 16 vols. Paris: Gallimard, 1948–1962.
———. *Contes du vieux-vieux temps.* Paris: Gallimard, 1970.
———. *Le Diable et ses diableries.* Ed. Claire Pourrat. Paris: Gallimard, 1977.
———. *Les Brigands.* Ed. Claire Pourrat. Paris: Gallimard, 1978.
———. *Au Village.* Ed. Claire Pourrat. Paris: Gallimard, 1979.

———. *Les Amours*. Ed. Claire Pourrat. Paris: Gallimard, 1981.
———. *Les Fées*. Ed. Claire Pourrat. Paris: Gallimard, 1983.
———. *Les Fous et les sages*. Ed. Claire Pourrat. Paris: Gallimard, 1986.
———. *Le Bestiaire*. Ed. Claire Pourrat. Paris: Gallimard, 1986.
———. *Contes*. Paris: Gallimard, 1987.
———. *A Treasury of French Tales*. Trans. Mary Mian. London: George Allen & Unwin, 1953.
———. *French Folktales from the Collection of Henri Pourrat*. Trans. and ed. Royall Tyler. New York: Pantheon, 1993.
Richling, Mathias. *Ich dachte, es wäre der Froschkönig*. Stuttgart: Spectrum, 1984.
Robertson, Martin. *The Sleeping Beauty's Prince*. Oxford: Robert Dugdale, 1977.
Rühm, Gerhard. *Knochenspielzeug*. Stierstadt im Taunus: Eremiten-Presse, 1970.
Rühmkorf, Peter. *Der Hüter des Misthaufens: Aufgeklärte Märchen*. Reinbek: Rowohlt, 1983.
Ryder, Frank and Robert M. Browning, eds. *German Literary Fairy Tales*. New York: Continuum, 1983.
Sangenberg, Georg (Hans Traxler). *Gänsehaut*. Frankfurt am Main: 1964.
Schädlich, Hans Joachim. *Versuchte Nähe*. Reinbek: Rowohlt, 1977.
Schami, Rafik. *Das Schaf im Wolfspelz*. Kiel: Neuer Malik Verlag, 1986.
———. *Der Wunderkasten*. Kiel: Neuer Malik Verlag, 1990.
Schleusing, Thomas. *Es war einmal . . . Märchen für Erwachsene*. Berlin: Eulenspiegel, 1979.
Schrauff, Chris. *Der Wolf und seine Steine*. Hannover: SOAK-Verlag, 1986.
Seidel, Ina. *Das wunderbare Geißleinbuch: Neue Geschichten für Kinder, die die alten Märchen gut kennen*. Reutlingen: Ensslin & Laiblin, 1949.
Seifert, Theodor. *Schneewittchen: Das fast verlorene Leben*. Stuttgart: Kreuz, 1983.
Sexton, Anne. *Transformations*. Boston: Houghton Mifflin, 1971.
Stepan, Bohumil. *Knusperhäuschen*. Cologne, 1971.
Stöckle, Frieder, ed. *Handwerkermärchen*. Frankfurt am Main: Fischer, 1986.
Traxler, Hans. *Die Wahrheit über Hänsel und Gretel*. Frankfurt am Main: Bärmeier und Nikel, 1963.
Ungerer, Tomi. *Tomi Ungerers Märchenbuch*. Zurich: Diogenes, 1975.
Viorst, Judith. *If I Were in Charge of the World*. New York: Atheneum, 1982.
Waddell, Martin. *The Tough Princess*. Illustr. Patrick Benson. New York: Philomel, 1986.
Waechter, Friedrich. *Tischlein deck dich und Knüppel aus dem Sack*. Reinbek bei Hamburg: Rowohlt, 1972.
———. *Die Bauern im Brunnen*. Zurich: Diogenes, 1978.
Wesselski, Albert, ed. *Deutsche Märchen vor Grimm*. Munich: Rohrer, 1942.
Wiechert, Ernst. *Märchen*. 2 vols. Munich: Desch, 1946.
Williams, Jay. *The Practical Princess and Other Liberating Tales*. New York: Parents' Magazine Press, 1979.
Wolf, Friedrich. *Märchen für große und kleine Kinder*. Berlin: Aufbau, 1947.
Wondratschek, Wolf. *Früher begann der Tag mit einer Schußwunde*. Munich: Hanser, 1971.
Yolen, Jane. *Sleeping Ugly*. New York: Coward, McCann & Geoghegan, 1981.

———. *Tales of Wonder.* New York: Schocken, 1983.
———. *The Sleeping Beauty.* Illustr. Ruth Sanderson. New York: Knopf, 1986.
Zipes, Jack, ed. *Spells of Enchantment: The Wondrous Fairy Tales of Western Culture.* New York: Viking, 1991.
———, ed. *The Great Fairy Tale Tradition: From Straparola and Basile to the Brothers Grimm.* New York: Norton, 2001.

INDEX

LaVergne, TN USA
11 April 2010
178876LV00001B/32/A